MARGARET LEE RUNBECK

A

Hungry Man

DREAMS

PEOPLES BOOK CLUB
CHICAGO

THIS BOOK IS DEDICATED, IN GRATEFUL MEMORY,

TO

Henry Scott Rubel

WHO INSPIRED GOODNESS IN MEN

BECAUSE HE WORSHIPED THE GOODNESS OF GOD.

AN EXPLANATION

A modern convention of capitalization would separate from other pronouns those which refer to God.

Believing that God is as close to man as his own consciousness, I have not set apart such pronouns with capital letters.

My authority for the conviction of the closeness of God may be found in the verse, "In him we live and move and have our being." (Acts 17:28.)

The Bible, also, is my authority for this lack of capitalization, as may be observed from the same quotation.

M.L.R.

A

Hungry Man

DREAMS

Books by Margaret Lee Runbeck

OUR MISS BOO

TIME FOR EACH OTHER

THE GREAT ANSWER

THE SECRET

HOPE OF EARTH

PINK MAGIC

ANSWER WITHOUT CEASING

A HUNGRY MAN DREAMS

CONTENTS

PART I

The father divides his living

1

PAPA loved to slap up quick billboard pictures with his big paintbrush of a voice.

"Mama's the pretty one of us. She's the only one in the family who doesn't look like me. The children should have been smart enough to take after her. Somehow their papa got in the way of their good looks . . . and *look* at them!" He would roar with mirth when he said this, because he knew that his children, though both were somewhat florid and large for their age, were going to be handsome in a careless extravagant way.

Every detail of their appearance had been stressed with a kind of exuberant flamboyance; flesh colors were just a bit more intense than one might expect, so that other persons looked pale and underdone beside them; each body line was prolonged and held until it seemed to collide with the next line. The masses and planes were all continued just a fraction farther than usual. The visual sum was one of energy and vitality.

Lucile, their mother, as a matter of fact, did *not* look as if she belonged in the family. She was a reticent etching hung incongruously among big high-colored oils. Papa and the children had splashes of carnation-pink across their cheekbones, innocent china-blue eyes, and embroidery-floss yellow hair, which blew weightlessly with very cleanness as they moved. They had large restless hands, tight-packed with wholesome-looking flesh. No matter how carefully they were tailored and furbished, their clothes always looked too tight for them after

3

the first wearing, and their shoes were noisier and quicker than anyone else's. They were all three big, generous, over-endowed persons who would brush noisily and cheerfully through any world they inhabited, upsetting small objects, both human and inanimate, and never being embarrassed at the wreckage.

Lucile, on the contrary, was a masterpiece of economy and omission. She was beautiful for what had been left out as Chinese prints are beautiful. There was never an extra ounce, or a completed curve, about her. Her own coloring was subdued, so that you looked twice to see it, and then found such cause for boasting in yourself because you had appreciated it, that your eyes lingered in enjoyment. Her hair was dark and shadowy against her cream skin; her eyes were a gray which never became blue or green; and when she spoke it was necessary that you listen attentively, for there seemed no extra breath in her to send her words out on a banner of voice, as the other members of the Our family spoke.

Lucile was someone who easily might have been overlooked, yet she seldom was overlooked because the discovering of her was such peaceful vindication of what was within the perceiver. She was a woman whose beauty had to be found in the beholder himself. But lying there, and once discovered, it stayed safe and inviolable.

"I knew she was mine because she was so quiet," Papa said when his son Jubal asked him how he came to marry the girl he had found teaching business composition in a Chicago night school.

"I am a noisy, impetuous man. All my troubles in life came from rushing ahead too fast and insisting too much. I knew when I first saw her that she was what I needed. She is my exercise in quietness, your mama."

His blue eyes softened as they always did when he thought about his great love for this small woman. "I knew that if I could speak quietly enough to make her hear me, it would be a good thing." He cocked his eye humorously at his son. "A good thing for me, and for you to. You understand me?"

"Sure," Jubal said.

Jubal had, in fact, great savannahs of understanding for his mother, in which the two of them often walked for hours with no words necessary. Papa, he used to think, was like a visit to Soulard Market in the chilly early morning, when your skin prickled with aliveness, and your nose and ears and eyes, and certainly your hunger, were assaulted with crude, wonderful impressions . . . the smell of marigolds, the clash of red shawls and green corduroy on the country people, the bite of sharp cheese offered from the end of a huge knife, the blue smoke of the charcoal fires in the open air, the fat ooze and bubble of laughter. But Mama was like lying quietly alone beside the almost hidden stream in Forest Park, with one finger dabbling in the cool water, and the sky unmeasurably high overhead. Papa was like the blast and blare of Wagner on the first night the opera came to St. Louis, with all your blood marching to the thunder of it. Mama was a page of Schumann so eloquently scored that one needed no piano to listen to it. Mama was melody one heard in oneself.

Sometimes when he came home from school, Jubal would bound up the great curving staircase and plunge down the hall to the closed door of her room, and then he would stop suddenly and stand there waiting. Much as he wanted to tell her some boyish scrap of news, he would suddenly be overcome with shyness and a strange unnamed respect. Sometimes he would turn and go away, not quite knowing why. If she heard him, she called out, or came herself and opened the door and bent down to kiss him quickly.

"Oh Jubal . . . I was hoping it would be you."

"Who else would it be . . . stumbling over his feet to get up here?" Jubal would say. "I ran all the way home to tell you...."

"Come in and tell me."

But sometimes when he was within the small intimate sitting room, with the fire chuckling in the green marble fireplace, and the solid gold clock which Papa had brought from Leipzig lisping patiently in the stillness, he had nothing to tell. As Papa said, what he had was not quiet enough to be told here.

Often he would see that she had laid down a book on her table, and when he glanced at it she would pick it up again without any insincere asking whether or not he wanted to hear. She would begin reading just where she had left off, and sometimes it would be poetry, the pellucid measures of Keats or Wordsworth, or the solid cartwheels of Whitman rumbling over quickly acceptable meanings. Just as often the book would be her Bible. Curiously enough, the Bible was the only book she ever hesitated to read to him. She had a strange courtesy about the Bible; she never shared it until Jubal himself had asked for it.

When once he asked her rather timidly about this, she said, "It doesn't do anyone any good, unless he wants it first. Other meanings come to you without being invited. But God's word waits outside until you beg it to come in."

"Preachers don't wait. The minute you get near one, he begins hammering away at you," Jubal said with a quick perverse impulse to tease her which he could not recognize as the ever waiting, impersonal enmity of the human mind against the still small voice of God.

She did not answer him when he said that. She sat and looked at him with gentle understanding; then she opened the big book at its very end, and read a strange violent story from the book of Revelation:

"And there appeared a great wonder in heaven; a woman clothed with the sun, and the moon under her feet, and upon her head a crown of twelve stars. And she being with child cried, travailing in birth, and pained to be delivered."

She lifted her head and looked at him, to see that he understood the words. "That is a parable. It applies to anyone who has a good purpose waiting to be born . . . a new idea . . . anything really good, Jubal."

"Yes, Mama."

She went on reading, "And there appeared another wonder in heaven, and behold a great red dragon, having seven heads and ten horns and seven crowns upon his heads. And the dragon stood before the woman which was ready to be delivered, for to devour her child as soon as it was born."

Jubal's face was flushed now, for his mother was reading to him about birth, and that was a painful fact only lately discovered. But she looked past the blush serenely, because she had something she must tell. Not to an embarrassed callow boy, but to a man who was going to need the wisdom many times in his life.

"You see," she said gently, "before ever the good purpose can be born, the world's evil waits to devour it. It is the oldest warfare in time. Evil waits to kill good . . . sometimes in the very man who is bringing forth the good."

"What kind of good . . . you mean preaching good?" he asked distastefully.

"No. All kinds. Inventors and discoverers are persecuted. One must have great courage to give a great gift. For the world usually begins by hating it and trying to destroy it."

"I don't know why anyone would bother then," Jubal said.

"You've got to love the world a great deal. In order to add to the world's good gain you've got to be willing to be hated . . . or to be ridiculous. . . ."

She closed the book then, and looked out of the window a moment. "I have told you something you are too young to understand, Jubal. You may probably have to live it, to understand it."

Often when she read to him from the Bible, she was not a

solemn woman. Sometimes she was full of mischief and fun, as if she knew God so well she had no formality or reserve in his presence. Once she read him the verse which says:

> For a man's life consisteth not in the abundance of the things which he possesseth.

Their eyes met, and Jubal puffed out his cheeks, and made his thumbs and forefingers into quick spectacles, so that he looked absurdly like Papa. They both burst out laughing, all the more happily because they understood the depths of fondness behind the caricature.

"Exactly," Mama said.

"But how he loves the abundance of things he possesseth," Jubal cried, and he began checking them off on his fingers. "There's my Lucile, first of all, and then there's my liddle boy Jubal, and Minna . . . well, we count Minna, but she's not much to count yet . . . and my *houze,* and the *blumbing* . . . and the good potato pancakes of Anna, and her Wiener Schnitzel. . . . "

"But his life really does not consist of these things," Mama said, suddenly serious.

"No. Papa's life consists of his big heart," Jubal said. "Papa thinks his life consists of stuff everybody can admire, but really . . . "

"Papa knows everything about everything," Lucile said, "but he doesn't know much about Henry Our. He's a much bigger man than he suspects."

"And, heaven knows, he suspects he's pretty big!" Jubal said precociously. But for once his mother did not rebuke him for his precocity. For once she crumpled over with delicious laughing.

"Oh Jubal . . . you have no right to be so funny. I think perhaps I ought to scold you," she said helplessly.

2

It wasn't the biggest house in St. Louis, but it was certainly the most beloved by the persons who lived in it. At the end of the day Papa drove westward along Lindell Boulevard in his brass-trimmed Standard Six 50-horsepower touring car. The sight of his own bloated red brick and terra-cotta house sitting solidly in the neatly barbered lawns behind the redstone walls smote him as if he never had seen it before.

It seemed to him too good to be true that such an impressive mansion could belong to him, and that in it were six loyal persons waiting for his homecoming as the climax of their day. Often when he looked up at the great shouldering bulk of the house with its cupolas, chimneys and balconies, and the brilliant green weathervane on the roof, he was guilty of unmasculine tears of joyful emotion.

Sometimes, sitting in imagination beside Papa on the slick black leather seat, was that brash twenty-year-old boy who had come to America in 1890, only twenty years before, with a pocketful of dreams and twenty-four dollars in cash. It was through his eyes that Papa surveyed this superlative moment of homecoming.

He wouldn't have believed it, Papa sometimes said to himself. But that was not correct, for that boy who had been himself had believed anything was possible. That was why it had become possible. It was, in fact, out of that boy's fertile lack that all this abundance had been created. Out of his own frugal aloneness he had peopled the house . . . Lucile and the

9

two children and the three strong German servants, always smiling and pleased. The high-ceilinged overornate parlor, with French furniture and glass-walled curio cases standing on bowlegged gilt stilts, came from his memory of the bare, creaking rooming-house cubicles where he had lived. The cold linoleum on those floors was responsible for the creamy Persian rugs scrolled over with a welter of guavas and cumquats. The sky-blue silk wall panels edged with gold-leaf garlands were a little more opulent than most St. Louis parlors had, because Papa had been so depressed by the stained, peeling wall paper of his youth. The chandeliers, which even Papa knew were too big and too lavishly sprinkled throughout the house, were in memory of the feeble gas jets under which he had squinted his way through an American education, such as it was.

This house and everything in it was Papa's retort to the blunt squalor which had greeted him when first he arrived in America. The richness of that transformation was the richness of Papa's love for America, and his lavish gratitude for what it had given him.

"America took everything poor and little and made it big for me, before my very eyes," he sometimes said. Only Lucile fully appreciated the ambiguous remark. She knew that somehow in the scuffle Papa had exchanged his awareness of his own ego with that of America. America, large and lavish, was really Papa himself, placed outside where he himself could view it. It was a case of sublimely mistaken identity. When she tried to explain this to him, he shook his head almost angrily, as if she were trying to detract from that romantic love affair between his new country and himself.

"The America you found was you, yourself," she said. "A small man, my darling, would have found this a petty, cruel country. Many have."

"No . . . you do not understand," he said fiercely, "because you have always had America for yours. Nobody born here could understand."

The sense of his great good fortune might have been complacency in some men, but in Papa it was too naïve and gaily shared by all his eye rested upon to be anything so ingrowing as smugness. An essential part of Papa's abundance was that it must be bestowed freely upon everything around him. There was a second helping of everything Papa experienced. He overbought, overpaid, overtipped, and overenjoyed. He filled his house with too much furniture; his wardrobe bulged (as he did himself) with too many elegantly tailored clothes; when he got up at dawn and went down to Soulard Market, his big touring car was not able to bring home the baskets of sweet potatoes, walnuts, and oranges, the four-inch steaks, the haunches of pork, the garlands of sausages. When he ordered equipment for the brewery, which his purchasing agent could not prevent his doing, he bought an extra of everything. If they needed an additional tyepwriter, he ordered two. If word got around to him that they could use another wash-tun, or wort-boiling pan, or forcing tray, he had several sent into the works.

He overpaid his men in the same way, and his colleagues who owned other breweries used to talk very seriously to him about it.

"You'll wreck yourself with wages like that, Henry," they said. But what they meant, of course, was that he would wreck them.

"I get bigger every year," he said with his maddening childlike beam. "I make more money, my men make more money, and America drinks more Our Brew. I got no kick."

When he took his family out to dine the whole dining room of the Jefferson Hotel sprang to life and every waiter's mouth watered, for Papa was almost delirious with his tips. Generosity was a holy superstition with Papa. He felt that nothing

must ever break the current which flowed so affectionately between himself and America. They had given their very best
to each other, and would continue to outdo each other in generosity, as long as they both should live.

Indeed, it *was* a kind of marriage between them, Lucile, his
legal wife, used to think when she mused affectionately upon
her big simple-minded husband. She fancied a marriage ceremony between them, probably performed on that distant day
when he had arrived at Hoboken on that little seven thousand
gross ton steamer, the *Fulda*. She pictured him on the ferry,
with his plump suitcase at his feet, and his eyes raised to the
skyscrapers in reverent awe.

"With all my worldly goods I thee endow," Lucile pictured
each of them saying, the city and the boy.

And so they had done, the country giving him everything he
could understand and use, and he giving back to it a growing,
sprawling business built out of a comical fusing of idealism
and shrewdness, of lyric realism and gross sentimentality, of
poetry . . . and beer.

He seemed never to think about his beer as other people
considered it. It was not mere beverage to him, but the benefi-
cence of the fertile earth, the rich black soil nourishing the
barley, the hand of the sunshine playing across it as across a
myriad-stringed harp. When he held up a foaming stein (he
abhorred anything but stone from which to drink his beer)
he seemed to see in his dark brew warmth and friendliness and
comradeship. Gemütlichkeit, with all its untranslatable comfort.

Much as he loved his family, it was not the circumference of
his great gregarious affection. His heart, it sometimes seemed
to his wife, was a big, vulgar circus tent, with barkers enticing
all passers-by to stop in and enjoy themselves freely. The more
effete members of St. Louis society laughed at that big circus
tent of a man; but that did not prevent them from being very
fond of him. Even the ones, such as the chancellor of Wash-

ington University, who betrayed themselves by snubbing the Ours when invitations went out, began with Henry Our when it was time to look for a contribution for some philanthropy, or for some civic leadership. It nettled Lucile that this should be so, but Henry himself never seemed aware of it, since he had more friends than he could possibly have time for. His only regret was that there was not more of him available to be thrown into the lusty business of living.

With all his worshiping of success for himself, Henry had no snobbery about success for others. He valued a street sweeper, if he happened to be a frisky thinker, as affectionately as he esteemed the president of the board of directors of the J. Kennard Sons Carpet Company. When he counted his friends, they stood equal in his eyes.

Everyone knew him by name, from the conductor on the new Grand Avenue pay-as-you-enter streetcar to Captain Robert McCulloch, the president of the United Railway Company. The curator at the Art Museum in Forest Park where Henry often took the children called him by name respectfully; the man who kept the boathouse at Benton Park called him Henry. The other Germans in the Liederkranz Club and the Schlaraffia, to which he had presented a handsome Bavarian pillar stove for their Old Heidelberg clubroom, loved him and honored him. He had a talent for making people love him, but he never realized that some persons always lie beyond the touch of that talent.

At Christmas time Henry was the busiest man in town, for he could not bear to think there was one person in the whole city's 700,000 who would feel forgotten, or lonely, or unhappy on this particular day. The Our Boys' Club really sprang from Henry's Christmas custom of giving a huge party for any boy who cared to attend. It was only a few steps from that to a weekly outing for the city's poor children, and another step to building them a gymnasium and clubhouse of their own.

"Don't scold me for spending so much money," he said

when first he told Lucile of his plans. "A thousand dollars isn't as big to me as ten dollars was once. I used to be able to afford generosity out of my ten dollars. I should still be able."

"I'm not scolding you," Lucile said. "I'm loving you, Henry."

The city had little it could give back to Henry Our, except its own heart. But in 1910 it did make a gesture. A committee of citizens raised a fund, and for once Henry's name was not at the top of the list of contributors. It worried him a bit, when he discovered that a pedestal for some kind of statue, about which he knew nothing, was being erected on a small triangular spot of grass near Vandeventer Place. He asked several people what was going up there, but nobody told him. He wondered if he ought to remind the Mayor that he was on the Civic Parks and Improvements Committee. . . .

But he found out, all right. One Sunday when the leaves were beginning to turn and Lucile had acquired a luscious wheelbarrow of a hat heaped up and spilling over with pink and purple willow plumes, the Mayor himself came to wait on Henry just after midday dinner, and escorted the family down to the unveiling.

There was a band, and speeches from schoolchildren, business celebrities and a college professor. At last two little girls in black-ribbed stockings and bunchy petticoats pulled a gold cord that lifted the bunting around the statue. There was a stone Henry, a little slimmer than in life, a shade more distinguished-looking. He was standing a bit self-consciously with one hand on the back of a massive chair and the other falteringly outstretched over the heads of the crowd, as if he might be asking a blessing. He had on a Prince Albert coat; a lovely sharp crease ran down his trouser legs.

There was a bronze tablet on the front of the pedestal, but Henry for the moment could not read what it said, because a mist had filmed his glasses just then. But the children read it, and Lucile, and a wave of murmuring approval went over the crowd.

> Henry Our
> Our Neighbor
> Our Citizen
> Our Friend."

It was the greatest afternoon of Papa's life. He behaved with proper dignity during the ceremony, but when they were home he became a bit maudlin. The whole family, in fact, was on the verge of uncomfortable sentimentality. But Jubal, who was twelve at the time, as usual stabilized the scene by making a joke. Jubal realistically pointed out that the sculptor had noticeably improved on Papa's generous figure.

"You mean I don't look as pretty as that?" Papa asked in great disappointment.

"Sermons in brooks, and compliments in stone, Papa," Jubal said.

When Papa looked utterly mystified by the allusion, Lucile said, "Education, dear."

So Papa nodded, satisfied. The word was a magic formula for explaining many things to Papa, and a most convenient device.

3

WHEN Heinrich Gustaf Auerbach got his first job in America, the Irishman who hired him had a big sprawling handwriting. That is how it happened that the best beer sold around the turn of the century was known as Our Brew.

The Irishman had, besides his wasteful handwriting, a Celtic derision for all Teutonic pomposity. So he scrawled as much of Heinrich's name as he could on the payroll, and the syllables which wouldn't fit on the blank line were lopped off.

"Heinie Auer, me boy," he said jovially, when Heinrich attempted to protest through his vociferous young mustache, "Ye'd better learn to wear your pants longer and your name shorter if ye want to git along in America."

He had to cut all expenses down to the bone during those months. He cut down on his sleeping and his eating, so it seemed believable to him that he also had to cut down on his name. But he intended to reclaim the last syllable as soon as he could afford it.

Every time he changed jobs, which was frequent because he was rising like a cork in a water tank, he was determined that he would write his full name on his application. But the references he had acquired seemed more vital than the lost "bach," so Auer he remained. The phonetic change in the spelling from Auer to Our was his amused concession to American commercialism which he came to admire and enjoy with all his rollicking exuberant humor. He installed on the top of his first small brewery a much-too-large electric sign which said Our Brew; thus commercialism gobbled up the first syllable of his name as surely as it had the last.

So complete was the transition that until Jubal was twelve years old he had never realized that the great family name had ever been anything but Our. Jubal's own name was partly a boast and partly a shame to his father. When Henry's contemporaries asked him how he happened to chose such an unusual name for his son he mumbled something about its being an old family name.

"From my wife's family, of course. Very educated people."

Henry might not have consented to the name, except that it caught him off guard, when his defenses were weakened, as any father's are when his first son has just been born. They had an agreement, he and Lucile. He was to name all the girls in the family and she was to name all the boys. (With one stipulation from him — there were to be no more Henrys in Lucile's life.)

So when the nurse had brought his son out to be inspected at the end of the worst day Henry had ever lived, there was a little note written by Lucile herself long before this day had commenced.

"My darling," (the note said, written in her primly beautiful schoolteacher's hand)

"This is to introduce our son

Jubal Rumston Our

"I hope he will look like you, and will inherit your breadth of heart. I have named him for the man who invented the first musical instrument the world ever knew. I like to imagine what kind of man he must have been, who first dared to make music on an instrument of twigs and thongs."

To tell the truth, Henry was quite superior about his son's name at first. By the time he found out where the name actually came from, it was too late to change it, chagrined and sheepish though he felt about the origin. For the name came out of the Book of Genesis. And Henry never could get over believing that only soft and weak people let the Bible influence them.

"But not women, of course," he apologized to Lucile when he tried to explain this to her. "Women are supposed to be soft and weak."

She let him clasp her protectively in his arms, as he said this ingenuous thing, and she did not deny it. But in her heart she was laughing to herself, for it had been her experience that the strongest and the most lasting things in the world were those which came out of the Bible. That was why she had rooted her son and his name in that Book. But she was far too wise to say so.

When Papa talked about his beer, there was a poet in the house. When the Ours entertained Papa's friends, most of whom were in the brewery business themselves, Lucile permitted no shop talk. But Papa had ways of getting around her gentle dicta. He had agreed to leave the commercial aspect of his beloved brewing outside the walls of his home, but he had devised sly ways of bringing it in through academic ruminations.

When some Otto or Carl or August would be dining intimately with the Our family, Papa would get a glazed and happy look in his eyes about the time the nuts and raisins had been laid on the huge table, and Lucile would know that he was about to wander back into the antiquity of the industry.

"I suppose you think that Germany brewed the first ale in history," he might say jovially, and his guests, who likely as not had heard all this before, would cock their eyes attentively and give him right of way, because after all he was their host.

"The source of primitive brewing is enshrouded in the mists of antiquity," he would say then, quoting verbatim some for-

gotten source and comfortably settling farther back on his pelvis
to give his crowded barrel of a stomach more working room
for the vast task just thrust upon it.

"Antiquity, hmn?" the guest would murmur.

"The ancient derivation . . . *cere-visiae,*" Papa would say
happily. "You know what that comes from, of course."

A decently amiable guest would shake his head encourag-
ingly, and a less tactful one would nod vaguely. But whatever
the response, Papa would always go right on, "*Ceres,* of course,
the goddess of corn, and *vis,* naturally, means strength."

"Naturally."

"Brewing reached its greatest development, probably, at the
height of Egyptian civilization," Papa would say thoughtfully,
as if he had been there personally and had compared all the
brews down through the ages. "But for a thousand years after
the decline of Egyptian gentility, the art of brewing lay
neglected."

Sometimes Lucile herself would come to his aid and ask the
question which would carry him safely on, before some other
impatient male could siphon the conversation off into another
subject.

"Is that so, Mr. Our?" Lucile would ask brightly, "And how
was the art of brewing rescued from oblivion then?"

Papa would look down the table at her with melting fondness in his blue eyes. In all innocence he believed that she had
never before heard the answer to this, and that she honestly
wanted to know.

"Why, that is a very interesting point," Papa would say.
"Brewing was revived by the large European monasteries to
provide entertainment and wholesome nourishment for the pil-
grims on crusades."

Then he was safely launched, and nothing could block him
from here on, so Lucile leaned back among her laces, with a
listening smile on her face, and her dark curls nodding atten-

tively from time to time, while her mind went window-shopping about its own feminine business.

"Yes sir, wholesome nourishment," Papa would say. "Beer is really food. A glass of good ale is approximately as nourishing as a glass of milk. The barley, of course. . . . " He had sundry excellent and tiresome statistics and these he ran through nimbly. When he had exhausted his hearers (though never himself, for he seemed built up into new strength just by thinking of the nourishment) he usually brought the conversation to a close with a high flourish by quoting John Milton.

"Yes . . . our industry has brought great comfort to the race. And such harm as we must answer for is the misuse, not the use. Milton himself says, 'No man denies that best things may be abused. But what does most harm in the abusing, if used rightly, does most good. And such a good to take away from honest men, for being abused by such as abuse all things, is the greatest abuse of all.' "

He liked that very much. He would gladly have said it again. He thought that if he ever built a new brewery, he would have those words carved in stone, or printed in gold, above the entrance, silent answer to those busybodies who sometimes talked about abolishing beer by legislation. As well talk of abolishing sunshine because sometimes men suffered sunstroke. . . .

The children were seldom present when Papa entertained. So about once a year, he permited himself to run through the routine with them.

"I want the children to be proud of my brewery," he often said to Lucile. "Jubal and Minna . . . I want them to know what an honorable thing it is."

"They're too young to think much about it," Lucile said.

"Children are never too young to think," Papa would say. "I want them to think in the right way. When Jubal goes to college I want him to learn all there is to know about our industry . . . maybe study chemistry and work out improvements. I would be pleased to leave something to the brewing industry which has our name attached."

"Must you wait for Jubal, darling? Why not have something invented now with the name of Henry Our attached?" Lucile would ask, with no mischief in her eye.

"Umn . . . perhaps," Papa would say very seriously. "Jubal will make industry history. I have had to learn from experience. Jubal will go on where I leave off. He'll begin with all I know and add to it."

Jubal, matter of fact, was very much interested in his father's business. He often asked intelligent questions, and received deluging answers. And later in the day, and with no visible connection, of course, out of the fullness of his heart, his father always gave him some handsome present. His first pony, a Victor talking machine with a big metal petunia from which the music roared, and various other gifts came by this method.

His mother warned him. "Jubal, I'm not going to have that happen again."

"What happen, Mother?"

"You know very well how Papa happened to bring home those new ice skates." Jubal looked at her measuringly, making up his mind whether or not they would be frank with each other, or go on playing the charade of child and adult.

"But it makes him happy, Mother," he said. "You know it does. And you. . . ."

"Jubal, that will do," she said sternly. "It's different with me. I'm his wife, and a woman is supposed to encourage her husband."

She saw that Jubal was thinking over and finally accepting that spurious difference between their two guiles. Then suddenly her lovely honesty asserted itself.

"We're both frauds, Jubal," she said. "We both do the same thing to Papa. The only difference is that women aren't expected to behave too sincerely. But people do expect little boys to be honest." She knew that honest was not really the word, and she thought to herself, At least people don't expect little boys to be astute enough to see through a man like Henry.

"Well, anyway," Jubal said, "I expect he gets more out of it than we do. We get the gift, but Papa gets the happiness."

"Never mind that," Lucile said sternly. "Don't try to pretend that you're doing it for anything but the gift, my young friend. It's deplorable to deceive other people, but it's despicable to deceive yourself."

Jubal thought that over. "If you're dishonest, be honest enough to know you're dishonest," he said with his wide, disarming grin.

"That will do," his mother said, and then her dimples showed him that they understood each other.

The boy could not help knowing that he was the apple of his father's eye.

"Don't be ashamed because your papa thinks you are such a fine boy," Henry would say, holding Jubal at arm's length and admiring him. "Your papa was hungry for somebody to love for a long, long time."

Occasionally after such an outburst, Papa would feel that he must balance the excess by stern disapproval. So Jubal would be punished for some minor misdemeanor. Papa was tortured by the punishment, while Jubal philosophically endured it, knowing that one extreme was as absurd as the other, and that neither had any real bearing on his own deserving. It was entirely Papa's affair, as Jubal saw it. Papa was the subject and the predicate; Jubal was only the object, he thought to himself, for he was studying grammar at that time.

But the streams of affection between the man and his son ran deep and strong, and the boy thought of his father as a rock of rightness and power. When Lucile read the Bible to him, it was Papa himself who brooded protectively through the Psalms.

"The Lord is my shepherd," Lucile read, and Jubal thought to himself, It's funny to think of Papa ever being out in a field taking care of sheep. That must have been before he came to America. When he asked his mother about it, she was shocked and tried to describe God as she conceived him. But that only left Jubal with the impression that once Papa had worn long whiskers instead of the silky skein of golden mustache which now decorated his face.

He loved to hear about the lonely early days in America, when young Heinrich had wandered up and down the uncaring streets of lower New York.

"The buildings were so high and noble," Papa said. "Higher even than they are now, Jubal, because I was lower then. You know how that could be possible?"

"Of course," Jubal said.

"And the people seemed lower to me then, because I was living on the mountains inside myself, the impossible mountains that every boy must have within, if he is going to amount to anything."

Jubal, even when he was still only twelve or so, used to suffer (deliciously from this safe distance) because of Papa's loneliness.

"I kept thinking to myself: Somewhere there are the sky-scraper people, and I will wait until I am good enough to find them," Papa said.

He loved hearing how his father had been pushed west by the dream of finding his own good life, how he had at last saved up enough money to buy a ticket to Chicago from a scalper who lurked in the shadows outside Grand Central Depot waiting for just such boys as himself.

"I took a chance that the ticket he sold me would be no good when I got on the train, and that the conductor would disgrace me and throw me off and my valise after me. But anyway, fourteen thirty-four it cost me to ride forty hours in a coach with orange peels and banana skins underfoot, and the cinders so gritty in the green plush of the seats that my face broke out like measles. But nothing dampened my spirits, neither the dirt, the noise, nor the ruffians who tried to bait me when they found out what kind of an innocent I was."

Jubal suffered and exulted through Papa's first job in Chicago, in a dark little basement office, where young Heinrich sweated and scribbled as a bill clerk.

"Six dollars a week they paid me, and another two dollars if I wanted to spend four more evenings working."

"And did you?" Jubal would ask, and his father would toss him a look which more than answered.

"I'd have worked nine evenings in the week, if I had known where to lay my hands on the extra evenings." His round drum of chest would rumble with mirth as he remembered the titanic zeal of the immigrant.

"And such meals as I ate!" he would cry, thumping his stomach fondly. "I paid five dollars a week for room and board, and the more food you could hold, the better bargain you got. But the typhoid fever cheated me in the end."

"It did?"

"Two weeks I had to lie on my bed without a mouthful of food," he said, looking lean in the jowl as he remembered it. "That was the way to cure typhoid fever in those days. Not a mouthful, not a crumb. I think the typhoid was pushed out by the starvation."

Jubal had a robust michievousness in him which often got him into trouble. Little Minna said she never knew when he was just foolin' and when she was supposed to believe what he said because he was her big brother.

"You can't tell by looking at him, Mama," Minna used to

whine when she got herself into a predicament because she had carried out some fanciful instruction from Jubal.

"Well, on the uncertainty, it's safest to decide that he's always fooling," Mama said.

"But Mama," the little girl insisted, "nobody can fool all the time."

"Jubal can."

Minna was the sober side of Henry, Lucile often thought to herself, and that was one reason the child's father was remorsefully indifferent about her.

"Dress her up pretty, Lucile. She's a good little girl, so she'll have to be dressed up especially pretty to cover up that handicap," Papa said when he was forced to concentrate on his small tiresome daughter. "Maybe we ought to give her dancing lessons. Her legs yet." (For his own amusement he lapsed into funny-paper German occasionally.)

"She looks like you, my darling," Mama said, "especially from the knees down."

"Well, I got a right to have bulgy legs," Papa said. "I'm a boy. But Minna, ach. We give her dancing lessons."

"You needn't worry about Minna," Lucile said. "She's a nice sensible child, and she'll grow up into just the kind of woman you yourself might better have married."

"Don't talk foolish," Papa said. "No matter what kind of man I would have turned out to be, I'd still have much better married you."

Whatever else in the universe Papa wanted changed and improved . . . and he had so much vitality that he was always instigating improvements, some madly radical and some thoroughly workable . . . one perfection stood fast: his beautiful Lucile, so quiet and gentle, yet so full of highfalutin nonsense in the head to which he listened without translating, the way one might listen to music.

"Pay attention to what your mother says," he'd sometimes say crossly to Jubal. But you could see by the dreamy look on his face that he was paying attention not at all to her thoughts but only to her face which he found so lovely and refreshing to his eyes.

"You talk so pretty. It makes no difference that you speak foolishness, Leibchen," he often said to her.

"What foolishness do I talk?"

"You know very well," he said craftily. "You use this question as a little door for me to push open. Then I find the conversation is inside the subject I do not wish to find myself in. But I'm too smart to push open the door."

"You're too smart for many things my Henry," Lucile said. "You have the smartness of the brain. But you also have good in your heart."

"That's right," he said contentedly. "And I leave religion to my wife. That's smart, right there."

If he had taken her views more seriously, her great spirituality might have warred with his genial materialism. But he had early found that the way of negating that was never to allow her to talk about the things he didn't want to bother with. "Those are for you. You take care of God, and I take care of the rest. That way our family prospers."

After he came home from the brewery, he liked to have a quiet little time with Mama in her sitting room. In the winter, she had a fire waiting for him there, and an oval tray with a Venetian glass bottle of sherry and two dainty glasses standing on a spindly-legged table. He liked everything in Mama's sitting room because it was fragile and deliciously ridiculous, and he could stamp around in the room making the chandelier shiver and glint and the small rosewood chairs shudder at the thought of his sitting on them. Sometimes the children could hear chuckles and whispering coming from Mama's sitting room, but nobody was supposed to go in and interrupt. When the gong in the hall below would announce dinner, Mama would come out pink-cheeked and prettily bemused, and Papa would be walking solidly on the balls of his feet and rubbing his hands together with good nature.

Papa loved everything about his home, and he loved it with bravura. So sincere was his conviction that everything in his house was wonderful, that he even tolerated Minna's sniveling piano music, and listened patiently while she sat with her plump legs dangling and thumped out simplified Chopin.

"It will improve," he said sometimes. "Minna will begin to see that music is something to be enjoyed."

One day, however, he had charged into the music room with a beaming face because he had heard genuine music coming from behind the closed door. Then he had stopped blankly, for it was Jubal on the piano stool, a brooding Jubal, with a serious face for once.

"But . . . do you take lessons, also?" Papa had stammered, and Jubal had jumped up guiltily from the stool and stood there blushing.

"I'm sorry, Papa. I thought nobody was home."

"You play some more," Papa commanded. He sat down in one of the brocatelle chairs, his feet planted squarely on the pink and cream rug, his plump hands palm-down on his knees. "I listen now, and you play me something."

Jubal said, "I can't really play, Papa. I just fool with it."

"You play."

So Jubal played again. This time he played with thunder and waves, and a bit of flourished elbows and galloping hands, because he never could resist a really appreciative audience.

"What is that? Mozart, Wagner?" Papa asked.

"It's nothing," Jubal said, standing beside the piano and trying to keep his legs from trembling with excitement. "I just make up things, Papa. For fun."

"Tomorrow you begin to study music," Papa said. "I listen every week to that Minna play baby music. And all the time in the house, we have something big."

"But Minna's so proud of her music."

"She finds something else to be proud of," Papa said angrily. "We don't waste time any more with that."

"You mean, you'll stop Minna's lessons?"

Papa flipped his hands crossly, for he didn't want to think of mediocrity when talent, that thing he most worshiped, was blazing in the house.

"Lessons or no lessons . . . what difference would it make?" he said with annoyance.

But Jubal couldn't let it rest that way.

"I can't take piano lessons," he said. "It would spoil it for Minna. Minna hasn't got much else, Papa. I've got everything. And anyway nothing could take the music away from me."

Papa got up from his chair and came over and embraced his son. "Jubey, you're a good fine boy," he said. "No wonder you got music in you which doesn't need to be taught."

"I'm not good," Jubal said in hot embarrassment. "I'm only saying it so you'll think how good I am, Papa."

"I understand," Papa said, refusing to be defrauded of his son's wonderfulness. "I know you, Jubey. So we won't take the music lessons. Maybe I get you a place downtown where you can play the piano whenever you want to. So Minna won't hear it. That Minna."

"That'd be fine," Jubal said. "But the music will wait for me. I don't see a piano very often. Where I can play it, I mean. But whenever I do, why it's just like we're old friends."

"Yah. That's right, that's right," Papa said, pleased to a mistiness of the eyes.

At the table, when the family was alone Papa listened to Minna's piping little inanities, but his real delight was to hear Jubal tell about some boyish exploit or other. Papa was a boy with Jubal, and he entered into the teasing and the mischief and sometimes even a quickly concealed immature obscenity. And Lucile, serene and mothering, watched over them both with rare understanding.

Once, when the children were present even though August
Glazer, the congressman, was dining with the Our family, Jubal
became intoxicated with the attention he was getting, and almost plunged to disaster.

Papa was about to launch into his exposition of the nourishment value of beer. He was sitting up very straight in his
massively carved armchair, his taupe vest with the festoon of
watch chain across it, thrust out like a rotund boast. He had
led up through the preliminaries which the family well knew,
and was about to open his mouth in the first syllables of the
main dissertation, when Jubal thrust out his own chest, and
pushed back the lapels of an imaginary coat.

"Mr. Glazer, I'm going to tell you something that will surprise you," Jubal said with dignity.

"What's that, my boy?"

"I wonder if you appreciate the relative merits of beer and
milk? Common cow's milk, that is." He held his head slightly
on one side, and August Glazer wondered how he had never
happened to notice before how many of his father's mannerisms
the boy had.

"A friend of ours suffered from a broken leg last week. A
regrettable occurrence. He's an elderly man, and he lives in
a small frame house over on Carr Street, which has a front
porch with a flight of stairs leading up to it."

Papa at this moment was looking in astonishment at Jubal,
but Lucile's eyes were downcast, and she was nervously fingering the lace of her bosom.

"Poor old Mr. Brandenburg . . . no relation to the Concerto,
of course . . . went out early in the morning to get the bottle
of milk which the milkman had left at the door. His eyes are
dim, and his feet are none too sure, and as he stooped over to
pick up the bottle, he slipped on a piece of ice. Before he
knew what had happened he had bounded down the whole
flight of steps."

Part-way through this recital, Jubal picked up an imaginary

gold watch chain from his own flat little chest, and swung it in his fingers as his father often did when he was making a point. This was more than Lucile could endure.

"Jubal, that will do," she said stiffly, not daring to look at the original of this burlesque.

But Jubal was so carried away by his own impersonation that he heard the interruption only as a cue thrown to him by one of the supporting cast.

"Lucile, my pet, you must not interrupt me," he said exactly as Papa had said it one million times in this room. He heard a drowning gasp from the other end of the table, but he was already so guilty there was no use in trying to back out into innocence. If he were going to be saved at all, it would have to be through laughter.

"To continue, Glazer, our friend broke his leg. And that shows you how much more beneficial to the race is beer than that evil-smelling, overestimated beverage which your constituents in the Anti-Saloon League are forever recommending."

August Glazer, enjoying the moment with all the accumulated malice of his long envy of Papa, roared appreciatively.

"But I don't see how that proves . . . " he said.

"You don't, Glazer?" Jubal pounced on the point delightedly, as Papa did when there was an opportunity to show his contemporaries that they had overlooked something quite obvious. "Why, if poor old Mr. Brandenburg . . . no relation to the Concerto, of course . . . had been a beer drinker, he would have stepped safely over to his little icebox cozily placed in the corner of his kitchen, and would not have risked his life in the stormy elements where the milkman leaves his filthy wares."

Papa was out of his chair now, his face popping with angry blood. "Why, you . . . I'll not have that son of yours, Lucile Rumston. . . . " Papa looked as if he were going to burst into tears of chagrin and mortification.

Jubal, still in his part, was looking at him quizzically as if he were some steamy peasant. Jubal, in fact, was looking just as Papa usually looked when anyone else tried to express too-violent feeling.

Papa stopped where he was, halfway around the table. For a moment the outraged original and the impersonator looked each other in the eye. Then Jubal crumbled, and put his shaking little paw up over his mouth in terror.

"I beg your pardon, Papa . . . I didn't mean . . . "

It was a moment of utter ghastly nightmare.

But suddenly, with one of his lightning changes, Papa burst into Jovian mirth. Papa laughed until the tears came to his eyes. He slapped his chest to keep from choking.

"D'ja hear that, Glazer? That boy of mine . . . did you ever hear anything like that? He's more like me than I am myself!"

Everyone in the room began to breathe again.

"Come here, you scalawag, and let me . . . " He was beaming with fond amusement now. But Jubal looked crumpled and pale, as if he were stricken with some excruciating physical pain. He ran to his father, and buried his face.

"You ought to punish me, Papa," he muttered. "You ought to do something terrible to me, sir. I don't know what got into me. I didn't mean to make a joke of you. . . . "

"Nonsense, Jubal. You were only having a little fun. You were entertaining us all," Papa said. "I didn't know you had it in you. I didn't know I had it in myself. . . . "

But Jubal was inconsolable. He could not explain to the roomful of people goggling at him with conflicting emotions in their faces. But he had never been so ashamed of himself, and so grieved in his life. He had hurt something inside himself, and that was the precious image of his father's dignity.

"There isn't anybody on earth better than you . . . and I made a joke of you," he said painfully, unable to meet his father's fatuous eyes. "I don't know how I could do such a thing, sir. Not to you."

"You did nothing to Papa, my son," Henry said tenderly.
"You only made your old papa laugh." He laughed again to
prove it.

"I did something dreadful," Jubal said. "I did it to myself."
It was a small and unimportant scene, and yet it became a
signet deep in Jubal Our, which stamped its shape eventually
in the biggest and most pervasive pattern of his life.

4

At the end of Jubal's thirteenth summer, he and Papa returned from their triumphal trip to Germany, two weeks after school had started.

"The boy has learned more in this three months than schools could teach him in a year," Papa said, dismissing the tardy enrollment with a snap of his fingers. "And I besides learned much," he added earnestly.

"You, my darling?" Lucile widened her eyes with mock incredulity.

"Nobody could associate with a young inquisitiveness without bursting his own horizons," Henry said.

"Then it was a good trip, and I'm glad you had it. But I missed you terribly."

"That is a sound for the ears like the sight of the Statue of Liberty for the homesick eyes," Papa said, and kissed her fingers. "Yes, it was a good trip. And besides, we brought back the finest *Braumeister* in Munich, descended straight from the brew master of Duke Wilhelm der Frommer himself."

Lucile's hand patted him at that characteristic sentence, so full of happy bombast, but ending as usual with its feet firmly on the ground.

Jubal said, "We had pretzels as big as kites. And radishes. They cut them in corkscrews and salted them just the way Anna does for us, Mama. They do so many things just the way we do them here in our house."

"They have heard of us, perhaps," Lucile said with gentle

33

irony. "They know enough to copy a good household, those Munichens."

"Don't tease the boy," Papa said. "He found himself at home, and that's the best feeling on earth. At home! Ach, what words." His eyes filled with quick moisture like the white radishes Jubal had described, which "weep" when enough salt has been sprinkled into their crevices.

"And Wiener Schnitzel, Mama," Jubal said, "and Sauerbraten." He bubbled along, telling all about the wonderful things they had seen and done in Munich, about the Hofbrauhaus with its noisy band concert in the cobbled square courtyard with singing family groups seated around tables which were really big beer kegs scrubbed nearly white. He was filled with anecdotes about the old Graf Lechberg palace where they had stayed, and where he had slept in a Biedermeier bed in a room with a secret door leading out to the fine carved staircase. Fräulein Liesecke and her sister, the Other Fräulein, the hostesses of the celebrated old pension, had pampered him prodigiously, and as usual he had emerged from the encounter knowing that being Papa's son was about as privileged a position as a boy could ask in life.

He had brought Minna a Kaiserlein Lebkuchen from Nürnberg, that toy city which is supposed to have spilled out of Santa Claus' pack. He was disappointed because to her it was only stale gingerbread with a crumbling sugar portrait of Kaiser Frederick III on the top. Minna would rather have had a good substantial doll, she said, and Jubal refused to comment on this stupid heresy. Dolls might be bought anyplace, since one had money enough. But only from Nürnberg could the Kaiserlein Lebkuchen come.

He waited until all the greetings which dissipate attention were over, and the whole family was gathered quietly at the end of the homecoming meal, and then he told about Papa's old town. He described it so well that Papa sat there with tears running frankly down his face, and one could not help knowing that this moment here at the table was better to Papa than the actual sight of the village. For this moment had all the implications and overtones of Papa's secure present locked within.

Papa's town was Rothenburg, so old, so storied, and so unchanged by the centuries.

"Except for one thing," Papa said quickly, "the *blumbing*." He caricatured the word as he said it, but that was to hide the fact that actually Papa had not been pleased that the town had come into the miraculous heritage of plumbing. He had secretly anticipated going home and telling about his bathroom in St. Louis, while neighbors listened, incredulous. But there the plumbing was, undeniably. Not excellent plumbing, of course, but adequate. Hot and cold.

They found the very house where Papa had been a boy, and sure enough there were goats nibbling in the streets, just as he had said there would be. Papa and Jubal had gone along the Kapellenplatz, with both their hearts pounding with excitement. And there at Number 4 was the Bierstube with men sitting solemnly around tables, playing chess or reading, with their steins beside them. The men had glanced up and then went on with whatever they were doing. So Papa stood in the middle of the room and said, "Does anyone here know of Heinrich Auerbach who used to live in this village twenty-five years ago?" (That was when Jubal first knew about their name.)

Some of them didn't bother looking up again, but a few old-timers glanced up quickly. And then one of them . . . Here Jubal had to act it out.

" 'Why . . . that's the Auerbach nose!' he cried. And he made a dive for the nose . . . but not on Papa," the boy said. "He made a dive for the nose on *me*."

"He did," Papa said. "He knew Jubal by the nose. 'It's

the same old wrinkle and dip at the end that old Jacob Auerbach had!' That's what they all said. Jacob was my grandfather, Mama," he explained. "I remembered, after they mentioned it. No wonder this Jubal here always seemed like a blood relation of mine!" He laughed tremulously at his cumbersome joke. "No wonder."

So then everyone in the place had crowded around them, and one by one the responsible middle-aged men took off their disguises and Papa recognized his old playmates.

After that nobody would hear of Henry and his boy taking rooms in one of the inns. The old friends fought and argued for the privilege of moving them from the Eisehut and taking them home. By night every house in the village knew that Jacob Auerbach's nose had returned, worn this generation by an American boy.

The Mayor, of course, had the honor finally of being their host, although his family had never done anything before but snub and humiliate the Auerbachs. But all that was tactfully forgotten now, and Henry would have been the most passionate in denying that it ever had happened. So for ten days they lived in the aristocratic old house in the Herrenstrasse, with its hidden courtyard painted in faded old frescoes showing the Ages of Man. The Mayoress loaded them down with gifts to be taken home to Lucile and Minna. These would be arriving throughout the next exciting weeks when the rest of the trunks caught up with the travelers.

"And now for the Meistertrunk story," Jubal said, and his quick eye glared at Mama and Minna, to warn them that they were not to say, "But Jubal . . . Papa's told us this story a hundred times. . . . "

He told it as if it had never been heard before, and they listened in the same spirit. The story was supposed to have happened during the Thirty Years' War, when Rothenburg was captured by the Imperial General, Tilly. All the city councilmen had been ordered hanged, for Tilly fancied the little city and decided that he would take it over and run it his own way. But while he was sitting in conference, someone brought him the three-quart Pokal or state beaker, filled with the town's best wine. The seven aides of Tilly passed the beaker round and round, quaffing deeply and wiping their lips on their sleeves.

Finally the servant who was passing the huge stein from man to man was heard to say, "Ah . . . you are puny drinkers compared to the good men of Rothenburg."

Tilly, a little tipsy by now, overhead the insult. "What do you mean by saying such a thing?"

"I mean only what everyone can see for himself," the servant said.

"What is that, you wretch?"

"Why, any man in Rothenburg can drink the Pokal at a swallow."

Tilly was furious at such audacity.

"All right, you filthy braggart, we shall see about that. Fill up the Pokal again. If any man here can drink it at one draught, I shall free the town," he said.

The Rothenburgers were stunned. Then the Burgomeister stepped forward and seized the Pokal in his trembling hand. He lifted it to his lips and drained the three interminable quarts, drinking and drinking until the veins stood out on his forehead and his upraised hands shook with the tension. The room was deathly still, except for the almost-sobbing gulping of the Burgomeister. Then the last drop was drained. He lowered the Pokal from before his face, and toppled senseless at Tilly's feet.

So the life of the town was saved. And best of all a tradition was born, and the town has forever a festival to be celebrated every year, the Meistertrunk festival which lasts a week, and makes the whole year worthwhile.

"And those are the fine men one finds in Rothenburg," Jubal said at the end of his story. "But none so fine as our own papa."

"No, none so fine as our own papa," Lucile said, and reached over her soft hand and laid it on Papa's.

But in the morning she added an amendment to her praise. For it was not until the next morning that she realized that Jubal had brought home for himself a passion which would have eclipsed everything else, if it had been mentioned first. Because this had been Papa's trip and Papa's homecoming, Jubal, with more than a boy's discernment and graciousness, had given Papa his great happy day with nothing usurping even the smallest corner of it.

Papa himself brought up the subject the next morning at breakfast.

"Jubal, you quite forgot to tell your mother," Papa said.

"Forgot?"

Papa looked at him in amazement. "Here I spend three thousand five hundred dollars for a toy for you, and you forget even to mention it!"

Lucile said, "What on earth, Henry?"

Papa sat back now in his chair, enjoying this morsel of his own rich generosity. "That boy of yours, Lucile! Wait until you see what is coming by express. And also technical men traveling by train out here to build a laboratory for your son!"

"What *are* you talking about?"

"A wireless, Mama," Jubal said, his face flushed with excitement now that the wonderful word was out.

"Such a thing," Papa said with maddening deliberation. "Well to go back to the beginning. You know America is not so smart about everything in the world as we sometimes think she is. There are other places, too, yet, where ideas are born."

"Yes, yes," Lucile cried impatiently, "we agree on that, my darling. But what. . . . "

"There was once a young German high-school teacher named Heinrich Rudolph Hertz," Papa said. "In 1877 . . . "

"Oh, good heavens . . . do we always have to go back into the mists of antiquity?" Lucile cried with irreverent impatience. Papa gazed at her as if he could not possibly imagine what she was talking about. "What's all this to do with Jubal? You tell me *instantly*."

"I am telling you," Papa said loudly.

Jubal himself cut through the confusion now. "Papa bought me a wireless set, Mama. I'm to have it for my own. There isn't another one as good this side of the Allegheny Mountains."

"But what on earth will you do with it? Wire . . . what *is* wireless, anyway? It's dangerous, isn't it? It's something wrecked ships have, don't they. . . . ?"

"Your son, my dear woman, has displayed signs of being an engineering genius," Papa said stiffly.

Mama burst out laughing then. "Oh, Henry . . . you get such extravagant notions! Of course he's not an engineering genius. He's only a little boy, and you just keep thinking up more and more grandiloquent ways of flattering yourself that your child. . . . "

"No, Mama," Jubal said quite seriously. "This is something different. I wouldn't be a bit surprised if maybe I am a. . . . "

"Jubal, you leave the room," his mother said. "I want to talk to your father."

"No, stay," Papa said. "When I get myself into a tangle and cannot tell your mama the names of the things which are wound up into this strange big box of wires and plates, you must help me."

"I don't want to hear about any wires and plates," Lucile said crossly. "Don't think you'll put me off and lose me in something you know I cannot understand. I want to hear immediately what all this has to do with Jubal."

"Stop fluttering your hands like butterflies, and we will tell you," Papa said placatingly. "Now. You have heard of Marconi, my pet?"

"I have also heard of Christopher Columbus. He discovered this spot on which we are eating our breakfast, but we do not have to begin with him."

"True," Papa said patiently. "But we must go back to Marconi. No further, I promise you."

Jubal came and stood close to his mother, unconsciously using that physical winsomeness of his. "It's the greatest thing in the world. Hertz discovered how to pick up waves from the atmosphere. You see, Mama, the atmosphere is like a great invisible ocean. Every sound lies on it like chips on the surface of the sea. The waves Hertz found a way of recording are very fast . . . too fast to carry voices or music. But an American has found a way of improving that. A man named Fessenden tried to build a generator. . . . "

Mama threw up her hands in resigned despair, but Papa put his finger on his lips and motioned for her to listen attentively to what their son was saying.

"Fessenden's generator was to smooth out the current and make it steadier. You see, he was trying to find a receiver that would translate impulses the way the telephone receiver does. Then we could have not only the dots and dashes in the code, but we might hear the actual sounds transmitted. Not a telegraph, Mama. But really a telephone . . . only without any wires."

"So?"

"Well, he has succeeded. Voices and music have been sent without any wires. Sent through the air itself."

"It should please you, Lucile," Papa said cajolingly. "The first words that ever were spoken in the test were from your Bible. 'Glory to God in the highest, and on earth peace and good will to men,'" Papa quoted.

Lucile was still cautious. "Even that does not prove it is a good thing for a child to be playing with," she said sternly. "The Bible has been quoted and misused throughout history

very often when men want to hide something they are doing."
But she was pleased, and her eyes were large and excited in
spite of herself.

They led her carefully through the maze, until she understood that Jubal was to have a wireless set of his own, and that
in addition his father had bought a collection of all available
materials so that he might begin building himself a crystal
detector for his own experimenting. They were sending home
an already obsolete Fleming valve, a deForest audion, and
fragments of galena and silicon and carborundum, and a tall
prop wound with wire like a Christmas tree with tinsel, which
was to snare silent signals out of the air and transform them
into voices.

The New York newspapers had found out about the prodigy
and his amazing collection of unassembled equipment, and
had sent reporters down to the Astor to interview him. Papa
had a picture of himself and Jubal posing in the bay window
of their suite. Mama glanced at the picture and the half-
column of printing.

"But it will be dangerous for a boy."

"I have seen to that," Henry said. "We stopped on our way
home and made all the arrangements."

"Arrangements?"

"Experts are coming next week from the Westinghouse
Electric Company in Schenectady. They will build Jubal a
safe place to work in. They will make him a small glass-walled
laboratory down at the end of the grounds where the carriage
house used to be."

"Papa has thought of everything," Jubal said.

"The place will be perfectly safe with insulation," Papa said
complacently. "You know that I would not ever let anything
unpleasant or dangerous happen to anyone."

5

BUT IN THE NEXT few years, dangers and catastrophes sprang up
against which Papa could provide no insulation. There was a
barbershop in a small continental city, and waiting tensely in
its doorway at noon on the twenty-ninth of June, 1914, was an
impassioned young student who fired two shots into a passing
automobile. The man and woman in the automobile continued to sit bolt upright, but when the terrified chauffeur had
driven the car to a hospital, attendants lifted out two lifeless
bodies.

Two dead bodies. War casualties. The first names to appear
on lists which now would grow and spread through the months
and the years until everyone alive on the earth had been drawn
into widening circles shivering away from those two shots at
Sarajevo.

Jubal was sixteen by this time. He had romped his way
through high school much too fast for anyone's comfort. The
big problem of the house was how to occupy him until he was
old enough to be sent to college. The solution seemed to be a
series of owl-faced tutors, young grinds delighted to be living
in the snug luxury of the Our mansion. A vast and bubbling
volcano of information seethed below the good nature of young
Jubal Our, so that by the time the chills and fever of war had
really gripped the world, he was one of the best-informed
uneducated persons in the country.

His curiosity was prodigious. Being entirely unhampered, it
was a wild animal; it differed from other wild animals only in

good nature. It was fierce and tireless, but its ferocity was benevolent.

"That brain of his is a pig," Papa said. "It eats all the time . . . a glutton. But a good glutton."

"It will become an epicure in time," Lucile said. "Now it wants everything it sees. Eventually it will choose and select."

When the first quiver of excitement shook the sunny complacency of that August day when Germany declared war on Russia, and France declared war on Germany, Jubal precociously recognized it as the world-shattering warning it was. Much of the globe secretly welcomed war as a great animal workout which could end only in victory (for each side . . . for such is the ambidextrous madness of world lust). America, safe behind its ocean, looked on as an unconcerned spectator. But Jubal, young though he was, knew it was the end of something gentle and innocent on earth.

At breakfast Papa read the newspaper account of the way the nations were going to war, chanting hymns and shouting patriotic battle songs through village streets decked with flags and flowers. No one was bored or lethargic now; the weary round of farm life, the cozy inanity of village life, the city's alert dementia were broken at last, and now there was a chance to wrestle and romp. It was a carnival for old hatreds and new loyalties.

"They have made a Hetz of it," Papa said, using that word which is untranslatable because the idea of a punishment-frolic is so uniquely indigenous to the Austrian psychology.

Lucile was sick and unhappy as she heard the reports. The newspaper said, "Unter den Linden filled with shrieking, singing paraders. 'War . . . give us war,' they shouted. 'Down with Russia,' they shrilled between verses of 'God save the Kaiser' and 'Deutschland, Deutschland über Alles.' " She lifted her troubled eyes to Papa, who was perspiring with excitement as he read the picturing words.

Lucile said, "They go to war with songs on their lips as if they didn't know what dying means."

"The Old World is hungry for a good war," Papa said. "Like boys who have to fight because they want the others to think they are strong. But not America. America is a younger giant. He *knows* he is strong. He doesn't need to kill somebody to prove it."

Papa's eyes became dewy as they always did when he spoke about America, his beloved. "Americans will not need to fight. President Wilson will see to that."

Jubal asked, trying not to sound eager, "But if the day comes?"

"If the day comes . . . you will fight," Papa promised firmly. "I am too old and too fat. But maybe they can find a place to use me in the war, if America ever needs me."

Everyone was relieved when the war finally began for America. Now at last everyone knew where America stood, and no more big fancy words to becloud the matter. A lot of editorial ink had been spilled, a lot of oratorical gales had been spent, but now at last on April 2, 1917, the President called a special session of Congress and said the word. America had ceased to be that "moral eunuch which was calling itself neutral."

They had stayed out of war with oratory; they went in with more splendid eloquence. The lighted dome of the Capitol stood out against the rainy sky like a rallying torch, and under the dome the President was announcing that "the German submarine warfare is a warfare against mankind, a war against all nations, a challenge to all mankind." The heaven-shaking words were revolutionarily new then; later they were to become the tritest cliché which the laziest editorial writer on earth could reach for and slap into his copy.

The President was pleading that this might be "war without hate," and people tried to picture such ambiguity. After all, they told themselves meekly, Mr. Wilson was a college president, and if he said so, why it must be possible. "These crimes were committed only by the German Government," Wilson said. "Their source lay, not in any hostile feeling or purpose of the German people, who were no doubt ignorant of them."

When Papa read those words, he took out his silk handkerchief and wept unashamed. That wonderful Wilson yet! He had found a way of making all this bearable to Papa. America would not be *fighting* Germans! America would be *freeing* them! Papa hugged to his heart the germ of idealistic imbecility which he could not foresee would finally convulse the whole world in blood and lust. Not fighting but freeing! Freeing people . . . even against their will!

By October, two million men were overseas, and before the year was out fifty thousand drafted men each month were swarming across the ocean by transport. Someone wrote a song called "I Didn't Raise My Boy To Be a Soldier." A few persons sang it wistfully, but many declared that it was a song only for slackers. Why, everybody knew this wasn't just an ordinary war! This was a crusade, you might say. This was making the world safe for democracy, wasn't it? This was the war to end all wars!

There had been tension and guilt for a long time, but now, thanks to the President, America was holding up her head and looking the world in the eye with a holy expression. The streets were full of rosy-cheeked boys, and bands playing in open trucks, and well-dressed women stopping strangers to sell them Liberty Bonds. Everyone was in it, heart and soul and body. The daughters of prosperous patriots were dancing ecstatically with farmers' sons and immigrants' sons and the sons of no fathers at all, in a unifying public embrace under the title which left out nobody, the War Camp Community. War in America was on at last, and it was a cross between a hysterical revival meeting in which everyone converted his neighbor, and a glorious, clean picnic. It was a kind of carnival of music and make-believe which had stepped down from Howard

Chandler Christy posters and billboards. War was young and innocent then, a festival of sentimentality and chauvinism.

Then editors began printing gruesome stories of atrocities in Belgium. But these were so horrible that practically everyone recognized them as falling into the category of that newly used word "propaganda." Even the Huns, as the Germans were now being called, couldn't be as blood-lusting as *that!* So a man named Raemaker sprang up who drew persuasive cartoons of the Kaiser leering with pleasure as he wolfed down babies with a sword for a fork.

But for Papa the war was always fought on the high plane that Wilson had suggested. On April 9, Papa gave a great public celebration which cost him thousands of dollars, to announce that Jubal had enlisted in the Navy as a wireless operator. Thirteen other boys from Our Brewery families signed up that night, and Papa went to bed strangled with emotion too complex to be unsnarled.

Lucile knew only that her son was leaving in the morning for the submarine base at New London, Connecticut, for six months of dangerous training which would eventually put him aboard a marauding ship to prowl the sea looking for other ships to murder. Her Jubal would be the voice of that terrible steel-skinned monster. She had known that morning when Jubal and Papa came home from Germany with their fine talk of words flying from an electrified wire through vacant miles of air to find another electrified wire . . . that this would bring no good to anyone. Words were meant to stay home and work peaceably. And so were men. But it appeared she was the only woman in the world who thought so. . . .

Jubal himself was scarcely able to contain his excitement and bliss. At last he was out in the world of men. Even the campus of the university where he had spent a winter in a school of engineering had been cozier than he wanted his man's environment to be.

Now he would be in his own world. The submarine training had been physically hideous. But horrible as had been the wet blankets, the cold food, cramped quarters, the ever-present stench of gasoline, oil and sulphuric acid, on the Submarine G-4, Jubal had found a quickening in the mental vigor of that life. The men had liked him; he had come through creditably, so he knew he could endure anything.

The new ship would be a paradise after the torture of that existence. He was assigned as radio electrician, second class, to a mine layer, the U.S.S. *Susquehanna*, three thousand five hundred tons, four hundred and sixty feet long. She was painted from stem to stern with great colored arcs and rhomboids for camouflage. He had seen her once in New London; he had loved her on sight; and now she was his.

Jubal at nineteen was a tall, good-natured boy who looked at least twenty-five because of the tight-packed maturity of his figure. For the past five years or so he had thought like a man, but he had cautiously concealed that fact from everyone but himself, while he presumed on the prerogatives of being still a boy. Ever since the day he recognized that Papa, who seemed like the lord of his own private universe, was in reality only a child secretly bewildered at his own competence and good fortune, Jubal had been the elder in secret viewpoint. When a child becomes the father of his own parent, he never again can be wholeheartedly a boy.

6

JUBAL was supposed to report to his ship by three this afternoon. As soon as his train got into South Station, he would go
over to Pier Seven of the Charlestown Navy Yard where his
orders said the *Susquehanna* was tied up. He would look things
over quickly, and then decide how to spend the next nine hours.
After all, there would be many months ahead in which to get
acquainted with the ship; Boston might not be at his fingertips
again for years. A man must learn to *take* things as they came,
to reach out and grab them when they present themselves.

He showed his orders to the marine sentry at the Navy Yard
gate, then strode across the worn planks of Pier Seven trying
not to look too eager and delighted. But his heart was bounding and leaping. A young pleasant-looking officer was in
charge; if they had met under any other circumstances, Jubal
would have liked the guy and would have told him so, probably.
But as it was, he signed on soberly, and was soberly told where
to stow his gear. Then he asked for a liberty card for the rest of
the afternoon. The young officer of the deck, standing at a small
desk, looked over at him enquiringly, so Jubal mumbled a
quick improvisation.

"My mother's at the Copley Plaza, sir . . . I've not seen her
for quite some time . . . she's come on from the far West, in
case I could manage a few hours before we push off. . . ."

The officer said nothing, but wrote carefully on the card and
then glanced up at him. Jubal saw in his eyes that the lie hadn't

been necessary. Possibly expected, but not necessary.

"As a matter of fact, sir . . ."

"Okay, Our. Let's leave it at that, shall we?"

"Yessir." He took the card; then left as expeditiously as possible.

He saw from the card that he was to have until midnight. That would give him plenty of time to see the sights and have the finest dinner he could buy at the Touraine, or maybe the Parker House. But first of all, he'd dash up to Symphony Hall for a ticket. He must have some music which he could carry off to war with him from his last night on land.

After the concert he telephoned to St. Louis to say good-bye. He got back to the ship at eleven-forty, his veins pounding with the music which filled him to the brim. Not German music, of course, since that was out of taste now. But this interval gave the French their chance, and Rimsky-Korsakoff, and the Italians. The second sight of the *Susquehanna* thrilled him even more than had the daylight view of her. She was tied up beside her tall sister, the *Monongahela*. The two of them, stately against the stars, seemed to be carrying on a silent queenly conversation. In utter joy he walked about the pier in the purple shadows listening to the creaking and scraping of the hawsers and the straining and moaning of the gangway.

After a few minutes a voice called down to him from the deck of the ship.

"Better come aboard, sailor . . . it's nearly midnight."

He went up the gangway then, and stopped at the desk of the officer of the deck.

"Name?" asked the officer shortly. It was the same man with whom the lie hadn't gone down.

"Our, sir."

"How was your mother? Fine, I trust."

"Yessir. Just fine," Jubal said, wondering if he was supposed to grin or play this deadpan. "And she sent you her love, sir, if you don't mind."

"I don't mind at all," the officer said, playing it straight himself. "There's nothing like the love of a good woman, I always say."

"Yessir."

"Better get below now."

Jubal knew exactly where his bunk was, for he had marked it down carefully this afternoon. He groped along through the blue war-lights until he found the steep ladder which plunged into the dank and heated darkness of number one hold, a triangular hell, shaped like a flatiron and nearly as hot. Directly above was the mine deck along which ran four long tracks. Five hundred mines would be rolled along these tracks as the *Susquehanna* delivered these high explosives to their charted spots in the great mine barrage that was being laid from the northern tip of the British Isles to the Norwegian coast.

Climbing monkeylike down the ladder, Jubal said to himself, We won't have a ghost of a chance in this hold if we hit anything. We're below the water line, below the mine deck and rammed up in the point of the bow where nothing could get out. Preferred position for suicide, *if*.

In the half-light the tiers of bunks looked like shelves in a morgue, with disorderly bodies laid in rows waiting to be claimed. The singsong of a bilge pump somewhere below whined as background music, but over that shimmered a cacophony of tired men's breathing and snoring. Jubal tiptoed between the iron-pipe beds counting off to his own bunk, number three, section six. He stepped as lightly as possible on the pipe railing of the bunk beneath his and hoisted himself up to his own pallet.

A long hairy arm came out of the darkness and explored Jubal's bulk.

"Plenty of you, ain't they?" the voice from below said. "I

allus draw the biggest guy on the ship to sleep in the canvas on top of me."

Catcalls and specific advice about where to go or else pipe down came out of the darkness.

"Okay, okay," said the man operating the hairy arm. Jubal took off his shoes and squirmed out of his clothes, then lay down on the stretched canvas.

The whisper from below continued, "My name's Carter. Been on this here ship three months. Ain't a bad little boat. Once you get used to the stink."

Jubal felt he should show some friendliness, so he hung his head over the iron edge of his bunk and grinned into the darkness.

"Why, this is a perfumed boudoir, after the submarine I been on," he said imitating Carter's own speech.

"One thing. We ain't got so many god-damned regulations as they have on the big battle wagons."

Somebody shouted, "Okay, you two . . . take your knittin' and go sit in the head where you can talk real good." A shoe came hurtling through the dark and struck Jubal's shoulder, just missing his face.

Carter said, as if the idea hadn't occurred to him before, "Maybe we oughta be more quiet."

"Maybe we ought," Jubal said, feeling his ear to make sure it wasn't bleeding.

The hold became quiet again, settling down to the normal rumbling and sputtering of the sleepers. Deep in the vitals of the ship, Jubal could hear the faint hum of a dynamo and the wheeze and thumping of the bilge pump. He lay on his back trying to sort out the smells and the layers of sounds. Bilge gas, he said happily to himself. Revolting and wonderful fumes; they meant he was on a ship headed toward war.

Perhaps it wasn't the safest place on earth. It was being said "on good authority" that submarine warfare was taking from eight to twenty ships every week. Twice as fast as new tonnage could be built, the Germans were sinking ships. Jubal knew that. But he wanted to be exactly where he was. Not for Wilsonian reasons; he wanted to be where he was, out of sheer love of excitement and novelty. He wanted to be where the Big Show was going on.

He woke up to a strange sound. There was no way of knowing whether it was midnight or midafternoon, whether he had been asleep fifteen minutes or ten hours. Engines were throbbing so that the hot thick air seemed to pulse like membrane. There was a long gasping metallic sound which he identified as the anchor engine rolling the chain back into the chain locker. Then the bugle tore through the tough fabric of noise and split it end to end, echoing and re-echoing throughout the steel corridors.

A barbed-wire voice shouted, "Out o' your hammocks, you guys. Hit the deck! Set the special Sea Detail."

Jubal reported to the Communications Office with the other radio men. The Chief, a red-haired Swede with a sulky underlip, looked him over disparagingly, then motioned him to stand aside for orders.

"You'll find your watches posted here, also duplicated in the radio shack. No excuse for not knowing when you go on and when you have relief. Missing a watch is a court-martial offense in wartime. That clear?"

Jubal looked over the equipment and talked with the other radio floosies like a man who had discovered compatriots. He would go on watch at noon, he saw from the schedule. So now he went out on deck to have a look at the Boatswain's Mates and the deckhands getting ready to cast off. There couldn't have been a better moment anywhere in the world. Everything was standing at attention. The *Susquehanna* and the *Monongahela* were almost unbearably beautiful ships, to the boy watching. Their high bows tapered back to low sterns and quarterdecks. They owed their speedy and cruiserlike style to their two masts and the slight rake of their stacks. Each ship had two tugs fussing around importantly, glittering and white in the slashing sunlight. The tugs would never really go anyplace, so they could afford to be white and uncamouflaged.

The ships were moving smoothly, like floating swans. Their tugs, four nautical mermaids, were guiding them out into the harbor, and the buildings and warehouses lining the piers and docks were gliding backwards, silent as a picture. The whole ship was strangely quiet as if every man aboard was secretly saying an inner good-bye to everything he had known up to now.

After a few hours the life of the ship caught him up and became the only order he could remember. The ship was everything; all that had been before in his life was a dream and a rumor. When he was alone between watches, he tried to think of Papa .... dim and improbable as a character in a novel read long ago. When he thought of his mother, she was a poem whose lines eluded him. He had the rhythm in his heart, but the words had sifted from his mind. It shocked him that it should be so.

Because he was young to be a radio floosy, the men on the ship were forever trying to corner him to find out where they were going. Jubal amused himself by looking as if he knew; he wasn't above accepting some kind of bribe by appearing to confirm someone's cherished theory.

The Captain's orderly was a big Texas barber named Milton, a humorless guy who was always going around among the crew trying to save souls, as if he had to have a certain number of spiritual scalps to hang on his belt. Very confidentially he approached Jubal and tried to find out where the ship was going.

"Listen, Our ... you don't have to say yes and you don't have to say no. But I read a magazine article that said the Mediterranean was gonna be the battleground. So *are* we?" Jubal let a bright alarm spring into his face, then muggingly made believe he was disguising his giveaway expression.

Milton breathed, "No kiddin'!" He paled above his slack mouth. "I hear the subs are thick as fleas on a hound dog out thataway."

"Now, don't say anything, will you, Milton? Just keep it to yourself," Jubal advised, looking as if he could hardly control his admiration of Milton for guessing. It was only a matter of hours before everyone on the *Susquehanna* believed the ship was headed for the Mediterranean. Jubal had suggested it so many times that he now believed it himself.

The days were filled with a ritual of orderliness; time was as tidy as a new, slick line. The pleasant mess before noon, the watches in the wireless shack with the headphones muttering their continual messages, the reliefs when he could hunch over a book, the forever yarning of the men who had put in three and even four hitches in "this man's Navy," as they usually spoke of it. It was a good life, Jubey thought; he'd never ask for better.

Being even then unable to resist any audience who would listen to his highly colored stories with even moderate credulity, Jubey added considerably to the legends that were always circulating. Sometimes he would give graphic accounts of battles between ships and submarines, full of technical details and emotional embellishments. He never exactly said he had been present in these fracases, but it was easy to surmise that he had been. His sixty roommates in the number one hold thought they were pretty lucky to have such a narrator available when craps and poker palled.

He had the ship's barber cut his thick curly hair cruelly short, but this didn't achieve the effect he had hoped for. There was something incongruous about his huge prosperous man's body topped by a youngter's pleased face.

I've just got to be tough, he often reminded himself. With a cherubic mug like mine, there's no choice. But he never could seem to remember. The guilty fact was that he just loved everything he saw. Loved it and laughed at it in his heart, in a merry affectionate way that seemed to him anything but manly. He considered it a hereditary disease contracted from Papa, and no doubt that was precisely what it was. But with Papa the disease had infected both his mind and his heart. Jubey knew that at the helm of his own soft heart he had a sharp-seeing mind. And he intended to make it even sharper.

He played various musical instruments and sang raucously, composing spontaneous songs as off-color as his healthy boy's mind could manage. His mates said of him, "Leave that kid alone a half-hour with any kind of musical instrument and he plays it like he invented it."

"It's nothing," Jubal muttered modestly. "Accordion plays me. I don't play it."

"Leave him alone with a dame, and I bet it'd be the same way."

"If you say so, sailor," he would grin, hoping someday it might actually become the truth.

Sometimes after they had sat for two hours on the mine tracks watching some blizzardly-appearing motion picture, Jubey would get up and rub his backside tenderly where the rivet marks were stamped indelibly and say something like, "Well, I tell you. That scene where the guy was hanging out the window by a rope would a been a lot funnier if his pet mouse, that he'd been sharing his cheese sandwiches with, had finally gnawed through the rope and let him drop."

His pals would consider his improvement a minute, and then they'd have to concede that Jubey was right.

"If you get back from the Suicide Squad, Jube, you better get a job writing them there movies," they'd say admiringly. "Or maybe even actin' in 'em."

"I wouldn't be caught dead," Jubey would say, adapting his way of speaking to theirs, as he always did in any conversation.

"Well, what are you plannin' to do if the war ever gets done?"

"I'm going to get me a nice little meat market when I get

back. I'm going to find myself a nice little wife who can make apple Strudel and potato pancakes, and I'm gonna sell the best meat you can buy. No matter what happens, people always want meat. Am I right?"

He was right, all right. For a youngster like he was, he was certainly right a lot of the time. And when he wasn't, he was probably only kiddin'. Sometimes you couldn't be sure whether he was kiddin' the shirt off you, or tellin' you something that just happened to be true. He sure loved to kid people.

There was always an undercurrent of rumors and accounts of ships going down in so-many minutes after the German torpedoes had struck. Nobody knew just where such stories started, but they grew and multiplied daily. You got used to them finally and stopped being afraid. Fear is a perishable commodity; keep it in the hot climate of a fevered skull for a few hours, and it melts like ice. Fear abates and fatalism sets in. They said over and over to each other, "If we're gonna get it, nothing can stop it. If we ain't, what's the use worryin'?"

The morning they did get it was an innocent masterpiece of weather. The last of the stars were just paling in the sky, and a circle of the sea began to emerge from darkness. The sky had a crescent of light on its eastern rim, as Jubey, taking notes for the Log, jotted down that the weather was fair, the temperature forty-one degrees the sea calm and the visibility five miles. He saw Milton's feet going up the ladder with the Captain's coffee. The Skipper had left written orders that he was to be called at five that morning, and now it was getting on toward six. The ship was traveling a zigzag course, to throw off any lurking U-boats. There were lookout men on the bow and in the crow's-nest, and stationed on each side of the lower bridge, for everyone knew the ship was passing through one of ell's pastures.

The explosion came without warning. One moment everything was quiet and twilit, and the next a blaze of daylight ripped the eyeballs, and a deafening crash split the eardrums as the torpedo hit. It tore into the number two hold, sending up a mountainous column of water and debris which rained down on the bridge.

The bow swung down under the impact, thrusting the screw almost out of the water. Then Jubey heard the engines being put full astern. Hardly realizing that he was performing the act which he had rehearsed in his mind so many times, he was sending out the W/T S.O.S. signal. In a few moments he was adding to it the position the Skipper shouted down to him. Explosions kept coming, deep in the holds and the engine room, shattering steam pipes like soda straws, and scalding a score of men. The Communications Officer hurled overboard two bags of mail, and the secret code books and sailing orders of the ship.

Afterwards, when Jubey remembered those demented moments before he was off the ship himself, it seemed to him he must have been only a disembodied eye gazing here and there at pictures which he never could forget. He had no memory of his body running from place to place; but he carried for months, as entonic vision, brilliant vignettes of the death of his ship. He knew exactly how the explosions had ripped through the beautiful anatomy of the *Susquehanna*, piercing the refrigeration pipes so that men reeled blind and choking from the fumes to die on deck. The ship was blasted from without and from within, as the mines were set off by the torpedo. Some men were killed by fire, some by laceration, and many, trapped and unable to escape, went down with the ship.

Within minutes the Skipper had ordered the boats away, but some of them couldn't be got to, for they were only bashed-in wreckage buried in debris. Over the turmoil and noise, Jubal heard the big-lunged powerful voice of the Skipper ordering him to leave ship.

"I can't leave, sir," he called back in a dream. "I might get a signal from some convoy that could help us."

"You leave, Our," the Captain shouted back at him. "I'll take the signals."

"You can't, sir," Jubey said.

"Neither can you, you crazy fool," the Skipper said. "In ten minutes we'll have no ship to pick up any signal."

The next Jubey knew, he was being dumped into a boat, and Milton, jibbering prayer and terror, was clambering in behind him.

"Jesus, take my hand, sir," Milton was saying, and Jubey thought the "sir" referred to the Skipper, and looked around expecting to see him. Then it crossed his mind that in a few minutes Milton would probably find himself promoted ... still an orderly, of course, but an orderly to a him with a capital letter.

Hope he does as good a job as he's done for this skipper, he said to himself. Though for my part, I'd prefer an orderly who sniveled less.

The boat swung out on its davits, and began lowering jerkily from the shipside. Jubey could see that the lifeboat was dangerously overloaded; every face was stunned and emptied of expression, down to the dregs of itself, the imbecility of terror. Eyes looked large and floating, and skin was stretched tight and green over sagging jaws. Almost every face in the boat was bellowing some nonsense which no one troubled to hear, listening only to his own.

Then in a sickening, helpless way the bow of the lifeboat caught immovably; the stern wobbled a few moments and continued to drop, so that everyone slid in a screaming heap, clutching at other bodies and trying to grip on to the boat which was determined to spew them out into the emptiness. The little boat, absurdly unmanageable, hung like a pea pod on a vine, and one by one the occupants lost their grip and plunged feet first into the sea.

No one, except the others in the doomed lifeboat, noticed what was happening, for everywhere something terrible and unpreventable was taking place. Jubey clung to the gunwhale quite a while, and when he let loose it was because Milton had gone, and he felt that someone responsible ought to be there to help the poor guy.

It never occurred to him that he himself wouldn't come out of this experience alive. He felt almost as if Papa were beside him, robustly rejecting such an impossibility as Germans killing *his* son. There was such manifest contradiction in that circumstance that it became impossible. He kept hearing Papa's hearty laugh and his naïve assurance that everything was "going to be all right, and nobody must feel bad." In a smear of confusion, Jubey wondered if this might be the kind of comfort people like Milton have from prayer. He explored the curious analogy, and decided that it would hold. Probably people who had faith in God felt the same fond amusement that he himself felt about his faith in Papa. One knew such faith was completely without foundation in fact, and yet. . . . Perhaps faith was one of the realities which lay beyond the realm of fact. Deliberately he occupied himself trying to make this distinction clear, while he was tumbling through the air and striking the water, then boring into the icy darkness below the surface.

For a few moments he felt he must just let his bursting lungs collapse, and sink down into the welcome nothingness of the water. But the thought of Papa rallied him again, and he knew he could not sink; he would have to struggle through somehow. Papa would be very angry if he didn't.

I won't let myself be killed, Papa. Never fear, he was saying in the center of his brain. You wouldn't understand that happening, Papa. So it won't happen.

Now he began to look around him. He realized for the first time that it was broad daylight. His notes would have to be amended to read "Visibility Fifteen Miles." The big brilliant sun was now striking its scarlet swords through the waves, seeming to gather them up like sheets of paper along rapiers.

The ship was wallowing ignominiously in death, and Jubey

knew that in a few moments she must plunge under the sea. When she did, she would drag all she could with her. That aroused him and he began swimming away from her, as many other men were doing. There were a few boats around him, overloaded with huddling figures. Some of the men in the water were crying piteously for the boats to pick them up, but no one seemed to hear or care. This was no time for depending on anyone at hand. Here you could depend on no one but yourself, and what had gone into the making of you.

He swam for what he felt must have been fifteen minutes, and still the ship at its demented angle seemed dangerously close. Suddenly she began to slip bow first into some chosen slot in this churning sea around her. Her whistle gave a long bass blast as the air was squeezed through her. The stack crumpled like paper. Then there was a smothered groan and rumple, and a curious cloud of dirt blew up from her, and she was gone. Although Jubey had always heard about the great suction of a ship sinking, which reaches out and clutches all it can grab to carry to death with her, he felt no pull from this beloved ship. She was too much of a lady, he thought deliriously; she'll take her death alone.

There seemed to be fewer boats in the sea now, and those were far away, and one couldn't be entirely certain whether they were lifeboats or fragments of the ship. There was no plausible hope that anything would pick him up, yet he knew he was not going to die.

He swam about aimlessly for a long time. It appeared there was no one else in the whole universe now. At first the sea had been full of crazy debris, galley equipment tangled with wearing apparel, a sailor's white cap skipping madly across a wave, a long ribbon of toilet paper, a tilted orange crate filled with sodden bread. But by now everything that wasn't buoyant had sunk, and the sea looked as if she had no acquaintance with men and their untidy ways.

The last of the lifeboats had disappeared; there seemed no

one alive but himself and the blazing, unanswering sun in the sky. The loneness he felt was as cosmic as that the earth itself must feel reeling down the wide avenues of the firmament. He had lost all account of time. He could not be sure whether minutes or hours had passed since the ship had uttered that last insane blast and had lurched into oblivion. Once more he consulted the unreasonable certainty deep within himself, and once more he knew he was not going to die. Unless this aloneness which he was feeling *was* death.

A splintered plank suddenly catapulted down a wave and just missed striking him. He reached out feebly to grasp it, but with satanic caprice, it swerved away from him and careened out of his reach. Then he saw there was a man clinging to it, his head lolling between his clutching arms.

A giddy exuberance surged up in Jubey. No, he was not dead. Two men couldn't be occupying the same nightmare, and the guy on the plank was as assuredly in it as was Jubey himself. He tried to give a shout to welcome that other occupant of the mirage, but only a bleat came out of his tight throat. He tried again; this time he shouted words, characteristic words.

"Hi there . . ." he called. "Man overboard, bud."

The lolling head paid no attention, and Jubal swam after the timber which the wave was carrying farther from him. He called out again, and now the body raised its head uncertainly as if it couldn't be sure it had heard a human voice. The face was dead with fright and fatigue, yet there was something familiar about the terrified eyes. When he heard what the man was muttering, he knew it was Milton.

"Oh Jesus."

"Sorry, bud, but it's only me," Jubey said, getting a firmer hold on the cruelly splintered timber.

The big Texan shifted his grasp on the plank and tried to clutch at Jubey, muttering hysterically. Jubey knew enough about drowning to elude him and managed to get himself around to the other side of their timber. He felt a long draining weakness all through his body, and it seemed to him that he would save himself a lot of anguish if he just let loose and sank. To keep his mind from that persuasive thought, he talked to Milton.

"What's all that praying you're always doing?" he said. "Seems to me if you've got faith enough to do it, you ought to have faith enough to trust it to take care of you now."

Milton tried to focus his eyes on Jubey's grimacing face. Obviously he, too, was trying to concentrate on something which might ease the moment.

"You're Jubey Our, ain't you?"

"That's what I *think,* Milton."

The Texan seemed to doze a moment, then he roused and said in a loud strong voice, "Have you been saved, Jubey?"

"Saved?" Jubey gasped, deliberately misinterpreting the word. "How's it look to you, buddy? Sure I'm saved. We've got a nice big plank we can live on for the rest of our lives if we want to."

"I mean *saved,* Jubey . . . are you a Christian?" Milton muttered, almost too breathless to get out the words.

Jubey was about to answer in some outrageous way which might anger the older man enough to rouse him from his lethargic coma. But before he thought of any words, he saw something between the waves. It was the submarine just surfacing. She showed no periscope, only a conning tower and the harsh black level of a gun. She lay quietly, small and sinister, and it was hard to believe that anything so insignificant and ugly could have destroyed a large and beautiful ship.

Jubey couldn't judge how close the evil thing lay; it might have been two hundred yards or fifty. Milton, too, saw the U-boat now.

"They're going to shoot us, Jubey," he squealed in a soprano squeak. "That's what they do. They come up and take turns shooting whatever they can find alive in the water."

"Don't be stupid," Jubal said angrily. "They wouldn't waste shots on guys who had one foot in a watery grave. If they're going to do anything, they're going to pick us up." He tried to lift himself up on the plank so that he could be sighted from the U-boat.

"Hi there . . . Sprechen sie Deutsch?" he shouted, hoping the absurdity of his greeting might intrigue them. He went on shouting other German remarks. But there was no way of knowing whether or not they had been sighted.

"We'll have to swim for it," he said to Milton. "If you want to come with me, you're welcome."

Milton, splashing and floundering, tried to get around to Jubey's side, with some mad idea of holding on to him to keep from being left.

"Okay, then, we'll swim. Keep hold of the plank."

Suddenly they knew they had been sighted, for the submarine was putting out one of its tiny dinghies, and two men were climbing into it from the narrow deck of the U-boat.

"Now's your chance, Milton," Jubey said. "You pray and I'll do the talking."

"Praise God," Milton said. "He's heard my prayers."

Jubey began calling out to the dinghy in German, then seeing that they obviously couldn't hear him from the distance, he saved his breath. As they came nearer, one of the two men in the dinghy shouted across in fairly good English. Jubal answered in German, matching tact with tact. "Thank you, gentlemen, for coming to pick us up," he said.

He could see that one of the men was an officer, a blond handsome chap in his forties. "Don't get up your hopes, my friend," the officer said. "We have not decided to rescue you by any means."

"Come closer and let me persuade you," Jubey said, trying to infuse all his personality and winsomeness into the words. Milton, groveling and whimpering was crying, "What're you saying, Jube? What's *he* saying? Oh God, please look down on us with mercy. . . ."

They shouted back and forth for several minutes, the officer asking questions about the ship, and then about Jubey himself. How did it happen that he spoke good German? Then at last the officer said, "Well, I'm sorry to have to leave you, my young friend."

"Don't leave us, sir," Jubey cried, his voice breaking at the danger. "Don't come close so that we can see the kindness in your face, and then leave us."

"We have no room for you. This is no pleasure cruise," the German said regretfully. "Unless . . ."

"Unless what?" Jubey called out. "Whatever it is, we'll do it."

"Today is our Captain's birthday," the officer said. "We're going to celebrate this evening."

"And?"

"Well, I was wondering. We have a handsome accordion on board. But nobody can play it. If one of you . . ."

Milton, a plea in every pore, was begging for translation, and Jubey gave it in a few words.

"They've answered your prayer, son. All you have to do is play an accordion for the Captain's birthday party."

"I can't play. You know I can't play nothin'."

"Certainly you can play," Jubey said sternly. "If that praying of yours could bring up a submarine out of the sea, it certainly will give you skill enough to play an accordion."

"I can't play *nothin'*. I can't even carry a tune. Oh God, please help me."

"Don't ask God to help you. If you have any faith in him, you'll trust that he *is* helping you," Jubey said angrily. "You haven't any faith in him."

"I have so."

"But none in yourself." The boy's scorn would have blistered fresh paint. It was inconceivable to him that Milton couldn't have played by sheer unction of necessity. "I'm giving you one more chance, Milton. Let me tell him you can play and they'll pick you up."

The officer and the man from the U-boat were losing their patience. "Very well. I am sorry, my friend. Good luck to you," the officer called out, as they began to maneuver their dinghy about.

Milton croaked, "They'd find out as soon as I tried . . . they'd torture me."

Jubey said, "All right, then. If you don't want the chance, I'll take it." He lifted his voice and called out. "It just happens, sir, that you're talking to one of the finest accordion players in the American Navy."

"Which of you?"

"Your humble servant, sir. Me."

The officer hesitated as if he suspected some trick, then as Jubey reassured him, he turned the boat and came about to a position where they could pick him up. When he tried to climb into the boat it was evident that his strength was almost exhausted, but the two Germans dragged him over the side. Then the officer said to Milton, goggle-eyed with despair at what was happening, "I am sorry for you. But this is war, and men cannot do exactly what they might wish."

"You can't leave me," Milton said. "Your wickedness would haunt you the rest of your life."

"I have already enough wickedness to haunt me, if that were possible," the German said with serious courtesy. "This will add nothing appreciable to it."

Jubey kept from looking at Milton's agonizing face. The man would have to die believing his prayers had failed. But where prayers fail there is sometimes a chance that something else can succeed . . . some nimbleness of wit, some charm of manner. . . . In a wordless second an old familiar picture floated before his eyes; he saw himself a guilty culprit about to be punished by Papa, and then through his blurting out some audacious nonsense, he saw the whole scene change, so that Papa burst out laughing, and everything was saved. Yes, that was it. He needed only to get his fingers on some winning foolishness.

"On second thought," he said, still barely able to speak above his breathlessness, "I remember now. I cannot possibly play the accordion . . . unless I have a good man to turn the sheets of music . . . so will you please . . ."

The officer looked angry for a second. Then just as Papa's face used to do, his countenance flooded with color and he burst out laughing.

He said to Milton, "All right. Scramble into the boat, you. But I shall be ashamed of myself." He clapped Jubey on the shoulder companionably. "I should know better than to involve myself with you, you young rascal . . . what did you say your name is?"

"Auerbach," Jubey gasped, restoring the lost syllable where he could see it would do the most good. "Heinrich Auerbach."

"Ja . . . ja . . . and mine is Jimmy Smith," the officer said delightedly.

Milton lay on the bottom of the dinghy panting and gasping and weeping. Just as they reached the submarine, where now several officers were standing on the deck watching the little boat, Milton said in a mutter to Jubey, "See . . . my prayer saved me after all."

"*Your* prayer? How do you figure that?"

"God put kindness in your heart and wit on your tongue. Those sure enough saved me."

Jubal looked at him in comic exasperation. "Milton, you win," he said. "Nobody can defeat a praying man."

"That's right, Jubey," the Texan agreed without humor. "That's the way God meant it to be."

"Nope, you can't beat a praying man," Jubey said again. But he made up his mind that next time he wouldn't be a part of the dubious transaction. If God wanted that kind of fearful souls, he'd just have to save 'em himself.

When they were safe on the submarine, they found themselves unexpectedly welcome. In his quite realistic way Jubey

knew that with any luck at all he could easily become something of a pet or mascot to the officers and crew. The fact that
he spoke perfect German gave his wit a well-built bridge over
which to run back and forth between the two languages. Before
anyone had a chance to break out some dry warm German
apparel for him, he was surrounded by men asking questions
about America. How did the Americans feel about the war?
Did they possibly think they could defeat the Fatherland? Did
Jubey happen to know a musician named Smaltz who played in
a little restaurant up on 63d Street in New York City? Jubey
did, of course. Jubey had an opinion on every subject, and the
information he had to fabricate was always a bit more colorful
than facts which came ready-made.

Milton, as soon as he was dry and warm, fell into a coma of
fatigue. But Jubey took only a small rest, and then was up and
about, cementing affectionate relations between himself and
everyone else, especialy the blond torpedo officer, Lieutenant
Kurt Geitzen, who had rescued him.

The seven officers and thirty-eight men on the craft were in
excellent spirits, having just bagged a mine layer. If their
Captain hadn't happened to have a birthday, they would have
celebrated anyway. But the birthday gave a special freedom
and polish.

"You really can play the accordion?" Geitzen asked Jubey
cocking up one blond eyebrow.

"I said I could, sir."

"You want to practice first?"

"Not necessary. I play by ear, and I can hang garlands
around any melody you mention."

"We have also a violin and a guitar."

"I can play those."

"Individually or collectively?"

"Whichever way you wish, sir. You name it, and I'll perform
it if it kills me."

The submarine cruised around a while, traveling at about eight knots, hoping to find an undefended little merchant ship which might be shot at and then rifled for fresh provisions. When a smudge of smoke appeared on the horizon, the U-boat submerged, traveling cautiously at a slow speed, until it was discovered that the smoke came from a Norwegian steamer. They came so close to this little ship that the vibration of her propellers could be felt. After she was passed, they surfaced again and cruised pleasantly.

As the afternoon was drawing to a close, the Captain said, "Close the hatches. We're diving."

The big submarine seemed to be looking for a comfortable level, and when it found what it wanted, it quivered and rolled a bit and then seemed to sigh like a huge bird snuggling into its nest.

"Now we'll celebrate. Officers and men together," the Captain said with an expansive beam on his round German face. Dressed in their heavy leather submarine suits, they crowded into the tiny messroom. There was a magnificent cake for the occasion, but the other food was strictly submarine fare, canned fish, potato soup, hardtack and dried peaches. But an abundance of rum transformed the tasteless meal into a banquet. There were speeches from everybody who wanted to talk, including Jubey. The messroom was crowded and smelled abominable, but there was noise and good cheer and boyish humor.

Once again, because Jubey had the ability to live only in the event which was at that moment happening, he found himself quite at home. He played the accordion until he nearly dropped, and sang until his voice was a mere croak. He would have gone on playing, except that Geitzen ordered him to bed.

"I want you to get your money's worth, sir," Jubey said. "Never let it be said that an Auerbach didn't live up to his obligations."

"Your obligation is to stay alive so you can amuse us tomorrow," Geitzen told him, not unkindly.

As soon as he had this permission to collapse, his nerve left him, and still holding the big ornate accordion, he slithered to the floor. A great red-bearded sailor raised him up by the armpits, and Jubey said, "Sorry, sir . . . I've had rather an exciting day. If you'll excuse me. . . ."

Two sailors dragged him to a bunk, next to which was the mound of inert matter that was Milton. Jubey motioned for the sailors to stop a moment while he looked into the Texan's naked face, hatchet-sharp but untroubled. Jubey tried to imagine how Milton felt about this bizarre day, but the tentacles of his imagination found only a smudgy smear as the essence of the religious man.

"That guy," he muttered to himself. "You can't get the best of a praying man."

The sailors shrugged agreement, not knowing what he had said, and then gently dumped him into bed, where he had not another thought for the next fifteen hours. But it was sitting on his chest waiting to look him in the eye when he finally woke up. Now his annoyance was gone, and all that was left was a sly pleasure that he had played a joke on God.

Throughout the next years of his life, the words about the praying man were often in his mind, sometimes with one inflection and again with another . . . most often with sarcastic accusation, but finally with unwilling, astonished tribute.

"You can't defeat a praying man." It was a trivial-seeming sentence, but it became the fugue of the contrapuntal quarrel which was his life's unwelcome theme.

IT WAS many months before Jubey got home again. He came home through various stages, for it was a long journey. But the physical travel, sometimes headed homeward, sometimes with his face set only on further wandering, was as nothing compared to the involute emotional journey he was making. He had two reasons for the strange pilgrimage: there was the feeling that he was being beckoned here and there by his own inward growth which he must not deny on penalty of the death of growing; and almost as strong as that necessity, was the warning that he dared not risk facing Papa until he had some stable conclusions of his own with which he could "protect" Papa. The "protecting" of Papa was a strange and reciprocal need. He never phrased it to himself, but he recognized that it had been forever written into him, more indelible than thought.

Papa's idealism was a kind of magnetic force, a gravity which held upright all the items in Papa's world. Nothing must happen to this idealism, or everything else would lean and shift and topple. Jubey must somehow preserve his father's great childlike faith in the rightness of the order, so that same faith might support Jubey's own world. The boy must uphold his father's faith, so that it could uphold Jubey.

For many months after the war was over he was not sure he could uphold an obsolete faith in a good and beautiful world. Mama, who was a spirit compounded wholly of faith and goodness, he never thought of as in danger, for Mama's trust was in things imperishable. Mama's confidence was not based on anything the eye could see, so nothing the eye could see would ever menace it. But Papa was different. Papa's faith lay in his wonderful toys, in the brewery and the strong, jolly men who were his genial competitors, in his snug, overheated household, in the rich people of St. Louis and the aristocrats who tolerated the Ours indulgently without bending an inch to include them. Papa had faith in the great solid structure of America which he knew. Values invisible could not add nor subtract one iota of the tensile strength of Papa's almost physical confidence. That put the whole structure gravely in danger, in the direct ratio of the perishability of the outer world. Everywhere he went, both in Europe and in his own country, Jubal could see that the physical world was changing. The very ground on which Papa was standing was quivering with an incandescent stirring of spirit which ultimately in ten years or fifty would destroy that ground.

Henry Our would certainly see that knowledge in Jubey's face, and not understanding it would grieve Papa. He would think that something sound and sure had collapsed in his son. Until he could clarify his own conclusions, Jubey dared not take himself into Papa's presence.

So he delayed his homecoming, trying to find some logical yet compassionate way of explaining to the middle-aged child what was happening in the world. He knew that if he returned prematurely, he would not have in him the simple wisdom that could build a safe bridge for his father to cross. Unless there was a firm core of understanding in himself, he would only anger and alarm Papa. And separate the two of them forever.

One sequence he knew he could have explained in a way that would reinforce Papa's naïve belief that great fundamental good lay under all naughtiness (for this was the word best describing Papa's infantile conception of evil). He knew Papa would have loved hearing about his experience on the German U-boat. His blue eyes would have glistened with tears of gratification as his boy told about the long days and nights on the submarine, when the men read aloud from the small but choice supply of books, Goethe and Schiller, and even fine translations of Shakespeare and Swift. Papa's head would have kept time to the memory of music as Jubey told about the hours of singing; his eyes would have shone with pride about the English lessons the boy gave the officers and the crew, and the long searching talks about America.

That submarine in mid-ocean would have seemed to Papa not enemy ground on which two captives were held, but a fine island where men might learn about each others' countries, a place of momentary peace where men of good will could understand each other. From such states, however unpropitiously they had come into being, would finally spring the great unity which would make all men at home wherever they found themselves.

It would have been difficult to describe the hours in which he and Kurt Geitzen talked together. In what might have been considered hostile and unnatural surroundings, it might have been easy for a boy to miss the meaning of such a man. But somehow Jubey saw beneath the urbane and worldly exterior, even before conversation confirmed perception.

One night they were on the small deck together looking at the stars which Geitzen pointed out by name. Jubey said, after quietly listening awhile as the German explained the great stately pavane of the constellations, "You're taller than you look, sir."

Geitzen saw the full meaning which the boy was too shy to speak, and nodded slowly.

"A man needs the great heights or he suffocates," the torpedo officer said. "The world presses him down unless he knows a reverse force of gravity which draws him upward from his small self and his small companions, and the world."

In a panic Jubey thought, Is he going to talk religion? But

Geitzen only pulled on his cigar and added nothing, so in spite of himself Jubey asked, "Have you been drawn upward, sir?"

"I've been drawn every which way . . . is that your American idiom? I have tried everything that beckoned. And finally I lifted up my eyes."

Jubey, not sure whether they were discussing religion or astronomy, asked timidly, "To the firmament, you mean?"

"To the firmament within," the older man said reverently. After that, it was almost a guilty secret between them. They spoke of it seldom, but it was always present.

Once, when the big German was telling Jubey some episode of his student life, he said, "That was when the two of me were still wrestling together."

"The two of you?"

"The angel and the devil within. Haven't you discovered them yet?"

"I haven't that combination in me," Jubey said. "Not the angel anyway."

"I saw the angel the morning we picked you up," Geitzen said with a stern face. "You would have given that poor whimpering Milton the chance to be rescued, and you would have gone down yourself."

"He was praying," Jubey said seriously. "If God wasn't going to take care of that, somebody had to."

"So you became God."

"Do you mean to be sarcastic, sir?"

The officer smiled slowly, and Jubey saw a hidden trap had somehow been laid for him, and he had been caught in it.

Geitzen said, "I apologize. You see, you have more respect than you admit."

"Just the usual amount," Jubey protested, unwilling to be accused of goodness.

"We'll start again. So you became God's ambassador."

But the boy wouldn't even agree to that. "If prayers are going to be answered at all, human beings probably have to answer them for each other," he said stubbornly.

"Ah, you see . . . it *is* the angel and the devil wrestling in you." Geitzen smiled good-naturedly. "The angel in the deed, and the devil in the explanation of the deed."

But Jubey still persisted. "All right, sir. I'll grant you the wrestling. But in me the wrestling is between a devil and a clown."

Geitzen patted him roughly on his shoulder. "You think so now," he said thoughtfully. "But watch them both and you'll discover what they really are. Give them twenty-five years, and then see."

Jubey went back to the other man's phrase. " 'God's ambassador,' " he quoted sceptically. "Why doesn't God do his own work, if he's so all-powerful as his friends claim he is?"

The officer looked at him as if to see whether this question came from honesty or impudence. After a minute he said, "Why doesn't the principle of mathematics do its own work?"

Jubey grinned in the darkness. Then Geitzen went on, obviously enjoying himself. "You don't like God's keeping his eye on you, do you? Well, I'll tell you. This is his life you're living. You think it's yours, don't you? But he's only loaned it to you. To get certain work done."

"Suppose I don't feel like doing the work," Jubey said rebelliously. "I've got my own ideas, Lieutenant."

"All right. So you'll choose. You'll think you do the whole choosing, but in the end you'll realize what really happened. You *can* listen for his directions. If you don't like that and you insist on going your own way, you won't know what's happening. But willingly or not, you'll be doing God's work in the end. You'll be either the blind devil or the seeing angel. . . . But both of them serve God's purpose."

"We're caught either way," Jubey said.

"We're caught and held," Geitzen amended. "Maybe it will

take us half of eternity to recognize that we're held . . . safe in the big plan."

"You and me on this U-boat?"

"You and me," Geitzen said. "Six hundred men were drowned. But you weren't. A certain number of officers in the German submarine fleet. I was there to pick you up. God had it in mind."

No, that was no conversation that could be described to anyone. But it became indelible in Jubey's memory.

There were many anecdotes about those days on the submarine, however, which Papa would have loved hearing. Especially he would have been touched by the courteous way the officers dealt with the crews of some of the ships they sank, how they boarded the ships and talked with the officers, and gave them a chance to collect their valuables before their vessels were torpedoed, how they helped launch their lifeboats, and made certain there were adequate provisions. The sly impudence of the Prussian good manners would have been misinterpreted with benevolent idealism by Papa.

He would have loved hearing about the day which finally came, when Jubey left the submarine. Lieutenant Geitzen had said, "If I keep you with us until we go back to Bremerhaven you will be a prisoner of war. I would not like to see that happen. This way . . . well, at least God will have his second chance with you."

"Are we asking that Gentleman to take a hand in my business again?"

"Asking or not asking." Geitzen shrugged his shoulders. "After the war is over, you will write and tell me how he managed everything." He gave Jubey an old silver cross, ornately covered with leaves and small flames, with a tiny bird singing among the leaves.

"This looks quite valuable, sir," Jubey protested.

"Only to those who believe what it has to say," the German

replied. Then he went and asked the Captain for permission to put Jubey and Milton into a lifeboat from the next ship they had the good fortune to sink.

That is how it happened that, in order to save young Jubal Our, a certain motor launch full of men was spared from going down with a ship off the coast of Ireland.

After the two captives had been transferred from the U-boat to the launch, Jubey called out to his friend, "Lieutenant . . . come back and get me. I don't want to take my chances with the other Gentleman. I'd rather take them with you, sir."

"That's blasphemous, boy," Kurt Geitzen said gruffly.

After a moment's thinking, Jubey said, "Thank you, sir."

"Do you understand what it means?"

"Not yet. Maybe some day."

"Work at it until you understand it."

Papa would have enjoyed hearing about the way the motor launch made its landfall on the frowning coast of Norway, and the way Jubey traveled around the country and finally got to England on a tanker, and at last boarded an American battleship just before peace was declared.

As soon as he reached New York he talked by telephone to St. Louis, and Papa wept into the telephone.

"You start home tomorrow, Jubey?"

"Not tomorrow, Papa. I have to do some things first."

"What kind of things? I send out one of my men to do them for you. You come home and tell me."

"Nobody else could do them, Papa."

"Why not?"

"They're things that have to be done to my mind."

There was a long patient silence, then Papa said with a shade of the old weary meekness which that particular word always caused him, "You mean *education,* Jubey?"

"That's it."

"Couldn't you be educated here with me? I could help yet."

"No. It's because you *would* help. This I have to see for myself."

It was then that Papa explained that Mama could not speak to him at all because she had one of her bad spells of tonsilitis. That tonsilitis almost brought Jubey bounding home. But then Papa relayed what Lucille wanted to say, and now Jubey himself wept, for what she wanted to say was that he must not think about how much they wanted him at home; he was to stay as long as he needed to.

"Mama says if it's education, you mustn't cut any corners," Papa said. "Mama says if it's time to learn something, you listen to what it is. But I don't say it, Jubey. I say come home because I haven't seen you for thirteen months and a week."

Jubey understood then why it had been Papa and not Mama whom he had missed and worried about all the time he had been away. That fragile, pastel Mama could take care of herself; it was big highly colored, blustering Papa who was vulnerable, and hence must be thought about and missed. Mama would understand even if Jubey told her that he had never worried about her . . . that he had scarcely thought about her, knowing she was as fixed in his firmament as the eternal North Star.

With his terminal pay he bought an old car and some workman's clothes. In the back of his mind was some half-formed idea of "seeing America." He had talked about America by the hour to men who knew it only as a dream, but the fact was he knew little about its many layers of living. During his months in the Navy he had got to know men of every posssible type; now he must know what made those men as they were, children and satyrs, gullible and crafty, ignorant yet full of unaccountable wisdom.

He struck out boldly, not caring where he began, and before his wanderings were over he had lived with textile workers in the gray frame tenements of Lawrence and Lynn, and with lumbermen in the tall, silent Vermont forests; he had held a job on the chopping-out machine in a garment-maker's loft on the lower East Side of New York. He dipped into the steel mills and the coal mines of Pennsylvania and Ohio, and during a lunch hour in a cannery in Georgia he had tried to teach a herd of laboring children to sing, until one of them had thrown a rock at his head, mistaking him for a foreman. He had served for a couple of weeks as an orderly in the alcoholics' ward of a great city hospital until he could endure no more of that sterile agony. He stayed only a few days everywhere he went, like a man looking for something lost who soon discovers that it is not here.

Everywhere he went he phrased within himself a great clamor of protest that life should be both bleak and blessed in this land which knew such radiant plenty and such starving need. Through it all he kept looking and looking for some code which would translate the ambiguities. But he never found it, and he wished impatiently that he could give up looking and just fall asleep in indifference as so many other men had. He raged within himself sometimes at his self-inflicted poverty and loneliness, knowing that all he had to do was to go home and forget his wanderings. He knew there was some great piece of literature that told of a lad like himself who wandered and starved in a desolate country while his father's door stood open to receive him. He could not remember in what literature the epic belonged. Probably in Goethe, he thought, and he intended someday to find it and read it, and lay it against the pattern of himself.

He thought a hundred times of how it would feel to try to fit back into that safe household. When he was hungry, he closed his eyes and smelled the rich fragrance of that big warm house at dinnertime. When he was lonely, he felt the heat of the fireplace on his soles, as he and Papa sat in the anomalous library and talked. He tried to picture himself finally going back to his university to finish his education, although this plan felt almost as impossible as expecting to return to his own childhood.

To be certain he would have train fare at hand, if his ideas ever became clarified enough so that he felt he could go home safely, he asked Papa to send the money. He kept it in his breast pocket and often he took it out and looked at it yearningly, wishing he could accept the miracle it could work so easily.

When the winter was almost over, just when he was ready to take that defeated miracle, he met Rose Kramer.

PART II

He journeys to a far country

1

He had no idea where he was, but he knew that he was surrounded on all sides of his consciousness by pulsing pain and darkness. For a second he thought he was drowning in the fathomless water after his ship was torpedoed; then he identified the rhythmic rumbling noise and motion as a moving car. He got his eyes open and saw that the darkness was splashed by a dim light, and that a strong-looking small pair of hands gripped the steering wheel of the car. They seemed to be boy's hands, and in the darkness above them glowed a cigarette clinging to a lip. But it was not a masculine lip, by any means.

A pure and lovely profile rose above a lifted throat, and as his burning eyes accustomed themselves to the shadowiness, he made out a golden knot of hair on the back of the neck, and a flowerlike cluster of very blond curls over the ear and across the cheek. He didn't have to see too clearly to know this was a woman beside him driving his car determinedly as if she knew where she was going. He moved his hand, as heavy as stone, and tried to reach his head which seemed to be reverberating as if it had just been pounded like a great iron bell.

"Coming back, buddy?" The voice was surprisingly husky, but there was a friendly lift of humor to it.

"From a long way, feels like," Jubey said vaguely.

"It was a long way, and no mistake. They knocked you out about eight o'clock. We're pushing midnight now."

"Knocked me out? Fists or . . ."

"A little of both," she said. "They gave you a Mickey Finn

first. Then when that didn't make a rug of you, they polished you off with some fancy fist work. That's what you get for carrying money around on your person."

"Whyn't they ask me for it?" Jubey said in a dreamy, pain-soaked voice. "I'd rather have given it to them."

"I doubt that. You look like a fighter to me."

"Depends."

"Anyway I got your car for you. And I got what's left of you."

"We going anyplace in particular?" he asked, sensing that this would not be a girl whom you could thank easily.

"Well, in a way. We're not so much going *to* some place, as we are getting away from somewhere."

"I see." The memory of the fracas was beginning to come back to him. He had gone into a restaurant down in Scollay Square in Boston; later he expected to sign up for a job in one of the hiring halls, until he sold his car. He got to talking with two men who were also looking for work. They had bought him a drink, then he had bought them one, and all he could remember after that was his own voice talking in loud circles, and his own laughter flapping like crazy banners. He had tried to quiet down, but somehow he couldn't control his voice. Even then he had thought there must be something strange in the drink. There had been a blond waitress in the place . . . yes, this was the girl.

"That's right," she said, as if she had followed his fuzzy memory through the dazedness. "I saw what they were doing to you. You were bragging, you know, and showing your money . . . I couldn't get you stopped."

"When I brag, I'm like Niagara."

"So I just had to wait until they'd finished with you. I told 'em you were my boy friend, and that this was my car."

He put his hand surreptitiously in his pocket where the fat wallet should have been. Yep, it was gone all right. So was his watch. Not the watch Papa had given him, of course; that was at the bottom of the ocean. But this was a pretty good watch. Except that it leaked. He could see that his brain wasn't meshing quite right. Maybe he'd better just let himself drop again into the black gnashing waters of semiconsciousness until he felt a little better.

"Put it here, if it's more comfortable," the voice was saying to him, and the boyish-looking hand which smelled pleasantly of tobacco and some kind of flower perfume guided his wobbling head over to a rough slender shoulder. "You just sleep, and let me take care of things," she said in a soothing voice. "You can be the boss tomorrow."

He tried to say something bright and reassuring to show by his cheerfulness that he appreciated her, and by his wit that she would eventually find him worth having rescued. But no words seemed to come out. His face felt as if it were made of stone. Stone that had been hammered by a powerful mallet.

The next time he woke up, there was daylight filtering through the darkness. Through the windshield he saw the raw March countryside, streaked with stingy snow and penciled with gaunt trees. The car was lurching to a stop against a low stone wall, and a wan electric sign over a doorway said "Food and Beer."

The girl's voice said, "Well, you got your little peepers open! How's it feel this time?"

"Like hell with the damper down," Jubey said, and tried to grin.

"How'd you like some coffee? I'll bring it out. Or, if you've got your legs back, maybe you'd like to come in. You're not as badly banged-up as you feel. It's mostly the Mickey Finn."

"I'll make it . . . if you don't mind being seen with a guy in my condition."

"I picked you, buddy," she said, and this time she turned her full face on him and he saw that she was unusually beautiful, in a rather touchingly common way . . . like a sunflower. Like a sunflower making no attempt to be an orchid or anything else, but affirming exactly what it was, without apology or pose.

She ran around to his side of the car, and opening the door, reached in and tried to help him, as if he were old and infirm. He could see her better now. She had a pink scrubbed-looking face, with carefully shaped dark eyebrows and brown eyes which were a surprise under her blond hair. She was dressed in a wide-shouldered trench coat, slimly belted around her waist, and with a neat white silk scarf tied in an ascot fold around her neck. On her head was an overseas cap. Probably given her by the last man she had rescued, he thought, and then disliked his cynicism. On her middle finger was a big thick ring with a twist of crude gold serving for a setting. He summed her up in one swift appraisal, of which she was not unconscious.

"*You* don't look your best, either, buddy," she said gently.

He found he was able to walk easily, and in a few moments the cold bright air of the morning took hold of him and lifted him up out of the haziness and ache. He walked up and down a few turns before they went into the shabby eating place. Suddenly he was happy, and pleased about everything. A banged-up head and his money stolen seemed a small price. After all, he had never before been rescued by a girl, and driven through the night while he was unconscious. His experience with girls had been alarmingly meager; that fact had worried him sometimes. But he had compensated for his lack of experience by a lavish serial of daydreaming which went on under and over everything else he thought about.

So now here was a daydream out in the open! Here was a daydream on its fanciful own. He wasn't the author of this one; now, as he had always wanted to be, he was only an obedient actor, following wherever the daydream led.

The dreary little lunchroom was empty except for the proprietor who was dozing with his feet propped up on a chair. As he heard customers pushing open the door, he patted his stomach wearily, and then got up.

"Sorry to wake you, Buster," the girl said with what Jubey soon came to know was her customary kindness. "Fact is, if you need your rest, I can heat up the coffee myself."

"G'mornin' . . . not at all. Just having a bit of a snatch. Time to wake up anyway," the big man said in a slightly Cockney accent. "What'll be your pleasure, miss?"

"Coffee, like I said . . . and maybe an egg or two, if you've got some handy."

The man was looking enquiringly at Jubey, who was suddenly a little dizzy from the warm air of the lunchroom. "Anything the matter?" he asked uneasily.

"My brother had a slight accident," the girl said. "Fell asleep while he was driving, and bumped his head."

"Your car all right?"

"Oh sure. Our car feels right at home when it's in trouble," she said cheerfully. "What's one more dent among a couple dozen?"

The lunchroom man laughed, then turned up the gas and clapped a small skillet on it, all in one perfected motion.

"Lucky you didn't get killed, the both of you. *And* the car."

"People like us don't get killed," the girl said, loosening the white silk scarf around her neck and smiling at Jubey. "That's right, isn't it, Bill?"

"That's exactly right, Clarabella," Jubey said, and winked heavily at her.

She ate quickly and nervously, with a healthy appetite, and when she saw he wasn't going to make use of a scribble of bacon on his plate, she asked for it with eyebrows and forefinger, and accepted it with a grin.

"Missed my dinner last night. On your account," she said in explanation. "Guess you wish you had missed yours, don't you?"

"Matter of fact, I've just been thinking this is worth all the rest." He saw a look of caution come across the girl's face, and he knew she was thinking she was going to have trouble with him, so he diluted his remark with an explanation entirely innocent. "I like not knowing where I am or with whom."

"Whom?" she asked. "Is that education, or just something you picked up?"

"Something *I* picked up? I thought you said you did the picking up."

She blushed, and then to discount the blush, she slapped a cigarette against her lower lip, and expertly flipped off the head of a match with her thumbnail.

"That's a pretty good switch for a guy with a Mickey Finn under his belt," she said with an exaggerated drawl.

When they were getting back into the car, Jubey said, "Well, where *am* I going? And with whom, if you'll pardon my grammar?"

"I'll pardon it. Matter of fact, I like it," she said. "I always meant to take on a little myself, when I get the time. We're going up to Portland, Maine. For no particular reason except it's as good a place as any, I guess."

"And with whom?" he insisted.

"Well, the name's Roberta Rose Kramer, if that's what you're digging for."

"Roberta Rose Kramer? I'll call you Rose, shall I?"

"I can't remember that anybody ever did before. But okay, if you want to."

"Rose," he said, testing it on tongue and ear. "On account of that's the kind of woman I need most right now."

"Don't get any false notions, buddy," she said in a matter-of-fact voice. "Just because I happened to let you lend me your car for a trip north."

Jubey laughed a loud sudden peel. "You don't know how funny that is, sister," he said. "Nothing could be farther from my mind than a false notion. But thanks for the implication, anyway."

"Okay," she said blandly. "Mean anything you want to by that remark. Just so you get the point."

They rode along in silence a few minutes, then he said, "How did you happen to take me along with the car?"

"Well, I couldn't *steal* the bus," she said ingenuously.

"So you kidnaped the owner. What made you think I wanted to leave Boston?"

"Why, I figured you'd probably stolen that wad of money, and the best place for you was somewhere else."

"Good reasoning," he said, "except that I didn't happen to steal it."

"Where'd a guy like you get a wad like that? I mean honestly?"

"My old man sent it to me. To buy a railroad ticket."

"For crying out loud," the girl said in amazement. "What's the matter with your old man . . . rich or something?"

"Nope. He just wanted me to come home."

"Imagine that," she said sarcastically, on guard now. "What kind of a guy *is* he, anyway?"

"Just a nice kindhearted old German," Jubey said slowly.

"What's he do for a living?"

"Works in a brewery."

"Well, that's more like it," she said in some relief. "My old man used to work in a coal mine. What a stinker *he* was! That's how I happened to get the Roberta hung on me."

"Your mother must have thought he was all right."

She threw him a disgusted look. "*She* knew all about him. I guess she figured naming me after him might keep him from beating me whenever he thought of it. But it didn't. It just made him all the madder at me, on account of I wasn't a boy." She was quiet a long moment, then she said almost to herself, "I tried to be a boy."

"I expect you still try sometimes," Jubey said. For some inscrutable reason that made her blush unhappily.

She changed the subject then and began telling him about the way she had managed to get him into the car last night.

"I saw you when you drove up and parked," she said. "You know what I thought? . . . 'Now, there's a nice kid. If I had a brother, I wouldn't mind having him like that kid.' Funny thing was that only yesterday morning I made up my mind I wasn't going to stay on in that dump another day if I could help it. I even put my stuff in a suitcase, so if something turned up."

"And it did," Jubey said companionably. "You know that's what Shakespeare said."

"Shakespeare! My word," she remarked accusingly. "Are you showing off, or something?"

"*You* brought up the subject."

"I hate a guy that shows off," she said, and then, "Okay. So what did Shakespeare say?"

"He said, 'The readiness is all.' "

"Sounds goofy," she said resentfully, and then, "But I see what he means."

"Sure you do. He means your suitcase."

"Yeah. That's kind of wonderful, isn't it? When you think of Shakespeare saying something maybe four or five hundred years ago or whenever it was he lived . . . and having it come right down to my suitcase."

"That's education for you," Jubey said solemnly.

"Yes. It certainly is," she agreed. "Well, I always said, like I told you, that when I have time, I'm going to . . . "

"Yep. So you packed your suitcase."

"Just in case. And later when I realized you were probably in trouble, on account of having so much money on you, I thought maybe we could both kind of help each other get away." She looked a little flustered and timid now, so Jubey said heartily, "Sure. And that's exactly how it worked out. Only . . . what're we going to use for money?"

"I've got money. I've got forty-two dollars," she said candidly. "That ought to last us until one of us gets a job."

"Good luck my gear's in the trunk, so at least you won't have to buy me some clothes," Jubey said. "But I guess I'll have to draw on the treasury for a telegram to tell my old man I'll be delayed awhile. Of course I could ask him for some more train fare."

"That wouldn't be right, after he sent you the money once," she said. "We'll have to make that up some way when things get going for us."

2

PORTLAND seemed an open book to Rose. She knew exactly
where to go looking for a rooming house that was both clean
and cheap. In the full daylight she was older, probably thirty.
But her skin had a pink and dewy freshness which made the
sketched-in wrinkles around her eyes seem a touching imposi-
tion of nature against innocence. It hurt Jubey that she was
older than he had thought; he knew with a terrible premonition that he would pity her and that this pity would lead him
into grief. The time to harden himself against her was early,
he thought angrily; but he knew it was already too late. The
daylight had probably shown her, too, something about her
companion's age, for she was assuming a careless superiority.
She was at the same time freer and more indifferent about him,
because she found the boy in him in greater majority than the
man.

"You let me do the talking," she said when they went up a
short flight of brown wooden stairs to a mud-colored door on
which a room-for-rent sign was hung.

"Don't boss me, little woman," Jubey said, more to restore
her spirits than to exercise his own. "Where I come from the
man does the talking."

She laughed at that, and knuckled him a good-natured punch
in the ribs. The door opened just in time for a dribble-haired
little woman to see the punch.

Jubey said respectfully, "Morning, ma'am. If you've got two
rooms, we'd like to look at them. My sister and I, that is."

The woman hesitated a long moment, looking them up and down. Then she opened the mud-colored door uncertainly. "I've got one with an alcove," she said. "It's got portières."

"That won't do," Jubey said. "My sister snores something awful. And I'm a light sleeper." The woman considered this grimly

"I've got an unfinished room in the attic," she said at last. "The children sleep there in the summer. But it's right cold now."

"We'll look at it," Rose said. "We like the neighborhood, and probably there's a view of the harbor from the attic."

"D'you spose so?" the woman asked, as pleased as if Rose had discovered buried treasure in her house. "It *is* real pretty up there, if a body don't mind the cold. I'll give you plenty of comforters and quilts."

"It's as good as rented," Jubey said, "unless the icicles cut off the view."

It was the alcove which really closed the deal, for behind the portières stood a small kitchen table covered with yellow oil-cloth. On a shelf near by was a two-burner gas stove, and in a hanging bookcase were two of every kind of dishes anybody could want, cups and saucers, soup bowls and dinner plates.

"Of course you'd have to keep your butter in my icebox downstairs," the landlady said honestly, not able to bear the bliss in Rose's eyes.

"Unless we keep it under my pillow in the attic," Jubey suggested.

"I couldn't allow that, on account of it might draw squirrels in the attic," the landlady said. Then she realized it was a joke, and said so heavily.

"My brother is quite a joker," Rose admitted gloomily as if it were an affliction nobody could help.

"Well, be that as it may," the landlady said, to show she was broad-minded . . . on most subjects.

They went downstairs to the dining room, and Rose counted out the first week's rent and turned it over cheerfully.

"One more thing," the landlady said, now that she had the rent in her apron pocket. "This is a respectable house. Very. I'm sure I don't need to say any more than that."

"Then let's *not* say any more," Jubey said, trying to sound as stuffy as possible.

"I only mention it, because . . . well, frankly, Miss Kramer, how do I know this *is* your brother?"

Jubey said, "We've got our birth certificates tattooed on our backs. At least I still have. I haven't seen Rose's back since we used to take our Saturday night baths together in our mother's washtub."

"Hush your mouth," Rose said crossly, and then to the paling woman in the apron. "Would I be traveling double with a *kid?* Anybody could see he's my brother!" She became more and more righteously indignant. "He's not only my brother, he's my *baby* brother." She drew up her five feet one and performed the miracle of looking scornfully down her nose at Jubey's six feet two.

They put in a fine day, settling themselves in the house and the neighborhood and the town. They made the mistake of wandering into Loring, Short and Harmon's where Jubey went a little mad in the back room where the second-hand books were stacked. He picked out an armful with reckless exuberance.

"That tells me about you," Rose said gloomily, "a man that would rather have books than new clothes."

"The law prevents indecent exposure. But it's up to you to see that your mind doesn't go around nekkid as the day it was born," Jubey told her.

"I'm not complaining," she said. "It's just that I know what I'm up against. Besides, who knows? . . . I might get to reading, myself, some day."

"It's a contagious disease," he warned her. "You're liable to catch it if you get too close to an open book. Especially if somebody reads you snatches while you're cooking at the end of a long hard day, with the cozy evening stretching ahead."

"Go along with you," she said quite happily, falling into the brogue of his thought.

Just before they went "home" in the late afternoon, they bought a nude-looking stewing hen and a big paper bag full of groceries.

"Nothing starts off housekeeping on the right foot like a good stewed chicken and mashed potatoes," Rose said. "I may have my faults, but I'm the best furnished-room cook in America."

"And to think you picked me," Jubey said.

While the chicken was stewing, they went up to the attic and hung quilts over the more apparent cracks in the walls.

The twilight was purple and pink outside the window, and beyond a sloping plateau of roofs and chimneys shone the sullen harbor. The icicles Jubey had joked about hung in sculptured crystal from the edge of the eaves. They caught Rose's lamplight and unraveled it from the prismatic skein, so that each icicle was like a needle threaded with brilliant silks.

It was a window from the frontispiece of a boy's adventure book, with the dim masts of ships and the span of a bridge in the distance, and the house roofs close at hand. In that window and in that moment were the two most primitive lures the heart must always choose between, the need for wandering and the need for finding home. Rose, in her gamin's practical way, believed she had fused them both in one snatched handful. Jubal, in whom the two needs would battle forever, knew that any momentary truce between them, any synthesis of their fulfilling, would always be delusion and mirage. You might believe you had found a way of having both, but in the end you would have to choose, and take the consequences of your choice.

But for tonight, at least, there was the attic window to remind you, and the furnished room with the toy dinner cooking, to make you forget.

The dinner was all that Rose had promised it would be, although by the time they were eating it, she had become shy and gruff about its goodness, and was trying to pick a quarrel to hide her happiness. The strangeness of their situation was just beginning to impress her, and gradually she was becoming self-conscious and embarrassed because it was she who had taken the initiative. She had put on a pink blouse; then discovering that it was very feminine and much too affirmative of her reluctant delight in this phase of herself, she had canceled it sternly under an unbecoming gray sweater.

"Afraid to be pretty?" Jubey asked, when he saw her fiercely buttoning the sweater up to her chin.

"Course not," she said crossly.

"Sure you are. But who're you afraid of . . . you or me?"

"You eat your mashed potatoes," she said as if he were ten. He saw that stressing his juvenility, also, was a precaution, and he admitted resignedly that probably this state of affairs was best. For the moment, at any rate, he added to save his masculine self-respect.

When the meal was over, he reached into his coat pocket and brought out a volume of Dante Gabriel Rossetti's poems, tipping back his chair on its two hind legs and beginning to read aloud. She sat staring at him with her elbows on the table, and her hunger in her eyes. When he looked up from the book and stopped a moment to read her face, she quickly rose and gathered up the dishes. With a minimum of noise she filled a pan with scalding water from the little teakettle steaming on the gas burner and began washing the dishes.

Jubal got up from his place and walked around the tiny room with exuberant delight. Everything was right and good, and he was as happy as a child. No, as happy as a man, he amended joyfully. Last night at this time, he was just strolling into that shabby eating place, barely noticing that the neat waitress in the limp white uniform was a blonde . . . and here tonight . . . If you took life as it came, you were sure of adventure. And more astonishing adventure than you could possibly compose for ~~yourself. Men wrote poetry; but Life lived it!~~

"What're *you* supposed to be doing?" Rose asked gruffly, not raising her eyes from her small dishpan.

"I'm just thinking how absolutely wonderful everything is, if you'll only let it be," he said, going near to her as if he knew this banally sublime thought could never be phrased by words but only by the necromancy of presence.

"Well, stop galloping around like a pony . . . get back to your chair and read some more."

"You like it, Rose? You like poetry?"

"It's all right," she said grudgingly. "It's as good a way as any to keep from helping me with the dishes." But she softened all that with a long, sweet look over her shoulder.

After that he read no more love sonnets, but let his voice ring out on Alfred Noyes' *The Highwayman*. She turned from the dishpan, forgetting what she was doing.

"That's all people need," Jubey said when he closed the book. "A safe place for the body to enjoy, and a journey for the mind to make."

"You talk too fancy," Rose told him. "But I'm not complaining."

She fell into silence then, and he could see that she was trying to get something difficult ready to say. Her rough, small-boy's hands lay revealed on the table, twisting themselves in a torture of effort. He pretended to be looking through the table of contents of his book, while he watched those hands, knowing they were her autobiography, and that sometime he would have to read them whether he wanted to or not.

"I suppose I owe you some kind of explanation," she said,

taking her words unconsciously from some piece of fiction she had read some time. "Doesn't seem fair for me to kind of kidnap you, like you said, without telling you how come I wanted to get away. And things like that."

"Tell me if you want to," Jubey said, half in fear that something would destroy this odd idyll whose beauty would surely be lost in sordidness if it had to be described. "As far as I'm concerned, it doesn't need any explaining."

"Yes. It needs plenty," she said doggedly. "And the time to tell you is now. Later . . . if there turns out to be any later . . . it would only be harder. Now, we're just strangers."

"Are we?" Jubey asked. "I got the idea I'm your brother."

"You know what I mean. Really and truly."

"We never were strangers. We didn't have time to be. We skipped the first chapter, and maybe a few others. How could people be strangers when the little one of them dragged the big one out of a fight and took care of him? And is still taking care of him? Feeding him and getting him some books, and talking sweet to him so that his heart is running around like a puppy wagging its tail?"

She blushed through this speech, and could find none of her roughness to cancel it out as she had canceled out her pink feminine blouse.

"But I gotta tell you anyway. I don't want you to think I'm any better than I am."

"All right, Rosie. Tell me how bad you are."

"Not bad, exactly," she said. "Only terribly lonesome sometimes."

"Like everybody is," Jubey said, trying to divert her.

"No. Not like everybody. Like a woman gets lonesome. For somebody to need her. Not just part of her, either. But all of her."

"I know, Rosie," he said, as gentle as a father.

"D'ja ever think about lonesomeness? I don't guess you have.

You being just a boy, and a kind of jolly boy, the way you are."

"Jolly people are the lonesomest," he said. "Jolly people are the most scared of it. That's why they act jolly."

"Yes. I guess that's right. I never thought of that, Jubey. But I guess that's right." She twisted her hands again, trying to find the way to say what she needed to. "People think there's only one way of being drunk. Well, there's lots of things besides liquor that make people act like drunks. Lonesomeness does. It makes you believe everything's going to be dandy. Or else it makes you so blue you just sit and let tears trickle out of you. I've seen plenty of drunks, and I've felt plenty lonesome, and as far as I can make out, there's not much difference."

"So?"

"Well, so then you do things you wouldn't do when you were sober. You look at some bragging broken-down, good-for-nothing, and you say, 'Why sure . . . he's a good guy. All he needs is me to kind of straighten him out.' You know what I mean, Jubey?" Her face begged him to understand, and he put out his big rough hand and gathered hers into it.

"You don't need to tell me anything, Rosie," he said again. "I know you as well as if I'd made you myself."

"You do?" she asked incredulously. "You mean you wouldn't be shocked if I was to tell you . . . "

"I wouldn't be shocked if you were to tell me *anything*. So, for that reason, you don't have to. Except the way things kind of get said between friends, natural and easy, when the time comes for them."

"Yeah," she said thoughtfully. "Like when you're sloshing chow around, not thinking about anything, and all of a sudden you begin remembering something you just hate to think about. And you remember awhile, kind of not able to stop yourself, and all of a sudden you think, Why sure . . . I can see how that happened. The guy was frightened to death — or Certainly! That nasty old woman just had to have the money and she didn't care *who* suffered . . . and the next time you think about it, it's all explained and it doesn't hurt you any more."

"That's it," he said. "If we're going to travel double . . . wasn't that what you said to Mrs. Turello?"

"I said that was what we *weren't* doing," she corrected him primly.

"Well, if we're going to travel double, let's just let what we tell each other come out when it wants to. Let's just take each other as we are . . . the way you took me last night when you saw I needed somebody."

"Okay," she said . "That's the way it is. I've already done that, Jubey. It's only that . . . "

"It's only that you've got to trust me to do the same."

She nodded, and then there were tears in her eyes. "There's one more thing, Jubey."

"Okay."

"There's something about this . . .you know, you and me . . . that I like. I wish it wouldn't have to go the way everything always goes, Jubey. I'd like it awful well if we could keep this from having hell drip into it. You know what I mean?"

"Sure I know what you mean. What'd you think I am? A kid?"

"I'd like it if, maybe two three years from now, I could look back and say to myself, *There* was one thing that stayed right. You don't know how I'd like it if I could say that."

He got up from his chair and stretched his arms up over his head and yawned a big masculine yawn, to keep a mistiness out of his own eyes.

"You talk fancy yourself," he said, bending over to grin into her face. "But I'm not complaining."

"No, but honestly," she insisted.

"You want it in writing?"

"Don't joke, Jubey. This is awful serious to me."

"It's serious to me, too. You want me to promise?"

"I guess that's what I do want. You promise for both of us. Because I can't always depend on me, Jubey. I get to thinking oh-never-mind . . . and first thing you know . . . " The tears now splashed down on her hands, and he saw by the way her hands pulled away that she detested tears.

He patted her shoulder. "You're crossing bridges before we come to 'em, Rosie."

"We'll come to 'em," she said desolately. "We'll come to 'em all right. Only safe time to think about 'em is right now."

"All right. So we've thought about them," he said. "So now I'll bid you good night, madam, and mount to my apartment in the attic. Sleep well, and dream pretty. And tomorrow I'll go out and find myself the finest job in the city, and on payday I'll bring you home a gold watch and chain. Or at least a mouth organ for me to play you songs on."

"You're such a fool," she said, whisking the tears out of her eyes.

"But you're not complaining," Jubey reminded her with a grin.

He lay on the lumpy cot in the attic and looked out across the slope of other people's roofs down to the harbor, bright now in the moonlight. He thought back over the whole good day, and all it lacked was someone to tell its beauty to. Only there would be no one who would see it as he did. Not even Rosie. Least of all Rosie. She would have her own description of this day, and he doubted if he would recognize the day if he met her description.

He felt happy and nourished along the whole young length of him. The waves of the poetry were still washing lazily on the shore of his under-mind. His head felt clear and good again, for most of the soreness from the battering had receded. His flat young stomach was filled and lulled by Rosie's excellent food. And there was an imp of mischief peering from behind a tree in the center of his good intentions. He had promised, to be sure. But after all, everything was a matter of definition, and what was "bad" today can sometimes be seen as "delightful" tomorrow. He'd take charge of that department. The only consideration would be for Rosie herself. She wanted something she could remember happily two-three years from now? Well, he'd see what he could do.

3

THE DAYS went swiftly, like the make-believe they were. Rosie got her job first.

"People always eat," she said disparagingly when she brought home her first day's pay. "Drop me down beside the North Pole, and I'd be a waitress by noon."

"That's because you're so pretty," Jubey said. "People digest their food better when it's handed them by a blonde."

His own job was harder to find. He had discovered early in this wandering that a man's occupation is dictated by the clothes he owns. The best accountant in the city wouldn't be hired as a bookkeeper while he was wearing corduroy pants and a sheepskin jacket. The jobs Jubey could have handled most easily, he couldn't dress for. That disqualified his head from working and left only his strong back and arms to earn his wage. But he had wanted it that way, until the moment came when he wished Rose to see she had a good man to take care of her. Then it irked him that the doors at which he was supposed to apply for work were off alleys, into warehouses, ice plants, machine shops. But Rose was unaware that this dilemma was the cause of his impatience.

"Keep your shirt on. You'll get a job," she said. "And in the meantime, there's me."

"That's the point," he muttered disgruntedly.

He finally did get something, of course, unloading cargo down on that dock that looked so romantic from his attic window. Jubey wore canvas gloves, but even so his hands were cruelly hurt by the heavy work. He held the job a week, and then was tipped off that a vaudeville theater needed a clean-up man. He took that job without even asking about the pay; after all, he had always wanted to be on a stage, hadn't he?

He watched the shows round and round four times a day. But he wasn't seeing what was actually on the stage; in his mind he was watching a constant revision of the simple-minded comedy material, raising the broad coarse jokes to a higher and higher attenuation, and trying to get up his courage to suggest even one improvement to the players.

The strange dizzy week started something whirling deep inside him, something he couldn't mention even to himself. The mouldy, sweet dusty smell of the theater had been breathed into his nostrils and something new was created in him. One more stranger within him, to wrangle with the others who couldn't seem to find out what they wanted, or how they meant to get it.

The night before he lost that job, he slipped Rose through the stage door, so she could see the show. Afterwards he sat at their little oilcloth-covered table half the night, going through all the routines, showing her what could be done, even with such old chewing gum as the material was. Most of the turns he acted out, and sleepy as she was she laughed so loud that Mrs. Turello came up to see what was happening. He went easily from the aged red-haired ingenue to the Jareth Brothers in top hats and tails. Even the performing dogs he "impersonated," and then it was Mrs. Turello who had hysterics that woke up the other roomers.

"Well, whyn't you tell *them?*" Rose kept saying. "Why waste it on us, Jubey? We don't know anything about it. You tell *them,* honey."

"That's what I'm going to do," Jubey said excitedly. "Maybe I better just pick out the best ... the Jareth Brothers, maybe ... and give 'em an idea. ... " The next day just before the theater opened, he knocked on the Jareth Brothers' door.

That's how he lost that job.

Rose did her best to console him. "The thing is, you're too smart for your own comfort, Jubey," she said when he got home. "You got to get up above where you are now. You shouldna been born down here with us. You got to get up where there's some chance for you."

"You don't know what you're talking about."

"No. I mean it. You'll always be nothing but a dumbhead down here. But if you could only get hold of some good clothes, and get acquainted with some clever people, I bet you'd amount to something."

Sometimes she would sketch out large and touchingly ignorant plans for him. How about them just working like fiends ... well, you know people can *always* work harder than they are ... and maybe not spend as much money on food and stuff as they were spending ... and try to get a little money ahead so Jubey could ...

"Don't talk crazy." Jubey could barely keep tears from his eyes because she was so good and so helpless with all her poor bravery. "You talk like my mother or something," he would say when he couldn't find any other words to divert her.

"Well, I might as well *be*," she'd sometimes answer back, stung by an anger whose name she didn't know.

The strange part of it all was that Jubey seemed to forget that this situation was only anomalous make-believe which could be dissolved at any time he chose to dispel it. He worried and fumed at its restrictions and chafings as sincerely as if they were genuine ones which could not be changed.

Sometimes they quarreled like children and Rose called him names, and said she wished he had never laid her eyes on him. Then both of them would be thinking the same treacherous thing ... that before tomorrow came each of them would be alone.

One night when he saw her beyond his printed page sitting and glaring at him, he knew she was wishing she had never picked him up out of that fracas.

"*I* think of running away, too. Don't forget that," he said to the sullen determination in her transparent face.

"Go ahead and run. Nothing's holding you."

"*You* run. You picked it up. You lay it down," he said with unexpected gentleness. "That way you'll have nobody to blame but yourself."

At other times each of them would be contrite because of the angry disloyalty that had snapped between them like an electric charge. Each knew why this anger was, but neither wanted to speak about it, for they knew that the surest way to destroy the precarious safety between them was to discuss it.

Sometimes for no immediate reason, Rose would burst out crying, and when Jubey would put his arms around her shoulders and try to smile into her face, she would push him away angrily.

"I hate this neither one thing nor the other."

"You wanted it this way, Rosie."

"Sure I want it this way. But it makes me furious that you're so beastly cheerful about it."

"I'm not cheerful about it. I'm gnashing my teeth."

"Like heck you are. You don't even know what I'm talking about. You're insulting, that's what you are. You're so safe you're insulting."

"All right, I'll show you," he cried, and yanked her to him. "You come here and I'll show you. I'll show you in a way you'll never forget, my little so-and-so."

It was just about then, fortunately, that she would hold him away by her strong thin arms, and twist her face out of his reach. Then, when she had got away from him, she would say contritely, "Jubey ... I told you you'd have to watch out for me. I warned you that I'd get around you sometime, if I could. Only don't let me, Jubey. You promised me you'd take care of it."

Jubey would wipe his brow and try not to meet her eye. "But for gosh sake, Rosie ... what do you think I'm made of? I can't be on both teams at once, you know."

"Yes you can," she would say unreasonably, all softness and goodness now that the passion had been scared out of her. "You have to be, because you promised."

"Well, I take back my promise."

"You can't. You said I could think about this when I get to be an old lady."

"I'll give you something really to think about," he said.

But he dared to say it only because once again, below all her surface weakness, there was that strangely prim "good" woman who had made up her mind to protect him, in spite of them both.

4

THEY GOT RESTLESS when the first warm wind of spring came. The forsythia bushes along the park were suddenly fountains of gold, and that night the rooms that had seemed cozy through the weeks of cold March and rainy April were only small and cramped. They went out and walked, though a waitress' feet can think of better pleasures than walking.

"Let's pull out tomorrow," Jubey said suddenly. "Let's go places."

"I shouldn't of let you get that new clutch put in the car," Rose said. "Where'll we go?"

"Let's start south. I'd like to see spring come tearing up from the south. What'd you say?"

"I say sure."

They woke up the Chinaman and got back their meager laundry; they dutifully left Jubey's books tied with twine at the door of the public library; they gave Mrs. Turello a week's rent instead of "notice," and by seven o'clock in the morning they were on their way.

"We'll strike south, and the first one that sees a jonquil gets free beer," Jubey said.

They drove for several days, nursing the decrepit car watchfully. Sometimes, so comfortable was their understanding, they didn't speak for hours. Unexpectedly, as they drove along the Hudson and saw the George Washington Bridge flung like a volley of jewels against the twilit sky, they decided to stop over in New York City for a couple of days' diversion.

"I'd spend my time in vaudeville shows," Jubey said. "But what would you do?"

"I'd find plenty to do," Rose said. "I might even take a quick course in manicuring, so I could wear callouses on another part of my anatomy."

They found a hotel which they could afford and which Rose decided was clean and decent enough. When they registered for two rooms on different floors, the sly little Filipino behind the desk was shocked that they should be so extravagant. But Jubey silenced him before Rose understood what he was trying to suggest.

She had never been in New York, and she was exhilarated and off guard. They opened their suitcases and got out the best clothes they had, and then went out to walk the city. Rose could not keep from crying when they reached lower Fifth Avenue and she looked up at the giant buildings, dark and ghostly after the working hordes had deserted them. Jubey held her hard little hand tight in his jacket pocket; by this time she trusted him so much that he didn't even have to pretend not to see her emotion.

"Go ahead and cry, honey. No extra charge for finding it *that* wonderful."

"It isn't the city," Rose said with a gulp. "It's seeing it with you, you dope."

They smiled at each other and walked along in silence for several blocks. At last Rose said, "There's something I've been thinking of asking you, Jubey."

"Yes?"

"Would you . . . would you be willing . . . to ask me to marry you sometime?"

He thought for a moment that she was teasing him; then by the tension of her face he saw she was deadly in earnest.

"I'll ask you right now, Rosie."

She shook her head vehemently. "No . . . not now. It

wouldn't mean anything now, because I ... well, I really backed you into a spot where you couldn't help yourself."

"All right. I'll find the right time, and then I'll ask you."

"You don't have to, Jubey. I mean, if you don't want to, you don't have to."

"You let me handle it, Rosie. You just be a little woman and let me take over the project."

After that she couldn't find anything to say. He could see her, in her shame, wishing she was dead, and that touched him so much that he stopped on the street and made her face him.

"Do you really want to get married, Rosie?"

"Oh, forget it," she said. "You've always got to talk everything into a pulp."

"We don't have to talk about it. I can say willya and you can say yes, and that will settle everything."

She dabbed at her eyes, acutely conscious that passers-by were mildly interested. Jubey took out his handkerchief and handed it to her, then he turned her face up to his and looked into her eyes.

"Listen. I don't know why I never got around to telling you this, but ... "

She cried in fear, "Oh Jubey, don't tell me! I might have known somebody would have got hold of you before I saw you."

"Hush. That isn't it. But I have to say it, Rosie. I have to tell you ... this funny little time with you has been the happiest time I've ever known."

"Do you really mean that, Jubey?"

"I mean it. And so, I was wondering if maybe you'd ... like ... to marry me." By the time he got to the end of the sentence his face had burst out in perspiration, and he knew his voice was twice as loud as it should have been.

"Jubey ... I ought to tell you a few things."

"You don't need to tell me anything. I know all about you, Rosie. I know. ... "

"I'm eleven years older than you are," she said in a whisper. "And besides . . . "

"Besides nothing. Tomorrow we'll get a license, and maybe by this time tomorrow night . . . "

He felt himself trembling all over, as if he had suddenly witnessed a terrific accident, too vast for him to prevent or to help. The dream had suddenly been pierced, and here was sober reality. A dozen clear pictures like quickly dealt cards fell before his sight: Rose, with the cigarette hanging drolly from her lip; Rose and Lucile, heartbreakingly trying to forgive each other for being what each was; Papa explosively crashing through the amenities. . . . Where would he leave her while he went back to the university? Of course he must go back; he saw that now.

Everyone in the situation would be hurt . . . but Rose most of all. Between them, they would not be able to keep from destroying her. Unless he never went home again. Yes, that would be the way, the only safe way for all of them. He had chosen wandering? Well, he should have it for the rest of his life. His tongue was so dry that it clove to the roof of his mouth, and he couldn't speak. He could only grin crazily down at her, and hope that somehow she would misinterpret what must have been in his face. She was so good . . . so pathetically good under her shallow vice, that she would never be able to understand his complex tangle of loyalties and desires and aims.

"Jubey, you're a good boy," she said in a strangely maternal way. "No wonder somebody like me can't help loving you."

"Nobody . . . except you . . . does," he said doggedly, as if he could erase all the agony of the future by that childish denial. "Nobody ever did . . . much. So if you want me . . . "

"I know," she said with incongruous sadness.

They strolled along, out of step and suddenly very tired, as if they had each climbed a mountain. They talked brightly about what they saw on either side, but their voices were hollow and frightened, and each tried to believe that was only the way the other's voice was being heard.

At Union Square they saw knots of people collected in the broad street, and Rose cried, almost in relief, "Must be something wrong, Jubey! Let's us go over."

They ran to join a group, and Jubey welcomed the pace broken between them. As they drew near, they realized what was happening. No accident, but only orators sprinkled here and there with a restless circle of listeners around each.

"Just talking," Rose cried in disappointment. "Some of your kinfolks, Jubey, talking themselves black and blue."

"We'll listen awhile."

"Oh, for gosh sakes," she said, "I get plenty of this at home." She was exuberant now that the awkwardness was over, and she nudged him playfully in the ribs, and stood on her tiptoes to see what kind of man was behind the big angry voice booming forth.

"Wouldn't you know . . . a half-pint man!" she said disgustedly.

"Pick any size you like. They're all here," Jubey said, equally relieved at the change of subject.

They drifted around the perimeters of several of the harangues, and finally settled on a big red-faced blond man with a tattered felt hat and no necktie. He was shouting criticisms against the administration, beating the stupid crowd over the head with a cat-o'-nine-tails made of their poverty and unemployment, and rumors of great graft. His castigations were as old as the upward trudge of mankind itself. He was bending double and shaking his black-rimmed finger in their faces, shouting questions to which their blank, miserable faces were the only answer. They had crowded together tonight for the bleak comfort of mere animal warmth, but he was belaboring them with their lacks and their dooms, so that they were becoming poorer and more discouraged by the syllable.

Rose and Jubey listened ten minutes, and Rose said, "He's right, the red-haired so-and-so." She was angry at him, because there was no other way of localizing the injustices one wanted to be angry about.

"But don't you see . . ." Jubey said to her, his compassion shining in his face.

Before she realized what he was doing, he had jumped up on the stone coping that ran around a dismal little park. He began talking, to nobody in particular. He lifted his face to the fragment of sky overhead and talked to it, and at first Rose looked around in embarrassment, expecting someone to pull him down and ask if he had a permit.

"They're telling you you're poor, aren't they? You're not poor. You're the richest people in the world. You have a bank account in your name so big you never can spend it all. Where in the world did you get such a thing? Why, your forefathers left it to you. Had you forgotten that? No need to forget it. They wrote your inheritance in documents to last forever, so you could put your hands on it whenever you need it. They said they were providing you, for all the years you lived on these shores, with life, with liberty and with the pursuit of happiness. Remember that? Life . . . what kind of life is that, do you suppose? Well, I'll tell you. I'll tell you the way I described it to a submarine full of Germans not so many months ago."

He went on talking, his voice a strong, proud stream which Rose hardly recognized, pulsing with honesty and passion. Sometimes he laughed as he talked, and the crowd which had collected one by one laughed with him and nudged each other roughly and said, "He's right . . . the kid's sure right."

He had gone back to the beginnings of America, and was describing those men who dreamed the big dream. Against the backdrop of the tall dead buildings, and the dwarfed leafless trees of the park, he was painting in the figures of the women who worked beside those men. He was coming down through

Jefferson, and Lincoln and Wilson, and was explaining their
noblest aspirations in terms this sodden crowd could understand. In thrilling cadences he was talking to them, but also
he was reminding himself. He was begging them to wake up
their minds, to shake themselves into aliveness, so that food and
drink and daily play would not satisfy them. He was making
them feel the eternal thirst for knowing, and the ecstatic aliveness that comes from supping even a thimbleful of the divine
elixir of knowledge and the freedom knowledge bestows.

"You're scared to death. But you don't have to be. The head-
lines keep telling you that nearly six million men are out of
work, and you think, Tomorrow I'll be out. Tomorrow has got
you by the throat, so you can't think straight today. But you've
got to think straight. And you can.

"A man who is thinking has on a secret armor. People don't
push around a man who knows how to think."

Black drops of humanity dripped off the edges of the other
masses and fastened themselves on the crowd around Jubey.
They cried to each other as they pushed into the crowd, "Say,
the guy over here must be giving something away."

A man up close growled over his shoulder, "He *is* giving
something away. Shut your mouth and listen."

"What's he givin'? Hot peanuts?"

"Naw. Hot hope."

The crowd stirred and grinned as one man; they muttered
among themselves, half afraid of being found guilty of believing
what a youngster was saying. Then they shushed each other
and listened, and Rose was pushed farther and farther back in
the crowd until she was on the outer edge. Her face was lifted
and full of joy, and she was crying to herself strange imprecations and blessings and cursings. She was saying to herself,
That's what he's got those long arms for, to wave up to heaven
while he talks! And that voice of his . . . how come I never
noticed before what a voice the kid has? Makes ants crawl all
over you . . . and I thought . . .

The tears were coming fast now, but she barely noticed them. She brushed them off as if they were only impersonal rain, and no blame to her. A baggy-bodied old man said to her, "You and me both, sister." Then when she looked at him in bewilderment he said, "You don't often hear a guy talk like that. Makes you homesick, don't it?"

"Homesick for what?" Rose said crossly.

"For all kinds of things good."

She looked at him with all the hostility she could find in the sum of herself. "Go get yourself a free bath in a flophouse," she said.

"Why, lady! I don't know what you're mad at *me* for."

"I got plenty of reason," she said, but even to herself she did not know how to phrase her case against him. She knew only that she detested the poverty and the weakness and the victimhood of him. She could not go beyond that knowledge to seeing that the reason for her anger was that he was an ambassador from all the weak and poor who had stolen Jubey from her. And eventually would steal him from his own life.

She walked smartly around the rim of the crowd, while her heart was on its knees begging her not to do what she knew she would have to do. She stood in the tangled shadow of a starved little tree which a tall street light was keeping awake; she was not able to hear Jubey's words now, only his voice. It came down across the river of cacophony like a tall ship bearing new cargo. In her wordless way she saw that picture and almost understood what it meant.

"Oh, be done with it," she said aloud, and ran away on her high heels, floundering and stumbling like someone wounded mortally.

The crowd kept him until his voice was gravel in his throat. They asked him questions and he found answers he didn't even know he had. He kept thinking to himself, Where on earth did that come from? It seemed to him that some ancient creature had suddenly come to life in him, brushing aside the crude youngness and the egotism and uncertainty and blame. Without benefit of Jubey, it was speaking of itself. Of all the listeners in the crowd, no one was more amazed than Jubal Our.

The thought of Rose crossed his mind occasionally, but it was always as if she were a figure of a long-finished past. A woman I used to know . . . a good woman I used to know. . . .

It was almost midnight when he began walking south through the tall empty streets, dragging his crowd behind him like a huge encompassing shadow of things to come. Several of the other street orators had joined this band. Only the hardy ones were with him now; the ones with the tough and flexible minds inside their shabby bodies, the Jubeys-grown-old who had missed their destiny along the way.

Each had his pet grudge, his piercingly original case against God, or else his euphoric dream that kept him nourished and warm in the midst of his ruin. There was the white-haired giant that wanted to do away with all the mentally incompetent ("beginning with me, naturally," he said jovially) and the Irishman who was working to have colleges open for free education for anyone over fifty who could keep up to scholastic standards. There was the Negro who spoke not a word but listened with his soul in his face to everything that was said, and the red-faced man with the cough who believed this would be a better world if everybody who wanted one was given a small farm. They strolled along the streets, and sometimes, like a clutter of trash drifting downstream, they got caught on the sharp prong of an idea, and forgot to move ahead.

There was a different Filipino behind the desk in the deserted hotel lobby. Jubey held up his key, and asked if Miss Kramer had come in.

"I sink so . . . but I only come on duty at eleven," he said. "Want I ring her room, please?"

"Don't bother her," Jubey said, and ran up the linoleum covered stairs to the second floor. As he walked down to his door, he heard the telephone ringing, but before he got the key in the lock the phone was quiet. It must be a wrong number. Who would be calling him here? He tore off his clothes as fast as he could, scarcely realizing what he was doing, so vehemently was he thinking about all that had happened to him tonight. His flesh was warm and alive with excitement and joy.

If only Rose were here. . . He wanted to go over it again. She would laugh at him, and tease him a bit. She would say, What's so wonderful about talking to a lot of bums on a street corner? But she would have seen . . . she must have seen that something great and new had happened to him. It was as if secret rooms had been discovered in what had appeared to be a small and mediocre building. The men in the crowd couldn't have known that, but Rose saw it happening, just the way he did.

What had caused it to happen? Surely not just that moment of overwhelming compassion he had felt for the crowd! Yet it seemed that moment had unlocked the secret beautiful rooms in his mind. That moment had unleashed a torrent of strength and energy and power in him. Could that be the discovery of some law of living?

The long-necked telephone standing on the bare table rang again. Perhaps it was one of those talkative cronies, wanting to hammer home one last point. He grinned to himself, picturing the guy, ragged and probably vile-smelling, spending a cherished beer nickel just to make some point, political or religious.

He grabbed the telephone eagerly. But it wasn't a self-appointed messiah's voice. It was Rose.

"Jubey?"

"Say. I've just been thinking about you. Why did you leave so early? Slip something on and come down. . . ."

"Jubey, listen. I'm not in the hotel, honey."

"Why not? Where are you, anyway?"

"I'm in a bus station. I'm leaving, Jubey."

"What're you talking about, Rosie? I'll come get you. Didn't we say . . . "

The weight which the glorious evening had lifted fell upon him again. She didn't say anything for a few moments, and he had to speak her name again to make sure the telephone connection hadn't been broken. Then he knew she was crying.

"Rose, please. Please don't. I can't do anything from here. . . ."

"I don't want you to do anything," she said in a smothered little voice. "Jubey . . . I heard you talking. . . ."

"Didn't you like it, Rosie? Weren't you maybe a little bit proud of me?"

"You don't need me to be proud of you," she said with some of her old spirit coming back into her voice. "You're plenty proud of yourself, you big bragging so-and-so."

"Don't scold me, Rosie," he said, the way he often did. "I'm just a little guy trying to get along."

An operator's voice came in saying flatly, "Your three minutes is up. Signal when you're finished." Rosie, restored by her blithe anger, said, "Get yourself off the wire, operator." Then, reinforced by that remark, she went back to Jubey.

"I suppose you're so full of yourself you didn't even hear what I told you. I'm leaving. I'm going back to Boston."

"But you said that tomorrow you wanted . . . "

She interrupted, as if she couldn't bear the way he was framing the words. "I only wanted you to . . . ask me, Jubey. I just wanted that much, to kind of remember you by."

"You mean you don't want to . . . "

"Oh, for crying out loud!"

"You mean you don't love me?"

"Of course I don't love you," she said. "You're nothing but a kid, and you're so full of wind you'd sail if you held up a handkerchief."

"But, Rosie, you said . . . "

"Aw, tell it to the crowd," Rose said. "I've got to have some-body my own size to pick on, and you're too . . . "

Now she was really crying. He heard the tough child's sob catch in her throat, then she hung up. He tried to signal the operator, but only the Filipino at the desk came on and shad-owboxed about the call until Jubey himself hung up.

He lay face downward on the bed, trying to realize that Rose was gone. He thought back over their strange shabby little idyll. In his mind was her face, beautiful and touchingly com-mon. The sketched lines about her lovely eyes hurt him so he could not bear to think about them. Her body was angrily boyish because it was afraid of the fierce love that betrayed it. Her tight little body was tireless and eager and always a sleep-less traitor dogging her life.

But inside that enigmatic body there was the spirit of a gladiator. A tough brittle spirit, ashamed of its strength and afraid of its weakness. She led with her heart . . . doubled up like a fist. If you dared suspect that it *was* a heart, you got bopped on the jaw with it.

She was gone now, and there would be nobody to tell about her. He had lost something dangerous and dear out of his life, and the only person who could mourn that loss with him was Rose . . . and Rose was gone.

He was crying like a kid, and there wasn't any need to con-ceal the fact. The whole thing revolved slowly in his mind. The weary excitement had ebbed away like carousel music after the park has closed. It had been nothing. You could say it in one short casual sentence, and it would be nothing. Yet to him it had meant coming of age. He said the ugly, simple sentence just once, "A kid falls for the wrong girl, and that makes him so sorry for everybody that he breaks out in oratory."

But over that sentence, as he tried to bury it once and for all below the surface of his mind, was springing up a strong wild sprout from a dormant seed. A thrust of intention, undeniable as a spear of stubborn growth burst open in the center of his mind. *He would start home tomorrow.*

Now he could face Papa with no danger of hurting him by the teeming contradictions within. He could not phrase any simple certainties . . . perhaps one never could. But he had seen enough and felt enough so that now Papa's innocent credulities were safe in his presence. He could "protect" Papa without damaging his own integrity. The irrational sum of all that had happened to him . . . Milton and his cowardly prayer . . . Kurt Geitzen and his kindness . . . the poverty, the patience, the anger, the joy of the working people he knew . . . Rose Kramer's goodness, and that skyrocketing compassion tonight which had given first eloquence and then wisdom . . . all these somehow were welded together for a strength which would keep Papa's faith in a simple world from collapsing.

His wandering was over now. Tomorrow he would pick up his own life again and carry it forward.

5

THIS TIME Jubal did not announce his homecoming. He searched again to remember in what literary work he had read the pattern of it . . . the boy who wandered and starved among husks while his father's riches waited for his return. Still he had not been able to identify just where that classic plot originated. But he remembered its climax, when the boy turned his face homeward, and the father ran to meet him and put the best clothes on him, and a ring on his finger. He knew that was how it would be with him, and once he had started on the homeward trip, he could barely wait to reach that ornate brick house with cupolas and balconies hung on it like jewelry. All the hours he was riding in the daycoach from New York to St. Louis, he was picturing his own arrival, and was varying it until it suited his mood.

The train would come in a little after three. Even if neighbors happened to be in the railway station, no one would recognize him for he was still wearing his workman's clothes. And he felt, besides, that he had probably changed beyond recognition, through all his experiences.

He would take a taxi, and get out on Lindell Boulevard a block before the Our mansion. He would slip through the wide "grounds" always kept so beautifully shaved and barbered, and would enter the back door of the house. Anna in the kitchen would look at him, and her stupid dear face would collapse, and her round mouth would open in a small scream. Then as she recognized him she would run and gather him to her bosom.

He could smell the sweet nutmeg and cinnamon fragrance of that bosom now, for it had eased many a little-boy sorrow. She would smuggle him up the back stairs and into his own suite, and there he would bathe luxuriously with the fine English soap. When he was dressed in his excellent gray suit with the Alice blue necktie which Mama liked best, he would open his door, and standing in the middle of the room, he would give a gigantic roar.

Hail the conquering hero is home, he would shout (or some such banal nonsense). Or perhaps he would only lift up his terrifyingly big voice in one of the old German songs they all loved. The house would catch its breath, then doors would open all at once, and Mama would come running out . . . and Papa, probably having his small rest before dinner, would bounce out of his room shouting that he must be dreaming . . . but he thought he heard Jubey. . . . And Minna, too, would dash into Jubey's room, clutching a kimono and crying excitedly. Minna would be grown up! Perhaps even pretty.

At any rate, they would all be there, weeping and laughing and scolding him fondly for not letting them know he was coming. Lucile would cling to him with probably not a word, and he would look down into her eyes and tell her he understood her quietness.

The dream of the homecoming was unbearably sweet to him.

But it had no similarity to the reality as it came about. It was raining when the train came into the station, a cold, chill unwelcoming rain that made everything look dirty and poor. He checked his unwieldy gear in a baggage room, knowing that Papa would send a man down tomorrow to pick it up. He wanted to forget it, to walk up Lindell Boulevard swinging free arms.

The taxi had to pull over to the curbstone and stop when they got almost within sight of the pink mansion, because a

cortege of funeral cars was coming slowly towards them down
the center of the street, and the traffic law required this respect.
So Jubey got out and paid the driver, while his eye automatically counted the big brass-trimmed automobiles creeping at
about four miles an hour. There was a great number of them,
so he knew someone important was dead. Behind the sleek
black hearse were four opened cars heaped with flowers, un-
speakably trite and ineffectual in the rain. He stood behind his
cab and watched with dismal protest this parade so out of mood
with his homecoming. It was no doubt some elderly neighbor,
and Papa and Lucile would probably be sitting gloomily in one
of these shrouded cars, so that all his plans would fizzle out.

Or would they? He had no idea how long funeral services
last, but perhaps it would work out just right. He would be
dressed and ready for them when they returned. When he
heard the front door open, he would let out that big roar that
was impatiently waiting in his throat. They would be all the
more delighted because of this dreary interlude.

He walked along the boulevard as fast as he could, his head
down so that his eyes wouldn't have to watch the procession. As
soon as the procession had dropped behind him he felt better;
he could scarcely keep from running. The rain against his face
felt gritty; he would give himself a good shampoo when he
bathed. . . .

Here was their house, looming up as it always did, big as
Papa's gratitude, flamboyant as his good fortune. The catalpa
tree had buds on it, and the rhododendrons were shiny and
splashed with white reflections in the rain. The big front door,
behind its narrow ugly stone piazza, was closed and blank. He
ran now, as he had often run the last hundred yards before he
reached home, his feet ringing on the sidewalk that encircled
the low redstone wall topped with ornamental iron lace. Here
was the place where he always vaulted over the wall and scur-

ried through the break in the shrubbery beside the back entrance. Down at the back of the land, he saw the laboratory Papa had built for his wireless.

The doorknob filled his palm in the old familiar way, and turned willingly in his hand. He remembered there was always a vision of Anna's cookies that came to him just here. What a childhood he had had . . . nothing but food and kindness and love. Nothing but welcoming and pride and indulgence showered on him . . . and he had chosen exile!

He stepped through the wide back-entry hall, sniffing the lovely familiar smell of apples which clung around the place. Before he could even see the kitchen through the door which led to it, he could hear Anna's big clock which she had always told him "ticked with wooden shoes on yet."

But above it, he heard something else, something that struck him like a sharp blow in the pit of the stomach. He stopped in the door, afraid to look, for something told him what had happened here today.

At the kitchen table Anna was sitting, her red arms blotting out her big bosom, and her face hidden in her hands. Trickling from between her fingers was the weary gutteral grinding of weeping which has gone on so long that it doesn't care how it sounds. She looked up when she heard him, then resumed her untidy crying. "Go away. We don't want nothing. Can't you see?"

There was another woman in the kitchen, a stranger with protruding teeth and black hair scraped back from her forehead. She was sitting on a kitchen chair with her shoes off. Her black unfriendly eyes crawled over Jubey like inquisitive beetles.

"Anna . . . what is it?" he whispered. It was a totally unnecessary question, for he knew.

She looked up at him again, and now her red arms dropped from the table and she burst out crying harder than ever.

"Oh, Jubey . . . it's your mother . . . it's your saintly little mother. . . ." She wallowed out of her chair and rolled herself into his arms, sobbing with indecent abandon. She was jabbering almost out of control. He held her and dully patted her shoulder, towering above her and thinking numbly that this was somehow wrong since she had always been the big one who hovered over him when there was trouble.

"We tried and tried to reach you, Jubey," she said. "Your father spent hundreds of dollars trying to locate you while she was sick. First one city and then another . . . where *was* you yet?"

"I was lost," he muttered.

She pulled him to the table, and made him sit down, then hunched across from him talking in tumbled emotion, telling him a snatch of this and of that, and scrubbing at her eyes. The whole scene felt so completely out of the realm of plausibility that, except for the funeral procession, he could have believed it was all one of her old superstitions and ghost stories.

Inevitably she thought of food for him, and rose up in the midst of her noisy damp dream, and going to the refrigerator, she blindly took out a ham and some tomatoes, and began slicing and arranging them on a plate. She pushed it across the table to him without seeming to be concious of the food or of her preparation of it. But he shook his head, and got up and left the kitchen, for there was gathering in him a hurricane of grief.

The house had unnatural twilight in it; even the thick white doilies and crocheting with which all horizontal surfaces must be covered had taken on a subdued grayness. He avoided glancing into the parlor as he passed, fearing to see rows of thin-legged folding chairs, or emptied containers that had held those bleak flowers he had pitied in the rain. The big winding staircase reached out arms to him, and he went up dully. Just as he had thouasnds of times, he went first to Lucile's room. He put up his hand to knock as he always had; it was the irrevocable obsolescence of that gesture which finally brought the storm of tears.

He opened the door and stepped into her room. Nothing was changed. The green marble fireplace, the chair where she read, the rosewood table with the Venetian glass decanter and the tulip-sized glasses, the sentimental water colors she had painted when she was a girl . . . all were the same. The rest of the house had been submerged in a green twilit sadness. But this little room had a golden light in it, which seemed to come from nowhere, unless it was from memory itself. He looked around slowly, then he realized he was holding his hands palms up as if they were expecting something to touch them.

He remembered how through all the homesick picturing on the train, he had felt Lucile clinging to him and saying no word. That had been the only true part of the imagining . . . He remembered how he had looked down into her eyes and had told her that he understood her quietness. He told her again in his heart, and listened for her reply, so that it seemed to come to him.

You had to stay away, my darling. There was something you had to learn first. I know. So don't scold yourself, Jubal. Just take what you learned, and later you must . . .

He waited for the next words, the next important words. But none came. He said the broken sentence over to himself. Just take what you learned, and later you must . . . What gentle command was beyond that connecting word? He tried to frame it for himself. But it waited. With an upsurge of prescience he knew that it would wait stubbornly until the years themselves brought the clause and fitted it to the link.

Then deep within him, he heard her voice, and it was reading a verse which sounded like a Bible verse: Wait for it, for it will surely come. It will not tarry.

He searched and his memory could recall no such verse. But he was so sure that her voice within him was saying it that he turned to the low table beside her chair and picked up her Bible. The leather felt almost warm to his hand. He opened it at random, but he was afraid to look down on the page. If the words had been there, it would have been insupportable to him. To have manifested such facile coincidence would have been beneath the dignity of the three of them, his mother, himself, and the Bible. He tucked the Bible under his arm then, and kneeling before the lowest shelf where her books stood, he reached for her Concordance to see if there were actually such a verse. Yes, it was here, the third verse of the second chapter of Habakkuk:

> For the vision is yet for an appointed time, but at the end it shall speak and not lie; though it tarry, wait for it; because it will surely come; it will not tarry.

He sat in her chair, not grieving now, but going back through their lovely days together, as if they were written forever in him, like a psalm. After awhile he heard the gravel spitting on the drive, then the heavy opening of big car doors. In a few moments there were subdued voices downstairs, and he knew that the funeral party had returned. His first feeling was that he must somehow escape, for he could not join in any heavy crape conventionality of grief.

Then, flooding over that reluctance, came his great love for Papa. This strange communion he had just known with his thoughts about Lucile gave him a large benevolence, tender towards Papa and even towards himself. He remembered how he had wanted to "protect" Papa, in a boyish and smug way. He saw now that his need for "protecting" Papa was dwarfed and ridiculous, for Papa had been grappling with sorrow so big it must have blotted out the whole world for him, and brought maturity beyond any measuring which his brash young son could do.

He went downstairs as fast as he could. From the voices he

knew the group had gone into the small back parlor, full of green leather and plush and brass lamps. All through the years in this house, the room had always been filled to bursting with Papa's laughter and jokes, and the appreciation of his friends. The room had been the funnybone of the house, Lucile used to say. . . .

The friends were here today, sitting uncomfortably on the edges of the chairs, their plump legs bulging out of their tight black trousers, their derbies held respectfully, and their eyes, in hammocks of wrinkles, maudlin with sympathy.

Papa looked small and shrunken. He was huddled in his own chair, and the late afternoon gloom falling on his cockscomb of blond hair showed that it was no longer blond, but white. And no longer an arrogant cockscomb, but limp. The other men were still, but Papa was gallantly talking. He was no doubt continuing a monologue bravely begun in the shrouded car coming back from the cemetery, telling about the early days when he had first come to St. Louis. He was mentioning Lucile, just to show that he could do it. Handkerchiefs came out again at the mention of her name, but Papa held up his old round head and talked on.

Jubey went into the room, and Papa looked up into his face, and for a moment forgot what he was saying. Jubey walked over to his father's chair and put a hand on his shoulder. Papa reached up his warm soft fingers and patted it. The men spoke to Jubey in mumbles, and the boy recognized each with a word. The staunch mourners got up almost as a man, and said they must let Henry rest. As they were leaving, they collided with a tall plump young woman in black carrying a large tray.

When she recognized Jubey, Minna gave a little cry and fresh tears spurted from her eyes. Holding the big tray she was helpless to brush them away, so they ran down her face distressingly, until Jubey went over and tenderly touched them with his handkerchief.

Then she picked up her new duty as the hostess of the hous·.

"We've some nice drinks and some sandwiches. We can't let you go without . . ."

"No, Minna," Papa said authoritatively. "Nobody wants any food today."

"But Mama would be so ashamed," Minna said piteously. Papa considered that a moment and then agreed meekly, "That's right. I ask you to excuse me for not thinking."

"We'll go back to the dining room, Henry," one of his friends said kindly. "We'll have the nice sandwiches, and you and your boy just rest here and talk."

"Ja, Ja . . . thank you very much," Papa said, and motioned for Jubey to close the door. He went back to his father's chair and bent over and kissed his cheek. Papa reached up and patted his face. That double gesture was all that was needed for repri-mand or explanation.

"You didn't look surprised when you saw me, Papa."

"No. I expected you."

"You expected me?"

"Mama said." He bent forward to see Jubey's face better. "We didn't hear from you for such a long time."

"I didn't know what to write, Papa." He never could ex-plain that dilemma. Papa nodded slowly, as if he did under-stand.

"So Mama said you would come at the right time. That was almost the last thing she told me."

"How did she know?" Jubey brought out the question in a suffering whisper. Papa waited a few minutes as if he must make sure the words would not be lightly heard.

"Mama was often talking to her friend God," he said simply. "She told me she asked him to send you back, and she knew you would come just when I . . . needed my son," he explained with a gentleness which was new and foreign to the vigorous independent monarch who had thought he himself ruled his own universe.

"Yes, Papa," Jubey said, accepting all of it just as it was.

6

THE NEXT DAYS were difficult for everyone, except Minna. Under their very eyes Minna changed. She had been a somewhat listless plump girl, occupied with senseless predilections involving embroidery silks and handwritten notes whose addresses began with a flourishing "Miss," and long serious telephone conversations, and the creaming of already perfect skin, and the exploring of the perfection with a magnifying mirror. Now she was a stern and tyrannical young woman who glistened with importance. No doubt she patterned herself after Lucile, but there was little resemblance.

Papa, who not-too-secretly had shared Jubey's temptation to ignore Minna, now gave up entirely and let her push him around the domestic routine as if she were someone hired for the purpose. When he did remember her, it was always with guilt that spoke itself in a five-pound box of Lowney's chocolates, or two dozen long-stemmed American Beauty roses. She absorbed these attentions graciously, but was not deceived about them. "Poor Papa's *sweet,*" she always said with a matronly little sigh.

With this new authority, Minna was actually less attractive than before. But strangely enough, her mimicking domesticity was believable to two suitors who seemed to spring up from nowhere. For a while her life was a sober contest between the thirty-year-old bachelor son of one of Henry's associates and a pallid young widower with an infant in his foreground.

"Minna will get married yet," Papa said whenever she became too much of a nuisance, and his tone was always a complacent hope lifted into a command to some nubile destiny to manifest itself soon, and get the matter over with.

The house was shrouded with mourning that seemed to get into one's lungs like actual dust. Minna never spoke of her mother as anything but "poor Mama," until Jubey could bear it no longer and said to her, "Please stop calling her that. She was farther from being 'poor Mama' than any woman on earth."

This, naturally, melted Minna to hot tears of self-pity, so that Jubey had to pat her shoulder and apologize.

"Mama meant happinesss," he said to her, "and you're doing everything possible to miss her meaning, and try to make us all forget it."

"How can you say such cruel things? You didn't understand poor Mama. You stayed away, doing all kinds of shameful things, I'm sure. Just when you should have been home, sympathizing!" she said angrily. "Now you just want us to forget our sadness. And you want Papa to forget."

"I only want him to forget the sadness so that Mama's joyousness can come back to him," Jubey said painfully.

He thought sometimes that it would be better if Papa could get away from the house for a few months. Perhaps take a suite in one of the downtown hotels. But Papa stayed on in the big gloomy house, and when he spoke, it was often in a dead whisper. Sometimes in the middle of the night Jubey heard his heavy step going down the hall, and he knew that Henry had gone into Lucile's sitting room and was communing there with his quiet laughing little love.

There was much to worry Henry Our these days, for something terrible was threatening America. It had hung like a cloud over his country for many years, but Papa had never imagined the cloud could burst into a deluge that would drown and ruin so much that he believed in and loved. There had always been the hum and whine of what Papa thought of as mere gnats and mosquitoes . . . the Anti-Saloon League, the W.C.T.U., and other groups which he couldn't possibly understand. He used often to talk about them with Lucile. How could people make such a noise about something which was all friendliness and good will? "They got no jolliness in their bones," Papa used to say with benign gentleness. "Maybe they didn't ever have enough good fun, such people."

But Lucile would not gloss over such a viewpoint. "No, that's not it, Henry. They fight against the tragedies which liquor causes."

"Then they better call themselves the Anti-People League. It's people that cause the harm, and we shouldn't blame the liquor."

But Papa was by no means blind to the tragedies. In his own way he analyzed them quite sincerely. Sorrows and loneliness and unsureness and unwantedness were the wrongs, which drove men into the forgetfulness which liquor offered. In some good future, the causes of men's unhappiness must be dealt with. Meantime, it was only breaking off branches to berate the liquor, Papa felt. In a world of happy people, there would be no need for dark and ugly drinking.

As early as 1915 Papa had quixotically tried to reform the saloons. He spent hundreds of thousands in wasted attempts to make the dingy saloons more like the old German beer gardens he knew and loved, places of sunshine and moderation and good will.

There were cartoons about these attempts in the magazines and newspapers which championed the fight for prohibition. They pictured Henry Our as a stupid fat bartender, offering lollipops and beer to children, urging young mothers and their infants to make themselves at home in the reeking atmosphere of the corner saloons. These cartoons completely mystified Papa, and he tried all the harder to show what he meant. He had built a reproduction of the Bierstube, set in a courtyard where drinkers might play games on tables with their steins beside them. He had engaged a good noisy German band, and for a few weeks there was music and joy to be had with the Our Brew. But then even the Germans in the community began shunning the place, for patriotism was cutting the heart out of all German innocence and making it seem somehow bad. So the place had to be closed. . . . But only temporarily, Papa always said to himself. Only until all this trouble about war blows past.

The United States Brewer's Association realized at last what Henry Our had been preaching for two years. Then they voted a huge appropriation to advertise their campaign "to promote temperance . . . a genuine temperance which means sobriety and moderation; not prohibition which will prove a fallacy and a failure."

All kinds of false issues attached themselves to the onrush of grim determination. Hot oratory spurted freely, and liquor became somehow confused with German treachery and with shortage of food and with other extraneous matters. Papa read the newspapers as well as the bulky reports issued by his own Association, and shook his head. He knew that America was the home of sound thinking and good feeling, and now all this jerking of truth back and forth from one camp to another confounded him. Right, it now appeared to Papa, was on the side of those who had the most money to buy the biggest billboards and newspaper pages. The friends of prohibition were spending thirty-five millions in their crusade. The outraged brewers and distillers were throwing their private fortunes together and hacking recklessly at everything in sight. They blacklisted companies who dared be unfriendly to the brewing interests, so that no one who earned his living through beer dared eat a Heinz pickle, or send a Christmas package by means of Delaware, Lackawanna and Western railway freight. It was a tangle of ineffectual malice, and it made Papa's head ache to think about it.

But by September of 1918, the deadly fight had become more than just a nuisance. For an emergency Food Control Law suddenly closed all breweries, in order to save food and labor. A drought had damaged crops, and there were some who shouted that was God's way of slamming shut the doors of those brewers who were consuming millions of tons of innocent grains which were needed to nourish starving children.

Then the war was over, but the talk was not. What had been called a war emergency measure lingered in effect. Figures blazed out the news that eleven million loaves of bread a day could be baked if the grain was denied to the liquor manufacturers. Humanitarians pointed out that this hypothetical flow of food would be enough to supply the entire bread relief program of Belgium.

So now for nearly nine months Papa's beloved plant had been silent and deserted. Except for Papa's own office, in the heart of the building. From there he tirelessly waged his war against Congress, against the legislatures of those states which were attempting to ratify the amendment, and against that strange faceless horde of reformers which he pictured as tall half-human scarecrows determined to sweep the working man's pleasures out beyond his reach. Papa never doubted that he would win the fight. He felt quite certain Right was on his side, and Papa had a sentimental faith in right.

7

THE INCIDENT of Papa's statue on Vendeventer Place shocked the whole city. Papa himself was not spared one detail of its ugliness.

On a fine August morning he and Jubey were being driven down to the office in the silent brewery. A moment before, Jubey had thought, The good old man is more cheerful than he's been since I came home. Mama would be happy.

They neared the triangular plot of grass where the now old-fashioned monument of a slimmer and more elegant Henry Our stood with one hand grasping the back of a handsome chair and the other benevolently extended over the heads of his beloved fellow citizens in perpetual blessing.

Suddenly they were aware of a commotion in the street around the statue. A crowd had collected, which two policemen mounted on tall sleek horses were trying to dispel. Jubey thought at first that it must be some street accident; then he saw the pavement was littered with handbills.

"Some agitator yet," Papa said, suspecting no connection with that handsome stone image of himself.

Then, inescapably, Jubey's eyes lifted to the statue, and his blood pounded with quick anger. Red paint by the gallon had been thrown across the head and face, running down across the plump and noble figure, to drip and smear in rivulets across the bronze tablet on the front of the pedestal.

A postscript had been added to the tribute on the bronze which said

Henry Our
    Our Neighbor
    Our Citizen
    Our Friend.

The new words painted a foot high in hideous crude red across the stone pedestal said "Our Disgrace."

Jubey thought in a panic, I must get Papa out of this before he sees it. But already Papa had stepped out of the car to enquire what the excitement was about. He never asked the question. His eyes took in the defaced statue at a glance. His knees sagged under him and he would have sunk to the ground, except that two men caught him.

"I don't feel so good," Papa said.

"Don't you worry, Mr. Our . . . the police are going to find out who did that. We'll see that they're punished right and proper."

The crowd converged around Papa then, and some people shook his hand and tried to sympathize. But there were others, whom Jubey recognized, who spoke behind their hands to other bystanders, while their eyes, cold and gratified, roamed over the scene with malicious delight. Papa got back into the car feebly, and they drove on without speaking.

At last he said, "I don't go to work this morning, Jubal. I think maybe I better go back home and rest."

"That's a good idea," Jubal said, and the chauffeur, without being spoken to, turned the car homeward.

Not until he was safely inside his own house did Papa break down. He had sat erect and silent as they drove back through the streets, but once inside his own door, he began trembling uncontrollably.

Anna, by now, had seen the shameful news across the front page of the morning paper, and she came running towards them, crying and cursing.

"Oh, Mr. Our, God will punish such people. But the police must punish them first. That's public property already."

Papa kept shaking his head in mute denial of what he had seen.

Anna said again, taking off his straw hat as if he were too ill to lift his arms, "They ain't got no right damaging public property."

Papa tried to smile. He reached up and touched his chest where he supposed his heart was, and he said in German, "No, Anna. What they damage most is private property . . ."

Jubey said, "Rats with it, Papa! They haven't touched you."

Papa looked at him like a child.

"That's right," Jubey said, improvising as he went along. "Didn't Mama ever tell you the story of Constantine when a mob broke the head of his statue with stones?"

"So tell me."

"He felt his own skull. 'That's funny,' he said. 'They haven't touched me. No bones are broken.' " But Papa refused the meaning of the story. Or perhaps he heard only one word in what Jubey had said.

"This is the first time I can be glad Mama is not here," he said. "She could not bear such a thing, my Lucile."

Jubey went on trying to point out to him that public approval and public treachery are equally unimportant. "When you're in public life, you've got to understand that."

"I don't understand it. I loved the public, and they used to like me back," Papa said simply. "I'm no different now. I'm just like I always was. But now they don't like me. How can I think that is nothing important?"

The telephone rang all morning, and all the loyal friends offered consolation and indignation. The police commissioner came personally and sat with Henry awhile in the library, drinking some of the Our's fine spirits and trying to persuade his old friend that the disgrace was not to him, but to the paint slingers.

"We've good reason to believe they're not St. Louis people," he said staunchly. "Some prohibition people from Chicago. That's what we think."

No one told Henry that before daylight the police had taken down a big placard which had been stuck up in the grass denouncing him in explicit terms and suggesting he be sent back to Germany.

During the next days the matter of covering the shameful, obscene mutilation of the statue became a public issue. Editorials said it was indecent to leave it exposed to public sight. The police department, when interviewed by the press, declared they had no provision for erecting any kind of concealment. News services in other cities picked up the story, and humorists wrote delightedly about the dilemma. Cartoonists suggested means of preserving the modesties . . . a kimono or fig leaves. . . . But finally, unknown to Papa, Jubey himself wrote a check to provide a canvas barricade behind which painters might work at removing the desecration.

It was several weeks before the monument was presentable. But never as long as he lived did Papa ever have his car driven down past Vendeventer Place again. It was never spoken about in his presence. When the tribute had been erected ten years before, the sculptor had made Papa look ten years younger than he actually was, "and much prettier," as Papa himself said. But now the statue, which he had seen in that one shocked glimpse with blood-colored paint across it, had made Papa look ten years older than he had ever looked before.

When the whole story was finished, and Jubey could bear to look back over it, he knew that the morning when Papa saw the monument was the moment when he began to die.

The end began to pile up quickly. The tragedy was that none

of them recognized in time what all these external happenings were doing to the gentle, good-natured, pervertedly idealistic boy who lived inside the aging frame of Papa. That boy, so long frisky and optimistic to the point of absurdity, was dying by inches. The sunshine which was compounded of approval from others and benevolence from himself seemed entirely cut off from him, and he could not live without its invigorating rays.

Papa had so identified himself with what he thought of as his great gift to his America that he could not survive the hurt of having that "gift" rejected and defamed. If America no longer wanted that, it no longer wanted him. Somehow everything had been reversed. He had been living in prosperity and generosity; now his very success had become an affront, and a public offense. He was guilty of the very qualities for which he had been praised and loved. Ruthless judgment had fallen on him from all sides. He was banished now from everything he knew as good and innocent, so he must find a way of taking himself out of sight.

There was no one around who understood what had happened to Papa. His associates and competitors, angrily banded together by the common threat of prohibition, did not suffer as he did because they felt no rebuke in the events. They had a shell of worldiness to protect them, a kind of insulating cynicism. They were disgusted at the sight of their great silent breweries locked and sealed with Government bonded seals. They lamented the turning off of the vast spigots from which had spouted their personal prosperity. But none of Henry's friends seemed aware of any personal and inner disgrace, which was the dire malignancy from which Henry Our was suffering . . . and more than suffering. He was indeed dying from within, of that old-fashioned inoperable malady which used to be called "a broken heart."

It was no less cruel and real because it could appear as either

comic or extravagantly deserved, depending upon what judgment was brought to look back on it after the ailment became
fatal.

Jubal had no desire to go back to the university. But Papa
insisted, when fall came. Papa said conclusively, "I promised
Lucile. She would not understand."

Jubey said, "I'm too old for that kind of education." But
Papa was not fooled by that halfhearted reason. Lucile had expected her son to distinguish himself somehow, and education
must be the first step. Papa did not know how to explain that
Jubal must have all the foundation which education could
give, so that his life, unlike Papa's, would never topple and
shiver upon uncertain foundation.

"We've a big fight on our hands," Jubey said. "I could help
you here."

But Papa shook his head vehemently, and didn't need to add
that he was past all helping, for the statement was inscribed on
his shrunken face and in his halting walk.

In the end Jubey gave in for a negative reason. Minna decided to marry Earnest Schumacher, the fastidious bachelor
who had been competing with the widower. The widower Jubey
felt he could have ignored with an easily managed courtesy. But
Earnest was a talkative, conspicuous bore who endowed with
tiresome common sense any space he occupied. Earnest had
made an accomplishment of being uninteresting. The rightness
of his presence was consummate nuisance, for he had a deep
rich voice which pleased him expansively as he heard it utter-
ing banalities with stressed conviction. His very handsomeness
made the picture only more boring, for one could find no way
of softening impatience by pity for some physical deficiency.

Minna's admiration was pathetic. Her love was a smudgy
sheet of carbon paper which recorded on her personality everything Earnest thought and said, multiplying the obvious by two.
Earnest, of course, came to live in the Our mansion, so that he

could reinforce Minna's gentle tyrannies by his own unanswerable common sense.

After the Schumachers took over the house, the discussions about whether or not Jubey would finish his university work ceased. There was no actual moment when he gave in to Papa's insistence; he simply found himself getting ready to leave, and counting the days.

8

IT WAS a strange autumn for Jubey. He was twenty-two years old, but by now he looked as if he were nearly thirty. His large-featured face was lined about the eyes by laughter and about the mouth by pity which he knew no way of speaking. His body still seemed to be too big for his clothes after the first or second wearing. His hands, decently manicured, still looked like the hands of a laborer, and always would, for his sympathy spoke through those.

The first few weeks on the campus he found himself utterly alone. Then he realized that this shunning meant an uncomfortable respect from his classmates, all younger than himself and much less experienced. After he recognized this state, which at first was a relief from the congested emotions he had found at home, he knew that sooner or later he must remedy it. It was characteristic of him that he knew he could pick his own date for terminating his isolation. He would give himself ten more days, then he would be finished with solitude.

He turned up at Glee Club practice, and though tryouts had been settled two weeks before, he stepped into the baritone section without explanation. After the first stanza, the conductor, a nearsighted little man, demanded to hear the baritones alone, tipping his head critically as he listened.

"What has happened here?"

There was a moment of nudging and turning, so that even the nearsighted leader could see from where the unusual voice had come. At last Jubey, squirming with embarrassment said,

142

"I beg your pardon, Mr. Wolff. I found this voice running around my bathroom this morning. I thought I'd better turn it over to the authorities."

A guffaw went up from the group. Mr. Wolff considered the situation a moment. If the voice had been less interesting, he would have reprimanded the intruder and sent him out, for his cheerful impudence. The weighing was visible in the Wolff face. Then musicianship won and he said kindly, "My boy, let me hear you sing bars nine to twenty-one." Jubey sang the passage, with an exaggerated meekness on his face, as if apologizing for the interruption which was embarrassing him, and delighting the other students.

"You are a singer," Mr. Wolff said almost accusingly. "We must do something about that. You've studied, of course? Where?"

Jubey said, sounding like a Kansas farmer, "Aw, fer pity's sake, Mr. Wolff . . . I just wanted to get into the noise with you fellows."

"I am not at all sure you will fit into the noise," the leader said sulkily. "The voice is too big for the little noise. We'll probably have to make it solo. Stay after the practice and we shall talk."

Overnight Jubey began popping up all over the campus. Within hours he became a fad. His bright red socks were copied by two kinds of students, those who seriously admired him and his humor and those who regarded his sudden popularity with tongue in cheek. He was quoted vociferously; a particular twist of humor became known as a Jubeyism; and the favorite eating spot on the rim of the campus advertised a Jubey-wich, an egregious sandwich which he often ate, which was made of pumpernickel, sauerkraut, and ham with white radishes sliced over the ham. With this, if you too had a stomach like an electrical food chopper, you drank coffee, and felt hungry again in two hours.

Most of the clubs on the campus gave him a rush. But, for a reaon which he couldn't explain to them, he joined none. The reason was a strangely lugubrious integrity which would have shocked him if he had dissected it for himself. He knew that this Jubey which he had constructed so successfully for private and public amusement was a synthetic creature, a fictitious character he had "written" just as deliberately as he would have written improved parts for the naïve vaudevillians in the Portland theater, if they had allowed him the privilege. The clubs were bidding him in all sincerity, believing what they saw and heard. So he could not foist off on them as genuine this spurious creation, however much they enjoyed him. A fine line of honor was involved, and he could not violate it.

There was one club, however, which pursued him in spite of his jovial refusals to join. It was called the Jaundice Club. On the surface it appeared to be merely a group of hardheaded sceptics; actually most of the men were undeclared atheists. When they talked about themselves to prospective members, they said they were against the rape of honesty, wherever it occurred.

"Especially in skulls," they said. "Particularly our own."

The brothers would gather in Jubey's room, late at night, and talk their adolescent brand of philosophy while they smoked and drank near-beer. Strangely enough, Jubey did little of the talking. When they prodded him, he pulled on his pipe and made some farcical contribution.

He would draw down his mouth in pontifical mugging, and after a few moments of weighty silence he would say, "Well, that requires explicit penetration. It's not a question of verisimilitude entirely, although . . . wasn't it Sir Paltry Thundercrumb who said that all indecision is ablative? That accounts, presumably, for the integral misanthropy which the Hanoverian philosopher . . . what was his name . . . ?"

He would snap his fingers and look around the circle in a dis-

mayed attempt to get the name off the tip of his tongue, while
the others would crinkle their foreheads gravely as if they were
joining in the futile attempt.

"Oh yes . . . Wrastleworst, of course . . . now what *was* the
point I was making?" The others would glance at each other in
chagrin, hoping that somebody could paraphrase the elusive
point. Then, one by one, they would catch Jubey's sly grin
spreading over his lined, mobile face, and realize that he was
pompously ridiculing them. After that, they'd usually break
up and go to bed in lively spirits, anything but jaundiced.

"The trouble with you, Jubey, is that you don't need a club.
You *are* a club," one of them said one night as they were leaving. "We think we're trying to get you to join *us* . . . fact is,
we're trying to join *you*."

While he listened to their intellectual trapeze work, he often
kept one hand in his pocket. He made no comment to himself
about this gesture, but somehow it gave him a wry comfort to
be grasping that little silver cross with the carved leaves and the
singing bird which Kurt Geitzen had given him during their
last moments together. *There* was a man who had no fear of
being soft because he had faith in God. If religion was a crutch
for weak persons, as these half-baked young atheists were constantly implying, at least there was one strong man in the world
who looked God squarely in the eye.

Sometimes while his friends were vaporing through their
intricate cerebrations, Jubey would think, remembering Geitzen's quaint figure of speech, Which is winning the wrestling
match in me, the devil or the clown? And he would feel a
strange loneliness for certitude, which he could endure only by
improvising more outrageous comedy.

There came a time, at last, when the Jaundice Club insisted
upon an answer to their bid.

"Either you're with us or you're not," they said bluntly.

"I can't be sure which I am," he said in genuine sincerity.

"You certainly aren't going to stand there and admit you believe in God," one of them accused him.

"Well, I may not believe in God," he said slowly. "But I do believe in the people who believe in God."

Christmas came and went and Jubal dutifully went home and smirked his way through a false brotherliness-in-law with Earnest Schumacher. He allowed himself to be bullied by Minna, who bossed him dotingly with one eye on her new husband to make sure he saw how attractive she was in a smotheringly maternal role. Papa was doing his best to celebrate Christmas in the proper way, but it was painful to watch. The annual Boys' Club party, which had always been Papa's delight, was now an ordeal to be faced.

"You take charge, Jubal," Papa said with heartbreaking cheerfulness. "I'm too old yet to romp and frolic with the kids. Besides . . . maybe they don't want me any more."

"Nonsense," Jubey said. "The party wouldn't be any good without you to be Santa Claus."

"I just pay the bills, and somebody else be Santa Claus," Papa begged. "I don't feel like Santa Claus too much."

"You will," Jubey said. "Once you see the youngsters, it will all come back to you."

But somehow it didn't. Papa was a pathetic Santa Claus. His clothes seemed too big for him, and his voice was wavering and uncertain, so that the roomful of boys couldn't be kept quiet through his announcements. The party would have been a dismal attempt if Jubey had not been present to whirl it into liveliness when it was about to perish.

The hours they spent alone were the best, for both of them returned to the happy innocent days. Once when Papa was shouting with laughter at something Jubey had said, he stopped suddenly and cried, "It is just like our trip to Rothenburg! You and me. That was the best time of my life, Jubey."

Then he grew thoughtful as if he had been disloyal to Lucile, so he had to explain, "A man is many men inside himself. He is one man with his little boy, and another with his friends, and then he is someone who dies forever when his wife dies."

Papa still could not accept defeat in the fight against prohibition. "You wait and see. Something will happen," he said. "The people will rise up and demand their rights. The people were asleep when those Anti-Saloon folks pushed through their plot. But they will wake up. You watch and see."

"But Papa . . . " Jubey would try to explain. But Papa only shook his head and repeated his assurances.

"I know my America," he said fiercely. "When you love something the way I love this country, then you know."

At the end of the vacation Jubey got on the train for the East with a dismal sense of foreboding. Up to the last minute, he was protesting about going back, but Papa was still firm about what he had promised Lucile.

The morning of January 16 dawned bleakly, for it was the first day of what some were hailing as Dry America. All during the day of the fifteenth and up until one minute before midnight, there had been wakes and convivial parades and funerals mourning the death of John Barleycorn. The campus reeked with the festivity, for no one seemed to believe that it was anything but a national prank. Jubey had kept to himself all day; suddenly he felt he must go home and help his father through the first difficult hours.

Just as he was, in his velvet smoking jacket and his famous red socks, he shrugged into his overcoat and went down to the railway station without telling anyone he was leaving.

He got a local over to the main line, and finally managed to connect with a through train for St. Louis. He had expected to pick up a berth somewhere in the long line of sleeping cars. But everything was occupied. So he gave the porter a big tip, and made himself comfortable on the scratchy green plush sofa in the washroom. It was one of the rare nights in his life when he couldn't sleep. Not because of physical discomfort, but because of the uneasy knowledge that Papa was passing this night in the depths of personal defeat. He kept wishing he had made this trip the day before. . . .

About three o'clock the porter looked in to see how his private passenger was resting.

"Sorry you ain't sleeping, suh," the kindly Negro said. "Maybe you might res' better if you had a little nip of whisky I happen to have handy."

Jubey didn't especially want the drink, but it gave him something to think about that the new law was so easily and unabashedly broken.

"Believe I will," he said. Neither he nor the porter mentioned the fact that the familiar gesture had now become a federal offense.

At six the train stopped at a railway station and took on some supplies for the dining car. The porter put in his head again and said, "How'd you lak a nice mornin' paper, suh?"

Jubey tossed him a quarter and accepted the paper. It was still dark outside the twin windows in the dreary, hot little compartment. He spread out the paper and stifled a sleepy yawn at the same time. Then the headline struck him like a crude, unannounced blow: HENRY OUR SUICIDE, and under that the idiotic words, "Brewer ends life in rage of protest."

That was how Jubey found out.

9

ON THE THIRD DAY after the funeral he found Papa again. Exactly where he should have looked first for him, in Lucile's room. There was a sealed envelope with his name written on it, just under the cover of Lucile's Bible. If Jubey had not touched bottom in suffering, so that he picked up that book for the mere comfort of holding it in his hands, he might have missed the hour which shaped the rest of his life.

For through the lens of that simple letter Jubey found his own uncertain gropings focused. The letter was only a few lines, written in Papa's elaborate schoolboy's hand. It said:

"Please don't think hard of me, Jubey. I am too ashamed. Everything turned against me. I tried to be a good man, but only out of the good in myself. That is not enough. Lucile knew. She taught you. But I would not listen. You think about her life, and not your papa's. You make your life good, out of God, however that is done."

At first as he read the words, a hot rash of shame seemed to envelope his body. That Papa, so proud and independent, should have sunk at the end into such apology! He would never show the letter to anyone, for it was his father's ultimate ignominy.

Then the most angry rebellion rose up in him. How could anyone worship a deity who permitted a good, simple man to torture himself with vague recriminations? This one flaming indignation surmounted all the tempestuous protests which Jubey had piled up unadmittedly against God. A helpless tirade

uncoiled in his brain. In his mind was a blazing minute image
of himself standing in an empty place shaking his fists at heaven
and shouting imprecations. He let them go on for a long time;
he gloried in the cosmic audacity of himself, silently screaming
his accusations.

At last they seemed to stop, and the arena in the center of his
mind emptied itself of the dark fermenting crowds, and he
thought the tirade was over. A drench of astonishment came
over him now, for he recognized the memory of his conversation
with Kurt Geitzen. The devil . . . and whatever else was in him
. . . wrestling for supremacy. The clown had lain prostrate
while the devil leaped up and shouted what he had to say.

Then, in spite of himself, he read the words of Papa's letter
again, and now a long unclenching of his own pride and stub-
bornness and sufficiency released itself throughout his whole
body and mind, and he wept. A new stream of irresistible
thoughts began flowing through his mind, and the beaten-down
ego huddled quietly and listened. It came to him almost as
poetry.

Who are you, little one, that you argue against me? A man
has made a chaos of his life because he would not know me. He
has told you that. His life has told you, and you choose to turn
the meaning wrong-side out. He could not live without me;
and you cannot.

Jubey cried out in abysmal silence in the midst of himself:
Who is this speaking? I dare you to say! But there was no answer, except this: You know who. Never mind asking, for you
know.

Then a strange thing happened to him. He shouted his silent
accusations again, but now in his own cause. Look at *me*, Jubey
Our. Never mind *him*. Look at *me*, now. I'm a humorous man.
You'd say that was true, wouldn't you? Well, let me tell you
something. I'm humorous because inside myself I am so sad
and sick that if I didn't shout my way through everything, I'd

lie down and weep. I've too much pride to weep. I wouldn't give you the satisfaction of seeing me. So I laugh. I twist my little brain so that everyone around me may laugh too. "That jolly old Jubey" . . . that's how jolly he is. Did you know that?

And the voice came back to him, Yes, I knew that. But why do you bother making them laugh, little one?

I just do, he said sullenly. It's just something to do.

No, that's not the reason. Could it be that you love the strangers around you?

No. I love myself, Jubey said. I have my pride. You can see my pride, surely.

Yes, I see it. It is a grain of sand. But your love of the stranger with the bent back, and the bent heart is greater than the grain of sand.

You're leading me off my complaint, Jubey said furiously. That's an old trick of yours! You're not above flattery even, if flattery will lead me off my complaint.

What was your complaint, little one? I forget.

You're darned right you forget! But I don't. My complaint is that I've never been happy . . . and at home . . .inside myself.

Never at all?

Then the memory of a glowing hour came into his mind, and he quickly hid it away. Because its meaning . . . if it had any meaning at all . . . was an intrusion in his case. Those hours, those few inexplicable hours so filled with excitement and joy, were not to be talked about here. They were the exception in his life; they were the exception, to resuscitate a cliché, which proved the rule.

But he did not hide those hours quickly enough, for he heard the voice laughing. Not with malice, but with infinite fondness.

Yes, of course. *I* knew that wonderful night. That was the best of your whole life, wasn't it?

Jubey could not frame a scornful word to deny that, so he only bent his head in acknowledgment.

Do you know why that was? Because the love in you swept everything else aside that night, and spoke out of you any way it chose. You could hardly believe what you heard yourself saying to that poor crowd in the street. That's true, isn't it?

Again he bent his head, but whether that actually was a physical motion or only inner gesture, he could not say. But he did not need to say, for the conversation was going on too importunately to be stopped by quibbling.

That was *you*, little one. And me with you. That was you, for once in balance in the universe. Of course you were happy then. And you can be satisfied in no other way. You may fight and argue and postpone, if you wish. . . .

He ran to Lucile's little window, and threw it open, for suddenly he felt that something was strangling him. The poor letter of Papa's was still in his hand, as humble as a simple seed. A seed beside wagons heaped with harvest. His whole body was drenched and trembling, as if a great fever had broken. As if something painful to bring to birth was present now, and ready for growing.

PART III

No man gives to him

1

GAY SAVANNE happened to him near the close of the twenties.

She was a dancing gleam at the end of a long tunnel through which he traveled ... stumbling and running, and trying to retrace, but finally finishing with a bound. Since it was not a road, but a tunnel he was traveling, it offered retreats but not detours. Actually it was a journey within himself, from which there was no escaping.

A great deal was happening around him, a ferment of circumstances which overturned all that was familiar and kept everything in a boiling turmoil, where items from past and present seemed to pass each other or whirl side by side for a time, in the way the fragments from the torpedoed ship had consorted dementedly before they sank under the waves. At last in the seething test tube of his personal upheaval, the foam's bubbles burst and subsided, and the sediment shaped into new crystals.

The Our fortune, for one item, ended by being only a handful of suds. When the gigantic accounts were balanced, even the house, from which the life and spirit had already evaporated, had to be put up for sale. It was marked down and down in price until finally it came within the grasp of one of the very charitable organizations which Papa had loved. Their Board of Directors said rather grudgingly that even at the reduced price the house was not a very good buy, because remodeling was most expensive. The lush flamboyancy had to be stripped off, and the large rooms had to be divided into cubicles to which delinquent boys could be thriftily assigned.

The furniture was auctioned off quite early in the debacle; much of it was bought by friends who wanted "something to remember the Ours by." Jubey himself kept Mama's little rosewood table on which her Bible always stood. It was characteristic of the befuddlement of the moment that he kept the table for the sake of the Bible, but then forgot to reach for the Bible itself. So it went with the rest of the "second-hand books" to a dirty-faced little dealer, who propped up a rickety pigeon-hole in his roll-top desk by shoving the Book under it.

Minna and Earnest Schumacher, confronted by this seismic collapse in their affairs, were prostrated. Their ubiquitous common sense could find nothing solid enough to grasp in these mistlike shiftings and dissolvings. Minna and Earnest were shaken to the foundation fact of their natures, which fact was that there is safety and surety in what the eye can see and the hand can count. These events seemed a cruel revoking of law to them, and they never quite recovered, but carried to their graves the superstition that even solid facts can sometimes turn against one, if some unknowable, cabalistic precautions are not observed.

But the collapse and its reasons were perfectly clear to Jubey. The totality and completeness of it was the visible forthrightness of Papa's conviction. He had put his everything into what he believed, and so his very all, including his own plump joyous body, was disseminated back to oblivion, to start again in new forms. Papa had had no mental reservations, and so he had provided no canny loophole of escape for himself, his children or his possessions.

When everything was settled and sold, and the debts and obligations were paid or written off as uncollectable, there was little left except a few expensive gifts from Papa to his children. Minna wept over her salvage, and moved it into a staid, steam-heated house which Earnest found and rented because of its shiny hardwood floors and the solid stone walls of its foundation. Jubey took his possessions and liquidated them, all except one valuable square emerald ring which he had never worn except whenever Papa asked, "Maybe you don't like it yet? I get something else for you?"

Actually Jubey had no need of his possessions, for their essence had already entered into the substance of his bones and sinews in the metamorphosis from inanimate to living. The dead possessions lived in him and he was the sum of them all, and also of those other possessions, such as Rose Kramer, and the children in the Georgia cannery, and the stars above the narrow deck of the submarine, and the eternity-sized hours in the ocean with Milton and the plank. He kept the square emerald ring, actually, because it had *not* entered into him in any palpable meaning; he held it, so to speak, until it could be read and absorbed.

When the liquidating and counting was over, he found he had not quite enough money on hand to finish his university work. And now, because of the determination that had come to him about what he intended doing with his life, he knew he must have a degree, and must go on from that point. There would have to be some kind of scholarships won, and there would be the choice between being a studious solemn grind, as he felt he was within himself, or a personality so winsome and persuasive that opportunity came and ate out of his hand. He was certain he could get what he needed by the latter course; he wished with all his heart he could afford the risk of the former. He felt it would have been a splendid and mature step to have been able to trust work and merit; but at this point his faith was still in the power of laughter and charm. The clown was still champion, whoever it was with whom he wrestled.

So he finished at the university with a minimum of work and a crescendo of popularity and fun. Sometimes in the night, or when he was working alone in the tall-windowed library, an ancient weariness would sweep over him and he would think,

I'd like to be a dull dog for a year. I'd like everybody to let the dull dog alone.

Into his mind would come a picture of that chap, himself with a sagged expression, luxuriating in glumness. He wondered often why he imposed the odd necessity of humor on himself. Why couldn't he just allow the dark solemnity within him to seep through to the rim of himself which touched the world? What difference did it make if there was one more serious oaf going about among his fellows, declaring by his presence that all was accidental and inane and without plan? Why must he thrust himself across the line of the ledger into the column that promised delight and safety whether or not it ever could deliver them?

The voice within had accused him of making this effort because he loved. What was it he loved so much that he had to make his living an iteration of promise? Was it God? No. He scarcely knew that Gentleman, as Kurt Geitzen called him. Then it must be man himself, brave, ridiculous, audacious, tragic man, always reaching for the light as if it were something to clutch in his own hands, and then doing little with what he had grasped.

Sometimes when he came to this point in his thinking, a fragmentary quotation sprang up uninvited, "For God so loved the world ... "

One day it occurred to him that he and that Gentleman had something in common. They both "so loved the world." Would that bond be a basis for understanding between them? He wasn't sure. God, of course, could do what he pleased about the way he so loved the world. For Jubey's part, he saw that he would have to express that strange so-loving of his, or perish. He must find a way, a vocabulary of living which would say his love most clearly.

For a while he thought that way of speaking his life would be through medicine. But he shrank from that. Perhaps he had better go on with his engineering and learn to build decency for the poor, comfort for the in-betweens and beauty for the rich. But gradually he veered away from that course, also, for it seemed to him it lay along the fork of the road which Papa, in the depth of his defeat, had warned him against. Papa had pinned his faith and life to improved material circumstances, he had gloried in them and had tried to share them. But in the end they had mocked him because he had neglected the meaning within. A lonely man is no less tragic whether he has a new improved refrigerator or none at all; on the other hand, a man whole and in balance within himself needs not to be added to or augmented by any mechanism, however excellent.

So finally he rejected engineering, because, he said to himself, it just doesn't go deep enough.

What did, then? Education? Perhaps. Yet this nebulous constructing towards which he was groping, must touch more than the mere mind. What was there more than mind? The answer to that rudimentary question eluded him for months. Or if it came, it was garbed so humbly that it was not recognized, and the door was not opened.

The summer after he was graduated from the university, he took a job in a settlement house in New York City. The smell of fumigation and soup, and of boys' rubber-soled tennis shoes clung about the first few weeks. One night he went to the theater and sniffed with displeasure the people sitting next to him, because they, too, smelled of carbolic acid, beef, and rubber soles. When he realized that it was he and not they who were offending, he sat there chuckling, and put the episode away as a parable to be used some time against self-righteousness.

The summer was almost over before he realized what was his next uncertain step. Without discussing it with anyone, he got on the subway and rode up to West 116th Street and Broadway, and hurried along four blocks with fast-beating heart. Then he walked slowly all around the two blocks of the Union Theological Seminary buildings, trying to make up his mind to go in. The perspiration poured off his body, for he knew this was the day on which his life pivoted.

Across narrow 122d Street stood the Juilliard School of Music. Once he briskly crossed the street and started to enter the doors. But something said, No, Jubey. He argued with it in his mind, humorously. He said to the sounds of practicing filtering from the windows, Rescue me or I perish. Somehow he couldn't go in. He knew that this moment was deciding the style of his life, but he felt helpless about casting a dissenting vote.

He looked up at the massive square bulk of Brown Memorial Tower, and wished he knew how to pray for help. But if he had known how to pray, there would have been no need for praying. For that was his prime dilemma, and his insupportable guilt.

He had devised a private religion which had man in it but not God. It was based on the great love of man for man, and upon the goodness and the deep lakes of idealism which lay below man's surface ready to be tapped like rich oil wells. Jubey would need all the skill that had been assembled through two thousand years of preaching, in order to present this heritage of man to himself. He must find a way of showing men how to go back into their own goodness so that they could stop groping out toward some uncertain hypothesis. He believed their goodness was sufficient for all their needs once they learned how to use that goodness and trust it, instead of tragically attempting to create a god for themselves.

His immediate problem had been to conceal this guilty aim sufficiently so that the erudite, kindly man who interviewed him for admission to the Seminary would not guess. The tall, shabbily dressed boy who had suddenly remembered that he meant to get a haircut might look like good minister material from the outside. But Jubey knew that, from any standards but his own, he was actually a Trojan horse, carrying within these sanctified walls an army of revolution.

And yet, like all armies of revolution, the angry convictions and determinations hidden behind his good appearance, were all dedicated to freeing and saving. Through later years he always remembered how he had kept his mind from phrasing his intentions, as if their presence could be seen in his face. What he kept in his mind as he talked to the Dean about his admission to the Seminary, was the line of Dante which speaks of "the love which moves the sun and all the stars."

He knew there was a denial of his own thesis in this quotation, but somehow he couldn't quibble with it at that moment. Instead he held to it, irrationally, balancing on definitions as on shining trapezes, twisting and turning and seizing the flying bar just in time for survival. He felt in no position to say where that "love which moves the stars" came from; he only knew that it was the one trustworthy moving power on earth, and that he had to put himself within its jurisdiction. In later years he felt that it was the underwriting of this honest intention in the jungle of his contradictions which got him past the admission board.

The seminary years were strange and baffling, and yet somehow exciting. Ambiguities poured in on him, but he learned a technique for riding over them, as one rides a surfboard. When other students made themselves ill battling through some theological jungle, Jubey would sometimes say, "Don't gag on the botany. Just enjoy the flowers."

A great deal of the seminary experience he handled with delight. He freely told his colleagues that he wasn't a "damnationalist" and this automatically exempted him from many of the darker discussions.

"I came into this subject to explore light and not darkness," he sometimes said, when he was backed into a corner.

"You'll make a popular preacher, Jubal," he was told grudgingly by the man who taught Old Testament 105–106. "Congregations would much rather hear about the love of God than about His anger." There was a smile that went with the accusation, but Jubey caught the rebuke. Even so, he dared say what he thought about that.

"It's never seemed sound to me, sir, that God couldn't keep his temper. If he can't, who can?"

"You'll have to watch yourself, Our," the reverent man said in displeasure. "You've a tendency towards familiarity verging on blasphemy."

"I'm trying to become familiar, sir," Jubey said meekly. "I conceive that to be the aim of religion."

His necessary association with the various professors was a series of high-voltage shocks to himself and to the older men. They came to a kind of undeclared peace, for none of the faculty had the courage to eliminate this obviously inspired man, head and shoulders above the rest of his class in that rare combination, originality and teachableness.

He learned to conceal his exuberance like an infectious disease, but he found a hundred ways of enjoying what he was doing. His best device for continuing to think as outrageously as he pleased was to become letter-perfect in doctrine. He memorized a glib avalanche of definitions and distinctions from Boyce's *Theology*, the current textbook, and whenever there was danger of his lawlessness being exposed, he would retreat behind a barrage of brilliant dead scholasticism. He made himself beyond reproach, so that he might live through the revolutionary dilemma which was his obsession.

Of all the men in the seminary, there was probably none carrying on such a battle within himself. Often he felt that the jest against God was too tragic to be enjoyed, and he yearned to abandon it, and forget the whole assignment. But now it was too late to repudiate that subversive program of helping mankind to believe in itself while he appeared to be persuading it to believe in God. He found no choice but to go on.

As breathing space and relief from this conflict, he became a tireless mission worker, through the slums and the waterfronts of the great city. He worked off his restless mental surplus by keeping more than busy with outward errands. Though he was still only a lay reader, he had a license to preach, and did so whenever he could find a circle of listening faces.

Sometimes it saddened him that his preaching should have been so acceptable to the poor wretches who listened. He gave them what he had, which was his authoritative voice. He used to model that as if it were some plastic substance, raising it to peaks of passion and then rocking it in a kind of lulla-bye of tenderness, letting it spurt up in indignation or break into the joyous sound of praise. But all the time he was listen-ing to his voice perform these gymnastics, he would be talk-ing gibberish. He would be tangling reason into nonsense. Yet so eager were the listeners to be comforted and reassured, that they would laugh or weep or nod their heads sagely as they saw what was indicated. Even the tired social workers, or the men who had come down with him from the Seminary to observe, were not immune from the spell of his empty oratory. Afterwards, they would grasp his hand and look at him with naked gratitude in their eyes, and he would think ironically, You can't cheat a praying man. If he comes to hear a sermon, he hears a sermon.

Sometimes he felt as if there *must* be something wonderful being said through his voice, something which everyone but himself could hear. It would be a howling joke on him, wouldn't it, if the Beatitude actually were true, which said, "Blessed are the pure in heart, for they shall see God."

Back in the subway on the way uptown, he would slump in his seat utterly defeated and depressed because he knew how to preach to everyone but himself. He knew how to comfort all of them, but he himself could find no consolation. Except in the great pitying love he felt for the world; that was his solace and his rebuilding each morning when he started the day on its lumbering, heavy way.

If there had come a moment when he despised the listeners,

or scorned them because they could not discriminate, he would have destroyed himself. If he had questioned the goodness of men as he did the goodness of God, he would have been lost completely. But for as long as the love within him stayed alive, he could endure. . . .

During those years, he did much more than merely preach to the poor and the devalued. He worked around the wards of an overcrowded hospital, and spent his afternoons in jails and courtrooms. His world was the teeming universe of poverty, and his habitats were the spots where trouble coagulates in black clots of misery and hopelessness.

When his fellow students asked him why he drove himself so hard in these undemanded ways, he knew exactly the right answer. But when he asked himself, he found no sensible reply. "Except that they're so beastly pathetic . . . and so good. Somebody's got to do something for them. And if God won't. . . ." It was precisely the explanation he had given Kurt Geitzen about Milton's tearful prayer. Somebody *had* to take care of them.

It was through one of these self-assignments that he met Gay Savanne.

One night after some particularly dreary "entertainment" in one of his missions, Jubey got the idea of having a real vaudeville show for his people, not with broken-down amateur talent, but something bright and worth seeing. He would go to the best theaters and agencies and ask for talent.

His co-workers discouraged him. "You'll waste your time," they told him. "What can you offer any dancers and singers to get them down here? They keep away from this end of town, as everybody else does who can manage it."

"*We* don't keep away," Jubey said patiently. "You think we're the only decent guys in the city?"

He went around to the stage doors of several revue theaters and talked with the doormen. They were sympathetic but not too encouraging.

"Well, I'll tell you, padre. Your best bet is an animal act," the old Irishman at the stage door of the Music Box said honestly.

"So animals have kinder hearts than humans?"

The Irishman nodded, pulling down his long upper lip solemnly. "You must have obsairved that long since, sir. Except that you're still young, begging your pardon."

"All right. Is there an animal act in the house?"

"As pretty a one as you'd ever expect to see. Little Irish terriers, God love the race. Keenan's Canines, they're called."

"Could I go in and speak to them?"

"Well, begging your pardon, sir, that's against the rules. But I tell you what could be done. I could speak to them. I could sound them out for you, and thin they could leave word with me that you're to come back and arrange the details."

The details were "arranged" and before the week was out, Jubey had picked up from here and there seven acts that promised to appear for him the following Sunday afternoon.

The director of the mission said cheerfully, "Seven promised? Expect three to show up. The poorest three."

"You'll be surprised," Jubey told him. But, in spite of his reassurance, he himself prepared two "acts" which he could do on short notice, one a bit of clumsy magic depending heavily on the patter that went with it, and the other impersonations of various neighborhood celebrities, the policeman's horse, a schoolteacher, the old-clothes man, and a politician visiting his ward. At the last moment he deleted his best impersonation, which was a drunk assisting another drunk, remembering just in time that if word got back to the Seminary, that wouldn't be considered suitable.

The Sunday turned out to be cold and rainy, just the day for avoiding the drearier side of the city. Even Jubey himself was discouraged when the rain continued throughout the afternoon.

He muttered disgustedly to that unnamed adversary with

whom he so often kept up a one-sided quarrel, That's your idea of co-operation? I beat my brains out trying to do some small thing for these poor people, and what do you contribute? Any harder for you to throw down a decent day than all this filthy rain? What are you, a grouch or something? As usual no answer came back.

He went down early to the mission hall, and when the door was opened a hot, shabby smell came out, so he knew that already the audience was assembling.

"Too bad, Our," was the director's grim greeting.

"Any of the actors here yet?"

"Sorry to say, none."

"They'll come."

"If they don't, we've got an old moving picture about the missionaries in India."

"We won't need it," Jubey said. "These poor little guys have seen the thing ten times, and it wasn't any good the first time."

"I'm only offering what we have."

Through the window Jubey saw a taxi stopping at the curb-stone. Straggling children and adults headed for the mission house began running excitedly down the street to greet the taxi. The door was opening and a little man, as dapper as a penguin, was alighting with difficulty because five well-tailored terriers, each on a different-colored lead, were cavorting around him, tangling his spatted feet.

After he had been paid, the taxi driver began lifting out sleek strange-shaped theatrical luggage, obviously containing props for the act. When it seemed that the taxi must surely be empty, one more item stepped out. An unusually tall girl, in a simple tailored suit, with a small cloche hat and a large-meshed veil pinned smoothly over her glowing face. She had a single carnation in her lapel, and white gloves that matched it for freshness. The whole entourage, man, dogs and girl, were strictly black and white.

With his comprehensive eye delighting in the sight, Jubey seized an umbrella and ran out to the curb, thinking with gratitude that even if nothing else arrived, they could make the afternoon abundantly of what was here. His desire to give these poor people something to talk about and think about for weeks and months was so burning in him that he felt confident that it would somehow transform his own inexperience and ignorance into a definite talent for dealing with dogs. He laughed within himself for sheer happiness, recognizing this old pattern in himself, the brash confidence he always had that the need would somehow miraculously create an ability to meet it handsomely.

Another car was pulling up at the curb now, and other performers were there, two Japanese men, practically identical, who had promised to do acrobatics and wrestling in white silk tights; also an aging woman in walnut-sized pearls who had brought her large, fruity voice to stun the underprivileged. With her was her accompanist, and a young man in a gray derby (whose partner was a bit under the weather, he said) who'd be glad to dance solo, if that was all right.

In the excitement of trying to greet each performer as the top-billed star of the day, Jubey got confused about the umbrella, so that it ended with the dogs being escorted in dry, while everyone else had to scurry across the pavement with heads sunk into shoulders, as people hunch under rain. Jubey was acutely conscious of the tall girl in the dog act. She didn't look like a show person, for one thing. She looked, rather, like some family's pampered daughter. He dismissed with horror the notion that she might be related to the dapper little man who obviously owned the dogs.

Half the audience, discovering that the performers were

arriving, had left their seats and were clogging the hall so that it looked as if the actors would have to fight their way through.

Jubey shouted at them, "We know you're glad to see these people. But act like an audience. Get back to your seats, or we won't have any show for you."

Obediently they ebbed back to the musty-smelling hall, and Jubey took his performers upstairs to the crude little clinic which seemed the best place to lay out the show. Before time for the performance to begin, six of the seven acts had made good their promises. It was when each act had found some room in which to dress that Jubey discovered that the tall girl who had arrived with Keenan's Canines didn't belong in that act.

"Thank goodness," he said to her.

"Why 'thank goodness'?"

"I don't know. I'm just glad you're not a dog trainer," he said with embarrassment. "What *do* you do, anyway?"

"Well, I . . . I dance," she said, blushing for some reason. "I happened to hear about what you were doing, and I . . . tagged along."

"Are you a professional?" he asked, and was amazed that the question came from some upwelling wish in himself that she would say no. Then he said superciliously to himself, But what difference does it make to me whether she's a professional or not? But he was not deceived. He knew it made a great difference.

"Of course," she said. "Don't I look professional? Or, to put it another way, how do professionals look? Like Patricia P. Birmingham in the pearls?"

Jubey said in some confusion, "To tell you the truth, I've never really known any professionals until this moment."

"You'll like us," she said. "We're the dearest people in the world. We live out of our hearts."

He liked the expression and wondered if it were original with her, or if she had heard it said a thousand times around the theater. She saw him wondering about that, and she laughed. "The words just came out," she explained. "I never heard them before. But they're really pretty true about us. You'll see, Mr. Our."

"Matter of fact, it's what I've been learning to do myself," he said slowly. "I expected to live out of my brains . . . I intended to make them pretty good brains."

"Then something happened," she said in a matter-of-fact way.

He nodded, thankful that she had briefed the turmoil of his explanation.

"I guess it's the best kind of living there is," she said seriously. "But people don't seem to realize it. Most people, that is."

They both remembered then that there was work to do, so Jubey backed out of the drab classroom where she was about to set up her make-up mirror and get into a costume.

"Maybe after the show. . . . " he suggested vaguely. She nodded, keeping her gray eyes on his face, without giving him that brilliant smile which was her standard equipment.

The show was a great success. It would have been a success if the performers had done nothing more than appear in their costumes. But they did much more than that. They gave the best they had, unable to help giving the best, in fact, because the magnet whose drawing is the strongest is appreciation and applause. And never was there more extravagant response from an audience.

Naturally they liked the dogs best; naturally of the dogs, they liked best the one who always missed his cue and muffed his trick and fell flat on his face. They, too, had missed their cues and had fallen on their faces, so it was good to see that it is a thing which can be laughed about.

Next to the dogs, they loved the identical Japanese acrobats, for whom Jubey played an improvised accompaniment on the piano. They liked the dancing of the tall girl whose name

Jubey hadn't yet learned. But better than her dancing, they adored the accordion-pleated chiffon skirt made of rainbow colors, with diamonds around the whirling hem.

She's good, Jubey said to himself, sitting at the piano and following her rhythms easily. She's probably a whole lot better than she suspects. He found he was saying it rather gloomily to himself, and did not stop to wonder why.

Throughout the show the audience clapped and shouted and stamped on the floor, and when each act was finished, the spectators rose from their seats and made flattering personal remarks.

"Is them pearls the real McCoy, lady?" they shouted up to Patricia P. Birmingham. "They sure look lovely."

It was almost impossible to bring the afternoon to a close. Only Jubey's announcement that there would be coffee and cupcakes in the basement finally dispelled the admiration. At his voice, the whole room took flight, like a scattering of city pigeons when a car backfires.

The performers, expanded now by their own benevolence, lingered until the last cupcake was a crumb, and Jubey was in an agony of suspense for fear this radiant and demure girl, who had such subtle style to her dancing, might have forgotten her half-agreement of a date after the show.

But finally, the Keenan Canines could linger no longer. Keenan said, "Well, if you're ready, my dear . . . " and Jubey thought, She'll leave, and that'll be the end of it.

But he underestimated her ability to do exactly as she pleased.

"Mr. Our is driving me uptown," she said pleasantly. "I knew you wouldn't mind, Mr. Keenan. I seem to take up a lot of room in a taxi."

"Why, there's plenty of room," Keenan said vigorously.

"Really? Well, then maybe you'll take along my bag?"

"Delighted," he said, looking anything but.

So at last they were all disposed of, and the mission was cleared of its raucous echoes and scufflings, and Jubey and the girl looked at each other a long moment and then smiled understandingly.

"What a wonderful time," she said.

"It was, to me."

"When it seems so easy to make people enjoy themselves . . . we ought to manage it more often," the girl said.

"You probably manage it every day," Jubey reminded her.

"I do. And I love it." Her eyes, gray and large and rimmed about the iris with a dark outline, seemed to deepen with sincerity. "Sometimes I can't believe it's really happening to me, because I love it so much."

"You sound as if it hadn't been the usual struggle."

"No. It hasn't," she said. "It's been grand all the way. I feel guilty about it sometimes. But that's the way it seemed to fall out."

"No starving, no tramping around from agent to agent?"

"None of that. I just wanted to dance. So I danced." She smiled at him, then started to say something and stopped.

Jubey said, "You realize I don't even know your name? You see, I didn't have you on my list with the others."

She glanced up at him to see if he was serious, and then looked down. "That's right," she said, "I was the unwritten postscript."

"So the name is . . ."

"Gay," she said. "Gay Savanne."

He repeated it after her. "Sounds all right," he said. "It'll probably be easy to remember when you get to the top."

"Will it?" she said demurely.

The conversation seemed to come to a halt then, so Jubey said energetically, "Now let's see . . . hadn't we better have some supper somewhere?"

"I ate two cupcakes."

"Even so. We could talk better. Unless you've got to hurry home."

"Home's just a room," she said. "Two very nice rooms."

They let themselves out the locked front door, and Jubey put up the umbrella, realizing he should have telephoned for a cab from within the building.

"Your veil will go limp," he apologized.

"How would you know that?"

"My mother wore veils. And white gloves, too."

"That gives us a childhood in common," she said. The umbrella over them made everything much cozier than it otherwise would have been; the deserted streets added their bit, also, to the pleasantness of the moment.

"It's a long way to a street where taxis cruise," Jubey said apologetically.

" I like walking."

"We can have a more sumptuous supper if we skip the taxi," he said honestly. "I've been worrying about it."

"Don't worry about money. Ever. I've money to burn."

She opened her small handbag, and a rumor of perfume came up from it. She held the bag up jauntily and he saw a froth of lace on a handkerchief, and something twinkling like a key. But no sight of bills.

"I guess you've already burned it," he said.

"Don't worry anyway. But if you're poor . . . "

"I'm not poor," he said. "I'm studying to be a minister. There's quite a difference, except on the surface that shows."

She looked at him with honest admiration in her face. "I want to hear about that," she said. "I've never known a minister. Except from a distance, when he was standing on the bridge of his ship, so to speak."

"Now's your chance, Miss Gay Savanne."

"I'll take it," she said, laughing at him, her eyes almost on a level with his.

Up a flight of stairs they found a rather forlorn little Syrian restaurant, practically empty of customers, but full of a wonderful grapy fragrance. There were green and red jewels of Turkish paste in a sad little showcase, so Jubey took the taxi fare and bought a half-pound for the girl. They sat at a table in a far corner of the dimly lighted room, and ate a long lazy meal. Gay leaned on her elbows and listened, and sometimes asked good questions and sometimes only nodded understandingly. Then it was suddenly late, and obvious that the plump dark-eyed woman at the showcase was falling asleep. Jubey paid his bill, having to borrow a quarter from Gay, and they went back down the long flight of stairs into the rain again.

"Now you'll *have* to see me again, to restore my masculine dignity."

"Oh?"

"The quarter I borrowed."

"Plus two dimes for the bus we are about to take," she reminded him.

He got back to Hastings Hall just before midnight. His suite mate, a serious boy from Denver, was reading for his Monday classes.

"How'd it go, Jube?" he called out as he heard the doorknob.

"Great."

"Any acts turn up?"

Jubey came into the room, lit his pipe, and dropped into one of the big shabby chairs, eager to talk the whole business over, even if it had to be with this dull Westerner.

"*Did* they? We had somersaulters, trained dogs, a soprano with a cracked ceiling, a magician, and a girl named Gay Savanne."

"*A girl named Gay Savanne!* I like that."

"What'd you mean?"

"Don't you know who she is, you creeping preacher?"

"Who is she?" Jubey asked, his mouth dry.

"Well, she just happens to be the toast of the town at the moment."

Jubey said, "You're kidding."

"Don't you read newspapers?"

"I guess I don't," he said sheepishly. "And I was planning to ask her to marry me next week!"

2

HE WENT THROUGH the next days in a state of alternate elation and despair. What difference did it make if she was momentarily famous? Dancers come and go, but love goes on forever, he reasoned valiantly. As long as he kept it in the realm of fancy, it was easy to dream off on a blithe arpeggio. But when he made the mistake of going down to the theatrical district and walking past the Music Box, and seeing her name in proverbial lights across the marquee, and unmistakable pictures of her along the intimate lobby, he saw that the whole thing was out of all reason. Just an adventure, to be tucked away and told as a stodgy anecdote when he was a graying minister of the gospel. A fairly stock episode, in fact . . . the minister and the chorus girl; only, to be sure, Gay was no chorus girl. But he knew the pattern; he had encountered it in first-year college psychology. It was too patly typical to be interesting.

Except that he could think of nothing else by day or by night.

Word of it scampered around Hastings Hall like a family of mice. For a few days, whenever two students met, the greeting was, "Heard about Jubey Our and Gay Savanne?"

He was asked over and over, "What're you planning to do about it, Jubey?"

"Do? What'd you mean, do?" he usually answered querulously.

"Boy! I'd think of something to do, all right."

"Okay. So it didn't happen to you, fella," Jubey would say good naturedly. But he didn't feel good natured. He felt foolish, and cheated, and deflated.

Then something wonderful happened. A telephone call came just at dinnertime so that he had to be paged through the Charles Cuthbert Hall refectory.

Several of the more facetious brethren called out as he went past the crowded tables on the way to the telephone booths, "Give her my love, too, Jubey."

"Probably only my unwed mothers' club over at the settlement house," he said briskly over his shoulder.

But sure enough it was the carefree voice of Gay Savanne waiting in the black cage of the telephone.

"I thought you said you were going to call me," she said. "This hurts my pride."

He couldn't think of anything to say for a moment, and she said, "Is that you, Mr. Our?"

"It's me all right," he said. "But I'm speechless."

"You? Speechless?" she laughed at that, a good friendly laugh.

"Fact is, I found out who you were," he blurted out.

"Oh? You mean you don't like the idea?"

"I'm embarrassed. I'm not accustomed to being such a yokel. You probably laughed your little head off."

"Nonsense. I thought you liked me."

"You knew darned well."

"I thought you said . . . "

"I did. And I'd have said a lot more, if I'd had time. Only now . . . "

"Now?"

"Well, now it's ridiculous. You're somebody biggety."

"I'm just the same as I always was," she said contritely. "If you're going to be a good minister, that's the first thing you had better learn about people."

"You'll have to teach me," he said with what even he recognized as sophomoric banality.

"When do I begin? Tomorrow? After the show?"

He went back through the refectory trying not to look smug.

"The unmarried mothers?"

He put the expression on his face of a man telling a boastful lie. "Nope. Gay Savanne."

"Oh sure," the sceptics said, and one wag cried out, "That reminds me . . . Marilyn Miller phoned me this afternoon."

It was not a successful evening. Gay Savanne might have been the same person, but Jubey could not be. He had drawn a reckless sum out of his slim checking account, and he made up his mind that he would refuse to think about what that would do to his next week's living. Rather stuffily he insisted upon their going to the Plaza for their supper.

"You can't afford that," Gay said sternly.

"I'll find you more attractive, my dear young lady, if you let me manage that department," he said, trying to look down at her.

"I think it's only fair to warn you this is my big meal of the day."

"I'll leave my overcoat if I haven't enough to settle the bill," he said. "It's the last of my Brooks Brothers wardrobe."

"No, but really."

He walked her firmly up the broad steps, seeing in the tall doorman's eye that she was recognized.

She had on the same tailored suit, with a creamy silk blouse frilled at the neck and cuffs. Her dark hair was in smooth ringlets around her ears, and a soft knot was tucked neatly under the narrow brim of her gray felt hat. Of all the women in the room, she was the most simply dressed; the very simplicity was a boast. Looking at her, Jubey thought with a rush of homesickness such as he had not felt for years, Mama would have loved her clothes, and Papa would have loved her. He could almost hear Papa's pleased chuckle at the thought of this moment. My boy Jubey can't be lost so bad after all, Papa would be saying, if this pretty dancer has hold of him.

She raised her eyes from the two-foot-high menu, and then laid it down. "Where are you, Mr. Our? You've left," she said accusingly.

"That's right."

"What're you thinking about?"

"I'm thinking my father would have been in love with you on sight."

"If you can see it, you can do it," she said with her carefree laugh. "That's what they used to tell me in dancing school."

"You'll get yourself in trouble someday, saying such things," he warned her.

But she only laughed again, and went back to the menu. "That's what I'm hoping for, Preacher."

While she was eating her lusty main course, a middle-aged little man with a permanent blush came over and spoke to them.

"I beg your pardon," he said, "but I'm here from Chicago ... it would make me pretty proud if you'd give me your autograph, Miss Savanne."

"It would make me pretty proud, too," she said delightedly, scrawling her name across the Music Box Revue program he thrust at her.

"It's for my son," the Chicagoan said. "He thinks his old man is a stick-in-the-mud."

"We'll show him," Gay said. "I'll write 'love to Horace' or whatever your first name is."

He blushed even more deeply at that. "Well, I don't know. You see, my wife's a rather ... "

So Gay handed him the program with no mischief written in.

Jubey said, after the fan had left the table, "You really like all this, don't you?"

"I love it. Is that wrong? It gives a lot of pleasure to other people, also."

"Don't push me into sounding disapproving," he protested. "You probably couldn't find anyone on earth who understands and approves more than I do. When you know me better . . . "

"So I'm going to!" she said, and impulsively put out her hand and patted his arm. "That's all I want to know."

When they came out of the Plaza, Jubey had to admit that the night was "criminally beautiful." The late crowds had thinned out and the circle in front of the big hotel was a private garden in which they sat a moment on a stone bench and looked up at the Pulitzer fountain.

All but one of the horses and carriages usually dozing at the curb had gone home to bed, and the upper reaches of the skyline were blurred and lost now, with only a window here and there illumined.

"I live only across the street," Gay said.

"That room you mentioned," he said reproachfully.

"I said it was a *nice* room. The prettiest suite the Sherry-Netherlands can offer. But it isn't a home. I don't need a home just now. I'm between homes, my family's and the one of my own not yet arrived at."

She raised up her arms in an exuberance of delight, as if the whole indulgent city was her home, surrounding her with love.

"I'll walk you over any time you're ready, if you're not too tired," he said dejectedly, for suddenly the audacity had leaked out of him and he saw that this was a preposterous accidental touching of a world that could bring him nothing but discontent and regret.

"But first . . . " she said as they were crossing the pavement towards the one sleepy horse at the curb, "but first . . . we'll have a drive, shall we?"

"I haven't money enough," he said heavily. "I've no idea what they charge. But I know I haven't money enough."

"Who said 'money'?" she said scornfully. "The horse is my friend. He sends me a bill on the first of the month. I'm a good customer of his. And this is my treat."

She stepped over to the horse and put out one white-gloved hand toward his down-drooping head.

"Good evening, Edgar," she said to him. A tall-hatted figure, huddled in the seat of the hansom, stirred and came to life. The round little snowman in a flapping overcoat jumped out and came around to the horse's head.

"I thought that was you, Miss Savanne," the cabby said. "I said to myself, God love her, she's going to have one of her little rides tonight. Am I right?"

"You're right, Henry," she said, "provided you can persuade my friend the preacher, here, to go with me."

"A preacher, huh?" he said doubtfully. "Well, it's a pleasure to meet you, sir." But the words didn't disguise the "it takes all kinds" tone in his voice.

3

THE NEXT few days, as far as Jubey's duties were concerned, were a complete blackout. He went around in a frowning trance, and when anybody spoke to him, he grumbled some irrelevant answer. Up to now he had had a few conventional romances here and there; he knew his way around nimbly through the labyrinthine theorizing about sex which was the main theme for discussion among his contemporaries. He had done a self-respecting amount of observing, and had drawn some handy conclusions.

But this was the first time he had found himself helplessly in love. Always before he had tried to sell himself a bill of goods, but now, in spite of all common sense, he was precariously at the mercy of Gay Savanne. And she, it appeared, was completely lighthearted and irresponsible about it.

She assumed, with no coyness at all, that naturally he *would* be a little in love with her. There was only one normal masculine reaction, wasn't there? They talked about it on their second date. She said, "But Jubey, life's so much nicer when you're a little in love."

"Umn," he said glumly. "That's English for the Indian word 'ugh,' meaning 'you don't say so!' or 'tell it to the marines', or some similar expression of disbelief."

It was only a matter of days before he realized that this unforeseen friendship into which he had been projected so involuntarily had placed him in a brotherhood of squirming and worrying males, each of whom believed he had discovered

181

something indispensably unique. He ran into one or another of them every once in a while, either at the beginning or the end of one of his own hectic dates with her. In their faces as in a mirror, he saw the chaos of elation and despondency which was in himself.

"You seem to have an awful lot of friends."

"Yes, I do, don't I."

"You're just too darned nice to everybody, Gay."

"You *can't* think that," she said reproachfully. "Why, Jubey, you're looking almost . . . *jealous!*"

"Jealous! Why should I be jealous? I'm only telling you for your own good. You're frittering yourself away."

"Frittering? In what way?"

"Well . . . none of this will amount to anything. There's too much of it on hand."

Her large gray eyes looked with honest dismay into his. "But, Jubey, I like them," she said. "I'm not trying to make anything amount to anything! I just like them."

"Don't you ever expect to marry?"

"Good heavens, yes," she cried. "But not for ages, of course. I want to have a long exciting career, and then I want to marry some nice man with curly hair, so I'll have pretty children. And besides the curly hair, I'd like him to have . . . "

"A curly bank account."

"Certainly. But also, a big family of relatives we can visit at Thanksgiving and Christmas. . . . "

"Well, having looked over the pack, do you suspect this paragon is in it?"

"He *could* be," she said with dancing eyes. "There are some nice boys around at the moment."

"And every one of 'em thinks he's the only one," Jubey said angrily.

"*You* don't," she reminded him.

"I'm just an innocent bystander. I don't count."

"You do too count," she insisted. "You're one of the loveliest men I've ever known, Jubey. I'm only sorry . . . "

"That I haven't got curly hair, so to speak," he said bitterly.

Her delight in her own attractiveness was completely innocent. It was so wholehearted and so generous in its good will that it was utterly inoffensive. Assuming no credit for what she was, naturally she had no hypocritical modesty. She seemed constantly amazed and pleased that everything around her should be so wonderful. One could scarcely resist joining in her delight, for you couldn't resent her any more than you could begrudge a child its naïve beauty and winsomeness. There was no grain of malice in her anywhere, for she had nothing within to conceal and knew of nothing without to fear.

Once when Jubey was trying to get at the bottom of this unusual phenomenon of personality, he asked, "Don't girls dislike you?"

"Girls? Why, I don't think so," she said in surprise, as if he had asked a question as absurd as "Don't ants resent you?" Then it troubled her that he *had* asked such a thing. "Why, Jubey? What makes you think they might?"

"I just wondered."

"But how *could* they? I always like them first, so they just have to like me back. That's a law, isn't it? Pete says so."

"Pete, for crying out loud?"

"My father. My fine father."

"You appall me," Jubey said. "It's indecent to be so tickled to death about the human race."

"Is it? Well, maybe I've only met up with the darlings." She looked almost troubled that he had pointed out this defect in her. "Perhaps I'm a moron. In the way I enjoy people anyway."

"Or a genius," he said. "I'll let you know later, when I've studied the case further."

"So you're going to study it further? Every time I see you,

I'm scared it's going to be the last time you'll want to bother. Except that we do have fun, don't we?"

"In a suicidal kind of way," he conceded.

"Suicidal? To whom?"

"We'll see," he said gloomily. "Probably to me."

"Don't talk like that," she said quite seriously. "You sound like those people in books, cynical and everything. If I can't bring you some happiness, I just haven't any right to be near you, Jubey."

"Well, don't worry about it," he said. "Not that you would."

"I would so. I'd feel perfectly terrible. Then I'd get pale and haggard, and it would show in my dancing, and pretty soon I'd lose my job, because who wants to buy a ticket to see something sad at heart leaping around a stage? And I'd wander around awhile and starve, and finally I'd have to get into the bread line at one of your missions, and you'd come down on Thursday to cheer people up the way you do, and there *I'd* be. And you'd have to cheer *me* up . . . so you might as well do it now and save us all that bother. . . . "

"Exactly," he said, laughing in spite of himself.

She invited him many times to come to the theater and see her dance, but he always refused.

What's the use of my putting myself through that? he asked himself sulkily.

But he heard plenty of reports on her dancing. After she had come to their attention, practically every divinity student who could afford the price of a seat in the gallery went to the Music Box, and came home enamored or else just so plain jealous that ridicule was the only consolation.

One night, when he could stand it no longer, he got himself a ticket at the last moment and slipped into a seat halfway back in the audience. The scene took him over immediately as theater always did. The very smell of the plush seats and the well-dressed audience, the face powder and the dust from the orchestra pit, seemed to breathe into him the breath of life, "so that man becomes a living soul," he paraphrased blasphemously to himself.

When Gay Savanne came on, dressed in a demure white costume of knowing simplicity, the audience went mad. But Jubey sat slumped in his seat, utterly dejected by her beauty and the incarnate skill of her presence. He realized then that he had been forlornly hoping her success was just some kind of myopic illusion, some whim of the public's taste which would tire of itself and pass.

But he saw now that this was no accidental charm she held for them; this was predestined talent which she would have in that long slender body of hers as long as she lasted. She danced with thoughtful elegance. But Jubey, hardly able to keep tears of despair out of his eyes, said to himself, It's pure forgery . . . the girl doesn't pretend to be able to think.

When the chorus came out and danced behind her, they were permitting themselves to become vulgar and stubby by comparison. Everything about them was "too." When Gay Savanne glanced over her shoulder at them, her lovely face, which up to now had been in a rapt reverie, was suffused with love and goodness and a chivalrous appreciation of their efforts. A clever director had perceived that this friendly magnanimity was the final perfect embellishment to his star. If you had been able to resist her up to then, at the sweet graciousness of that look over her shoulder you succumbed. You loved not only the tall dancer, but all the excellence of the race wherever it occurs. You wanted us all to be "nice people" from that moment on.

Jubey had intended slipping out of the theater as he had come in. But after her dancing he couldn't be pettily protecting his silly dignity. Nobody could be churlishly thinking of himself in such gay good presence! An usher, seeing him blundering around a fire exit, helped him find his way backstage with an if-you're-a-friend-of-Miss-Savanne's-you're-a-friend-of-mine eagerness.

"You must have to pilot people back here every night, don't you?" Jubey asked the beaming lad.

"That's right. She's something, isn't she? And she never acts like a star, either. She's everybody's little sister."

The usher rapped on a door, and said, "Miss Savanne? There's a man who says he's a preacher here."

There was a moment's silence, then Gay cried out, "There can't be! He said he wouldn't want to come."

Jubey said humbly, "He wanted to, tonight, Miss Savanne."

The door was flung open and she took him in delightedly. A middle-aged woman was working among her many costumes. Gay had on an unflattering schoolgirlish bathrobe, like a student interrupted at her home work.

He found her dressing room not as he had expected it. It was no luxurious boudoir, but only a plain pleasant little room with no extra places to sit down. Gay was sitting before a big workmanly shelf with a lighted mirror behind it.

Without self-consciousness, she was working on her face with quick deft thoroughness. He leaned against the wall and watched her in the mirror.

"Oh, Jubey . . . you liked me!"

"Who said so?"

"Or you wouldn't have come back."

"I loved you," he said. Her gray eyes met his in the mirror, and for a moment she looked as if she were going to burst into tears. Then she seemed to read some casualness in his face, so her innocent smile came out and saved the moment. They talked about the dances, and her technical seriousness delighted him.

"You know what you're doing," he said. "I thought you just danced."

"Nobody just dances. If your head isn't in it, it's mere mediocrity."

That encouraged him to confess that he'd had a thought himself. "It may not be worth anything," he said. "But I was thinking . . . part of the surprise . . . the playing against the mood . . . which gives you so much style . . . is the look of thoughtfulness you put on. How would it be if, when those big gray curtains part for your first appearance, they opened on you with a big shabby green book, and your head bent as if you had to catch the last possible moment for reading, and maybe even a big pair of tortoise-rimmed students' glasses on? You wait a few seconds, not realizing the curtains have opened, then you take off the glasses, and put a bookmark in the book very deliberately. Then you bow a slow dignified bow. Not hurrying at all, you know. Then you smile the way you do, kind of taking the whole audience . . . gentlemen and scholars, you assume . . . into your confidence. Would that be anything?"

She had swung on her bench to listen and consider, and now she was nodding her head.

"We'll try it," she said, getting up and going over to the wardrobe where the maid had just hung the costumes. "Go outside a moment, Jubey, and I'll dress again," she said in a businesslike way.

"You mean now?"

"Of course now." She picked up a telephone which was sitting on a low table beside her make-up shelf, and asked for somebody named Charles. "Could you come down, darling? I think we've a nice idea."

When she was dressed, the three of them went out to the darkened theater, while the stage manager, a genial man in green shirt-sleeves, operated the footlights and the spots, and the parting of the gray curtains. They went through it twice, and Charles made a slight improvement in the timing. Then he clapped Jubey on the shoulder.

"That's good," he said. "In three minutes, with a pair of big horn-rimmed glasses and a book you've given Gay Savanne an education."

"Education?" Jubey said deliriously. "That gal's got more real education in her little finger than most college professors have in their whole carcass."

Charles looked dubiously at him, as if he thought Jubey were pulling somebody's leg. Then he said, "Well, you may be right at that. Didn't Gay say you're a preacher?"

"Not quite yet."

"How come you get ideas like this?"

"Maybe preaching and acting aren't as far apart as you might think." The director shrugged at that, indifferently.

But indifference didn't bother Jubey now, for at last he had accomplished what had been itching in his brain for a long time; he had got one of his ideas up on its feet and had seen it walk across a stage! His backbone was humming with pleasure.

During the next days Gay blew up the idea he had contributed, as if she believed it were the best item in her whole routine.

"It's not that good, Gay," he sometimes said sheepishly.

"It starts off the thing with tone," she said.

She made the most of insisting that he must spend time with her whenever he could. "In case you think of anything else that's good. Do you mind?"

"Something awful," he said.

4

Most of the time, she insisted on their taking their fun in Jubey's customary world instead of in her shiny one. There were no twilights and no evenings in her life, because of the theater, but there were plenty of midnights and afternoons, and Jubey could always find some novel side of New York to show her. She liked walking along the Battery streets with him. She went bowling in a basement alley he patronized, and afterwards there was no food that could compare with that served in Eddie's Diner over on the Jersey flats. They enjoyed Brooklyn Bridge on a windy morning, and the pushcarts on Grand Street.

"Don't think you fool anybody," he told her. "A baby could tell at one glance that you're an expensive pink-and-pretty from uptown seeing how the other half lives."

"The same goes for you," she said astutely. "The only difference is that I'm down for the afternoon, and you're down for a couple of years."

She was a wonderful listener for his tortured self-arguments. He would think disloyally, She's so safe to be around when you've got to blow off steam. She looks at you with those big inhaling eyes of hers . . . and she doesn't understand a word you're saying.

Sometimes he would come dangerously close to baring the ultimate treachey on which his private theology was based. He had a feeling sometimes that if he could just express it to her once, if it could be said daringly out in the palpable air, something in him would ease.

He tried it one night when they were riding back and forth on the ferry. It struck him as characteristic of her that she should be enjoying this ferry ride without benefit of Edna St. Vincent Millay, who had lately charted the exact blueprint of this delight. It seemed exquisitely humorous that this Gay Savanne, who was full of the hedonistic ecstasy Millay purveyed so eloquently, had never read a line of her; probably the only woman of her generation who had not, Jubey chuckled to himself.

It was a cool April night, and the late commuting passengers were glad to crowd inside the cabin of the round-nosed plodding boat. Gay and Jubey huddled together on the lee side of the deck where the shadows were long and dark. His woolly scarf which Minna had knitted and sent at Christmas was tied warmly around Gay's throat, and her hand was tucked in Jubey's overcoat pocket. Her celebrated long legs were stretched out lazily before her, and the moon ran a bold silver stroke from her ankles to the flutter of skirts at her knees, then picked up the line again across the lift of her breast and along her throat to her chin, adding one swift touch of light at the end of her nose. Her eyes, when she tipped them to Jubey's face, were shimmering with excitement and sprinkled light.

"You're smarter than most people, Jubey," she said. "Whatever made you decide to be a preacher?"

"I like to hear myself talk."

"No. But really."

He said seriously, "I love the poor little guys."

"Of course. But why not invent new card games for them, or a better five-cent cigar? Why not give them something they know they want?"

"You wouldn't mean by any chance 'something they'd be willing to pay for'?"

"Possibly," she admitted. Then she had the honesty to say, "Yes, I guess that is what I mean, Jubey." She squeezed his hand in apology. "But preaching seems such a strange thing for you to want to do."

"It is a strange thing," he said slowly. "I wake up in the night sometimes and I think, Who is this guy that's taken over my skin? Can't be me, surely. But it is me, Gay. It's me, all right. In the thing up to my neck."

"Up to your heart, anyway," she said.

They were both quiet a long time, and the scraping of feet ebbing toward the doors warned them they were nearing the ferry's slip.

"God's such a long way off," Gay said, "and there are so many other things right here at hand."

"Who said anything about God?" he asked. She looked at him as if she thought she had misunderstood him. So then he dared to say the rest, to hear how it would sound in bald words.

"I'm not in this thing for God, Gay. I'm in it for poor little bewildered mankind. When I preach to 'em, I'm going to tell them how good *they* are; I'm going to try to help get that good in them from where it's hiding, so they can see it and use it better."

"That's all right," she said. "God would certainly be delighted with that, I should think."

He shrugged heavily, with angry impatience. "Delighted or not," he said. "That's up to him."

"That doesn't sound reverent," she said gently as one would reprimand a good child for appearing to be naughty.

"I'm reverent all right," he said pugnaciously. "But I'm reverent about something right here, not a long way off, the way you said. I'm reverent about the good people. That's the kind of worship I believe in."

"And what made them good?" she asked in gentle enquiry, not knowing she had fingered a touchstone of theological quarreling.

"They made themselves good," he said. "By love and sacrifice and the terrible tenderness they always show when they're right up against disaster."

She shook her head in denial of that, and with her free hand she reached over and patted his cheek as if an ancient instinct in her pitied him.

"You call it anything you want to," she said. "God has a lot of stage names."

Then after a baffling silence from Jubey she went on, "There's a legend Pete told me once when I was a youngster. I don't know where Pete heard it, because both of us are uneducated people, Jubey. But anyway. Seems this was way back before the world was. Whoever it was that made the world was getting everything organized and put into proper shape.

"Well, one big problem that came up was where to hide the secret of God's goodness in the earth."

"Why did it have to be hidden?" he asked indolently, half intrigued.

"Well, I'll tell you. It seemed necessary at the time. And rather a good idea, too, because you know what would have happened, don't you?"

"What would have happened?"

"Why, as soon as people found out, they would try to do something to change it, or improve it, or maybe get a patent on it to keep the price up. Well, anyway, they thought of hiding it in the farthermost depths of the sea, and then they thought of hiding it in one of the darkest caves. Or maybe in the deepest jungle. But none of these places seemed really safe. Because you know how men are . . . they'd go looking. And the harder the place was to find, the harder they would look. That's men for you."

She was sitting up straight now. She had turned from half-leaning on his shoulder to facing him, and her eyes were big and full of earnestness.

"So what did they do?"

"Well, they found a good place to hide it," she said in a mysterious provocative whisper. "They hid it right down in the depths of man himself. A little scrap of it in each one of them. Because they knew that nobody would think of looking for it there. But *you're* looking for it there, Jubey. And now the thing is . . ."

He found himself suddenly deeply touched by this unexpected moment. He felt that strange unclenching of tension all along his mind which he had experienced that night in Mama's little room, a childlike upwelling of trust, as if something bigger than thinking had reached out gently and comforted his rebellion. As if that Something said, Don't worry, Jubey . . . you're coming along the right road. Keep watching for the way-marks. I've got my eye on you, son.

But Gay still had something to say. "But the thing is . . . darling, you've got to call it by its proper name. It isn't just mankind, Jubey. It's man-and-God sort of meeting there."

He turned then and looked at her; not the cocksure Jubey who amused her, but the bewildered one, lost on the journey.

"Gay . . . I wish you were a homely little seamstress living in a room on Morningside Heights."

"Why, Jubey . . . what a thing to say! If I were, I doubt if you'd even look at me."

"I'd ask you to marry me," he said, taking hold of her shoulders and shaking her almost angrily, "and when I couldn't think of anything to preach about, you'd tell me what to say."

"Now you're making fun of me," she said. "I don't think you ought to be making fun of everything all the time, Jubey."

5

ALL THROUGH the spring the thing went on, and neither of
them mentioned that when the Music Box closed in June, and
when Jubey got his divinity diploma, the world would be
ending.

Both of them were looking for jobs, and that gave them a
new bond. All kinds of offers came to Gay, brought by her
eager agent, and rejected one by one for some special tailor-
made reason of her own. After looking over all the prospects
she decided to have a quiet summer at home with her family.

The offers that came to Jubey were pretty meager and hum-
bling. A church out in Idaho would pay his traveling expenses
for a month's trial without salary, if he cared to submit his
presence to their scrutiny. Every man in his class was aiming
at getting an assistantship in some important city church, where
he could exercise charm over parishioners, all this to lead
eventually to his becoming a pastor. A visiting Bishop who
had happened into the Union Settlement on East 104th Street
one afternoon, and had listened to Jubey conducting a service
there, offered him a mission station job as Bishop's chaplain
designate in a rural diocese in West Virginia. That would
have meant traveling around between three missions, preaching and ministering to farm people and miners.

He knew why he couldn't accept that job.

Even the letters I sent her from such a place would be grimy
by the time she got them, he said to himself.

They separated without knowing when they should meet

again, and if that troubled Gay, it certainly didn't show in her radiant good-bye. But Jubey was sick with despair and help-lessness.

She laughed at him. "My heavens, you sound as if trains were never going to run, or telegrams be delivered, or telephone calls be put through."

"Those conveniences are all fine for your plutocratic *suit-ors*," he said bitterly. "But I'm going to be a poverty-stricken minister. How many long distance calls do you think I can afford out of a hundred and fifty dollars?"

"Why, I think that's a very good salary," she cried, opening her eyes. "Let's see, in a month that would be . . . four times a hundred. . . ."

"Gay, that *is* the month," he said crossly. "And even that, of course, depends on my *getting* a church to hire me."

"Well, I'll have to telephone to *you*, then," she said, unper-turbed, as if that solved everything.

He wrote her a letter every day, carefully frivolous and with no suggestion of their being love letters, except that his heart-sickness emphasized the frivolity as a dazzle is made more bril-liant by shadow.

He moved into an old-fashioned room in a walk-up rooming house in the West Eighties, and continued his settlement work while he scrounged for an appointment. The country seemed to be swarming with young men with divinity diplomas. It wasn't a good year for religion anyway, for the nation was filled with the hilarity of dizzy prosperity. These were the years when materialism was a cajoled god in a benevolent soft mood handing out to laborers silk shirts and fur coats and refriger-ators, with no end of its reign in sight. Who wanted to be thinking about religion, except the poor and the ill? And when were they ever in a position to appoint ambitious young preachers to good posts?

Without Gay New York was a different city. There was

nothing to do in it, only days to be spent, and nights, trying to get tired enough to sleep. He tried to remember what he had enjoyed doing before he found Gay. But the interest was gone. No wonder the streets were thronged with dead-faced people; and the park benches filled with slumped-over scarecrows staring into space. No wonder the movie houses had herds of dispirited ghosts sitting in rows, hoping time would somehow pass. The city which had been full of entertaining and fascinating strangers was now turgid with seedy, indifferent, inescapable living. And all because one bright, laughing presence had withdrawn.

One night when he had finished his work and couldn't quite face his hot tight-walled room with the squirmy-patterned brown wall paper, he walked over to Union Square and lost himself in the jostling crowds of listeners.

He imagined himself telling Rose about this Gay Savanne, and he could see her honest eyes on his face listening, and her head nodding. It was somebody like that I had in mind for you, Jubey, she would say. Only for Pete's sake, why did you have to start at the top? Couldn't you have found somebody like her, just a little ways up, within your reach?

Nope, he said to the Rose in his mind. It's part of what Gay is that she'd be at the top.

All right then, get hurt, Rose would reply angrily. If you haven't got any better sense, you'll just have to get hurt.

Okay. Who's complaining? he asked fairly. I'd rather be hurt about her than happy about somebody else . . . or is that a popular song?

He listened to the orators, but now there was no temptation to leap upon the coping of the little park and take things over. He had heard too much preaching in the last few years to believe that words could change things, as he had believed that night. And that night, out of the passion of his believing, words *had* changed things. Would he ever again find in himself such passion and such faith? Probably not. Dr. Eustace Thorndike who taught Doctrinal Preaching, said that most ministers experienced one or two occasions in a lifetime of preaching when a higher eloquence seemed to envelope them, and that the rest of the sermons had to be compounded with more or less deliberate skill.

The old man had said that once or twice in a lifetime the minister is converted by his own sermon, and the rest of the time he must be content to watch inspiration touch others and pass him by. "It is the test of humility that the minister turns away hungry from the feast he himself has spread."

But that faraway night in this square nobody had been turned away hungry. A fantastic thought suddenly struck Jubey. Could that have been because it was not he himself who had spoken that night? Could there have been a greater Orator using his voice? He remembered how he had "listened" to those glowing words. He had spoken, but mostly he had listened to what was being said. That had been the secret of the great exhilaration of that night; he had felt himself "taken over" by something magnificently bigger than himself.

He stood now on the very same spot, almost praying to know what had happened, almost daring to pray.

The weary years of poverty and study that had grown from those moments had been but a long wavering shadow cast from that Light. Would the rest of his life be dwindling shadow as that Light receded into his past? Tonight he possessed the mental equipment, the knowledge and education and the trained skill; tonight he had all that a disciplined mind set to a task could accomplish. But there was something else; there was a spark which could not be simulated, which could not be forced into being. There was something which could only be "given." Just when he was nearly ready to accept the meaning of that awkward thought, it slipped into a prepared groove of familiar theological cliché. The gift of grace.

That angered him so that he lost the whole thing. He had vowed he never would accept those finger-marked expressions which invalidate most religious vocabularies . . . and here he was slipping into it! The gift of grace, indeed! He'd have none of it.

Yet he knew that on that most stirring night of his life, in an absurd episode which defied analysis, he had had exactly that gift and that grace. It had been but a grain of some indefinable substance, but it had changed his existence. Not immediately, for it had been a delayed-action process which had remolded him from within. It had seemed to beckon the very events it needed for the remolding, as if by some secret power.

He had scarcely ever thought of it with his conscious mind without scoffing at it. Yet it had gone on, irresistibly shaping him and his existence as it pleased. He called it by insulting names to himself. That Thing, was the way he usually referred to it when it crossed his mind. There's that Thing again.

He heard Gay's voice saying as it had on the ferry boat, "God has a lot of stage names, Jubey." But he refused to admit the application. Instead he let his mind veer off to the lovely pastime of thinking about Gay. She had quite an original vocabulary, hadn't she. Maybe it was because she hadn't been exposed to much formal education. She didn't know the accepted ways of saying things, so she said them well.

One night when he couldn't bear his loneliness another minute, he went without his dinner and telephoned her family's house in Woonsocket, Rhode Island. It was a thoroughly ghastly experience, because Gay's mother answered the phone, and said, "This is Roger, isn't it?" and before he could make her understand that it was not Roger by any means, she said, "Oh Roger, we've all been enjoying the beautiful flowers you sent. When are you coming up again, dear?"

He tried with all his dignity and enunciation to make her realize who he was, but she seemed completely unable to grasp his identity.

She just never heard of me, he said dejectedly to himself. That shows you.

For days after that he fumed about Roger, who, with everything else he obviously had, had stolen even Jubey's dollar-and-twenty-cent telephone call.

But in the end Gay more than made up for that, for she telephoned to him.

"Jubey, I've been thinking . . . it must be hot in town," her clear expensive-sounding voice said. "Why don't you come up and have a weekend with us? You'll probably be bored, but . . ."

"Oh, Gay."

"There's a train out of New York at two. I'll meet you at our railway station on Friday. Don't expect much, Jubey. We're not interesting people."

"I know," he said. "You're so uninteresting that I don't think of anything else all day."

6

ON THE STATION PLATFORM he saw her before his eyes confirmed the sight. She was wearing a pink linen dress and white slippers, and everything around her looked subdued and muted as if to award her all the light there was in the scene.

She saw him through the window of the day coach, and her face lifted suddenly with pleasure. She didn't wave, or run to him. She simply stood where she was and let him come to her, and that struck him as characteristic. She would always let him make all the small advances he was capable of making ... and if there were large chasms to be crossed, why ...

She began rather nervously to explain that her mother wanted to come, but at the last minute ...

"An angel interfered," he said. "Gay ... it's been seven weeks."

"Has it?"

"Acting like years," he said. "There wasn't anybody to play with."

"What's in the box?"

"Flowers. For your mother."

"She'll like you, Jubey."

"Sure."

The house was a great surprise. Not until he was actually on the train did he realize that Gay had never talked much about her family. Except Pete. He found it was impossible to picture them, and this gave him a lonely, disloyal feeling, as if their friendship had no normal foundations.

Just before they stopped in front of a broad brown house, singularly ugly and dignified behind its lawns, he said, "Gay, you've never told me much about your family. I know you have some younger brothers and sisters, but beyond that . . . "

"There's not much to tell," she said. "You'll see for yourself in a minute. Just take it easy, Jubey."

The house had a smell of raisins and mothballs, when the big front door was opened. Gay called out, "Comp'ny, comp'ny," but she sounded forcedly cheerful about it. The door to the back part of the house opened, and an untidy stout maid peered out, said "Oh," then closed the door again.

"That's Carolyn," Gay said. "She's mad at everything."

Another door opened upstairs, a few footsteps sounded along a hall, and then a pleasant voice came down, "Is that you, Gay? And Mr. Our?"

"That's mother," Gay said in a normal tone of voice. "She's quite deaf, but she doesn't admit it."

"I know," Jubey said. "I tried my best to tell her I wasn't Roger."

She was coming down the stairs now, a beautiful woman with a mass of red hair elaborately dressed on her small head. Nothing of her was in Gay, except her radiant smile. She put out her hand and spoke to Jubey. Like many deaf persons, she didn't wait for his greeting but went on talking, since that was the only way she felt socially safe. She asked about the city, and discussed the train and apologized for the fact that her husband wouldn't be home until later; and all the time her restless beautiful eyes, not gray like Gay's eyes, but a dark grapy blue, were evaluating Jubey, past, present, and future.

"The children won't be home for dinner either. They've gone to a baseball game." Then she gave an unexpectedly girlish laugh, "I usually go with them. Just love baseball!"

They took him into a cool, darkened back parlor, furnished with old, quite elaborate cane-seated summer furniture. A squeaky tropical matting rug was on the floor, and a huge folded paper fan stood in the opening of the fireplace to signify that summer was in session. It was evident that this was the warm-weather costume of the room, and that when September was over, there would be a general upheaval, when the sour-faced maid and a handy man hired by the day would drag lumpy fat upholstered furniture down from the attic, and a thick Persian rug would be unrolled to replace the mat. All this would be in the sacred name of a mother-in-law's tradition, for Mona Savanne had impatiently inherited her ideas of housekeeping and had too little interest in the subject to reform it with the times.

The room opened out on the back garden, which now seemed to be filled with discontented birds, squawking and quarreling among tall delphiniums. Gay's mother looked out at the garden, and not able to hear the birds, commented upon the peace.

"I always think there's nothing more peaceful than a garden at twilight," she said, and Jubey knew that many of her sentences began with those three words, and that possibly her family had learned not to listen to whatever came after them.

A strange thing had happened to Gay. She had become silent and somehow awkward, as if her grace were an affront in this house. The most casual observer could have seen that here was a long-established truce between two women who might have fought each other. With horror, Jubey realized that at last he was seeing someone who thoroughly disliked Gay. He knew without being told that it was probably a prenatal enmity, a basic resentment because the birth of this girl had interrupted or interfered with something the mother desired.

The very perfection of her child angered the woman, as if she found herself entered in an unfair competition. He wondered protectively if Gay was aware of this, and decided that she was not. She said, "Yes, Mother" and "No, Mother" in an obedient voice which her mother couldn't possibly have heard, and sat with her ankles crossed with demure patience as if this all had to be gone through with, so it might as well be done willingly. Jubey raised his voice like an ensign in the breeze, and insisted upon making himself heard. After a few minutes, he realized this courtesy was doing more than the flowers to win Gay's mother.

When dinner was half over, and she had found herself laughing at some of Jubey's nonsense, she suddenly stopped and leaned toward him. "Why, my dear . . . I find myself *liking* you," she said ingenuously.

But as Jubey was briefly lapping up the cream of that, she mischievously turned it to acid. "I always like Gay's young men," she said with her brilliant smile.

"That's true," Gay said in the normal voice which her mother couldn't hear. "And it's only her deafness that has kept her an honest woman. Imagine trying to carry on illicit affairs at the top of your lungs!"

"That's right, dear," her mother said complacently, assuming Gay had been explaining that *they* also always liked *her*. "I suppose it's because I'm just naturally *simpatica* to men."

Jubey, shivering with mirth said to Gay, "Now I understand! You come from a long line of *simpaticas*. To men, that is."

Pete Savanne came into the house like the missing *x* in the equation. His mill, he explained, had its annual employees' dinner and smoker tonight; otherwise he would have been at the station. He liked Jubey, sight unseen, he said bluntly, although it wasn't necessary to say that in words, for his great kindness and sensitiveness warmed the whole ugly house from the moment he stepped into it.

The sight of Pete explained the nature of Gay. With her father in the room everything became safe, or more explicitly, the dangers were seen as pretensions to be controlled by the higher knowing of love. The only half-hidden venom against her daughter was now put away, and Mona Savanne was transformed to a woman in love with her husband. A woman safe from herself.

Biblical words rushed in to be a commentary on what Jubey sensed was a familiar, lifelong pattern between these three.

"He prepareth a table before me in the presence of mine enemies."

He saw that the words applied equally to both women. For his wife, this remarkable man prepared peace in the midst of her own inner enemies; for his child, he equated all that threatened her so that she knew it was there without fearing it, or even believing that it was her responsibility to strive against it. In a flash of intuition Jubey realized that it was this safety, in the nullified presence of jealousy and malice, which had established in Gay the lovely traits that had made her safe and beloved wherever she went, even to the dangerous top of her profession.

A child could have seen the great love between Mona and her husband. But only a matured adult could have understood that the external deafness represented a deeper deafness which shut the woman off from accepting her own miracle. It was there for her, but she could not hear its persuasion.

Pete was a homely man, congenitally untidy. He had thick straw-colored hair which grew in several directions on his scalp so that it appeared to be blowing in private winds. His face was square and tossed together carelessly out of odds and ends of features, a too-big mouth, a crooked nose, and uncouth ears. But his eyes were Gay's eyes, and that made everything else forgiven on sight. He had large workman's hands, and a necktie which one knew must have been given him by some laborer who had to say his gratitude any way he could. His voice was loud and blunt, and this saved it from being a loophole through which he could have been robbed. You had to be a kindly person yourself, to detect the inexhaustible kindness that lay below the gruff exterior. That meant that only those who were harmless themselves entered into the peaceful valleys of the man, with no temptation to ravage what they saw. The ruthless and the vandals were held at bay by his gruff voice, hearing in it superior defence against themselves.

His younger children, two boys and a freckle-faced girl who seemed mischievously to have collected all the worst features of each parent, came home from the game about ten, hungry and excited. They went out to the kitchen and brought in glasses of milk and cartwheel cookies, and the little girl climbed upon her father's lap and spilled milk on his vest and crumb-fringed kisses on his chin. Their mother nagged at them about the lateness and the spilling, but they beamed at her as if it were they who were deaf, and went on with what they were doing. Gay, a quiet, happy Gay, saw that Jubey was enjoying the scene and let it go on as it was.

They were all in bed before midnight. Everyone in the house trailed into Jubey's room to make sure he was going to be comfortable. The red-haired little girl, whose name was Melissa, came in wearing pink pajamas, and carrying *Treasure Island,* in case he was somebody who didn't sleep well. "The way grownups sometimes don't," she explained engagingly.

At last the house was quiet, and Jubey was in a white-painted iron bed with brass balls ornamenting the tall head and foot pieces. Rectangles of moonlight lay before each old-fashioned window, so that the grim-looking dressers and the spinsterish rocking chairs were pleasantly visible. It was a room where time had stood still for twenty years or so; sleeping in it gave one the feeling of safe childhood. Jubey thought, I've not been in a home for years. I've been a wanderer. I thought I'd never get home again.

Unexpected as it was in quality, the evening was the happiest he had known for months. But the Saturday was even better, for he had Gay to himself. Everybody apologized about that; it just couldn't be helped; Mr. Our would have to understand, and forgive them.

"I'll try," Jubey said, playing it deadpan.

Gay took him upstairs during the morning to a sewing room on the attic floor, and showed him new costumes which were being made for her next season's work.

"Mother has a little Portuguese dressmaker we bring down from Boston. In the family for years. She used to do mother's costumes in fact."

"Was your mother a dancer?" he asked, thinking he must have uncovered the root of Mona's unnatural jealousy.

"Oh no. She was a singer in vaudeville. Quite a good one, though. Until love happened to her," Gay said. Then she amended that. "No, not love, really. Me. You see, after she married Pete, she became ambitious in a . . . well, in a different way. She wanted to sing in opera, or on the concert stage, anyhow."

"And you interfered?"

"Not me myself. But she began losing her hearing just before I was born."

"That should have given her a perfect alibi."

"Alibi? For what?" Gay asked guilelessly.

"In case she didn't make opera." He saw that she was distressed that he had analyzed the situation so cynically, and he was sorry he had spoken. But he felt quite satisfied with his own diagnosis. After all, if she could have sung in but one opera, she would have been Mona Savanne the opera star. Now she was Peter Savanne's wife who used to be in vaudeville. Quite a different personage.

During the rest of the visit, every time Mrs. Savanne was alone with him for five minutes she told him secrets in her beautiful loud voice. Did he know Roger Peatrie, Gay's awfully rich suitor? He was crazy to marry her. His family wanted to take Gay to Newport for a few weeks. What ailed the girl that she wouldn't go?

Jubey had no idea. "Maybe she just likes being home with you," he suggested.

Her mother seriously considered that and said no, Gay was just being stupid and stubborn. Or, on the other hand, maybe she was being smart, making the Peatries all the more determined. One couldn't tell, could one? Or had Mr. Our had much experience in such things; probably not. Jubey looked innocent of experience, as a fledgling minister should look.

Mrs. Savanne hoped, furthermore, that he himself had no notions about Gay. Notions? How could he have, he gasped, attempting a blush.

"Although it's plain to be seen she thinks you're wonderful or some such thing," Mrs. Savanne said impatiently. "You probably look quite distinguished in a preaching costume."

"Any kind of uniform, I suppose," Jubey conceded platitudinously.

Gay would be a most difficult and unsatisfactory wife, her mother said, unless she were married to a man of infinite patience . . . and means. Anyone could understand that; she'd been pretty badly spoiled. Her father, of course. And other people, too. "Even me," she said, and believed what she was saying. "When she was a small child, she adored me so that I couldn't dare punish her, no matter what she did. She simply wanted to die if I disapproved of her."

"Does she still?" Jubey asked.

"Yes, in a way I expect she does," Mona said with considerable satisfaction at the thought.

Later in the day when he and Gay were driving back from a view she wanted to show him, he spoke about her mother's running divulgences. She was undisturbed about them.

"I know," she said calmly. "But that's all right. I've nothing to hide from you, Jubey."

"Naturally not. I know all about you. And even if there were things I didn't know, they'd be all right, too."

"That's nice," she said, "and it wouldn't surprise me if it's the truth. Besides, one person never tells anything about another person. Only about herself."

"Who told you that?"

"Pete, of course. Pete told me just about everything I know. Except a few things you've told me, Jubey."

"What on earth have I ever told you?" he asked in honest astonishment.

She was quiet a moment, evidently rejecting a facetious reply. "Mostly things about God," she said at last.

She couldn't have found an answer that surprised him more. "God? I don't believe we've ever talked about him. Except maybe that once."

"It isn't talking that tells. It's being what you are."

"And you've learned something about God from me being what I am?"

"Of course. He's behind just about everything you do, Jubey. I never thought much about him before, but since I've known you, I've become quite well acquainted with him."

He shook his head in helpless dismay. The theme of this was somehow familiar. But he couldn't place just where a similar pattern had once taken shape, so he filed the conversation away to be thought out on the train going home.

There he traced it in a few minutes. His own derisive words came back to him from that long ago night when he had looked into the vacant face of that wretched Texan fast asleep in the submarine after they'd been picked up. He had appropriated an answer to that whimpering prayer of his, when Jubey knew ... he would have drowned except that ...

"You can't beat a praying man," Jubey had said disgustedly that night after he had played the accordion until he couldn't stand up any longer. "You can't defeat a praying man. He finds his answers everywhere he looks."

And now here was Gay, that sweet gullible Gay, thinking she was picking up clues on the subject.

He opened a Providence newspaper to the sports page and tried to get lost in it. Suppose he was going to spend his life surrounded by this repeated situation . . . himself smothering yawns and everyone around him tiresomely grateful to him for what they *thought* they heard him say!

My gosh, he said furiously to himself, wouldn't it be ghastly if I converted everybody I came near! A kind of spiritual King Midas, with a curse on me.

7

A TELEGRAM was waiting when he got back to his room just before midnight. He hoped it was from Gay, saying something like, "Darling, I find my career means nothing. Would you consider marrying me?"

But it said no such thing. It was signed by an unfamiliar name, one Samuel Hoppart, and it said, "Will you come for interview regarding appointment as assistant pastor Tuesday 3 P.M."

There was an address in a medium-sized Pennsylvania town. He went out to a drugstore telephone booth and sent a wire confirming the suggested interview. Then he walked along the river watching the lights and the shadowy boats, while he thought over the tangled ambiguities of his life which had brought him to this contrary moment, where he found himself hoping to get what he did not really want.

The interview was an enigma to him. He discovered it was being carried on in some secrecy. Samuel Hoppart was a mild-voiced, lanky widower who said frankly that he was the leading layman in the church, and that this was only a preliminary interview to sound out Jubey on certain theological matters, before recommending him to the church body. When he reached this point in his explanation he took out a sealed plain envelope from his vest pocket and wordlessly pushed it across his desk to Jubey, who understood this was Hoppart's tactful way of making himself financially responsible for the undertaking. He took the envelope with a muttered word of thanks, and put it in his own vest pocket, thinking, If the sample of my theology doesn't go down, I'll probably feel I ought to hand this thing back to old Hoppart.

He waited discreetly for the questioning to begin, but Hoppart talked along in his confidential voice about the various members and factions of the church, and of the town in general. There were singular opportunities here for a good lively assistant to the *present* minister. Each time he mentioned the pastor of Grace Church, Mr. Hoppart emphasized the word "present," giving it a joyful meaning which couldn't possibly escape the young aspirant.

"Ours is the largest congregation in town," he said. "If the pastor is the right kind of man he can be as important as the mayor, and more important than the chief of police."

The test of the theological purity was divulged rather suddenly, inserted between some business details of the building of their handsome new church and the matter of tax rate which gave businessmen in the town considerable nuisance. When he was sure he had Jubey off guard, he suddenly leaned forward and asked, "How do you stand on this distinction, Doctor Our . . . do you believe Christ died 'for us' or 'instead of us'?"

Jubey's first impulse was to burst out laughing; then he realized this was a matter of life and death, and that the eyes across the desk were pleading mutely behind rimless glasses. Jubey said to himself, He wants me terribly to be on the right side . . . and I sure want to be. If only I can figure out which side he thinks that is.

His mind riffled quickly through the lately thumbed textbooks while a picture of Dr. Bernard Barrows came before him, with his mouth drawn down between the wishbone-shaped wrinkles which testified to a lifetime of quibbling. He felt his own mouth assuming that authoritative shape, and his two hands came up before his chin, each fingertip arched against its mate exactly as the Barrows hands did during thought. He

could see Hoppart's face relaxing in approval of this panto-
mime, and he could almost hear the eager brain telegraphing
the good news that here was a young man who would give no
snap judgments.

From there on it was easy going, for Jubey's best skill was in
talking in bewildering circles around delicate subjects. He
split the hair neatly down the middle, and then explored both
sides of the narrowness. He called up references, some authoritative and genuine, and a few invented pontifically out of the
need of the moment. Mr. Hoppart was leaning back happily
now, his limp hands swinging contentedly on the watch chain
looped across his small round package of stomach.

"That's the way I rather hoped you'd see it," he said with
ripe gratification when he had consumed enough of this rich
fruitcake. "Now I think I owe it to you to tell you why I had
to ask this."

There was, it seemed, a disagreement among the members.
Dr. Eban Carruthers, the *present* minister, had stirred it up,
actually. Most unfortunate, too, especially when the whole
church had just succeeded in erecting such a beautiful new
edifice. That was the important thing, showing the town by
this visible sign that the church was unified.

Whether it is or not, Jubey commented to himself, while
he nodded unctuously.

So wide had yawned the breach however, that the dissenting
group had nearly succeeded in causing Dr. Carruthers to resign. They had taken themselves out bodily, conspicuously
staying away from services while they circulated nimble rumors
about all sorts of action they contemplated.

"What we really need," Mr. Hoppart said without humor,
"is an assistant pastor who can mollify both sides. Privately,
of course. Someone who can reassure each group and lead it
into working with the other for the good of the church."

"Tact," Jubey said. "Creative spiritual tact."

"Exactly," Mr. Hoppart said, a little dazed.

"I've encountered that problem before," Jubey said. "I've had quite an intimate connection with it." He didn't mention that where he had encountered it was within his own nature, which was torn like this church between two antagonistic factions.

But it struck him as poetic justice that the best position offered to him should be a large shadowing-forth of his own dilemma. And probably the same justice sent the warring congregation a man who was a thumbnail diagram of its own battleground. To the pure, all that comes is pure; to the muddled, what offers itself is confused. Could there be some law of arrangement, some inescapable balance which brings about such matching? If you could believe that, you would be conceding that what governs men's affairs is no haphazard chain of chance and accident. You would be saying, in fact, There is God in the design . . . a working God . . . a kind of infinite artist . . .

He realized with a start that he had recklessly fallen into a state of musing which had shut out all his expediency, then he saw that Hoppart was looking at him with respect and approval. The moment of unguarded honesty had been the most strategic expediency.

"I like a thoughtful, quiet man, Doctor Our," Hoppart said naïvely. "I'm frank to tell you I like your approach to this."

He took Jubey over to see the new church, a building unexpectedly large and very beautiful. The mortar between the bricks was scarcely dry, and the clean smell of new wood and new carpeting came sweeping out in a cool blast when the door was opened. Tall parallel gleams of the gold and green of ornamental organ pipes made beautiful the background at either side of the pulpit, and Jubey thought in a panic of wistful escapism, Maybe they'd let me play the organ . . . maybe I could say I'm a better organist than a preacher . . . yes, that would save me. . . . Then he steadied himself and shouldered his unwelcome destiny for which he had worked and sacrificed.

"I can see you like it," Hoppart said complacently. "We're told it's the finest church between New York and Cleveland."

"But how on earth . . . if the church wasn't pulling together . . . did they manage to build such a thing?"

"We bit off more than we can chew, to be quite frank. That's why we've got to find a man who can draw the breach together again. You see the money is just about split down the middle."

"Like the theological question itself," Jubey said so dryly that Hoppart glanced at him in alarm, and then gave a conspiratorial snort, perceiving that this young man was establishing comradeship.

The parsonage was not quite so pristine, but it was impressive, a big rambling frame house, porch-deep in bushes; huge green shutters hanging like setter's ears on all the windows gave a mournful expression.

"Will we meet Doctor Carruthers inside?"

"No. He and Mrs. Carruthers are on a week's vacation. A much-needed rest for all of us, I may say, under the circumstances."

Hoppart unlocked the door of a museum of cast-off elegance, ten rooms of heavily carved furniture and balding plush. The house, in fact, resembled no house Jubey had even seen so much as the Savanne dwelling in Woonsocket. If he had come here before he had made that trip, he would have burst out laughing at the thought of Gay in such a place. But now it seemed almost interchangeable with her family's own hideous mansion. Hoppart plainly admired the place, so Jubey said, "Looks as if all it needs is a heap of living."

Hoppart beamed, "Ah, I see you, also, quote my favorite poet," and checked up one more favorable point on Jubey's score.

He put Jubey on the New York train just before dinnertime, with a last admonition to say nothing to anyone, but to wait a few days for a formal invitation to meet the rest of the deacons. Before the month was out Jubey had another interview, and then received an official invitation to be the assistant pastor of Grace Church, in Tacoma, Pennsylvania, at a salary described to him several times by the deacons as "quite handsome, under the existing conditions."

8

GAY'S TRUNKS were being packed, and that was always a dramatic process in the Savanne house. The children enjoyed it because they loved everything their sister owned; this was their chance to see her shoes standing in a long line waiting to be put into shoe cases, and her frocks swooning on their hangers, while Mona on her knees before the theatrical trunks packed with suitable reminiscences of her own glory and glamour. This was their time for fingering the endless perfume bottles, and the half-dozen sparkling hairbrushes, and the big bath sponges; this was Melissa's moment for trying on hats and gloves, and even wrapping herself in the ermine stole, with its dozens of tails like exclamation marks, which people normally wouldn't let her so much as touch.

Even Peter Savanne was cheerful when his daughter was being packed up to return to her career, for he knew it was her chosen world. This was the third season she had been really successful, and it gave him boyish pleasure to have his associates mention it. Several times each winter he made it necessary for himself to go to New York on business. There was no man in the audience more enchanted than he when Gay Savanne danced. She ceased being his daughter for those few moments, and became all that was young and beautiful and full of delight in the world, someone untouchable and exempt from daily ordinariness. Within himself during the short moments while Gay Savanne danced, a secret poet stood upright and lived his brief life. He thought of it afterwards with shyness bordering on mysticism. The outside of the experience of having a star for his daughter was gruff boastfulness; but within there was a vision of a golden moth whirling in unearthly moonlight, evanescent and yet eternal.

Mona Savanne had never seen Gay dance since she had become a star. It seemed rather a strange coincidence, she often said, but whenever she had planned to see Gay dance, at the last moment something happened to prevent it. Once she even broke her ankle and had to spend the next ten weeks sitting on a pink chaise longue, with everybody running around waiting on her. She had made up her mind that this year nothing was going to interfere.

"Because heaven knows Gay will probably be marrying one of these days, and the career will be over," she often said with a sigh. "I know how it was with *me!*"

So now they were getting her ready to go back and the whole house and the whole neighborhood was racked by it. People who remembered her as a happy little girl kept running in to ask if there was anything they could do to help. Gay, whom Mona always said was utterly useless when it came to packing, was darting in and out of the house, urging sherry on callers, escorting visitors back to their cars, dashing off notes and signing for deliveries. She knew the leave-taking was all being overplayed a bit, but she threw herself into it because it gave everyone delight.

The children usually answered the telephone, pelting downstairs and shrieking as they ran, "I'll get it . . . I'll get it. . . ." They loved the excitement of assuring the operator that this *was* the right number, and waiting hopefully for the call to turn out to be a long-distance one which seemed to add personal stature to them.

But when the really important call came through, it happened to be Mona who answered. She reached the telephone first, but almost immediately everybody else in the house converged upon it, the children to listen shamelessly and Gay because she heard her mother's high, rich voice intoning, "Why Roger . . . how wonderful to hear from you . . . we thought you had forgotten us . . . what, my dear? . . . well, Gay's right upstairs. . . . "

She turned and called upstairs, not perceiving that Gay had already arrived, "Darling . . . it's Roger, so hurry. I didn't catch where he's calling from."

The little boys wanted to speak to him, to say they had made a bow and arrow, but needed some elk-skin thongs; did he have any idea where they could get hold of some? Firmly Gay reached over them and took the phone from Mona.

"Roger? . . . oh, how nice . . . " Gay said, and after a moment she turned her back upon the other listeners, trying to establish a bit of privacy.

"Of course I'll listen," she said in a melted-down voice. "You just talk, and I'll listen."

Her mother was prodding her gently and mouthing a question impatiently, "What's he saying, Gay dear?"

She was completely unaware of Mona; everything about her was concentrated on the voice in her ear. She looked as if she were going to weep. "But of course I do," she said at last. "You must have seen that all the time. I didn't ever try to hide it."

There was an agonizing silence while she listened with bright eyes. "No, that's not my attitude toward everybody. It's only my attitude toward you. You wouldn't have any way of judging I suppose, because you never saw me any other way except in love."

Mona said, "Gay, please speak up. Your diction gets worse all the time. You've never learned to breathe decently."

The children said disgustedly to each other in a voice of strong carrying power, "Mush-talk! This'll go on for hours. Ask him about the elk-skin, Gay. Just ask him."

Finally she could bear the surrounding distractions no

longer, so she said into the mouthpiece, "Will you wait just a minute? There's so much noise around . . . and I've got to hear what you're saying. . . . "

She turned upon them fiercely. "Listen, all of you. A man is asking me to marry him, and you're making so much noise I can barely hear him."

"Oh Gay . . . how wonderful," Mona cried. "Let me speak to him, dear."

"I will not let anyone speak to him. I expect this to be the last proposal I'm ever going to listen to. In my whole lifetime. So I'd like to remember what he is saying. If you don't mind."

"Oh, how utterly sweet of you," Mona said, practically in tears. "I must remember that so I can tell his mother."

"His *mother*," Gay said. "What have mothers got to do with this?"

"Mrs. Peatrie will be just as pleased as I am," Mona said emotionally.

"Mrs. Peatrie!" Gay cried disgustedly. "Why on earth should *she* be pleased?"

Then she gave up, and seized the telephone on its long wire and carried it into the pantry, shutting the door firmly.

After a moment of stunned indignation, Mona said to the children, "Your sister is being very rude." Then she got her teeth into the nuisance which was immediate. "But *you* had no business to be here listening and gabbling. This is something very private, and the only person a girl would want around at such a moment is her mother."

The children said, "We can't help it if we're around."

The pantry door opened after a few moments, and a pale Gay put out her head, still listening to whatever was being said. Her habitual concern for everyone got the best of her even at this excited moment; she smiled wanly at the three offenders in the hall, asking them with her eyes to forgive her. Then she spoke into the telephone.

"Is that all, darling? You've spent three minutes telling me why I'd be crazy if I married you. But I'm going to, anyway. I'm going to, and nothing's going to stop me. Not even you, Jubey."

She was crying now, and the two little boys said "Gosh," trying to adjust themselves quickly to the loss of their elk-skin thongs. Mona, half reading her lips, and half knowing by horrified intuition, burst into tears herself.

"*Jubey!* I simply can't believe you'd do such a thing," she said. "After all our sacrifices and hopes, to think you'd throw yourself away. . . . "

The call was over now, and Gay was trembling. She came out of the pantry, and hugged everybody indiscriminately.

Her mother said accusingly, "That utterly peculiar man . . . and all the time there was the wonderful Peatrie family just *begging* you. . . . How *could* it be Jubey?"

"How could it be anybody *but* Jubey?" Gay said unsteadily. "He's the one I really need."

9

GAY, with all her trunks and her engagement as a dancer at a chic new supper club, came down to New York just as she had planned. Jubey expected to be at Grand Central Station to meet her train. Then three hours before it was to arrive, Hoppart telephoned, saying he was in New York on business and wanted to drive Jubey up to Tacoma to spend the night.

"I'd like nothing better," Jubey said hesitantly. "But you see . . . the fact is, I've taken your advice, Mr. Hoppart, about being married."

He could imagine Hoppart's thin face flushing with dismay at the other end of the line. A nervous cackle came over the wire. "Well, my boy . . . I see I'll have to weigh my words a bit, won't I? You mean you've got yourself married in the last few days?"

"No. But I've got myself engaged," Jubey said, grateful that this was being carried on by telephone. "My new fiancée is arriving in New York in a few hours. I wanted to meet her train."

Hoppart was quiet a long dreadful moment. Then he said, "I'd like to give you the benefit of my own experience wherever I can, Doctor Our. I've taken quite a fancy to you."

"I'm very glad of that, sir," Jubey said, realizing this sentiment was only a pleasant preamble to unpleasant advice.

"It's been my own practice to take care of duties first. I've found then that my mind was free for enjoyments and such."

Jubey tried to rally to that trite advice. "You have a sound principle there, Mr. Hoppart. No doubt about that."

Suddenly he felt a necessity for taking some kind of stand on his own principles. If he were going to work with this didactic little bore, he would have to establish stout boundaries between them.

"The thing is, one has several duties, Mr. Hoppart," he said. "I'm afraid you'll have to trust me to decide which has precedence at this moment."

"Well . . ." the Hoppart breath came out in an indignant explosion. But after a few moments' wait for Jubey to repent of his audacity, the dry voice said meekly, "Well, I guess you must choose that for yourself, Doctor Our."

Just before they broke off the conversation, Hoppart had an awkward inspiration. "I'd like to meet that fiancée of yours," he said with unexpected joviality. "Sooner or later she and I will have to join forces behind you, I suppose. How would you and the young lady like to be my guests at dinner tonight?"

"You mean you'd stay over?"

"It might be worth doing," Hoppart said. "As long as I'm actually your sponsor in this new undertaking, perhaps I'd better get the whole picture."

"You'll realize how well chosen are your words, sir, when you see Miss Savanne. She really is a whole picture, and no mistake." Jubey tried to sound hearty since some encounter with Hoppart on this tremulous day seemed unavoidable.

"Pretty, hmn?" Hoppart said with a delighted snort. "Well, I've never been averse to a pretty girl. Though plenty of religious people seem to be. Sour grapes, I always say."

They settled the details of meeting for dinner. Hoppart said ever since he'd been a boy, the Brevoort Hotel had seemed to him the best place in New York to celebrate, whenever celebration was necessary.

Gay's train was due around three, but Jubey was at the station shortly after two, pacing up and down, bumping into people and stumbling over luggage, blind and deaf and slightly demented. A terrible feeling of premonition that Gay had come to her senses had taken possession of him.

He kept going over imaginary meetings with Gay, all of them grotesquely tragic. He would kiss her, of course; everyone kissed in railway stations, thank God. So she'd kiss him. Then he'd better say, giving her every chance, "I've been thinking it over, and I see how selfish it would be for me to expect . . . "

Or, being the honest straightforward kind of person she was, she would probably begin it, "Jubey dear, you really caught me by surprise the other day . . . I just wouldn't be a suitable wife for a minister." If she said that, suppose he said, "That's true. So I've decided that if you'll just wait for me a bit, I'll get started in something else."

Or . . . perhaps she wouldn't even be on the train. Perhaps at the last moment, she just couldn't face telling him. There probably was a wire right now waiting for him in his room. Jackass that he was, he had gone out early, and had missed it. . . .

Maybe her father would be on the train with her. In fact, that would almost make it easier. That good gruff man would say, "Jubey, you can see for yourself how wrong it would be for Gay. . . ."

And man to man, he'd have to admit it freely. He'd say, "Sir, I couldn't agree with you more completely. The thing is, I just got carried away by loving the girl so much."

About here in his torture, he had an idea. He would take a train up to the 125th Street stop, and get on Gay's Pullman. That would bring the whole horrible suspense to a climax fifteen minutes earlier. He would know when he looked into her eyes. . . .

But this plan only added one more agony to the nightmare,

because he nearly missed his connection. When he came thundering down the platform, having run down one flight of stairs and up the other on the incoming side of the tracks, the porter wouldn't let him in the parlor-car section.

"I've got to," Jubey said. "Life or death. Or worse even." He was fumbling in his pockets for some kind of tip, and chattering like an imbecile. "There's a girl in there . . . this is going to change the rest of her life. . . ."

The conductor, a round man in a spruce uniform, came up behind them. "Let him on, Will . . . I'll sell him a ticket."

So just as the wheels were beginning to turn, he scrambled up the iron steps and into the car, the conductor on his heels. He thrust a bill into the official hand and said, "Just take out the fare, and let me get on with this."

Then he dashed down the aisle of the first car. No Gay. The second car was equally empty, and by the fourth he was sure she wasn't on the train. Then he saw her, laughing up at a man who was entertaining her from the next chair. She didn't see Jubey, and he stood there overwhelmed by her beauty and the quality of her. She had on a dark suit and the tight little corsage of violets he had ordered sent to her this morning. Her white-gloved hands were crossed demurely in her lap, and those gray eyes were full of quiet mirth and appreciation. You couldn't look at her without knowing she was someone very special; she would have been a distinguished young person on a desert island, Jubey thought wordlessly. And he had presumed to think . . .

She lifted her eyes then to notice that a man was standing behind her train companion's chair and was staring down at her. Her eyes went through a small lifetime of feeling. They widened in quick pleasure, and then they seemed to waver and reassemble their light as a jewel sometimes does. The laughter went out of her face, and her teeth caught her lower lip as if unexpected delight had spurted through her body. Then her hands came out to him, and remembered themselves, and fell back in her lap.

"Jubey." That was all she said. But it was in a tone that melted away the man in the adjoining chair, and all else.

"I couldn't wait," Jubey said. "I was afraid . . ."

"Oh, Jubey," she said. "I was afraid too. You could so easily have changed your mind."

"*I* could have!" he said in a loud voice. Then they both laughed, and somehow the entertaining man must have appraised the situation and removed himself, for the next time they thought of him Jubey was sitting in his chair, leaning forward and holding both her hands in his.

"People are wonderful," Jubey said when they realized what had happened.

"It's the old chestnut about the world loving lovers," Gay pointed out tremulously.

"You sound like Hoppart."

"Hoppart? Some writer I should know?"

"Nope. Worse than that. Chairman of the board of deacons in my new church. You'll know him, all right. He's seen to that." Then apologetically he told her about tonight's inescapable invitation. She looked terrified at the thought.

"Oh, Jubey, suppose he doesn't like me?" she said.

Jubey laughed then. "A couple of hundred thousand people took one look at you and fell in love with you. So."

"But people like What's-his-name are different."

"You think so? Well, that's what we're going to find out in the next few years," he said soberly. "If they are, we're sunk."

"No, that isn't it. If they are, you'll have to change them, Jubey. Isn't that what a minister is for? To change people?"

"I hope not," he said. "I like 'em fine, the way they are." The train was in now, and the other passengers had drained out of the cars before they realized they were sitting alone, lost in themselves.

They went up the ramp, then Jubey excused himself and ran ahead through the gates into the waiting crowd. When she came in with the last of the tide of arrivals, he had his hat in his hand, and a burlesqued welcome on his face. With appropriate ardor he took her eagerly in his arms and kissed her.

"Oh, darling . . . I thought you'd never get here," he said. For both of them the shattering reality of the kiss broke the make-believe of Jubey's exaggeration, and left them helpless for a moment.

"This is what railway stations were built for," he said. "I couldn't let the architects down, could I?"

"You fool . . . you absolute fool," she said, half laughing and half crying at the kiss.

Her living room at the Sherry Netherlands was filled with flowers and telegrams and messages. Would Miss Savanne call this and that? Miss Savanne would call none of them. Pete had wired her agent she was coming in at six tonight to keep people from meeting her train. Would Jubey telephone the agent and say her plans had changed and that she was in but couldn't see anyone until tomorrow morning? Jubey would, with goose pimples.

Before he had hung up from the call, she came and sat on the floor at his feet. She put her arms around his knees and looked up into his face with utter earnestness.

"Jubey . . . there's only one thing."

"What's that, Gay?"

"I'd die if I did anything to interfere with your work."

A strange paragraph of unreadable fine print suddenly unrolled in his mind. He knew what it said all right, for it was the embryo alibi excusing failure which would make life bearable for him. Here was the clause of exquisite escape, usually sought at the beginning of enterprise to save face later, if success is withheld.

In a flash of relief he saw it: For my beautiful wife, I gave up the ministry, he heard his future, middle-aged voice saying. To his children? To his business associates? And most ignominious shame of all . . . to himself?

They couldn't appreciate Gay . . . so it was out of the question for me to continue. . . . Would he deceive himself when the moment came by mouthing such alibi? People did. Better people than he.

He glanced around the room, a setting utterly right for Gay, and far removed from anything he could give her. She sat at his feet in this defenseless attitude, her lovely face full of trust and expectation. All around her were the appurtenances of her success. And she was willing to give it all up for him! He knew this was a moment he would remember all his life. If things went well with them, this moment would be his secret treasure; if the whole strange destiny became a ghastly debacle as it so easily could become, this moment would be the hinge on which it swung.

Gay said, "I'd rather give you up right now . . . loving you as much as I do . . . than do anything to hurt your career."

He said with harsh honesty, "I'm walking on a tightrope at the moment. God knows whether I'll make it or not. If I don't make it, Gay, we'd crash together."

"Women who love their men always take that risk."

"Yes. But you don't have to take it. You've made yourself a wonderful life. And what do I do? With nothing but uncertainty to offer you, I'm ready to tear your career up by the roots."

"My career?" she cried in surprise, lifting herself in one fluid motion so that she came into his arms as soft and swift as light. "From today on, my career is you, Jubey. I've got to be a success at that. Or it will break my heart."

10

<hr style="border: 2px solid black;" />

THEY SPENT the hours before Hoppart's dinner talking about Jubey's visits to Tacoma. They avoided discussing the immediate steps that must be taken in terminating Gay's present obligations and contracts. "I'll get out of them honorably," she said. "Don't worry about it, Jubey."

When it was time for her to dress, Jubey went downstairs and paced up and down the lobby, trying not to look too conspicuously triumphant. In the street, there came the moment usually awkward for him, but apparently of no concern to Gay, when they had to choose between taxi and bus. He fought the small battle, and the future won, so they waited for the Fifth Avenue bus, holding hands secretly.

Gay said, "I feel the way I did when I went to see about my first job. Scared to death, yet pleased, too. Wishing I didn't have to face it, and knowing that nothing on earth could persuade me to dodge it."

"It's not as important as all that," Jubey said. "If that old alligator doesn't like you, we'll just go somewhere else and preach."

"But suppose the next place didn't like me either? Suppose they disapprove of dancers?"

"Then we'll join a circus and have fun. I'll be the barker and you can dance with trained seals."

"Jubey, be serious."

"It's too serious to be serious about," he said, with a lugubrious grin.

They found Mr. Hoppart sitting in the lobby of the Brevoort, his prim hat balanced on his knees and a small florist's
box on the floor beside his well-shined shoes. The sight of the
corsage box touched Jubey, and he thought with gruff affection, Guess *he* knows a thing or two, by cracky.

Hoppart got to his feet and put out his dry wrinkled hand,
taking the initiative in the introductions. "So this is Miss
Savanne. *Well.*" Beaming all over his face he looked posi-
tively waggish, as if Gay's beauty were a naughty indiscretion
in which he was about to participate. "I must say this is an
honor. I wonder if you happen to be related to that actress my
boy thinks is so wonderful?"

Gay said, spending one of her reticent smiles, "I used to be,
Mr. Hoppart. But I'm not related to her any more."

"Oh? Is that so?" Hoppart looked perplexed and at the same
time eager for some tidbit of gossip which he could carry back
to his son. Constructive gossip, of course, with a moral attached.

"We're giving each other up," Gay said, blushing a bit as she
realized the Hoppart reaction.

"What Gay means, sir . . . " Jubey began, feeling a trickle of
perspiration between his shoulder blades. "You see, the fact
is . . . "

"You see, I was the dancer," Gay said. "But I'm going to
give that up now, because I've got something much more important to do."

Hoppart took this in slowly, and his leathery face turned a
rich morocco color. "You mean you *are* the famous dancer?"

"Not very famous," Gay said. "Only around New York.
And only for the last few months." She was doing her gallant
best to discount and cancel out all achievement of hers.

"And you mean this young man here has persuaded you . . . "

"I persuaded him," Gay said. "I'd like to tell you all about
it sometime, Mr. Hoppart. You see, I have so much faith in

him . . . and I believe so completely in what he is going to do. . . . "

Hoppart took off his rimless glasses, and wiped his eyes meticulously. "Well, that's a very remarkable situation," he said at last. "I must say, my dear . . . " He bent over then and picked up the white box and handed it to her diffidently. "I've brought you a few posies. I'm afraid they're not the kind you're accustomed to, but I thought . . . "

She took the box graciously and opened it with dexterous ease, lifting out a small tight cluster of carnations and baby's breath, tied with an economical rosette of silver ribbon. "They're beautiful, and I thank you, Mr. Hoppart. I was afraid of you before I met you, but now I can see what a kind man you are. We'll be friends, won't we?"

He looked helplessly delighted at the prospect, and went into a flutter of arrangements about the dinner.

"I've reserved a table," he said, "so I guess we shouldn't keep them waiting." He led the way into the dining room, glancing neither to the left nor the right, and bouncing a bit on the balls of his feet.

He pulled back Gay's chair and seated her, blissfully self-conscious. Then he seated himself opposite her, smoothing down his sparse hair as if he felt it must be standing on end with excitement. Jubey thought to himself, I might as well not be here. That's the Gay of it, and it's wonderful to watch.

They ordered, Hoppart extending himself more and more, calling the headwaiter and asking about Hollandaise sauce, urging brook trout on his guests, and reminiscing about the baked Alaska that used to be his special treat when he was a boy. Led on by Gay, he had become quite a raconteur, enjoying himself to the point of intoxication.

Over the salad they became serious, for Mr. Hoppart wanted to explain to Gay something about the town and the difficulties of the church, and the precarious building expenses for which it was obligated. She listened with intelligence in her quiet eyes, and Jubey thought, Is this thinking, or only looking like thinking? What she says when he's finished will tell, all right.

Hoppart was nearing the end of the account, the steps of which Jubey knew well, from having heard it several times. "So you see, this young man's got his work cut out for him," he said. "No mistake about that."

Then Gay said something which caught Jubey utterly without warning. "But it's God's work," she said. "And God will do it. Jubey only has to do what God tells him to."

Hoppart's face flamed as if he had heard something slightly indecent. Then he recovered himself, and began nodding sagely. "Very true, very true, my dear," he said. "But of course I've been talking on the practical side."

"But that *is* the practical side, isn't it?" she asked without guile. "Anything else would be a kind of insubordination, wouldn't it? It would be like one of the office boys in an investment company deciding he knew more than the president . . . maybe investing some of the company's funds without consulting the expert. Wouldn't it be like that, sort of?"

Hoppart looked anything but comfortable at this. He laughed rather loudly and rubbed his hands together as if in appreciation of a rather clever joke. "That's quite an original way of looking at it, my dear. I can see you're very clever about things."

"But it's not original at all," Gay said, growing a bit pink herself in her earnestness. "It's the way Jesus looked at it, isn't it? Didn't he say, 'Of my own self I can do nothing. It is the Father who worketh in me.'"

"That's right," Hoppart said in an indulgent tone. "And it would no doubt be quite wonderful if we could remember that." But he looked positive that none of them would do anything so impractical as remembering it. He sought Jubey's eye in a comradely attempt to establish masculine solidarity in the presence of this delightful and absurd femininity. Jubey evaded his eye, hiding his face behind a hearty gulp of water from one of the heavy goblets.

But Gay was not to be put off by any patronizing and flattering big-man-to-little-woman attitude. Her sincerity was shining out of her and wouldn't be dimmed by superficial pleasantness.

"Mr. Hoppart, something tremendous has happened to me since I've known Jubey," she said.

"Well, he's quite a tremendous young man," Hoppart said, relieved to be on more solid ground.

"No. I don't mean that," she insisted. "Since I've known Jubey, I've found God. This summer I had a chance to work at it. I never used to pay the slightest attention to God. I guess I was saving him for my old age, or something. But since I've known Jubey I've begun reading the Bible. And even more than that . . . I've begun listening inside myself. I can't explain it very well, but I'm sure you know."

Hoppart was sitting back in his chair now, looking at her with a strange humility in his homely face. They both had forgotten Jubey. The stumbling words of Gay were only an echo of a silent conversation which seemed to be flowing back and forth between the two of them.

"I haven't any idea how people usually pray," Gay said, "so I've just been talking to God the way I talk to my own father. Then I listen to what he has to say to me."

"And does he say something?" Hoppart asked, as if he were the courtier talking to the child in the crowd who had innocence enough to see that the emperor was naked.

"Sometimes he does," she said honestly. "Sometimes I wait and nothing seems to come. But I imagine it's like anything else. I imagine you have to learn how to do it, how to listen, that is. It's a foreign language, in a way. Or maybe it would be better to say it's being spoken on some kind of spiritual wave-lengths that are higher than human speech . . . the way radio music couldn't be heard until we found the right kind of instruments and tubes and things. Do you suppose that's the way it is?"

"Probably," Hoppart said. "Probably something like that, my dear."

Suddenly, then, Gay remembered that it was Jubey who was supposed to be the authority. She looked at him in radiant apology, and impulsively put out her hand and touched his arm.

"Jubey?" she said questioningly. "Jubey?"

"I've just been thinking," he said, covering her hand with his own. "Maybe you're the minister in the family. Maybe I'd better take some dancing lessons."

Hoppart threw back his head and laughed with relief. Then unexpectedly he rose from his chair and excused himself. Jubey scrambled to his own feet, thinking irreverently of the old man's kidneys.

"If you'll excuse me, I'll leave you young people awhile to your own devices," he said. As Jubey sat down again at the table, he saw him speaking to the headwaiter.

"They must have moved the gents' room since Hoppart was a boy," he said.

She laughed and caught her lip with her white teeth. "Jubey, you have no respect . . . "

"But I've plenty of respect for you," he said, leaning toward her. "You handled that old boy magnificently. It was the best show I've seen in years."

She looked troubled. Then she changed the subject for a bit. But she couldn't leave it at that, so she came back to it earnestly.

"Jubey . . . you didn't really think that, did you?"

"Think what, darling?"

"That I was . . . handling him."

"Well, maybe that wasn't the prettiest word. But you were certainly giving him catnip. And he was certainly reveling in it."

"But that wasn't it at all." She looked as if she would weep.

"There's nothing wrong, Gay! We knew you'd have to win the old guy somehow. I just didn't think you had it in you to do it the way you did."

After a few minutes she said. "All right. Let's don't talk about it." He saw then that he really had hurt her. He was annoyed with himself now for being crude and blunt; usually he had enough appreciation for art and finesse not to dissect it, in such gauche and ugly fashion. He would have to make it up to her some way, but now was hardly the moment, for Hoppart would no doubt be back soon.

But instead of Hoppart, the headwaiter came to their table, and handed Gay a note, written on Brevoort paper and sealed in an envelope.

"The gentleman . . . your host, Miss Savanne . . . has been called away. He wanted me to extend his apologies."

Gay took the note and opened the envelope. She read it first, then passed it over to Jubey.

My dear young lady:

I thank you for taking time to dine with an old man on your first night in New York. Now you two enjoy yourselves.

Most of all thank you for telling me what you did. I will never forget it. Your friend,

SAMUEL HOPPART

Jubey read the note through twice. It was shy and clumsy, and yet it had more grace about it than he himself had shown.

"He's quite a little guy," he said contritely.

"Imagine him having delicacy enough to know that we

wanted to be by ourselves," Gay said, rewarding the apology which Jubey wanted to give, but which some boyishness made it impossible for him to express.

The waiter was bringing the dessert, a pink and white masterpiece, baked Alaska garnished with strawberries, the greedy dream of a departed child. Gay appeared now to have forgotten everything else but this rather touching gesture of their host.

But Jubey was thinking about her. He felt an unreasonable panic in him, because the invisible circle closing ever more tightly around him was suddenly seen to have a link in it which was Gay herself. He had thought of Gay as the link which would open and let him escape if this life became too intolerable; but now he saw that she might easily become the strongest chain of his bondage. The words in which this thought came startled him.

Then, without warning, a new and terrible yearning for Gay's own kind of simplicity swept over him with almost a nausea of forlornness. Why must I torture myself this way? he cried inwardly. Why don't I just give up? He's bigger than I am, so why do I try to fight him?

In a moment he got his unreasonable panic under control, and reworded his inner observation. He said steadily, "That girl! Here she is with a brand new talent! That's what it is . . . nothing mystical. Simply a talent like her dancing. A great adaptability, a supple way of fitting herself to whatever life she chooses. She's a dancer, inside and out!"

"What is it?" she asked suddenly, turning from the ludicrous confection and looking into his face.

"I'm just thinking how much you know . . . and what a dummkopf I am beside you."

"Now you're making fun of me," she said sadly.

A drench of relief and joy poured through him. This was no metaphysical adversary . . . this was his true love, his de-

licious morsel! He cried within himself in keenest mirth, This
is she! No mistake about it. She said that exactly the way
Lucile used to speak to Papa.

It was for him a moment of excruciating delight. But for
her, it was the first far-off alarm of a warning which she knew
she would not heed, because of her reckless love for Jubal Our.

11

By Christmas they knew Grace Church was suffering from a mortal illness.

The first days in Tacoma were easier than Jubey had anticipated. The curiosity of the town and the church members smoothed the way for him. Even if they were only giving him plenty of rope, as Hoppart platitudinously warned, both sides were going along with him. Both sides, in fact, courted him with not too subtle canniness. For a few weeks he was the most popular man in the community.

Dr. Eban Carruthers, a shy, innocent theologian whose aching integrity had brought about this division, was glad to retire behind Jubey's broad shoulder. Within a few days, the minister had turned over to him practically all his duties except the actual preaching of sermons.

The part of his job which Jubey liked best was now his, the personal part, the counciling and sympathizing. He was, in fact, a mission worker still. But now his cases didn't involve alcoholism and poverty and the slovenly small crimes which grow out of fright and lack; now he worked with more subtle misdemeanors. But it was still purely social work, and God didn't intrude much in it.

God minds his own business, and I mind mine, Jubey sometimes said to himself, when he thought about this. And let's keep it that way, shall we?

He was offered a very pleasant suite of rooms on the top floor of a house belonging to old stand-bys of the church.

There was a bedroom, a big sunny sitting room and study, and an old-fashioned bath with a marble tub big enough to teach ducks to swim, if the occasion ever arose, or so he wrote to Gay, describing it. There was also a kitchen on this floor, because the Temple's daughter and son-in-law had once kept house there. The kitchen door was now locked, but Jubey hoped that someday this winter it might be opened and Gay and a can opener installed.

The first evenings he spent in the apartment were strangely haunted by Rose Kramer and the shabby room with the cooking alcove where they had lived their odd abortive life. He wished Rose could see these rooms of his; she would admire them, and would explain them to him in a way which might quiet the uneasiness he felt in them.

He knew why he thought of Rose here. This was going to be his true home, just as that had been his false home. Nothing ever could erase the comfort of that false home she had made for him, just as no woman . . . not even his beautiful Gay . . . could ever take the strange evanescent place of that stern and ardent girl who had hurt herself by blundering out of her orbit into his. She had brought him so much more than she realized, for she had given him a sense of his own violent manhood. It never would be possible to explain Rose to anyone, nor the love he had for her. But he would never forget it, for whenever he thought of it, a surge of pathos and protectiveness made his very bones weak with gratitude for her.

The breach between the two factions of the church widened with the passing of the weeks. The theological controversy which had started the trouble was practically left behind, for once the spirit of division was given right of way, there was division on all opinions. Everyone disliked the persons with whom they disagreed, and justification piled up to reinforce dislike, until the whole town became a tumult of gossip and accusation.

Dr. Carruthers, cringing behind his closed study door, became more and more timid and confused, knowing that every word he uttered in his sermons was being weighed as a stone to hurl back at him. By the expressions on the faces throughout the congregation, one could identify the rock collectors; their lifted faces looked like slingshots, waiting.

One night a little before Christmas a committee visited Jubey in his rooms, a righteous, exhilarated group with fierce Old Testament quotations clutched in their minds to reinforce their anger. Their plan was to "take out their letters" from the church in a protesting body. They would meet in the Masonic Temple for the present, and they wanted to offer Jubey a call to be their pastor. Then they would bring suit against the other members for possession of the new church building, on the grounds that having departed from the true faith, the others had forfeited their property rights.

They had brought an attorney with them, a plump deliberate man named Blacken. He assured Jubey that he could make a creditable case, and that the young assistant minister was running no risk in joining them. After the others had left, he lingered a moment to emphasize a particular point. It might very well happen, he said, that this case could attract the attention of the prominent religionists of the country. Such things had happened before, Blacken said, and men found themselves "made" at the very beginning of their careers. Young Dr. Our might find himself in a most favorably conspicuous position.

"I don't want to be favorably conspicuous," Jubey said, trying to keep his distaste from showing. "I only want to get started in my work."

"Well, you think about it. If you were a bit more seasoned, you'd recognize this as opportunity."

"But I was hired to see that just such 'opportunity' wouldn't happen."

The lawyer said, "You might as well go along with it in the most sensible way possible. I'm frank to tell you that if you don't want to accept the offer, these people will find a young man who does. They're determined to get possession of the church building, and run it the way they please. You can't stop it."

With frightened intuition Jubey realized that because the very root of his own conviction was split, every act that grew from that root was warped and double. There had been a traitorous grafting upon a good tree, and the fruit was bitter to itself, however sound it might appear.

There was no way he could behave in a completely honorable way. If he told Hoppart that the dissenters were planning to bring suit in court for possession of the building, he was betraying the confidence of the withdrawing members; if he didn't tell Hoppart, he was protecting a confidence he had no right to possess. It was a dilemma demanding a Solomon who had the courage to propose dividing the contested "child" down the middle, in order to force those who really loved the church to protect it from being killed. Jubey felt like no Solomon. He felt, in fact, like the babe itself, claimed by two quarreling women.

If he had known how to pray, he would have prayed for an all-wise Solomon to save him.

12

In the end, however, the best thing that ever happened to him was brought about by the unhappy situation.

He had the big square emerald which Papa had given him set in a finely designed ring for Gay Savanne. Out of sheer boyish exuberance he showed it to Hoppart, who said, "You can't do less than take it down to her yourself, Jubal."

"Except that I can't afford a trip just now," Jubey said, flushing.

"Who says so?" the old man said gruffly. "If you were working for a lawyer or a banker, or even a grocery store, you'd think you were entitled to afford something decent once in awhile, wouldn't you?"

Jubey nodded, bewildered about where this was leading.

"The people who work for God ought to credit him with as much generosity as other employers, hadn't they?"

"I suppose so, sir," Jubey said dejectedly.

"Well, here then," the old idealist said crankily, fumbling in his vest pocket and thrusting several bills at Jubey in an angry accusing way.

"I can't take your money, Mr. Hoppart," Jubey said.

"It's my tithing," Hoppart said. "I call it God's postage stamps."

"But even so."

"Don't argue. Just let it take you down to New York to see that young lady. Don't know how you made her fall in love with you in the first place."

"Don't know either," Jubey said. "And thank you."

"Nonsense," Hoppart said. "I don't want to hear any more about it."

"Gay will love you for it," Jubey said. "She loves you already."

The old man shook his head protestingly, blushing like a boy. "I'm not supposed to get personal pleasure out of my tithing," he said.

"I don't think God would begrudge you Gay's thanks. Maybe we can credit him with courtesy as well as generosity," Jubey said, slyly amplifying the old man's remarks.

He gave Gay no warning that he was coming, but slipped into the supper club where she was dancing out a ten weeks' engagement. He got a table in an obscure corner, and ordered as frugally as possible. It was a charming room, with a slightly raised stage at one end. As soon as the curtains parted on Gay's first dance she saw him. He knew the minute she became aware of him, and he began to tremble with excitement. When the dance was finished, and she was taking her third bow, wearing now a cream velvet cape which covered her golden gauze costume, she suddenly put up her hand and stopped the applause.

"Will you forgive me if I tell you something?" she said to the crowded room in her grave sweet voice. She waited seriously until a flutter of approval came across the intimate footlights from the doting audience before she continued.

"If I'm dancing better than usual tonight, it's because the man . . . I love . . . is down there among you. I didn't expect him, but he's here."

A delighted murmur ran around the large room. Everyone broke into applause and looked around hoping some man would give himself away by embarrassment. Laughing, Gay shook her head. "I'm not going to tell you where he is," she said. *"Don't give yourself away, darling."*

Jubey, too, was now applauding and twisting in his seat as if to discover the star's lover. He felt that if anyone so much as glanced at him, his happiness would betray itself. But he was safe, for the audience was looking for a more romantic-appearing man than he.

Then she danced an encore out of her evident delight. Jubey slipped away soon after she had finished, sending back a note to tell her he would meet her at her hotel. He had news sense enough to know that reporters would spring up from nowhere, and he wanted to be sure Gay wanted the announcement made in this informal fashion.

She came straight into his arms when she opened the door of her little sitting room.

"Oh, Jubey . . . most people would be furious with me for doing that. But you didn't care."

"I loved it," he said. "The ham in me loved it, Gay."

"Of course," she said laughing. "It was fun, wasn't it?"

"Swell fun. And more than that. You understand the ham in me. If I didn't already know how good this stuff is going to be, I'd know now."

"It's going to be perfect," she said.

She reached for the telephone, and he said, "I've ordered. I asked them to send two of everything you usually have."

"It will shock you. I'm hungry as a horse."

"Nothing you ever do could shock me. It's fine with me that you look like a hummingbird, and eat like a horse."

"It's fine with me, too, if you think a preacher's wages can cover the situation."

"That's what I've come down to talk about," he said. "But first. . . ." He took the ring out of his pocket. No box, no wrappings, just the beautiful deep emerald set in simple plat-inum. He didn't put it on her hand with any graceful speech. He didn't put it on her hand at all. He simply thrust it at her with wordless sincerity. She took it with her eyes on his face, realizing that when Jubey really was moved, there were no words. She put it on her own finger, and impulsively lifted it and kissed the stone, then put her arms around Jubey's neck and kissed him.

"It's from Papa and me both," he said clumsily. "I kept wondering and wondering why he gave it to me. Then I found out."

During their supper he told her about the impossible situation in the church.

"You can't struggle with all that alone," she said decisively. "I'm coming up to help you."

"You mean . . . you'd marry me right away?"

"Doctor Our . . . what else could I mean?" she cried, making her large eyes even larger. Then she looked at him with delicious seriousness. "I've been looking for an excuse, Jubey."

"But . . . but . . . how'll you get out of things?"

"I've been getting out of them, one by one."

"And the salary, Gay. You've no idea. You know when I first told you, you thought it was for a *week*."

"I was young then, young and unrealistic. Now I'm a woman in love."

"Even women in love don't become thrifty overnight."

"Who said anything about overnight? I've been studying budgets for weeks. And practicing self-denial. And besides . . . we'll have all the important things, so why would we care about the things old money can buy?"

"Well, for one thing, you eat like a horse," he said gruffly, "and so, God wot, do I."

"It's too late to dissuade me," Gay said.

They settled down at last to discussing concrete plans. They would have a real wedding; Mona would never forgive them if she didn't have a wedding to engineer. And Pete, too; Pete would want to give her away.

"And your family will have to come from the West, Jubey."

"My family? I haven't any family," Jubey said. Then guilt-

ily he remembered Minna. "Of course Minna will want to be
there. Earnest too ... Oh, Gay ... does it have to be like that?"

"Just once in a lifetime, and the rest of our lives we'll live
as we please."

They settled on December 29, which was the Savannes' wedding anniversary. "That way, they'll always be celebrating
their own day, so they'll leave us alone on ours," Gay pointed
out.

"You don't fool me. I know you're just sentimental enough
to realize if there'd never been the Savannes, there couldn't be
the Ours."

"The Ours," Gay cried. "A toast to their 'forever and ever!' "

"A toast to Tacoma giving the assistant pastor a slight raise
in pay."

"A toast to our not caring whether they do or not."

He got the milk train back to Tacoma; no use wasting
money on a hotel room. After all, four dollars was a lot of
money for a man who was too happy to sleep anyway.

Minna wrote Jubey four gushing pages of complacency when
she received Mrs. Savanne's invitation to spend the week of
the wedding in Woonsocket. They weren't going to be able to
accept the invitation. They were, in fact, expecting another
"little stranger," she said.

That's one way of putting it, Jubey thought. But if I know
Minna and Earnest, it won't be such a *little* stranger. Probably weigh twelve pounds, stripped.

Marriage was going to solve everything for Jubey, Minna
said, just as it had solved everything for her. With clumsy
delicacy she hinted that Jubey's wandering restlessness had no
doubt been purely biological. Now he would find himself safe
and settled. Jubey read two pages, then let his eye bounce
down the third and fourth pages, lighting on only a couple of
perches before he folded the letter and chucked it back in its
sedate gray envelope.

Hostilities were briefly laid aside in Tacoma for the sake of Christmas. Nobody had any illusions about the armistice being more than temporary, but everyone was grateful for the momentary grace. The ugly town had taken on an ephemeral beauty for the holidays. A heavy snow fell two days before Christmas, a blank white sheet on which the gaunt houses, the towering telegraph poles, and the shivering, naked trees were drawn with bold beauty. A few sleighs came out of country barns, and deep-tone bells clattered and chimed on the thick necks of work horses clumping about the streets.

Jubey, as always in his delights, wished that Gay could see the little city as it looked now. By the time they came back to it after New Year's, drabness would have tranished the snow, and the townspeople, too, would have discovered once again that what was in the beribboned boxes was only sorry merchandise, and not some magic performed by giving.

He had promised Dr. Carruthers that he would stand by through Christmas, prepared to preach a sermon on the Nativity, if the regular minister didn't feel up to it when the moment came. He would get through Christmas somehow . . . anyhow . . . for on the twenty-seventh, he was going up to Woonsocket to be married.

The morning of the twenty-third he woke up early, and before anything else, he thought, In six days we'll be married. He tried to imagine Gay in this room. She would fit anywhere; she had some secret within her which made her at home wherever she was. And he, too, would be at home now because he would have her with him forever. Never homeless again, never unsatisfied and forlorn, as jolly men so often are in their innermost silences. Would she guess that? Was she capable of suspecting that he filled the air around himself with noise and good nature, because at the core of him was a silent and bewildered exile?

He should have tried to make her understand that before

she got herself into this marriage. Perhaps it wasn't fair to her, good simple child that she was. As so often happened, a fragment of Bible language brushed across his mind. " . . . unequally yoked together with unbelievers . . . " The stark word shocked him; yet it was the apt word.

He could not bear to face that word describing himself, so he veered from that to a contemplation of the mechanism of the human mind. How perfect was the filing system . . . the cross references . . . maintained by the meticulous human brain. He might have searched for hours through literature to find a quotation as fitting as that, as tragically fitting. Yet the wonderfully tabulated subconscious mind found it unerringly, and presented it so courteously that one might not even notice it unless one dared. Could one believe that there was some superintelligence latent beyond the upper mind? A robust, resilient thinker who made himself known only now and then, as agile antagonist when there was a point that must be made, or as resourceful ally, when comfort and support dared be given? Could that watcher within be what the saints identified as God?

He got up and drew his bath in the preposterously luxurious bathtub. He allowed himself to sing, not at the top of his lungs as he wanted to, but circumspectly, like an assistant pastor. Long icicles hung from the eaves above the bathroom window. He knew he never would see an icicle without thinking of the room in the Portland attic.

"I'm getting married in six days, darling," he said to Rose suddenly. "I wish you could see her. She's what you had in mind."

He knew this was going to be a full day, and he was glad of that. He had a scribbled list of errands and assignments on the top of his dresser, which began with a call on old Dr. Bennicker, noisily dying, and ended with a rehearsal of the townspeople who were going to sing carols on Christmas Eve. He had a gift for Mr. Hoppart, two fine old books he would be proud of owning and would never get around to reading. He would write a little note to tuck in with the books. It would be hard to tell Mr. Hoppart what he really felt about him, the gratitude and the strange affection, reluctant to be given because it was reluctantly received. But he must say it anyway, because he felt it.

He made the sick calls, seven of them. He had managed to find some small gift to take to each house, an old *National Geographic* to Dr. Bennicker who had been born in Labrador; a sprig of mistletoe to fasten on the headboard of the bed where the town's little milliner was recuperating in a becoming pink bed jacket she'd never before had time to wear; some excellent cigars to a farmer now on the mend. He found himself unexpectedly happy about the trivial gifts, and he remembered how Papa had beamed when he could assume the posture of giving. Giving was one of the refined pleasures. And the fewer worldly goods you had to bestow, the more exquisite was the pleasure when you managed. He would do a sermon about it someday . . . one of the unsung compensations of not being rich.

At three he went over to Dr. Carruthers to admire his notes for the sermon. Dr. Carruthers bleak face was pink and almost cheerful, for he had been associating with wise men and angels, and it was easy to believe there was peace on earth and good will among men, even in Tacoma.

"Christmas always smooths things out," he said hopefully. "Wouldn't surprise me a bit if the whole trouble was blowing over. Mrs. Stallings said good morning to my wife in the meat market yesterday." Jubey tried to agree with this optimism as they sat and talked into the early twilight. Mrs. Carruthers in a daisy-sprigged dress came into the library with a tray of fruit cake and tea.

"I don't know whether or not we've ever got around to telling you how glad we are you're here, Doctor Our," she said, sitting on the edge of her chair and sipping decorously.

"I'm glad, too," Jubey said, wishing it were entirely true.

At five he went over to the church, hushed and empty and mysteriously beautiful. The carol singers would begin arriving in a few minutes. But first he would play the organ. He had waited all day for this moment, this secret tryst. He would let all his happiness and his sadness and the richness of his love throb out in music. The organ was his best friend in this town. . . . He knew the organist resented his playing, but he couldn't keep away from the excellent instrument. He played much too easily to be forgiven by the perspiring professional. Whenever Mr. Mattox was in the building, Jubey tactfully fumbled and tripped and squeezed out thin trickling music. But Mr. Mattox was not here now, so he could play with full abandon. No thin watery melody now, but the rich wine of deep music, welling up and up until it filled the church and pulsed against the ruby windows.

When he finished, he turned on the bench and looked over the green curtain that was supposed to conceal the organist from the congregation. A row of listeners had gathered halfway back in the dark church.

"We knew that must be you, Doctor Our," one of the women said delightedly. "Nobody else plays the way you do. Like you just were bursting with happiness."

"That's just what I am," Jubey said. And this time it was more than true.

"My, I almost wish they'd let you be our organist," someone said shyly. "I always wished church music could sound . . . well, you know . . . pleased about things."

"I bet you'll preach that kind of sermons, too," someone else said in a burst of extravagant praise. "I just wish you'd get your chance."

He walked home through the lovely night, his overshoes squeaking on the crisp packed snow. The houses were full of lights, and along the streets figures were hurrying home. Some waved to him, recognizing him by his tallness, and he waved back, thinking, It's going to be good. We can stand it, because we'll have each other. We'll make a game of it. Gay and I will always make a game of things.

His landlady had asked him to have dinner with the family, so he ran upstairs and washed and glanced at the mail on his desk, and finding nothing from Gay, ran down again without opening any envelopes. Two shy children of the house were waiting at the bottom of the stairs for him, and he took them by the hand and went into the stuffy parlor and sat down with one on each knee to read them the funnies.

"You read good," one of them said when he paused. "I wish Papa read good like you."

"I'll remember that and tell it to my children."

"Have you got some children somewhere, Doctor Our?"

"Not yet. But I will have, Georgie. I sure will have. And I'll read good to them, too."

"Um-hmn," the little boy said in deep contentment. "Children like that."

Their mother called them and they all gathered about a round table steaming with mashed potatoes and turnips and a sizzling pork roast. Before anyone could touch a bite, all hands had to be in evidence, kneeling respectfully on the edge of the table, while Jubey said a grace. A short merciful grace, with one eye on the roast.

"You light your gas log tonight, Doctor Our," his landlady said with reckless generosity. "You just light your gas log, because it's real cold out."

"Man about to be married like Doctor Our don't know whether it's cold or hot," the landlady's husband said daringly. "No use wasting good gas on him, I expect."

The children still had pastework to do on their mother's Christmas present, so Jubey helped them behind a closed door, then went cheerfully up to his own domain. He would read awhile, then he would go out for a walk under the high new moon. He had a walk to do every night, because there was always a bulging letter to Gay that had to be mailed.

He lit the ugly gas log and sat in his deep chair, with the smaller one that would be Gay's pulled up beside it. A great richness was in him, from all the people he had loved this day. He saw that this was a good world. If this pinched, divided little town could seem good in spite of the angry currents that ran through it, any place could be good. All one needed was to know how to love what was present. To find the goodness in man, and hold it up to the light where it could be seen. There was a verse about that somewhere. He got up and took his Bible and brought it back to the chair. He searched awhile, never too sure of locations. Yes, here it was . . . in the book of Job:

"If there be a messenger with him, an interpreter, one among a thousand, to show unto man his uprightness, then he is gracious unto him, and saith, Deliver him from going down to the pit. I have found a ransom."

That is what poor bewildered mankind needs . . . an interpreter to show him how good he is, and to keep him from going down to the pit, as Papa had gone. He allowed himself to contemplate the excruciating pain of Papa's loss. If only he had understood then what he knew now, he might have prevented all that. If only anyone could have shown to Papa his goodness . . . if anyone could have shown to the citizens who had turned against Papa *their* goodness . . . none of that cruelty and agony need have happened.

He read the verse again. It was his secret dedication. In spite of all the theological ambiguities and the strange perverse quarreling he carried on with God, that verse made everything all right. It was his authority for this quixotic career he had embarked upon. Could he ever explain that to Gay? Did he need to make her understand? Would it only distress her to know the precarious balance of his mission. . . .

There was a knock on his door, a quick fluttery knock that couldn't be imagined as belonging to Mrs. Temple, the land-lady. Still holding the Bible, with his finger in the book of Job, he got up and opened the door. The hall was dark and for a moment he thought the tall, slight figure was one of the carol singers, a lonely girl who was always contriving to get a special word with him. Then the figure spoke.

"Merry Christmas, Jubey."

Suddenly Gay was in his arms, her hair tingling against his cheek, her eyes wide and full of happiness, her lips cool and curiously innocent in spite of their ardor.

"I'm your Christmas gift . . . I couldn't help coming," she said in a rush.

He took her into the light, and looked at her. She was wear-ing a long scarlet coat with gray fur, and her dark hair was almost covered by a tight fur bonnet. She smelled deliciously of cold, and of some spicy perfume. He couldn't find a word to say, so she cried, "Don't just stand there, Jubey! Say you're glad, or something." Then she saw the book in his arms, and her face muted from laughter to a tenderness he never had seen on it before.

"Oh Jubey," she said, and touched the book.

There was something in her being overwhelmed which an-noyed him. "I don't know why you're surprised about that," he said almost sullenly. "Nothing strange about a preacher being caught red-handed with the Bible." She put her arms around him contritely, then shook him with impatient delight.

"Or course not, silly. But I've never seen you with it before. It makes you . . . well, very attractive."

"Let's hope so," he said rather stuffily. "You'll probably be seeing me with it more or less regularly."

She loosened her coat, and looked around the room. "Exactly the way I thought," she said. "Except bigger."

He stood in the middle of the room awkwardly. There was a feeling of irritated shame which he couldn't quite shake off, nor analyze. He had expected Gay to see this room only after they had started on their life together. He realized now that he had had some wistful hope that things would look different to them both then.

"You're not glad to see me," she said.

"Of course I'm glad. I just don't know . . . "

"What to do with me? Well, I'll tell you." She threw off the handsome coat, and sat down on a hassock, and motioned for him to come back to his big chair. Her dress of some silver material was shimmering and flowing in the firelight, and all Jubey could think was, A dress like that . . . this is never going to work . . . I couldn't buy a thing like that if I saved for a year.

She said, "Jubey, stop fuming. We're here together, darling. This is *us.*"

"I've imagined it so long," he said lamely. "I just don't believe it."

"No, that's not it," she said and took his two hands and held them in her cold firm ones. "You've been making believe . . . you always do that . . . and now suddenly the make-believe has caught up with you. And you're scared."

"I'm scared to death."

"All right," she said, "I'm brave for both of us."

He leaned down and kissed her then, because he knew no words that could say what the kiss had to tell her.

"I had to come," she said. "I thought and thought about it, Jubey, and it seemed to me we just had to be married . . . in your church. It seemed to me a good way to make everybody happy about us. To give them all a little share in it, so they'd like it and want to help it along. It's such a good thing, Jubey . . . and we have so much . . . we ought to be able to give away some of it to the people in the church."

"Oh, Gay," he said. "Nobody but you would think of such a thing."

"Our wedding's the best thing I have to give anybody," she said earnestly.

"But . . . but . . . how will we manage it?"

"It's managed," she said. "Mr. Hoppart."

"In a word," Jubey said with a crooked grin.

"Exactly. I telephoned him. He said fine. I'm at his house. My bags and me. He's coming back to get me in an hour. That is, if you like the idea. . . . But if you don't, why I can go on home tomorrow morning before anybody sees me."

"What about your parents? They'll be furious."

"We'll just not tell them. We'll just have a second ceremony. Far as I'm concerned, I could marry you every few days, Jubey, for the rest of my life."

The wedding was at twilight on Christmas Eve. The whole church participated, though they kept a strict aisle between each faction. It was plain on every face that, though they felt fatuously friendly toward Dr. Our and his bride, they weren't letting that feeling confuse them into being friendly with each other. Things equal to the same thing, in this case, were certainly not equal to each other.

Everyone had brought Christmas flowers and plants and had decked the church. It seemed as if all of them yearned to give whatever they had to this venture. As Gay had foreseen, it now belonged to them, and they loved it.

As Jubey came down the aisle, he saw scores of faces he had come to love and understand in the past few weeks. Even the little milliner had got up from her bed and dressed to come, tucking her sprig of mistletoe in the skimpy fur collar of her coat. Looking around swiftly Jubey thought, These are my friends. They trust me. They think I have the Word. . . . Their faces blurred before his eyes, and for a second he struggled with an impulse to cry out, Stop all this. I'm deceiving you. All of you. I don't know anything about God. He's an unconfirmed rumor to me. . . .

But he knew he had no right to say that, for although admitting it might cleanse his own honesty, it would damage the people who heard it. He loved these trusting people too much to burden them with his own confusion. His step faltered a second, then his eyes swept up the aisle to Gay on Mr. Hoppart's arm, slowly advancing. She had on a simple gray suit, with a tight small bouquet of roses in one hand. Her head was lifted joyously, and her face had a future lifetime's happiness written on it.

She'll pull me through, Jubey cried in himself. She'll teach me. Then he said what might have been a prayer, Oh God, please let me learn.

Mr. Hoppart, his face parched and quivering with feeling, gave Gay into his keeping, and allowed himself a swift pat as he placed the bride's hand on Jubey's arm. Mr. Hoppart was easily the third happiest person in the whole church at that moment, and anyone could see it.

The organ music ceased then, and the two moons which were Dr. Eban Carruthers' spectacles shone blindly as the old minister turned his face upon his task.

"Dearly beloved, we are gathered here today," he said in his well-schooled voice, and the ceremony had started.

Afterwards the whole town crowded into the Sunday School room to meet the bride and wish the couple well. Someone had conjured up a towering white cake, which Gay cut solemnly. There were lesser, hastily baked cakes and coffee and sandwiches, and it was obvious that many a Christmas turkey had met his fate twenty-four hours earlier than was expected.

Jubey thought in a daze. All this reminds me of something . . . what is it?

Before he had time to remember, Gay said swiftly in his ear, "This is where we came in, darling. Remember the basement of the settlement house, and me passing out cupcakes . . . that first night?"

"We have come a long way," Jubey said, "and you'd not believe me if I told you that I knew then."

"I would believe you," she said. "Because I knew, too."

The unexpected climax of the reception was when Dr. Carruthers himself stepped up and handed Jubey an envelope.

"The church members have got together a little gift. And our good friend Samuel Hoppart wants you to take his car and start immediately on a wedding trip," Dr. Carruthers said, blushing with pleasure at the good will that had allowed him to be a cell in its circuit.

"But starting in our new home is the best wedding trip we can think of," Gay said.

"No, you're to go off for ten days," Mr. Hoppart said. "It's all arranged, Mrs. Our."

13

THEY DEVISED an elaborate scaffolding of explanations to conceal the fact that they were already married, so that Mona and Pete wouldn't have all their plans spoiled. The Savannes had expected Gay to arrive the day after Christmas because of her final performance in New York. Jubey was to come by train the following day.

They telephoned from somewhere along the road, the day after Christmas, saying that Jubey had got the loan of a car and they were driving up together. It was Jubey who did the actual telephoning, and when he heard Mona's bright voice on the line he said, "Mrs. Savanne, this is Roger."

"Roger?" she cried in amazement. "Why, what on earth?"

"Jubey has changed his mind. He's asked me to take over Gay, if you don't mind."

"Why, I never heard of such a thing," Mona cried. Then Gay seized the phone. . . .

As soon as Pete looked into Gay's and Jubey's faces, he said, "You two are married."

"Why . . . how . . . ?"

"Anybody would know it," he said gruffly. "It shows."

Mona immediately burst into tears, and Melissa and the little boys looked from face to face in horror.

"Gosh . . . who's going to eat all that food and stuff?"

Mona said, "How could you do such a thing to us? After all, we've been so broad-minded about Jubey and everything. . . ."

Pete said, "It was your own business, and I'm glad you managed it yourselves."

"But all the people we've invited . . . and Gay's lovely wedding dress that Olga has just finished . . . I simply can't bear it. Why can't you people do *anything* I expect you to?"

"We'll have the wedding, darling," Gay promised. "We just won't tell anybody." Then she had an inspiration. "Or better still . . . you and Pete can have the wedding ceremony . . . don't people celebrate anniversaries that way sometimes? And Jubey can perform the ceremony! We won't tell a soul until the moment comes."

"And I can wear the dress?" Mona cried like a child. "Oh Gay . . . I tried it on. It practically fits me, except that it's too long. Oh, I'm so glad I never let myself get all fat and puffy."

"I'm glad, too," Pete said. "I've been wanting to marry somebody, and it might as well be you."

The children looked helplessly at each other, quite out of their depths.

"Grownups," they said resignedly.

PART IV

He perishes with hunger

1

THE TROUBLE in the church came to a climax quite suddenly. The dissenters gathered their forces again, and this time they didn't ask Jubey to join them. This time, they brought in a vigorous red-haired minister from Vermont as their choice of an acceptable pastor. Before anyone could reason with them their attorney filed a suit in court, to show cause why the minority now holding the church building should not relinquish it to the majority.

Gay simply couldn't believe it was happening.

"Why, they all *like* us!" she cried, wide-eyed.

"That's hardly the point," Jubey tried to explain.

"But Doctor Carruthers is such a good man. And dear Mrs. Carruthers. And Mr. Hoppart . . . after all he's done for the church!"

"Get away from the personalities," Jubey said impatiently.

"But, Jubey . . . that's what a church is about, isn't it? People? And all getting along together?"

"Seems not," he said shortly.

"Well, you'd better go talk to them. You can show them."

"I've tried. I'm not half big enough for this job."

"Then God better take over," she said seriously.

"Maybe that's what has happened," he said. " 'He moves in mysterious ways his wonders to perform.' Isn't that the text?"

"You're not saying it reverently," she said.

"It's not a reverent situation."

Dr. Carruthers, aghast that the threat had at last fallen upon them, wanted to resign. Mr. Hoppart and the group behind him wouldn't hear of such a thing.

"We'll fight. If it's a fight they want, they'll get it," Hoppart said. "I'll spend my last dollar defending our right to this building."

But it turned out there was no opportunity for that, for the case came up quickly before a judge who was counting noses for re-election. Dr. Carruthers was put on the stand to defend his position with doctrinal authority. The judge drummed on his bench in boredom while the befuddled old minister shuffled through books and documents, trying to make his point.

Jubey took the stand then, and put on a brilliant dramatization of the theological disagreement. The judge stopped drumming and listened with interest. At the conclusion he said, "Young man, why aren't you a lawyer . . . or an actor?"

In the end it was a simple matter of numbers, and possession of the church went to the majority.

"We'll appeal," Hoppart said. "We'll take it to the highest court in the land."

But in the meantime, they had no church. And Dr. Carruthers and the Ours had no salary. Dr. Carruthers solved his immediate problem by retreating into the safety of a belated illness. His son, a prosperous replica of his father, arrived from Illinois and moved his parents out of their humiliation. Everyone who liked Dr. Carruthers wished the illness could have got around to rescuing him the year before.

Blacken, the lawyer, came to see Jubey; just to make sure there were no hard feelings, he said. "Sorry you didn't take my advice. You're the logical man for this job, now that we've shaken out the old mossbacks. I did my best to persuade you."

"I remember that you did."

"As a matter of fact, if you've something you could occupy

yourself with for a year, I think it could be arranged for you to come back. There's no question about how much these people like you, Doctor Our."

"I couldn't consider such a thing," Jubey said blushing.

"It's all very well to be loyal," Blacken said. "But this is a situation calling for a practical attitude."

"I've had enough of it," Jubey said. "I'm going to scrub out my mouth with soap, and find a place where I can be honest again."

"Don't decide now," Blacken said. "Just think it over. Perhaps you'd like to communicate with me in seven or eight months. You'll have cooled down by then."

"I hope not," Jubey said, grinning at him.

"Well, don't go on record about it," Blacken said. "This is a pretty bad time to be out of a job. In any field."

Before they packed up to leave Tacoma, Gay dressed prettily as always, called on practically everyone in the church, as innocently as a child might have done. She had no quarrel with anyone and no one could quarrel with her. She never had been able to understand what the battle was about; for her there was no battle. Watching her from the midst of his own torment, Jubey remembered what Socrates had said: "No evil can befall a good man, neither in this life nor in the life to come."

She didn't discuss it much, but once in a while at breakfast, she would gently prod Jubey with a question.

"The church has enough seats for all of us, hasn't it?" she might say thoughtfully.

"Not exactly, dear," Jubey would try to explain. "People with their prejudices bulging around them take up lots of room."

"But isn't that why we go to church, to have our prejudices dissolved?"

"My dear innocent, you're too logical ever to be a conforming dissenter."

"Words," Gay said, shaking her head earnestly. "It's words that double-cross you smart people, Jubey."

"Expect so," he admitted, going back to his newpsaper.

Under the circumstances, leaving Tacoma immediately seemed the most tactful behavior. Jubey would have been worried frantic about where they could go while they waited for another call, except that on the very night after the trial was finished, Gay said, "Isn't it wonderful I've got all that money saved?"

"All what money?"

"Didn't I tell you? Why, I've got three thousand dollars, Jubey. I began saving it the day after you had to borrow a quarter from me to tip the waiter in the Syrian restaurant."

He gazed at her in speechless amazement, then resorted to inadequate mirth. "What a woman! What a ghastly practical woman you are."

"Not usually. But I could see then that *somebody* would have to look ahead about money."

"And a scheming woman besides," he said taking her in his arms. "There was I, boyishly innocent."

"That's what I've always told you," she said complacently.

"So we've got money. And we don't need to starve. Or go home and live with your family." He couldn't begin to tell her how relieved he was, for he could see that in her was so little capacity and so little need for worry that she had no way of measuring the solid ground she had slipped under his feet so casually.

They went to New York, and registered at a pleasant small hotel on lower Fifth Avenue, to give themselves time to look around for an inexpensive apartment.

Gay said, "But before we go grubbing sensibly, let's take a couple of weeks and just have fun. I always wanted a honeymoon in New York City."

There seemed not much else they could do, actually. They

had a choice of enduring the uncertain period of waiting in anxiety, or of considering it a holiday. A holiday was always Gay's way. . . .

Jubey wrote careful letters to everyone he could think of; he invited a Bishop to a sedate luncheon; he called at the Seminary and told as many of the faculty members as he knew intimately exactly what had happened. They all agreed that he had done the only thing compatible with integrity. But they also agreed with the deduction of Blacken, that this was a bad time to be out of a job.

Tentatively, Jubey wondered if he might not get some kind of teaching post here, or in a small seminary. But he could see in the quick dart of eyes that this was an outrageous suggestion. He said to himself bitterly, The last thing they'd want to expose the divinity students to would be a guy like me. Attractive enough to people, but repulsive to God. He said the words blithely, but they hurt him unexpectedly, exactly as if someone other than himself had said them.

Word flew around that Gay had come back to New York, and every day or so would come some discreet nibble about a new engagement. She was apparently blind and deaf to any such idea, and Jubey felt it would be churlish to issue ultimatums when obviously none were necessary.

He did permit himself to say once, "Don't you get a little homesick, darling?"

"Homesick? For what?"

"Well, now that we're here in the city . . . doesn't your old life kind of nag at you?"

"How could it?"

"Quite easily. It nags at me, to tell you the truth."

"But, Jubey, I told you what was going to be my job. You. This is only a little in-between time for you. Maybe theater people learn how to wait between jobs more calmly than other people. We call it resting."

"Well, I don't," Jubey said. "I'm darned restless."

"I know you are, darling. We'll just have to think up some nice, interesting things for you to do. Maybe we'll look up some of our old friends."

"My old friends are either sheepish guys like myself that didn't get horses on the merry-go-round after graduation or else they're tiresome ducks that bore me stiff with their smug little superiority."

"That doesn't sound like you."

"It sounds exactly like me," he said childishly. "Only I say it less politely when I'm talking to myself about it."

The two weeks stretched into six, and the days took on a listless pattern. Over everything hung the pall of Jubey's humiliation and futility. He remembered Blacken's cynical good nature about not putting his noble refusal of the job on record; he even considered calling up Blacken and saying something like, Well, old man, you called the turn all right. If the red-haired wonder from Vermont doesn't turn out too well, put my name down on the list of applicants.

But the face of Samuel Hoppart rose before him, and he knew he never could inflict such treachery on the good old man. Hoppart had lost his church; he couldn't also lose his faith in Jubal Our.

Once in a while some of Gay's friends would invite them out to dinner. They would sit around a small table in some darkened noisy club, and the talk would be all of theater and gossip and lightheartedness as if there were no economic consternation in the world. Jubey would try to catch on and be interested for Gay's sake, but he felt excluded and awkward. He felt conspicuous by the very kindness everyone showed him. He felt surely they must be saying, This guy shore slipped one over on Gay! Why doesn't he let her go back to the theater where she belongs?

Anybody out of a job is a sensitive and uncomfortable sight, but a preacher out of a job is of all men most ridiculous, he paraphrased to himself. If he could have managed it without hurting Gay, he would have spared himself the humiliation of these evenings with her friends.

Yet it was through one of these evenings that the turn came. There had been a belated snow storm that Sunday in March, a long, persistent blizzard that began before dawn and blew into twilight. The city was held in its white clutch, as silent as a countryside. Six floors below their windows, they heard an occasional clanging of tire chains on a taxi roaming lonesomely through the paralyzed streets. It was weather that made any place a deserted village, with isolated groups either enchanted or frantic behind snowbound doors.

At eleven o'clock in the morning, their telephone rang and when Jubey answered, a pleasant man's voice said, "I'm Mike Pliven. Spose you're Gay's new husband."

"I better had be, or we've got a scandal on our hands," Jubey said, and then, "I've heard about you, Pliven. Hold the wire. Gay's washing her hair."

"Gay's always washing her hair," Mike said. "She's probably the cleanest girl in the world."

Gay, turbaned in a bath towel, came running in and took the telephone. "When did you get in, darling?" she cried as greeting.

"Been in ten weeks," Mike said. "Just found out you were back in town. Can you come down tonight, you and the guy with the purple-velvet voice?"

"We'd love it, wouldn't we, Jubey?" Gay said, her eyes doing a kind of *entrechat* of delight.

"We'd be nuts about it," Jubey said gruffly, though nobody stopped to listen to him.

Gay got the address and the other details, and hung up. "That's the most brilliant musician I know," she said. "Too brilliant for his own good."

"I know the type."

She looked at him seriously. "No. He's not like that at all.

You'll like him. You two could be brothers, except that you know where you're going, and Mike's always just wandered around in a wilderness."

"We *could* be brothers," Jubey said. "And I'd match my wilderness against his any time."

"Don't talk that way. Even in fun. One of the things I love most about you is that wide clear space in you like a broad valley full of sunshine. You have green pastures and still waters, Jubey."

"All right," he said, kissing her. "That's what I have. Officially, anyway."

The snow was still coming down like sacramental wafers as they drove south in their taxi. Gay was wearing her silver dress, and one of her fur coats, looking like anything but the wife of a minister out of a job. Or in a job, either, Jubey said unhappily to himself.

The address on Waverly Place was a tall grim-looking brick house; the lights spilling out of the windows gave it a festive but demented appearance like someone in mourning laughing hysterically. Beginning at this house a long queue of dark figures filled the sidewalk for half a block.

"What on earth?" Gay cried. Jubey opened the door of the cab and peered out while he was getting the fare from his pocket.

"There's an employment office in the basement," he said. He saw that some of the men in the long noisy line had snow shovels on which they leaned. "They're waiting for the storm to stop so they can begin clearing the streets."

"Oh, heavens . . . if Mike sees them, he's certain to invite them all to the party," Gay said. "You might as well brace yourself for a large evening."

The Plivens lived on the first floor, reached by a long flight of stone steps. As soon as they were out of the cab, Gay and Jubey could hear piano music.

"That'll be Mike?"

"And nobody plays the way he does," Gay said, running up the stone steps eagerly. "You wait, Jubey."

They stood in the hall and listened, not wanting to rap on the door before the music came to a pause. When it did, Gay turned the knob and they went into what once had been the high-ceilinged drawing room of the house. Lights came crashing from a crystal chandelier, but that was the only relic of grandeur. A hodgepodge of furniture was scattered about the room, and the thin, skimpy rug didn't begin to cover the wide-boarded floor. At the piano sat Mike, lost in his own music which still seemed to be suspended in the air. A small, straight-haired blond woman with an inquisitive-looking, turned-up nose was leaning against the piano studying his face.

"That's Ola. They're married," Gay said. Ola looked over at the door and saw them, and immediately she and Gay were in each other's arms, and Mike was up from the piano and had surrounded both women with his extravagant joy. They were all babbling at once, and it was obvious that they were old and intimate friends.

How come she barely mentioned them to me? Jubey thought, then realized once again that Gay seldom mentioned anything except the present place and time. She was dragging the Plivens around so that they all faced Jubey, and the two men shook hands, and Ola looked up into Jubey's face with troubled, speculative eyes, then rose on tiptoe and kissed him.

"That's because I didn't get to kiss you at the wedding," she said. "Gay forgot to invite us."

Mike was squat and dark, with black hair which sprayed out from a long, melon-shaped skull. His face was engagingly ugly, all except the eyes which were soft and expressive behind heavy glasses.

The others in the room had lapsed into a dozen intimate conversations which rose and floated toward the ceiling, with laughter and exclamation and question buoying them up.

Ola said, "Mike has been playing something new. You'd want him to finish?"

"Of course." The Ours sank down on a scratchy green divan, and Mike went back to the piano, and Ola went back to studying his face as she had before. The music was not quite as brilliant as it sounded. Jubey studied it carefully, and realized in the first five minutes what his affection for Mike would later conceal from him. Here was a composer who was not good enough for first rank, and yet was too marked and mannered by his own yearning for greatness to be acceptable in a popular way. He was that most tragic figure, an artist too good and at the same time not good enough.

When the music was finished, Ola disappeared into the kitchen and soon came running out balancing huge trays of food and drinks. She said gaily, "Now we have the hyphen between Mike's beautiful music and some fun."

It was a much more bohemian group than Gay usually knew, and Jubey felt utterly at home with them. They were more real to him than the glittering theatrical people; they were not so deliberately friendly, hence not so patronizing. He felt drawn to Mike immediately, and while they drank very poor homemade wine and ate big rye bread slices laid out with delicious cheese, they caught up on each other as if their friendship was long established and had been interrupted only briefly.

"Gay should have told me she was marrying such a good man. I thought she was marrying a preacher."

"I thought so, too," Jubey said ruefully, "but it turned out differently."

Gay kept running to the window to look down on the heavy queue of snow shovelers. "It's so cold out there . . . I just can't be warm in here."

Ola said, "We had to steel our hearts against them after the first week. Otherwise we die of misery."

"It's Sunday night, and we're all so happy," Gay said. "Couldn't we do *something?*"

"We could make coffee," Ola said resignedly. "We've done it all winter. I bought a big special pot.

"I'll carry it out to them," Jubey said. "Some of my best friends are unemployed."

Ola and Gay began making the coffee, and Mike stood on a chair and got down all the cups he could find, protesting that the party was now being ruined but unable to resist throwing himself into sharing their warmth and comfort, even in this inadequate way. Jubey carried trays of steaming cups out into the street. The very sight of him coming down the steps with the offering brought the line to life, so that the men called out cheerily and joked among themselves.

While they were waiting for the next pot to boil, Jubey suddenly began singing, leaning against a tall lamppost with his empty tray balanced on lifted fingertips. At first he sang a nonsensical song Papa had loved, then he picked up one of the banal ballads everyone knows, and soon the whole line was singing, "Row, row, row your boat, gently down the stream." They broke up into a round then, with Jubey running up and down from one section to the other leading them, and making a great clown of himself.

The Pliven guests opened the big front window and crowded close to hear, and in a few moments they, too, joined in. Neighbors hearing the strange music swelling in the street came to their doors and listened shivering, then dashed in and got coats so they, too, might join in.

The impromptu concert went on for more than a half-hour, then suddenly it was discovered that the snowstorm had stopped and the employment office in the basement, which had orders from the city department for all the volunteers they could supply at sixty cents an hour, was getting ready to open. Everyone in the line now felt warmed and cheered, for a fugitive friendliness was running up and down the street making an adventure out of a hardship.

"God bless you, sir," one of the men shouted to Jubey, and Jubey shouted back, "God bless all of us, bud."

Then he added, for fear that had sounded a bit sanctimonious, "If I had the clothes for it, I'd get in that line with you and ask for some shoveling to do. Happens I'm out of a job at the moment." There was all sorts of advice and condolence about this, as the line fed, man by man, through the employment office and then straggled up the street with a precious time card, to climb into one of the waiting city trucks.

After the crowd had melted away the guests came back reluctantly to the Plivens' party. Jubey sat down at the piano, now that his self-consciousness had thawed completely, and began to improvise. First he did an impersonation of Mike Pliven; not a malicious one, but an affectionate portrait of the dark little man breathing over his music in a curiously madonna-like attitude which was characteristic of him. The music, too, he imitated with subtlety and skill which astonished even himself.

I'm not this good, he kept saying to himself as he played the gentle burlesque. I guess it's just that I've not been happy for such a long time. I've not had much fun lately, and no music in me.

When he had finished, Ola ran to him and kissed him again. "That's because nobody ever understood my Mike as well as that before."

"Do you always have to write footnotes to your kisses?" Jubey asked her while everyone applauded. "I thought kisses were their own explanation."

Mike himself was frankly wiping his eyes with a big linen

handkerchief. "Where you been all my life?" he asked in the vernacular of the moment. "You're what I've been needing, Jubey."

Once he had started, his clowning couldn't be stopped. He sat at the piano and rippled out droll commentaries on the rakish stories that seemed to come to him from nowhere. He impersonated anything anybody asked for, with musical accompaniment, until the room was in an uproar of appreciation and mirth.

As a finale he said, "I'd like to dedicate this little impression to my wife, Gay, for these are the people who introduced us." Then he did a sad and hilarious sketch of the Keenan Canines, so that you saw each one of them, from the elegant lady terrier who did every trick immaculately down to the fuzzy little mop the slum people loved the best because he reminded them of themselves, that bewildered little chap who always missed the tricks and muffed his cues and bruised his dignity.

Now it was Gay who had tears in her eyes. "Where have you been keeping such things, Jubey?" she said. And now it was she who kissed him.

The party broke up a little after two, and just before the Ours were leaving, a big bald-headed man came up and asked Jubey to come out into the kitchen for a moment. Jubey had no idea who he was, but he remembered seeing him sitting morosely in a corner throughout the evening with little to say.

"You have something I think we could use," the big man said abruptly, without preliminary.

"Oh no, it's just nonsense."

"Sure it is. That's what I mean," the bald-headed man said. "I keep watching for the stuff, and I find precious little of it." He was fumbling in his vest pocket, and almost shyly he took out a card and handed it face downward to Jubey, who took it and stuffed it in his own pocket without glancing at it.

"Ever think you'd be interested in radio?" he asked.

"Sure I did. I was one of the earliest hams in the country when I was fourteen," Jubey said with a grin. He told the big man something about Papa's excitement about wireless, and how they had brought the great conglomeration of mechanism from Germany. He told about everything except the insulated little glass house which the men from Schenectady had built so that "nothing dangerous ever could happen to anybody." He never could bear to mention that little laboratory, for it was there that Papa had taken his own life. But he told the rest in a few quick sentences with his pleasure in the memory shining in his face.

"What have you been doing in the meantime?" the big man asked. "I'd have thought you would have come right along with us from the start."

"I would have," Jubey said slowly, the joy withering in his face. "But I got involved in a detour."

The man looked at him a long moment, as if he was trying to picture what had happened. "Well, you're finished with the detour now," he said with conviction. "Come down and talk to me tomorrow. Let's have lunch . . . one o'clock?"

"Sure," Jubey said. "But . . . "

"One then." He put on his fur-lined overcoat and a derby hat, and left, forgetting to say good-bye to anybody.

When Jubey and Gay were in the taxi, he took out the card. Gay said, "What's that?"

"A man invited me to lunch."

"What man?"

"That's what I'm going to find out," he said, holding up the card so that the passing street lights fell uncertainly upon it.

"Don't strain your eyes trying to read it, dear," she said with sleepy motherliness.

But Jubey had taken one glance at the card, and then had leaned back in the seat limply. "My gosh, I don't have to strain my eyes. I don't have to read it. It just happens to be the biggest name in radio."

Gay reached for the card, excited at the sight of Jubey's excitement. But he held on to the card, as if he was afraid it couldn't be real.

"It's George Irving Compton," he said. "What would a guy like that want with me?"

"Why, you said he wanted to lunch with you," she said in a matter-of-fact voice. "He probably knows of a church somewhere that needs a good minister."

He looked at her, and then he burst out laughing. "Are you out of your mind, my feathered friend?"

"Of course not," she said, not offended in the least. "Anybody could tell by the way you handled those poor snow shovelers that you have a wonderful way with people."

He took her unceremoniously in his arms and kissed her, out of sheer excitement. "My darling, if you *must* be as wrong as that, may you always have something as delicious as this to be wrong about," he said.

He was much too stimulated to sleep, so long after Gay had fallen quiet he got up and slipped on his clothes and went out to walk about the snowbound streets. The last of the shoveling was still going on, a nocturnal drama like illustrations to a German fairly tale, the bent gnomish figures silently shoveling white roofless tunnels so that when the city woke, it might move about as usual. Forty-Second Street had a few trucks and delivery vans threading through the narrow opened alleys in the snow. Occasionally a lighted window showed that the all-night lunch counters were doing a livelier business than usual.

Jubey strode along tingling with excitement and pleasure at what had happened tonight. The drab epoch was over; he knew it surely. He was finished with all the dreary mouthing, the unequal struggling to rouse the sleeping goodness which the boy had thought he glimpsed in mankind.

He remembered what he had told Kurt Geitzen long ago about the angel and the clown wrestling in him. Well, the angel, that battered sheepish angel, had been routed now and they would have to hear no more from him. The clown, a sly delighted fellow, was in the ascendant. He had had to lurk secretly behind that bedraggled, out-at-the-elbows angel for quite a long time. But he had his foot on the vanquished neck now, and from here on it would be his life.

His destiny seemed so obvious that he marveled that he ever could have fallen into what he had told George Irving Compton was a detour. It was worse than that. It was a run-around, a game of crack-the-whip. Whoever had led him on it must be laughing. He walked along for a block thinking about that "whoever," half angry that he was so often an intruder in his inner privacy. Who was he anyway? About all Jubey really knew about him was that he had been conceived in Jubey's own image and likeness. He was a large projection of Jubey, a prankster, sometimes tender and playful, and sometimes rough and ruthless in his games.

"Well, I'm finished with you now," Jubey said. "So go away please, and let me alone."

He stepped out of the shoveled path and kicked vigorously at the snow bank. "If there's anything a comedian doesn't need, it's you in his business. So good-bye, my friend."

2

HE CAME HOME from the interview the next day in a glow of anticipation. They had lunched alone, he and George Irving Compton (nobody ever called him less). Then he had been introduced to several executives and they had sat around discussing theories of comedy. Jubey had not realized he had any theories until that moment. Actually all he had to do was reach down into that deep reservoir of fun within him and bring up anything that seemed needed.

What these men wanted especially was the creation of a new character who could do just about what Jubey had done spontaneously the night before. Someone who could improvise on the piano to fit his own patter.

"Why limit it to a piano?" Jubey had asked.

"You mean you could work with other instruments?"

"Sure. I spose so . . . I never tried," Jubey said with a grin, borrowing the old joke. "No, the fact is, I can play anything. Invent a new instrument and I'll play it for you. Or does that sound boastful?"

"Certainly it sounds boastful. But if it's anything, show business is a form of bragging," George Irving Compton said.

At the end of the conference Jubey said, "I'll go home and think." He saw that these men would have more respect for a miracle that didn't happen too easily.

He intended to give Gay a dramatized version of the whole satisfactory encounter, acting out all the parts as he generally did when he told her about anything. But when he unlocked the door of their unpretentious suite, there sat the Plivens. Ola was unexpectedly chic in a green velvet suit and a small berry-red hat, and Mike was dressed as if he had just changed his house slippers for overshoes and had come as he was, with his hair looking as if it had recently composed thirty four bars of a symphony, and his trousers baggy and shiny from the agony.

Gay came running across the room and kissed him, taking his coat and hat in one of her charmingly womanly little gestures. He saw instantly that there was a warning in her face as she said, "Oh Jubey, Mike has come to talk something over with you. He's practically had an offer from a big radio company to do some composing for them. Let him tell you, dear."

"That's great, Mike," Jubey said cautiously.

"Don't know whether you happened to notice that large bald-headed chap who kind of kept to himself last night? Well, that's George Irving Compton. Maybe your work is too far from radio and stuff for you to recognize the name, but he's . . ."

"Everybody knows that name," Jubey said.

"He's been talking vaguely about it for months," Mike said. "I've submitted several ideas which they like."

"Awfully clever," Ola said nervously. "Mike can just do anything!"

"It's not what I want," he said apologetically. "But what the heck, these days?"

"I know exactly what you mean," Jubey said, his stomach shuddering.

"The fact is, when he called up and said he wanted to hear my new sonata last night, I really expected . . . "

"They always take so long to make up their minds," Ola interposed, very bright-eyed.

"Incidentally you didn't happen to notice how he took the sonata, did you?" Mike asked urgently.

"I did," Gay said impulsively. "Everyone else was chattering and applauding, the way people do. But I noticed him especially. He looked awfully impressed."

"He said he liked it," Mike said. "But what else could he say, me there with my tongue hanging out?"

They stayed about an hour, going over the situation several times. Finally Ola looked at her watch and said, "Don't you think we'd better get back, Mike?"

"We watch that phone till I hate the sight of it," Mike said with a disgusted grin.

The Ours invited them to dinner the next week and walked to the elevator with them, still reassuring them. As soon as the gold doors were closed Gay said, "Wasn't that ghastly? I suppose I ought to have told them instantly that you were out with that man. But somehow I didn't, and then it got worse and worse. *Did* he know of a church for you?"

"Church?" Jubey cried crossly. "Of course not."

"Then what was it?"

"He offered me Mike's job."

She looked at him as if she thought he was joking. Then she saw he was serious. "But Jubey . . . why, what on earth gave him the idea . . . ?"

"That I could handle it?" He shrugged, his vanity hurt by her amazement.

"Well, of course you were awfully funny, dear. You always are. But you're not *professional*." She gave a meaning to the word which drew a golden circle around just a few privileged persons in the race.

"No? Well, maybe we've just discovered a new meaning for the word 'professional.'"

"You mean he was *serious* about it?"

"As serious as a millionaire can be about comedy when it happens that comedy is his business."

They were back in their rooms by this time. She sat down limply, holding her lip with her teeth and frowning unhappily.

She had not even seen that she had offended him.

"Well, it will make an awfully good story to tell your parishioners some day," she said at last. "It really is quite a compliment, isn't it, dear?"

For the first time in their life together he thought, I've always known she was childlike. I've always loved that about her. But not this childlike. He was so annoyed that he couldn't bear to look at her. He went over to the window and pretended to look down into the street. The day and the world were utterly ruined for him.

He remembered that other time when he had given up his music because somebody else's little talent had to be protected. It had been Minna then, drumming pedantically through her scales, and counting off with her lips while she played nauseatingly silly little "pieces." He had felt quite noble because he had given up the joy of playing the family piano. Papa had got him a studio downtown, and that had been a guilty and delicious secret between them.

But Minna's playing had finally withered on the vine, so he had been able to come home and thunder out his music as he pleased. Nobody could keep him from music. It belonged to him, and now he was going to have it. Not great music, not disciplined proper music that had architecture to it . . . but his own brand of inborn music, as innate as his own humor and his own strange happiness. He was going to have it, and nobody had better get in his way.

Gay began to understand from his silence that something was wrong. She came over and put her arms around him, trying to make him look into her face. But he stubbornly stared down into the street.

"But Jubey, you wouldn't consider it, would you?"

"It's worth considering. Your friend Pliven is certainly hepped up about it."

"But Jubey . . . you have something so much more wonderful! There are a million comedians. . . . "

"And a million preachers. All of them, apparently, holding down all the jobs at the moment."

"But Jubey . . . "

"Don't keep saying that," he said angrily. "If you can't think, just don't talk."

More than his trivial vanity was hurt by this odd short-circuiting. Just when he had believed everything was beckoning him into his own good destiny, suddenly that jokester that seemed to be writing the script of his life had made his usual quick switch. You thought you had it in your hands, didn't you? Well, how about this? the circumstance was saying to him, and chuckling with malice.

It was the same old pattern; offering something good and then snatching it back. Why couldn't he come to some agreement with life, the way other men seemed to? Why did he have to go on fighting his way through this dichotomy?

Gay couldn't know all this. Gay thought it was only hurt pride. He had snapped out at her in the way hurt pride usually prompts. He had snapped out at her! He felt appalled; he couldn't let that happen between them. He put his arm around her, even though he still wasn't able to speak about all this muddled annoyance. She melted against him forgivingly.

"I wasn't very understanding about it," she said. "It just didn't occur to me that you would be flattered. You see, I think you're so big that no smaller men could flatter you, Jubey."

"It isn't a question of flattery," he said, sounding more pompous than he felt. "But naturally I'm interested when a man who isn't exactly an amateur considers I have a talent that might be a salable commodity."

"Don't use so many words, Jubey," she said, laughing at

him to restore his good humor. "You can't lose me whipping around corners with words, you know."

"Sorry. I try to keep things simple when we talk."

"Okay. Now we're even, dear," she said amiably. "So what did you tell him?"

"I told him I'd come up with a comedy idea tomorrow."

"You didn't! Doesn't he know you're a minister?"

"Am I?"

"You mean you let him think you would consider his offer?"

"Don't keep asking rhetorical questions."

She drew away from him and thought about this awhile. Plainly whatever mental process she considered thinking went on better a few feet away from him.

"But of course, even if you might be tempted to consider it . . . which you wouldn't be . . . now it's quite out of the question."

"I don't see why."

"You couldn't take Mike's job, Jubey."

"I'm not taking Mike's job. I'm taking my own job."

"That's quibbling. The job was practically in Mike's hands before you came along."

"You were practically in Roger's hands," he said trying to make up for his brusqueness.

"That was different. Don't confuse the issues."

His native good nature had suddenly melted all the difficulties. He saw it all quite clearly now, the outcome stretching pleasantly ahead of them as soon as they rearranged a few small matters. And inspiration could always move anything. Mountains, in fact. No, it was faith which was supposed to accomplish that feat. Well, he had faith. Faith in himself and in the spry ingenuity that always came to his rescue in some unexpected way.

He came over to her and kissed her warmly. "Don't worry about it, Gaiety. I've just had an inspiration that's going to fix up everything." She kissed him, then drew back, obviously suspicious of his inspirations.

"I'll take the job, all right. And I'll write a part for Mike into the act."

"You're joking."

"No. I mean it. We'll work together. Mike can be the straight man . . . the straight piano. His piano will feed mine the lines. And my piano will make the jokes. You'll see."

They didn't discuss it any more, and Jubey sank into a happy reverie, pacing up and down and pulling on his pipe and humming under his breath, obviously delighted with what was going on in his head.

Somewhere in the middle of the night he woke up and realized that Gay was not sleeping. He stretched out his hand, and she took it, and for a long time they said nothing.

Then, exactly as though they were resuming the discussion where it had ended, she said, "You see, Mike was awfully good to me when I was just starting out. If anybody really got me my chance, Mike did."

"I guess I remember now. You told me about him."

"He kept insisting I had style. And nobody paid any attention to him, and then finally . . ."

"But, darling, that doesn't change the situation, does it?"

"How can you say that doesn't change things?"

"Well, ethically George Irving Compton has a right to hire anybody he wants, and if he changed his mind that's his privilege. The personal element just doesn't enter into it."

"Of course it enters," Gay said gently. "Persons are all that matter, aren't they? Nothing is about anything, unless it's about people, and the way they feel."

"That's woman-reasoning," Jubey said.

"It's the way God reasons," she said. "He doesn't think anything is more important than people."

He saw it was hopeless to embark upon a discussion of ethics

with her, so he said patiently, "All right, darling. But even
so, Mike's going to have a fine chance. He's going to be better
off with me than he would be alone. I know how to bring out
the guy."

"But actually . . . that's not the most important half," she
said.

"Okay. Let's have the rest."

"The rest is you, Jubey. You have something wonderful to
do in the world. You can't throw it away on a lot of laughs."
She felt him twitch with the quisk rising tide of impatience,
and she put her hand against his face in a gentle, restraining
way.

"I gave up a good career, Jubey. Because I believed in what
you have in you. If it was a theatrical career we wanted in the
family, why, we *had* that. And if I do say so, probably superior
to this fly-by-night radio business."

"Oh, so now you're regretting."

"I'm not. I'm only reminding you that your great talent is
making people see that God is something real. The way you
showed him to me."

He sat up quickly then, and for a moment all the torrent of
his disbelief and his unadmitted humiliation because God had
not taken him into his confidence hammered dangerously. In
another moment he might have let it come pouring out, re-
gardless of consequences. But then she said something that
made it impossible for him to shock her with the truth.

"Besides . . . I want our son to have his father at his best."

He turned in the darkness and looked at her. She was nodding her head, and her eyes were wet. "That's the real reason,
Jubey," she said.

"Oh, Gay." He could find no words at all; he knew only
that there was nothing she could have told him that would
have meant to him as much as this did.

In the morning Jubey was bursting with plans. After she

had gone to sleep again, he had worked it all out. He insisted on keeping her in bed while he made the coffee in their little serving pantry. He parted his hair in the middle, put on a meek waiter's face, and brought in the small tray with expert flourish and a yes moddam, no moddam.

Then he immediately forgot his role, and sat on the side of the bed and sketched out the situation.

"Say we accept this for one year. We don't have any illusions about its being forever. We don't lost the path, so to speak. But we take the big chance that's been given us, to make some quick money, and get some good experience, and have a lot of fun."

"Oh Jubey, you really are crazy to do it, aren't you?"

"I never wanted anything in my life so much," he said; then he added, as she expected him to, "except the way I wanted you, of course."

"Of course," she said in a matter-of-fact voice.

"I've grubbed along such a long time, Gay. I've been having such a long hard pull. Except for you, nothing decent has happened to me for years . . . not since Papa, actually."

She reached out and took his hand and kissed the palm.

"I've been so ashamed and humiliated. There's so much I want to do for you. I'd like to buy you everything you want."

"I have everything I want."

"A man who can't buy things for a wife who is beautiful suffers like the devil. It's as if he has an impediment in his breathing."

"The best things there are, you've given me," she said. But he scarcely heard her, so vehement was his persuasion.

"And now there's to be the baby. I want him to have everything. We'll make some quick dough, and we'll pile it up like a good safe wall for a background. Then later . . ." he waved his arms helplessly.

"Yes, Jubey."

"Next year we'll be bogged down in parenthood, and we won't want this kind of life. We're going to throw ourselves into being champion parents; you know that. But this year..."

"This year you want to make music."

"I've got to, Gay," he said. "There's something in me that feels like a lion just let out of a cage into his own country again. I can't explain it." Her gray eyes studied him seriously.

"You have explained it, dear," she said.

"You mean you'll go along with me on this?"

"You know I will. I told you my career was going to be you."

"A man has to unwind his life from what is inside him," he said. "Sounds like a silkworm, doesn't it? But that's it."

"All right. We'll both be silkworms," Gay said. "And now call that waiter again, and let's order some more coffee."

"Right away, moddam."

3

NEITHER OF THEM mentioned the fact that the first year had passed. Neither of them mentioned that the second year had rounded out.

Time had gone fast, yet when it was looked back upon, it seemed as if a lifetime, a new bright lifetime, had been lived since George Irving Compton had taken them over. It had been an enormously successful venture for George Irving Compton; he was as proud of it as if he had created Jubey with his own bare hands. And in a sense that is what he had done, and Jubey was generous about acknowledging it.

"I walked on a tightrope the first six months," Jubey once told him. "The tightrope was your faith in my ability to keep going. And most of the time when you're out on a tightrope, you can't even see the swinging little thing under your feet."

"But you knew it was there," George Irving Compton said placidly. "You knew darned well."

Jubey had worked out better than either of them could have anticipated. The show built and pyramided from week to week out of sheer bounce and pleasure. Often, in the beginning, Jubey didn't even have a script, and sometimes he had only half an idea. He would come down to the studio with gravel under his tongue; his palms would be cold and damp, and he would think, This time, you're going to fall flat on your face, old boy.

But somehow, when the engineer in the control booth held up his thumb and forefinger in a circle, which meant that Jubey was "on," a gigantic calm came over him, a strange delightful timing, a magnificent leisure which got across the air and straightened out the kinks and the hurry in anyone who happened to be listening. It was the half-hour which added an extra hour to anybody's day. George Irving Compton himself stumbled on that description of Jubey's show, and so they used it in the promotion. It got to be a byword with the people who liked Jubal Our.

"Got to go home and pick up my extra Our," they said.

Inevitably the show was called Jubal Our's Jubilee. It began rather tentatively by being a matinée. Mike Pliven played a serious-minded musician giving listeners a music-appreciation lesson. Jubey played someone who had just happened into the studio, a window washer, stumbling over his bucket in his eagerness to learn, a messenger boy delivering a telegram, a hick from Kansas seeing the sights, an inventor who wanted to sell a device for straining out the sour notes.

Almost overnight mail began coming in, and then came homemade cakes from enthusiastic housewives, and soon letters asking if Jubal would mind if a new baby were named for him.

The program director told him, "You've got that strange thing which can't be imitated."

"What's that?"

"The thing that makes people like you. It's something you're either born with or you aren't, like lop ears or six fingers."

"Or two heads," Jubey said, "as in my case."

"Listen, Jubey, about that guy . . ."

"Don't worry about Mike. I've got a swell new idea for him. He'll work out fine. Just give him a little time."

"He doesn't add a thing."

"Sure he does. I've got to be talking to somebody. You know that. It's the oldest problem in comedy."

When the mail and the trade comments had grown to a

healthy stability, George Irving Compton said he wanted the Jubilee moved to a better spot just following an important newscast.

"It won't hold up there," his advisers said frankly.

"They're still people after they've heard the news. Or are they?"

It did hold up, and before that next year was out, it was given a place at dinnertime, dangerously near Amos and Andy on another network.

"That'll finish it. He's good, but not that good."

"You'll see," George Irving Compton said. "If I'm wrong, I'll go on the air with him myself and apologize."

After two and a half years it was building toward an evening show once a week. A major sponsor was considering it, and two of the top-flight script writers were working out more impressive formats. The growth had been phenomenal, a surprise to everyone but its discoverer.

Fortunately the Ours were nimble and resilient people, for their scale of living paralleled the rise of the show. The week after Jubey began his radio work, Gay moved them from the uninteresting hotel into a sunny little furnished apartment overlooking Gramercy Park.

The Savannes came down to visit, and Mona had to begin revising her ideas of Jubey. It seemed now that she had always known he was a winner. She had engineered the whole thing, in fact. If Gay would only think back she would remember. Gay remembered.

Pete liked the program, and showed a surprising flair for analyzing its appeal, and warning about its dangers.

"Your big talent, of course, is your appreciation for every scrubby little devil you've ever seen."

"He doesn't appreciate them," Gay interrupted. "He loves 'em."

"Sure," Pete said, "but I'm always scared to use such a big word."

"He makes fun without malice," Gay said. "He puts heart-beat into the comedy . . . Gosh, maybe I ought to be writing the publicity for it!"

It was only a question of weeks until she had begun looking into Sloane's windows, and thinking what kind of furniture she would want when they got ready to buy their own.

"As soon as you get your first raise," she had said to Jubey, holding him before her favorite window, and pointing out things she craved especially.

"My first raise buys you ermine, mink, chinchilla and points north," he said. "I've been jealous of every fur coat I've seen since the day I married you."

"I have fur coats. Now it's a wall-to-wall broadloom carpet I need, and a fireplace with two love seats."

When the raise did come, he telephoned to her, and that very afternoon she located a bigger apartment and a clever little decorator who came in during the next two weeks and "did" it from saucepan to front door knocker.

By the time the baby had arrived, it had been obvious that they needed an extra room, since they could afford a nurse. So, as long as they had to move anyway, Gay had decided they might skip a few rungs and go a bit smart and get into the East Eighties where their new friends were living.

What they wanted ultimately was to buy a swank apartment of their own in a co-operative building on Sutton Place at Fifty-Seventh. Might as well begin owning something, they said to each other.

"We're parents now, and parents should own property."

"If you could call one cell in a steel beehive 'property,' " Jubey said.

Later, when Jubey could tear himself away from the city, they would have a nice amusing country place somewhere in Connecticut, the way the really big shots did.

"But those guys have gray at their temples," Jubey protested modestly.

The baby had given them an excellent excuse for their concern about the style in which they lived. She turned out not to be the son they had expected. But that seemed quite acceptable, for she was a placid pretty child who sat in the midst of her good fortune and purred and beamed. It was Gay who named her.

"She can't be named for me, darling," Gay said. "So I want her named for the other woman in your life. Lucile."

That touched and pleased Jubey more than he could say. But it wasn't necessary for him to say anything, for Gay knew. It seemed unlikely, however, that the baby might ever grow to be like the original Lucile, the small fragile pastel. This Lucile was large and blond with rather light blue eyes and an incredibly perfect pink and white skin which smelled deliciously fragrant when you nuzzled your nose into her plumpness. She was everything a baby should be, obligingly happy and good, and sufficiently doll-like so that strangers stopped and talked baby-talk to her when the nurse took her out in her fine cream-colored perambulator.

On Sunday mornings Jubey himself did the honors, trying not to strut too much. When he came home with her, he always accused her of ogling the passers-by.

"She'll get her pop in trouble, winking at people the way she does," he said.

Sometimes he said delightedly to Gay when the baby responded extravagantly to approval, "She's pure ham, like her father." Jubey seemed to have forgotten that it was the distaff side of the heredity which might have supplied the theater sense. And Gay never reminded him. Indeed, it was possible that she did not even think about it herself, for her life in the theater seemed so far away from all this domesticity that she could hardly believe it had ever been.

Her old agent grieved publicly that the theatrical world had lost such a dancer. Once or twice a year he brought some excited producer to talk with Gay, and for an hour the two men sat on the edges of their chairs, excitedly laying out enticements and sketching in the part they had in mind for her. She woud listen with grave eyes, and would suggest the names of other dancers who might be interested.

Occasionally some young journalist would collect some of the beautiful old photographs from his newspaper's morgue, and would write around them a lament and a speculation about what might induce Gay Savanne to come back to the stage.

These stories usually were pasted by Jubey's secretary in his own bulging press books, because they always included paragraphs about Jubal Our, his career and his home life.

Before the first year had finished, Samuel Hoppart had come down to New York. He had telephoned Gay at her home, and asked if he might come up and talk to her.

"Why, Mr. Hoppart! There's nobody I'd rather see. Won't you come for luncheon?"

"I've eaten," he said with his blunt gaucherie. "I didn't want to be any bother to you."

"Well, come right away, and we'll have some coffee and dessert."

"Can't eat dessert. Been having some stomach trouble lately," he said. "But I'll come and watch you eat."

She was at the elevator to meet him when he arrived, and she linked her arm in his and walked him down the hall to their apartment, and then kissed his dry old cheek.

"You don't know how glad I am that you've come," she said. "You've heard about Jubey, I suppose."

"Yes I have," he said guardedly. "I felt real bad about it, too."

Not quite certain how much he meant by this, Gay said, "Well, you did all you could, Mr. Hoppart. It just seemed . . ."

"He's not to be blamed in any way," Hoppart said quickly.

"I heard the boy on the air. I could see he was trying awfully hard. And he deserves a lot of credit for making the best of a bad situation."

He sat down and looked around the living room admiringly. "My, you've got things nice here, I must say."

"It's fine," she said. "Jubey doesn't have as much time at home as we'd like, though."

"Jubey," he said sadly, and it was an entire, affectionate sentence. "That boy has a real calling, Gay. And here he is dribbling away, when there's God's work to do." He blushed as he said the word, as he always did. He talked most of his waking hours about the church and its affairs, but he seldom mentioned God's name, and Gay had intuition enough to know that it was her presence which made it possible for him. She could see from the discomfort of his face that it was necessary for him to say something more. So she waited patiently, an ability in which she excelled.

"I'd like to tell you something," he said at last. "You know I've been a religious man all my life."

"Yes, I'm sure you have."

"But I never really had a sense of worship. I can't explain the difference. But I guess you say it when you say I didn't know God. I knew religion, but I didn't know God. And Jubey . . . well, I don't know how he did it, but somehow he . . . well it was the way you said the first night I met you. Remember?"

"Of course."

"Jubey doesn't talk much about God. But you can't help thinking about him yourself when you see that boy at work."

"Will you tell him that, Mr. Hoppart? Jubey's had a bad time. He tried awfully hard to get a church. He wrote dozens of letters. And he talked to people. But it seemed there was just nothing open. . . . "

"I wrote letters, too," Mr. Hoppart said sadly. "Thought I

had quite a lot of influence here and there."

"Well, maybe this is all part of it," Gay said, looking earnestly into his face.

"Part of it?"

"Part of the way God is bringing him up. You know a mother has to watch her child go through unpleasant stages sometimes in order to grow up properly. Maybe God has something like that in mind."

Mr. Hoppart cleared his throat, and took off his glasses and wiped his eyes; then he brightened up, patted Gay's knee and changed the subject.

"The fact is, I've got good news for us," he said. "We think we see how we can start our church now. We'll have a small membership to begin with. We've gone in with the Congregational Church. They were going to have to close their church. If we can forget our doctrinal difference . . . and I guess most of us have learned a little discretion about that . . . I think we can make out."

Gay could guess what was coming now, and her stomach was trembling with apprehension that dared not be hope.

The old man leaned toward her and went on eagerly, "You see, what we expect is that if we can get a good minister, we'll draw quite a few members from our own church. People who were on the fence, who didn't really like the idea of taking our business into court the way they did. And if our minister could be Jubey . . . "

"Oh, Mr. Hoppart." She found suddenly there were tears in her eyes. She tried to hold them back, but they fell and she cupped her hand childishly about her mouth and caught them.

"We want him very much, Gay. We would be able to pay him a little more than we did at Grace Church. Several sizable contributions have been made."

"From you, I expect," she said in a whisper.

"Well, what difference does it make? I'm getting along in years, and what better could I do with my money? At any rate, we've worked out a budget, and we're prepared to offer Doctor Our two thousand dollars a year."

"I know that's a lot," Gay said.

"A lot for a minister," Mr. Hoppart corrected realistically. "But probably not much for a radio comedian." They talked then about the best time for Hoppart to go down to the studio and talk with Jubey.

"I've never been to a radio station. I wouldn't want to do anything that would embarrass the boy."

"Lots of people go to see him. He has an office. You call up first and they'll give you an appointment. He'll be awfully glad to see you, Mr. Hoppart. Jubey's awfully fond of you."

Just as he was leaving, he turned and came back. "Maybe I better not mention that I came and talked to you first."

"Whatever you think."

"Men are sometimes touchy about having their wife know too much about their business. Don't know whether or not Jubey's like that. But anyway."

"We won't mention it," she said. "Jubey likes to tell *me* things."

"Yes. I imagine he would," Hoppart said. A moment after he had gone Gay realized that was a clumsy compliment.

But this was one "thing" which Jubey evidently didn't like to tell her. For when he came home he didn't mention Hoppart's call, nor his offer. They went to bed without their old friend's name passing between them. Just before they fell asleep, Jubey permitted himself one question, and that was as close as he came to telling her.

"Gay . . . you're happy here, aren't you?"

"I'm happy with you."

"I mean, you like the way things are going, and everything?"

"I want you to have your own life, dear."

"Well, I'm having it," he said exuberantly. "And don't think I'm not."

"And no regrets?"

"Regrets? What a word! It's for the middle-aged, in the first place. And how could I have any regrets? What about, for Pete's sake?"

"I just wanted to be sure."

"Okay. So now you're sure."

The Plivens clung as long as they could, during the early part of the pyrotechnical display which was Jubey's rise. But it never seemed possible to Ola and Mike that such a skyrocket of a career would last. So for them, it didn't.

Ola sometimes confided to Gay that she was tucking away every scrap of spare money she could for the inevitable day when they'd all be "out."

"Does it seem wise to buy so many things, dear?" she sometimes asked when Gay showed her something new.

"We can afford it. So could you, Ola."

The little Dutch woman shrugged heavily. "I keep the money," she said flatly. "When you have to sell your good furniture, it's second-hand junk and you get nothing for it."

Jubey pulled Mike along by sheer determination. Before every program he had to breathe into Mike's playing the breath of life; but often there was so little conviction behind Mike's performance that the fan mail would mention it.

"What's the matter with the professor, got lead in his pants?" listeners would ask jovially. These quippish letters Jubey would sneak out of the mail before either Mike or George Irving Compton could see them.

"Can the Perfessor. We will all get along better mittout him."

When he read such frank complaints, Jubey took all the blame upon himself.

I've simply got to write him in better, he would say worriedly to himself. Then he would pace up and down the new long living room far into the night, muttering dialogue to himself, remembering Papa's old friends August and Carl and Otto, and trying to match Mike's lines to their inflections.

Mike had no confidence at all in the program. "They'll all wake up one of these days," he often said to Jubey furtively. "This stuff is just silly."

"Sure it's silly."

"It doesn't seem funny to me."

"Fortunately you're not typical. Look at the bushels of letters that come in. People are crazy about us."

"They'll get fed up with it," Mike would say miserably. "I feel like a fool. The piano is humiliated."

"The piano has got to remember who's boss," Jubey said. "What's it want to do, starve to death?"

"I think it would rather. And so would I. If it weren't for Ola."

"Ola's proud of you."

"She can't look people in the face."

"Now Perfessor, your ears are dragging."

"Don't Perfessor me," Mike said. "I want to vomit when I hear the word."

Jubey himself could play an unlimited number of characters. Sometimes in one program he would be a little boy taking lessons from the Perfessor, and a soprano-voiced woman trying to learn to sing, and a piano tuner taking the Perfessor's piano apart before his agonized eyes.

At the close of every week, he said to himself, Well, another week gone, and Mike's still not fired. I've got to make him better, the poor little guy.

But try as he would, he couldn't seem to create a real comedian out of the musician. He had so much guilt about it that if Mike had lost his job, Jubey probably wouldn't have been able to go on. It never occurred to him that George Irving Compton understood that, and kept Mike for that reason.

But in the end Mike solved the whole thing himself. He came into Jubey's office and threw his squat little body into one of the two leather chairs.

"Got some news."

"Good or bad?"

"Swell. I'm giving this up. I've got a self-respecting place on the faculty of Wheaton College."

"Never heard of it."

"It's a small college in Massachusetts. Very old, and very good. I'm going to teach harmony. I'm going to beg my piano's pardon and become an honest man again."

Jubey could see that the genuine musician meant exactly what he was saying, so he permitted himself to feel the relief that spurted through his own mind.

"I'm glad, Mike. You never liked this, did you?"

Mike didn't even have to answer; his appearance had been a silent statement of it every day. "I'll be earning about half as much. But at least I can hold up my head. You can have radio from here on, Jubey. I'm never even going to own a set. As long as I live."

"I'll miss you, son," Jubey said, perspiring with relief at this sudden rescue from his responsibility. "I've got so I really liked doing your script."

"You can't like it, Jube. You've got too much intelligence to like such nonsense."

"Nope. You overestimate my intelligence."

Mike looked at him frankly, hesitating whether or not to say what he thought. Then he decided there was no one else who could afford to do it.

"How long are you going to waste your life on this drivel?"

"I'm not wasting my life," Jubey said, considerably nettled.

"I thought you were a preacher, Jubey. I thought you had some serious hopes of doing something worth doing."

"Worth is a matter of opinion. I happen to think that making people laugh is worth doing. Especially in these gloomy days."

"That's what the monkeys in the zoo think," Mike said gently.

"Yes, but they're working for peanuts. I'm getting rich."

"Rich, hmn?" Mike commented meaningly. "What's money?"

"I could tell you, son, but I hate to waste gags I could use in the script," Jubey said with bravado.

"You've been wonderful to me," Mike said slowly. "Don't think I don't realize what you've done. I wouldn't have lasted a week except for you, Jubey. That's the reason I'm going to talk to you like a father. Even if it makes you mad."

"All right, Mike."

"You think you have talent. Everybody tells you so. I know what the trade papers say about you."

"So I have talent," Jubey said dryly.

"But you're more than just a comedian. You're a man with brains and a heart. You wanted to do something to help the world. I don't know why, but you did. You cared enough to put in several hard years getting educated to be a minister. And doing it the hard way, too, without anybody to give you a hand. Whatever made you do that must still be in you somewhere, Jubey."

"No. It's gone. And I'm better off without it," he said, almost angrily. "It was never anything but torture to me."

"Certainly it was torture. Any real ambition . . . any good determination is torture. My music is torture. That's the price we pay for trying to achieve. For trying to grow. Nothing that's worth anything is easy."

"I don't want any more torture," Jubey said, and Mike saw that he was trembling. But, just when he was beginning to hope something might come of this difficult conversation, he saw that the younger man was not going to let his mind linger a moment on that side of the subject. He hurried instead into the refuge of the trivial enjoyment of his work.

"I'd be a fool not to love this work I'm doing. I'm good at it, and I love it. It's play to me. If I didn't have to earn a living, and they'd let me come down here and do my program for nothing, that would still be jake with me."

Mike shook his head sadly. "You do enjoy your impersonations," he said. "I've watched you all this time, and I can see you enjoy them."

"Sure I do. They're the breath of life to me."

"But don't you see? You're impersonating all kinds of other people because you can't find yourself."

"What're you talking about?"

"You're trying to be everybody else, Jubey, because you don't dare be what you really are."

The room was terribly still for a long moment. Jubey's knuckles grew white and his eyes blazed with anger. But in a second he shook it off with a quip out of one of his own scripts.

"So now the Perfessor talks psychology already."

"So now the Perfessor tells you the truth. Like a fool," Mike said gloomily.

"All right. So I forgive you," Jubey said loudly.

"But one of these days when you grow up enough to listen to some sense, you remember what I said." He said it again, slow and maddeningly, to make sure Jubey wasn't going to miss it. "You make believe you're all kind of other people because you don't dare be yourself."

Jubey got up from his chair, and for a moment Mike thought he was going to strike him. But the comedian in the man was safely in charge, and the light touch could be depended upon.

"Okay. So now you've acted like a heavy father, and I hope you feel better, Mike my boy."

Mike got awkwardly to his feet. He had accomplished

nothing. He had chased his own blood pressure up ten or fifteen points and had made a fool of himself. As far as Jubey was concerned, he would go on living behind a high wall of his own building, and nothing anybody could say would reach him.

"Gay will want to have a party for you and Ola," Jubey was saying pleasantly. "We'll certainly want to give you a fine send-off for your new career."

Mike muttered something ungracious and stumbled out of the room. Jubey swung around to his typewriter where he was doing the first draft of a new script. With a vigorous pounding he ran a line of x's through the dialogue he had laboriously given to Mike. Then he ripped out the yellow sheet, wadded it furiously, and hurled it across the room. He put in a blank sheet and started over. The drudgery was finished now. From here on he would go it alone, and it would be good going.

Ola had already phoned to tell Gay the good news, so that he didn't have to go through the telling when he came home.

"They're awfully happy," Gay said. "This wasn't their life, was it?"

"I'll say it wasn't," Jubey said. "And now that it's over, I'm going to take off my rubbers and tell you the truth. I've had one heck of a time trying to keep Mike in the program."

"Maybe you shouldn't have tried," she said mildly. "Maybe the sooner a bad situation comes to a climax, the better."

"Well, that's fine thanks!" he said. "Who was it that brow-beat me into getting Mike the job in the first place?"

"There's no pleasing us, is there, dear?" she said, smoothing his hair and kissing him as if she were his mother.

"There was certainly no pleasing Mike," he said hotly. "I wish you had heard the song and dance he gave me today. He's a heavy-handed duck. He'll be fine in a one-horse girl's school up in the country."

Throughout dinner, he was in a jovial mood, full of anecdotes and quotations from his fan mail, so that Gay understood he had been hurt.

Then, at dessert, he grew serious.

"Read a very interesting article in the American Medical Association monthly today. One of the country's foremost psychologists was reporting the remedial effect humor has on mentally deranged patients."

"Normal people like it, too," Gay commented.

"I'll write the gags, Mrs. Our."

"I'm sorry."

"No. But seriously. Says they've put radios in the recreation rooms of certain institutions, and they find definite results. When the patients begin to laugh they begin to recover."

Seeing his need then, Gay looked intelligent and vivacious. "Yes. I guess that's right. Sick people don't often laugh."

"This chap said there was real therapeutic value in comedy. A society that cannot laugh is in danger."

"I see what he means."

"It gave me quite a thrill. The world *certainly* needs laughter these days. Maybe it needs humor more than some other things. I'm proud to be helping supply a little comedy. It's not a trivial vocation by any means."

"I'm sure it's not, dear," she said compassionately.

"You could say it's a pretty fine life's work. As much of a mission as . . . well, as anything."

Suddenly she wanted to weep at the urgency of him, his terrible need for being reassured. She kept her eyes on her plate, for fear he might see the pity in them. At this point pity would have driven him wild, for he was intoxicated with an elixir brewed of envy from others, and of chagrin from himself.

4

THE NEXT YEARS passed quite quickly. It seemed that all kinds of people were watching Jubey rise, the columnists, the rival networks, Gay's old friends from the theater. One lived in a circle of spotlight. And that was okay. Out of the darkness beyond that bright little tent of light in which one lived and moved and had his being came mailbags full of letters. Sooner or later all the persons Jubey had known in his life checked in through his mail. Old Anna, the cook who had served the Ours throughout most of her life, and then had retired to live on her ample savings, had her nephew write, because she wasn't sure such a famous man as Jubey could still read German. Old schoolteachers reminded him they had always said, etc; all the girls he ever had dated seemed to recall their association with ardent embellishments; the man from Schenectady who built the ill-fated little wireless laboratory on the back of Papa's land; everybody. Everybody except Roberta Rose Kramer. Jubey had never seen Rose's handwriting, but sometimes when a secretary brought in a pink or lavender letter to say this was probably something Mr. Our himself would want to handle, he'd think, This is from Rose. She's telling me how proud she is. . . . But the letter never was from Rose.

Even Milton, the Texas barber he had known on the *Susquehanna,* wrote to him: "Maybe you're too successful to remember me, Jubey. But once I saved your life by praying. Why don't you do a kind of sketch about that sometime. I think it is Christ's will that you tell the world about that time."

The letters from persons out of his own life he answered himself. But this one of Milton's he didn't answer. It made him too mad. That sniveling guy, he said to himself. You can't beat a praying man . . . why, darned if that's not exactly what I said when it happened! But it irked him that Milton had probably lived his whole petty existence in the glow of what he considered a miracle.

Let him have his silly old miracle, he scolded himself, you'd think you were just jealous, because *you* didn't get a miracle out of it.

But I did get a miracle, he reminded himself after a moment.

The arguing voice within him asked, What miracle, Jubey?

Why, the knowledge that if prayers won't, humor will, he said.

And you're living in that wisdom right now, aren't you?

Sure I'm living in it. And liking it fine.

Are you, son? Well, all right.

The climb to the top had been exhilarating; the clinging there was another matter. On the way up, each week brings new and encouraging developments, but when everyone is acknowledging that you are the best in your field, there are always some critics and listeners who attempt to prove their superior discrimination by finding subtle flaws in you which the rank and file may have missed.

Phoebe Tumulty, Jubey's brittle secretary, sometimes said, "When you're on top, where can you go but down?"

Tumulty, a tall, raw-boned woman who supported a sick husband without ever mentioning him, had seen lots of things in her lifetime, and most of them were discouraging. She had a genial pessimism which infuriated Gay, but which Jubey seemed to like as a balance to his own natural euphoria.

The three of them sometimes discussed the usefulness of Tumulty's function as the official deflater of the Our ego. Jubey always defended her function.

"Who could get conceited with Tumulty around?" he would ask largely, in such discussion.

"You could," Gay said, "on account of you have to keep telling yourself you're lots better than Tumulty thinks you are."

"She thinks I'm swell," Jubey said. "Don't you, Tumulty!"

"What I think of Our, I don't have to tell. Not even on my salary," she said, looking at him with adoration in her eyes while she puffed ferociously at her stub of a cigarette.

"But at least you'd fight to the death for me, wouldn't you?"

"Whenever you're attacked," she said. "But when you're riding smooth, it's up to me to keep you realistic."

"Okay, Pretty Thing," Jubey said, winking at Gay. "Whatever your system is, it works fine with me."

"But not with me," Gay told her. "You spoil the man so he's practically impossible to live with."

Tumulty blushed under her unpowdered freckles. "It's a country of free enterprise," she said, throwing her arm roughly around Gay. "Competition is the life of trade. There's nothing says you can't outspoil him, whenever you want to."

"And don't think I don't try it," Gay said, a bit more seriously than she intended. "When he's home long enough at a time, that is."

"What about all those fancy devices you've got for keeping him home?" Tumulty asked with her slow drawl. "Who plays on the nice new tennis court down in the country? And who rides the fancy new mare you gave him for Christmas?"

"I'm thinking of hiring an assistant vice-president in charge of enjoying life," Gay said. "The head man's got too much on his mind to be bothered about that little department."

"I'm enjoying life," Jubey said. "Make no mistake about that, you girls. It's enjoyment just to know you own such stuff, even if you don't have time to fool around with it."

"Never mind, dear," Gay said. "Some day you'll be nice and

old and nobody will want you to crack jokes, and then you can ride horseback and play with your five-year-old daughter. Only she'll be thirty-five by that time, and will have moved to Arkansas or somewhere."

"I play with Lucile," he said sheepishly. "I play nearly every Sunday."

"Not counting the last seven, of course," Gay said. "But that's all right. Lucile's crazy about the farmer on the place. He's got three kids of his own, if you ever happened to notice, and *he* plays with her."

"Next Sunday," Jubey said. "I promise. Make a note of it, Tumulty."

"Make a note for me too, Tumulty," Gay said. "Remind me to keep on loving the guy. If I have time."

"Time," Tumulty said gloomily. "That's the villain in the piece. Everything would be different, if it wasn't for time. Ever notice that?"

It was truer than it sounded as she said it. The fact was that though he devoted practically all his life to the Program (which they always spoke about with a capital, as if it were an irascible monarch), still there wasn't quite time enough to keep it appeased. It was a spoiled glutton, that Program; the more you gave it, the more it demanded. It was a jealous god, never quite satisfied.

As months went on and Jubey became more and more of a national character with a hundred radii emanating from his personality, there was not even enough time for him to write his own weekly show. That puzzled him.

"I used to dream up six shows a week," he said to Tumulty. "Didn't even have you to dictate 'em to. But in those days there was plenty of material. Everywhere you looked there was material."

"Maybe you don't look in the right places any more. Most of the people you associate with are slick professional people."

"That might be something," Jubey said. "I used to kind of mingle. I had time to be aimless and see things. But now I don't have that kind of time. Now, with one show a week, I'm swamped. And the three writers are swamped . . . and every Thursday night we work until dawn . . . and to tell you the truth, the shows aren't as good."

"Everybody's kept busy earning a big salary," Tumulty said. "You're a big mechanism now, Our. You're a monster with a dozen brains. And the brains all must have conferences with each other."

"Maybe it's the conferences that kill off the humor."

"Maybe so. You all have to beat the pore little jokes to a fine pulp before you finally pass on them."

"Things were funnier when I just tossed 'em out," Jubey said gloomily. "I wouldn't say this to anybody but you, Tumulty, but sometimes our stuff turns my stomach."

"Too much money cushions the whole deal," Tumulty said. "Money's not funny."

"Money's grim," Jubey said glumly. "You can't buy comedy with dough."

"You can spend a fortune every week trying to."

"If George Irving Compton just had the same faith in me that he used to have before I was a big item in the budget, I still could turn out a good show."

Tumulty yawned. "You're anti-social, Our. You're talking about depriving a half-dozen high-priced men of their liveli-hood."

"Yep."

But the show was pretty funny in spite of the agony that had to be endured to produce it. Naturally the funnier it was one week, the more agonizing the next week's work had to be in order to keep up with itself. And no one ever could be sure whether they had hit it or not until the actual hour in the studio, when the weary gags which had been put through the wringer of everyone's mentality over and over until they looked like wet wash suddenly came to life because there was a studio audience that whooped and roared. Then the humor leaped up from the smear of anonymous laundry, and strutted up and down the whole country. It was a metamorphosis which would have gone to the head of any comedian who had the power to bring it about.

After each show, all the people who had worked on the program studied the miracle. They ran the transcriptions over and over, dissecting each familiar joke and balancing the laughs.

"Now . . . what did it there, Jubey?"

"I got a kind of question into my voice. Gave the thing two meanings," Jubey would decide, perspiring with seriousness.

"The hat gag didn't do what I expected it to."

"That's a writer's joke," Jubey said. "Sounds good on paper."

And so it would go; the cold microscope of reason scraped over every square inch, trying to isolate and dissect the elusive spirit of fun, and found only a dead cadaver of mentality.

Gay said, "They none of them have had real theater experience. Everybody who's worked on a stage knows that the audience is responsible for at least fifty per cent of everything. They make their own jokes and they hear their own music. All you can hope to give them is a hook to hang something on."

"Okay. Then it's the hook we're worrying about," Jubey said in a dismissing tone of voice.

"Theater's pure contagion," Gay said. "You've got to have infectious mirth in yourself."

"I've got mirth," Jubey said glumly.

"You all work too hard at it. Something new every week is just too much. You haven't got time to learn to love each joke."

Once in a while Jubey would make a confession to her. "I never started a show without the cold feeling that this one was going to die on its feet. Never. I go over to the piano and I can hardly get my tongue off the roof of my mouth, and I think, Suppose they just sit there? This stuff isn't funny. They'll get up and shamble out."

"Don't you ever pray?"

"Good heavens, no."

"I do. I always do. Every week while you're on."

"That must be it," he said. "That explains it."

"No, I mean it."

"So do I."

But she saw in his face that it was only an affectionate remark, a kind of husbandly pat on the shoulder for her loyalty.

Each year he became more skillful in his work. But each year he became more serious about it. It had begun as a lark. It had begun with a strictly amateur viewpoint. He did it for fun! He did it because there wasn't anything on earth he enjoyed doing more. And people listened in the same spirit.

But now he had become an acknowledged professional, he had a different attitude toward it. He was afraid of other comedians. He jealously read all the reviews of everyone's work, and his skin itched and prickled when praise was too lavish for somebody else. He had privately decided to a fraction, exactly where he himself rated in the list of five top comedians. Sometimes at night he had a terrible dream that he was falling downstairs, and that Gay and someone he never could recognize were trying their best to break the fall but not succeeding. He'd wake up drenched and trembling; the dream was always too simple and undisguised for him to miss its meaning.

He tried to be interested in other things, but this enveloping career made that impossible. He bought a handsome and expensive telescope with the idea of having a good architect build him a little observatory somewhere on their Connecticut farm. He would make a real study of astronomy; he would have the best library on the subject that any amateur could collect. And then the traitor in him slyly suggested that it might even make good publicity. He saw a portrait of himself beside his telescope, with the ranged flight of impressive books as background.

But the telescope never got unpacked. There just wasn't time. . . . When he saw the wooden boxes and cartons which held it standing in his study, it was a wordless embarrassment and reproach.

I ought to give that to somebody, he said to himself. I ought to find some sensitive young Jubey . . . a kid like myself before I got swept into the tornado.

5

A STRANGE NECESSITY had been making itself felt in him lately. A terrible need to get away from the people who admired him, and fawned on his opinions and laughed before he had got out the first ten syllables of a sentence. He had a feeling of disgust and resentment against them which he couldn't explain and was afraid to analyze.

They pull on me, he said incoherently to himself. They think everything is just swell before it's half finished. I've got to get away from them before I do something dangerous.

He remembered the early days of his seminary life, when his mind had loathed the theological quibbling, and his heart had loved the simple people he found everywhere he looked. He thought back forlornly to that love which had been his constant climate, and he decided that was all only a part of being young. I just didn't know any better then, he said sadly to himself. I thought every little guy on earth was wonderful. I loved 'em so much. . . .

One morning the revulsion against his spoiled preferredness was so strong that he just couldn't face the studio. He drove around the city awhile, not seeing the crowding pedestrians and the impatient nettled faces of the drivers in the cars jammed around his. At last he got out of the mid-town traffic, and drove up through the dreary canyons around West Eightieth Street.

There were silent people shuffling along the streets or sitting dejectedly on the long iron stairs that led to front doors. People who had nothing particular to do, nothing particular to think. The sight of them turned his stomach, and he thought, I used to love them once. These are the people I got all peppered up about, because I wanted to tell them something. What in God's name was all that? What did I want to tell them? Jokes?

He felt suddenly alien in his own life, as if it had imprisoned him in a madhouse. Something had made a fool of him. At that realization he thought, I've not felt as sick as this since the morning I saw that headline in the train washroom.

Suddenly he felt that old helpless rebellion of struggling against an adversary so much bigger than himself that he could only beat fly-sized fists against a hundred foot wall. He felt that strange unwelcome presence with him which used to mock at him and goad him into anger.

I'm through with you, he reminded that presence staunchly. I haven't thought of you for years. Not since I began being successful.

But he couldn't seem to shake off the imminence. Rather than reason with it, he allowed himself to plunge into an abyss of wordless depression, as deep and void as the fathomless sea that morning his ship was torpedoed.

He stopped at a drugstore, plastered with patent medicine signs which never would keep their promises. Inside was the smell of iodine and chocolate ice-cream sodas. A pale and pimply old man in a dirty black alpaca coat looked up hopefully from a racing form spread out on the top of the old-fashioned glass display case.

"Something?"

"I only want to use your phone," Jubey said.

"Go right ahead," the old man said, motioning wearily to the dark rear of the store. "I thought you was a customer."

"I am," Jubey said. "When I come out, I'm going to buy some hair remover, some hair grower, some corn plasters, some ink eradicator, four gallons of deodorant, and a nice bottle of goat glands."

"What are you, wise guy or something?" the old man said unresentfully. "I was only asking you was you a customer."

"And I was only telling you, my friend, that good fortune just walked into your store in a size you've rarely encountered before."

"I think you're crazy."

"I shouldn't be surprised," Jubey said. "But I am also a man who cannot bear to see his brother man discouraged and defeated as you looked when I asked for the telephone."

"Business has been something awful," the old man said in explanation.

Jubey shut the door of the booth, and found a nickel in his pocket. Through the glass he could see the elderly drug clerk eyeing him a moment and then indifferently returning to his racing form. Somehow he felt quite cheered by the nonsensical conversation. At least he had found it possible to resume loving a member of the pathetic human race. *That was it;* when he was too harried by the too-muchness, he didn't take time to love 'em. And when he didn't love 'em, he dried up inside. I'm an engine that has to run on kindliness and love for the poor little guys, and I might as well remember it, he said to himself, while he waited for his call to be put through to Tumulty.

Her pleasant twangy voice came on, and when she heard him she said, "Where are you, Our? People are asking for you."

"I'm calling to say I won't be in today."

"Somebody sick?"

"Nobody but me. And I'm suffering from a malady it would take much too long for me to name."

"You drunk, Our?"

"Not at all. I'm just taking the day off. And if my family calls up, you can say I've just stepped out and you don't know when I'll be back."

"I don't like the look of it," Tumulty said.

So he reassured her by invoking the one word which always commanded undisputed right of way. "The Program," he said. "Fact is, I've got a terrific idea, Tumulty. I want a little time to myself to work it out."

"Oh, the Program," she said in relief. "Okay. And good luck."

In his mind he imitated her voice vindictively. "Oh, the Program, Our. Never mind what happens to you. But save the Program!"

He came out of the booth, and the suspicious eye of the clerk crawled up his face delightedly.

"I just figgered you out," the old man said. "We don't get many people that want to play."

"That's right, buddy. I notice that, too." He grinned at the old man; then took out his wallet and flipped out a ten-dollar bill.

"Give me something that costs nine dollars and a quarter," he said, "and keep the change for yourself, Pop."

The old man took the bill gingerly, with a sheepish grin on his face. If this was a gag, he wasn't going to act as if he had been taken in by it.

"Now let me see," he said. "What might you want?"

"You couldn't name an item that I don't need," Jubey said. "I'm in a state where anything you give me will seem like a panacea."

"A panacea?" the old man said warily. "I know we did have some, but where we put 'em . . . ain't much call for 'em lately."

He puttered around vaguely for a few minutes, and then decisively rang up a $9.25 sale on the cash register and dropped the change in his pocket. He'd be sure of that, anyway. He ran nimbly around the dingy shop picking up items here and there, and giggling with delight at his own anarchy. The last thing he added to the pile of mad miscellany was a dusty box of licorice drops.

"There you are," he said with great satisfaction, as he gravely wrapped up the bundle with pink shiny paper and tied it with sharp twine. "Come in again sometime, mister. Anytime."

"I'll do that," Jubey said. As he was walking out the door, the old man called after him.

"You wouldn't care for a cherry phosphate, would you? On the house, of course."

"A bit early in the morning for me," Jubey said. "But I'll certainly take you up on it sometime later when I'm passing by."

He got back in his car, tossed the pink parcel in the back, and drove off whistling.

"And now where?" he asked aloud.

He kept driving north and turned over to the river, not hurrying, not thinking, just driving along the way a youngster would who was playing hooky. He felt fine now, free and simplified. He had no plans for the day; he would just keep going, and if he saw a place he liked, he would stop. Maybe a park with a bench in the splashed sun and shadow under a tree. Or maybe, if he saw a place to fish, he would buy a line and take off his coat and his necktie and loll on the bank with some other truant.

Or was that a bit too idyllic for upper New York? Maybe on the Jersey shore you could find such a thing. Or even back in Jersey a way, where there might be lakes or ponds. He crossed the George Washington Bridge, liking the way the shadows from the great structure lashed across the moving car like huge whips. The river smelled good, slightly tarry and smoky, and with a suggestion of mud flats and kerosene . . . a man's smell. The smell a man on a holiday would like.

He began to be hungry now. What he wanted was a stack of wheat cakes, and a big thick slice of broiled ham. Two cups of coffee at least. He would like it in a diner, where truck drivers pulled in for a rest. He kept his eyes open for such a place, and at last he found it.

He took off his coat, with some vague idea that it was too

well tailored to admit him to the kind of companionship he
needed today. He wished his shirt were pink, the kind of pink
which hard-working men sometimes buy. He thought of stopping in a dry-goods store in the next town and buying a pink
shirt, then he said to himself, You don't have to put on an act,
Our. This is your holiday. Come just the way you are.

He sprawled on a high stool and leaned his elbows on the
counter and ordered his midmorning meal, and while he was
waiting for it, he talked to the woman behind the counter, and
to the two other men customers. There was a slow easiness
in all their voices, and Jubey loved the sound of it, and the
sound of his own voice. It reminded him of the days after he
had come back from the war and couldn't face home for
awhile. Those were the good days. He had thought they were
lost forever. But they weren't. They were waiting for you,
every place in the world, if you just had time to reach out and
take them. And the boy inside yourself who was capable of
living such days . . . he was waiting for you, too.

"Ever hear of a place to fish around here?" he asked the
spruce little middle-aged woman who was pouring out his second cup of coffee for him.

"Well, yes I did," she said. "They's a little lake kind of,
called Cedar's Mills." She began giving him directions, and
one of the other customers corrected her at one point, and they
argued good-naturedly and finally came to terms.

"I know, because my sister lived in a little town up that
way," the woman said. "Little town called Swiss Plains. Quiet-
est little dump on the map. But she liked it. Till she died,
anyway."

Jubey paid for his meal, selected a toothpick from a whisky
glass, stretched up his arms in animal contentment, scratched
his stomach delightedly, and said, "Well, I got to be shoving
along, miss. And thanks for the information."

He drove on, idly following the directions; not that he
wanted to fish particularly now; not that he wanted to find the

town where the woman's sister had lived; but because he had no other destination. Yes, there was the gas station where you took the road to the left. Willow trees, still young from the spring, blew gently, their diagonal sweep almost harplike. If you knew how to listen, a kind of melody might be heard from them. If you knew how to listen, there was melody everywhere to hear.

He found the town, just as she had described it. It seemed impossible that there should be such rustic quietness so near to Manhattan. A woman in a gingham apron was walking along the street, not hurrying. A cat was following her daintily. She turned into a yard where another woman was planting something. The cat arched its back and rubbed against her ankle. Jubey slowed down his car to watch the woman stand and talk and laugh.

He saw it was almost noon as he came to the town's school, a very pretentious brick and white-trimmed colonial structure rambling elegantly across landscaped lawns. It showed the town knew a thing or two about spending public money, getting federal aid, etc. He stopped his car in the shade of a big maple tree and inspected the building. European villages had cathedrals dominating them with their luxury and richness. But American villages had schools like this as their most expensive structures.

Twelve o'clock struck then, and the doors opened, and children began spraying out from the building. There was a surprising number of them, the town must stretch on for quite a way. Or perhaps the best of it, the residential part, was off the main road. He must drive around and explore. The children were well dressed, but not too well dressed. He tried to find a child who looked like Lucile. Then with some unanalyzed distaste he abandoned that idea, and began looking instead for children who looked like Minna and like himself when he was a schoolboy.

He found the park at last, with a big gold-lettered Roll of

Honor flanked by cedar trees. He read the names, good American names with syllables collected from many parts of Europe. There weren't many; fourteen. It might have been possible that he had known one of those boys. He thought about them; if this Adolf Tuesky, for instance, had not had to be lettered in gold on this white slab, what kind of life would he have led in this town? Who was better off, Jubal Our or Adolf Tuesky?

He shook himself out of that morbid and surprising thought and began walking along the street toward the small business section. There was a clean little real estate office with a man sitting at a desk. He went in, and the man looked up and said, "What can I do for you?"

"Just some information," Jubey said. "I was wondering how much property sells for?"

"Business or home?"

"Well, I was thinking . . . fact is, I was just driving through. I want to settle in a town about like this some time. I was wondering . . ."

"We've got a few fine buys right now," the real estate man said. "No use trying to disguise the fact that the depression hit us rather hard. The Arkwright Mills, you know. And other places, too. So if you wanted to, you could pick up a nice residence property at an inviting price."

"What I thought," Jubey said, "was that I might like to get a piece of land, and maybe build."

"That can be done, also," the real estate man said thoughtfully. "You got time to let me show you a couple of places now, sir?"

Jubey said, "Well, I don't want to impose on you, if you're busy. I haven't actually made up my mind, you know."

"I'm not busy," the realtor said without irony. "I'd be mighty pleased to show you what's around."

They went in Jubey's car, and as they drove, the real estate man, whose name was Simpson, told him about the town. He had lived here since he was a boy, he said. Except for one little stretch when he got the notion he'd like to live in a big city. "Come back here, though," he said expressively.

They turned down a tree-lined street with houses set far apart, old-fashioned houses with verandas and cupolas and striped, faded awnings. In one pleasant yard a hammock between two trees swung weightlessly and a dog sat wagging.

"That was our church," Simpson said, pointing with his thumb to a small white building with a modest spire.

"Was?"

"Hadda close last year. Kinda miss it."

Jubey looked at the church with instant antagonism. Weeds grew high around it, double crop, last year's ghostly gray, this year's rank and sassy. A hooded bulletin board stood on what had once been the lawn, with a blackboard underneath a little peaked roof. Nothing at all was written on the blackboard.

"What'd it die of? Having nothing to say?" Jubey asked truculently.

"What'd *what* die of? Oh, you mean the church?" Simpson looked heavily where Jubey pointed at the empty bulletin board. "Oh, that. Well, I guess it had plenty to say all right. It was us that just didn't listen, I expect."

They rode along in silence for a few moments, both uncomfortable about the conversation. Then Simpson pointed ahead.

"The place I'm thinking of for you is right near the end of this street. Hasn't got a thing on it except a garage."

"How'd it happen to have a garage?"

"Well, the man that owns it expected to build a house. He got the garage finished, thinking they'd maybe kind of bunk in that until the house was built."

"And the house didn't get built."

"Nope. Depression. He'd sell real cheap, I think."

They were drawing near to the land now, a rolling piece of land, sweet and sunny with spring growth upon it, a lilac bush in bloom, some heliotrope and irises set out hopefully but now crowded out by new weeds in which crickets sang. The two men sat in the car and looked at it sadly.

"A nice piece," Simpson said. "Too bad, I thought. They did everything they could. Set out plants and stuff, and the children worked. You can see from the garage he built that he was going to have a nice house."

"Let's go look at it," Jubey said, a strange excitement welling up into his throat. "You say there's living quarters in the garage?"

"Nothing elaborate. A little toilet and shower, and a place in the kitchen for a gas stove to be attached, and there's a sink. You could make out all right."

Jubey walked across the land, his feet loving the live feeling of the earth. The trees overhead were strong and good, and the little choked garden the children had built could be brought back easily.

He remembered when they had bought the farm in Connecticut. Gay had brought photographs home, and they had studied them; an architect had made recommendations about remodeling the house for more grace and style. At last Jubey had been taken out to see the establishment, all finished and bright and running, like a model under a Christmas tree. The farmer had everything in order; he was quite courteous about explaining things, but obviously you weren't supposed to interfere with what was going on.

It wasn't like this. This land had something touching and appealing about it. This needed you. About the same way you needed it. Simpson had come up behind him, and something kept him from talking. The two men stood there silently, each seeing his own chosen sight.

At last Simpson said, "It wouldn't be hard to swing." He told Jubey the price, and he said it in a whisper out of respect for the good land which had come to this shame in its old age.

It was a price so small that Jubey thought, One tree that Gay had moved on to the Connecticut lawn cost almost that much.

Then Simpson said, "I don't know what your business is, but if you could arrange things so you could live in a town like this . . ." and then he asked directly, "What business are you in, sir?"

Jubey heard himself saying, "I'm a minister. But I haven't any church right now."

"Oh, I'm sorry about that," the other man said, flushing painfully, for he knew better than to ask people about their businesses these days.

Then, as much to relieve his discomfort as anything else, Jubey said, "I couldn't build a house myself just yet. And my family and I couldn't really live here for the present. But I could come here and work sometimes."

"Yes, you could," Simpson said. "That's what the other people did." He wished immediately that he hadn't said that unfortunate sentence, so he rushed along to cover his clumsiness in drawing such a woebegone analogy.

"I don't believe I got your name, sir."

Jubey hesitated, then he said, "My name's Our. Henry Our."

"Our? Like Jubal Our? Don't happen to be related to him, do you?" He grinned in a flattering way, not really expecting an answer, only wishing to please.

"The name's spelled the same way," Jubey said. "But we're only very distantly related, as near as I can make out. Very distantly."

But now suddenly he was finished with the day. He took out his watch and looked at it, and said, "I've got to be getting back."

"Well, you think about this," Simpson said. "Nobody ought to buy anything in a hurry. Not these days." He felt chilled and disappointed. Something had gone wrong suddenly, and he wasn't sure just why. Probably those stupid questions he

had asked about the man's business. He ought to learn sometime! They drove back rather silently to the realtor's office.

"You take my card, Mr. Our. You call me up and ask me
anything you might want to know."

"Yes. Yes I will," Jubey said impatiently, stuffing the card in
his pocket. He opened the door and Simpson got out dejectedly, saying to himself, I'll never hear from that guy again. And
I thought for a moment I'd really sold the place. The guy liked
it. I thought he was going to bust into tears, he liked it so
much.

Jubey drove back to New York, fast and impatient. He was
tired now, deflated and a little ashamed of himself. What had
he been thinking of, anyway? Maybe he had better see Dr.
Cromer. Maybe his nerves were as bad as he suspected they
were. He would hate to have had anyone following him today,
tailing him, as they said in the scripts. They would have
thought he was definitely off the beam.

Maybe he needed a good vacation. Or, on the other hand,
maybe he *wasn't* so far off today! Maybe what he needed was a
hideaway, a place where he could go, and tell people he was
working on the program . . . and then just forget the whole
thing.

He could take books up there, the kind he never had time
for. He could make a garden and work in it. He could wear
old clothes and get to know the neighbors, and maybe sit in
somebody's kitchen at noon when the man of the house came
home to dinner. They would all talk and laugh, and nobody
would expect him to be any funnier than anyone else.

Through the next two weeks, the place kept haunting him.
He woke up in the night thinking about it, seeing the tall grass
blowing in the sunshine, imagining how a hammock might
hang between the trees. He would build a wall, the first thing
he did . . . a man had to have privacy. A man couldn't enjoy
coming out and looking for companionship unless he had sol-

itude to leave. So he would build a wall. Not an unfriendly one; a wall you could invite neighbors within.

And he would bring down his fine telescope and set it up in the garage. He would open a place in the roof, so that he could study the stars. He would invite the neighbors to come in and look at the stars with him. . . . But how would he be there at night? How could he manage that, quite? Well, no use bothering about that, at this point. He would have the telescope, and the library of books on astronomy which he had always intended to collect.

A man had to lift his eyes to the heavens. Who said that? A Psalm? No, it was Kurt Geitzen on the narrow deck of the U-boat. He saw now why he wanted to study the skies. Was it because he really wanted to find God? That he wanted God to be friends with him? Unexpectedly he found a shattering craving in himself.

He got up quietly and slipped on a robe and fumbled his way downstairs through the country house to the library. For a long time he fingered around the shelves, not finding the book he wanted. But he knew it was there somewhere. Had Gay given it away? Or would she have had any reason to take it to her room? He realized that the two diametrically divergent speculations marked the wide range of his ignorance about Gay. He used to know her by heart; that's the way they had said it. But now. . . .

Then he found the book he wanted, a big Bible. He took it over to one of the green leather chairs and turned on the reading lamp, holding the book on his lap. A Bible always rested on a lap differently from other books. Or did he imagine that, from seeing it first on his mother's lap when he was a child? He began leafing through the Psalms, a strange nostalgia gripping him. There were beautiful things here; no wonder they had endured while so much else had perished. At last he found the verses he wanted:

"The heavens declare the glory of God. And the firmament sheweth his handywork. Day unto day uttereth speech, and night unto night sheweth knowledge. There is no speech nor language where their voice is not heard. Their line is gone out through all the earth, and their circuit to the end of the world."

That was why he had wanted the telescope, to study the language of God. He saw it now, and the honest admission eased through him in a strangely peaceful way, like health stealing across a body that has been wracked by illness. All that brave defiance, all the futile splitting of man's goodness away from its Source, had only been a boyish, defiant shyness, the stubborn bravado of a boy too gruffly timid to tell his father how much he loved him. It would have been the same with Papa . . . except that Papa was an extravagantly affectionate man who came all the way himself. But with God. . . . Suddenly he remembered what Lucile had told him years ago, "The word of God waits outside your door until it is invited in."

In a flash of intuition, he understood himself and that curious religion he had tried to build for himself, based only on the love he felt for mankind. *But you cannot love the work unless you love the Workman!* The words said themselves within him, and left him shaken with their momentous meaning.

It would be fine to study that vast manuscript on high, to read with his telescope the mystic alphabet of that celestial love poem. But closer at hand was the greater, living manuscript, the race which God had fashioned to express his goodness and his bounteous variety. To love that without acknowledging its Author was an inner confusion, the niggardly ungraciousness which was plagiarism. No wonder God had rejected him until he could come into his presence with decent manners! All the time he was thinking these thoughts he was reading on through the Psalms, helpless to stop the flow of beauty through his mind, the tide of ancient comfort through his heart.

He had no idea how long he read, but suddenly he heard a

rustling whisper, and there at the door was Gay in a scarlet gown.

"I thought you'd gone down to get something to eat," she said. "Then you stayed so long I got to worrying."

She came into the room, and her eyes took in the book on his lap

"Why, Jubey ... what on earth are you doing?"

His humility was too new to bear the scrutiny. He felt his face flaming with shame, and the old familiar stubborn anger reared up in him.

"As you see, I'm reading the Bible," he said stiffly. "Anything wrong with that?"

"No, of course not," she said uneasily. "It just surprised me, that's all. Do you do it ... often?"

"Nope," he said, snapping it shut with an explosive bang. Then he gave himself the perverse relief of hurting them both. "Only when I'm using something from it for the Program."

"Oh, Jubey, you're not going to make a joke from the Bible, are you?" Her eyes were wide and wounded. Then she covered that with learned prudence. "Would that be wise? The public sometimes gets offended. . . ."

"Don't worry, my pet. I would never be guilty of offending my public," he said crossly. "Not while we all have to eat, and wear fur coats, and go to private school, and have our little teeth straightened, and take riding lessons, and one thing and another."

"Jubey, don't talk that way," she said sternly. "Besides, are there jokes in the Bible?"

"Certainly. There are jokes everywhere. Absolutely everywhere."

6

THE PLACE kept at him all through the spring. He went back several times to see it, carefully avoiding the main street of Swiss Plains, so that Simpson wouldn't get his hopes up for nothing. He lay under a tree and napped, and woke up holding on to the grass as if the earth were his mother and he must fill his hands with her beloved hair, to be safe.

Finally he fought it no more. He walked into Simpson's office and laid down a grimy handful of bills which looked as if a poor preacher must have been saving them for years.

"I want the place," he said. "I can't help it."

Simpson could hardly believe his good fortune. He had thought of Jubey many times and had cursed the bungling way he had lost the sale.

"Well, Mr. Our! I sure am mighty glad to see you."

"It's the kind of place I need," Jubey said. "It may take me years to get around to building a house on it, but I want the land. I'll work on it a little at a time."

"You're not making any mistake. I can tell you that," Simpson said.

As soon as the place was his, it became more precious to him. He went down to the hardware store and bought a lawn mower and a sythe, and that very afternoon he cleared a neat wide swathe around the garage. He took a shower without benefit of towel, shivering in the cold city water. But he loved every minute of the day, and he said to himself, Next week I'll come on Tuesday. Good and early.

Other people took vacations throughout that summer. George Irving Compton mentioned it to Jubey several times. But Jubey didn't want to go anywhere, he said.

"I like it here," he said. "Where could I go?"

Tumulty said, "I've never seen you looking better. If you need a vacation, a jackass needs two tails."

"Who said anything about a vacation!" Jubey asked quarrelsomely.

"Everybody," Tumulty told him.

"I'm happy," Jubey said. "That's the only vacation anybody needs. Happiness."

"What makes you so happy, Our?" Tumulty asked him, suspiciously. "Nothing's any different, and you used to be jumpy as a cat."

"I've got back something I love," he said. "Don't tell anybody, Tumulty, but I'm in love, and I don't know what I'm going to do about it."

"Oh my word," Tumulty said. "There's going to be trouble."

"If it ever comes up in court, you swear I never told you any such thing," he said mischievously, grinning.

"Don't joke about such things. It's bad luck," Tumulty said severely.

Throughout summer and into the fall he managed to save one day a week for his place. That's what he called it to himself. "I'm in my place," he said sometimes as he was working in the garden, and later harvesting his few squashes and cabbages and potatoes, and making them up into baskets to carry around the neighborhood to give away.

The garden, naturally, was just an excuse to be alone and busy and watching something come to pass in which he himself had only the humble part. Whatever a man did in a garden was the smallest part; something bigger decided what manner of creation would result. Working with elements so much bigger than yourself gave you a new view of yourself. The power which had the final decisions to make could not be seen with your eyes nor grasped with your mind, yet you felt it and waited humbly for its way with you.

It struck him often as he worked that the good thing about the kind of thinking he did down here was that it couldn't possibly be adapted for use on the Program. It was divinely unstealable. He remembered things he had read years ago which had been crammed away and locked up because he had no way of adapting them to this octopus purpose that dominated his life. Thoughts came out and communed with him in a wonderfully companionable way. Carlyle, for instance, had said somewhere that "the first peculiarity of original men is that they in some measure converse with the universe at first hand." That described it. One talked to the universe, and it talked back. Could that be God talking back?

Long before the summer was over, he got a Franklin stove and connected it to a stovepipe that joined the chimney with a neat black circle shaped like a porthole. He knew the stove was insurance against the time when winter would try to keep him from his place.

The neighbors remembered occasionally to ask about his family, but mostly they remembered only to talk about themselves, for Mr. Our had a wonderful way with them.

"You ought to go on the radio giving advice to families in trouble," they said sometimes. "You seem to know just what people ought to do."

"I don't know a thing," he sometimes said. "You're really asking God's help when you ask a minister . . . even a minister out of a job."

"Yes, I suppose we are," they said. "Well, anyway."

It was only a half a block from his place to the church, but it took him until August to go there. He said to himself that it was the lawn mower and not the man which went the first time. Seemed too bad to have the grass so tall around the locked-up church. Any stranger who passed would have a discouraged feeling, seeing a church out of business. So he decided to cut the grass, and tidy up the place. He spent a whole morning on it, opening up the almost submerged path which led to the front steps, and trimming back the bridal wreath bushes that had gone straggly and unkempt.

All kinds of people stopped their cars and called out to him gladly, "Oh, Mr. Our . . . does that mean we're going to have our church back again?"

"I'm only getting it ready," Jubey said. "I'm only doing the caretaker's work."

"We miss the church. Seems too bad we couldn't keep it going."

"Why couldn't we?" Jubey asked, hardly noticing that he had identified himself with the town, past as well as present.

"We just didn't have enough attendance. Seems like we didn't ever have a preacher that could hold the interest."

"What kind of preacher would that be?"

"Well, you know. Some ministers sort of make you think about *them,* and whether they're good preachers or not . . . and some just make you worship God."

"Maybe we have to want a minister awhile before we get one," Jubey said. "I've heard that sometimes you have to want a thing awhile, so you'll appreciate it."

"That could be, Mr. Our. That well could be."

7

THEN GAY took matters into her own hands and insisted that Jubey must have a vacation.

"What would I do that's more fun than working?" he protested.

"You might get acquainted again with your family," she said, trying not to sound accusing about it. "We miss you, Jubey. You used to be such fun to have around the house."

"And now I'm not fun?"

"Now we never have you around the house. Couldn't we just take a trip somewhere, the three of us? Maybe be cooped up in a nice cozy Pullman compartment where we wouldn't have a thing to do except enjoy ourselves?"

"You don't ask for much," he said, not knowing whether or not to laugh at her simplicity.

"I always remember a trip Pete and my mother and I took once," she said. "I was about nine, and all I could think was 'I have the two people I love most right here in this little room with me, and nothing can take them away from me, or interrupt us.' It was heaven."

"And you think it would be heaven again?"

"I'd have the two people I love most in the world," she said. "Jubey, take the time."

"I'll do it," he said.

But the weeks stretched by, and at the end of each one he said, "Gay, I'm awfully sorry about our trip. I thought surely we could manage it next week."

But finally Tumulty told George Irving Compton, who picked up a phone and arranged this and that, including a reservation at the Broadmoor in Colorado Springs because he himself had once been there and had enjoyed it. Within three days, then, the Ours were on their way, Jubey amiably taking two other peoples' vacations.

The Ours were shut up cozily together in a Pullman drawing room. But they weren't entirely alone, for word had got around the train that Jubal Our was traveling on it. And besides, George Irving Compton had messenger boys meeting the train at every possible stop, with long worrying telegrams asking Jubey's advice about the replacement program they were scheduling while he was gone.

As long as they were going to "use up" so much time crossing the United States, Jubey decided they might as well stop off in St. Louis for a few hours and see the old city. He said he thought it would be nice for Lucile to see her grandfather's statue, and the wonderful old house where they all had lived. Actually it was he who was homesick for the sight of it all. There seemed no way they could manage it decently without spending the night with the Schumacher family, which by now had grown to five.

Minna, inevitably tall and solid and wearing violet scent, was determined not to be awed by Jubey. But when she saw the retinue getting off the train with all the miscellaneous luggage, including two typewriters, and when the local newspaper reporters who had heard somehow that the famous comedian was passing through his old home town, closed in upon them, Minna found herself suddenly overwhelmed. Earnest, however, was undaunted, and rushed up and kissed Gay before anyone could explain to her who he was.

"And this is little Lucile," he said, patting her head heavily. "I'm your Uncle Earnest, darling, and these are your cousins, Atlee, Sherman, and Marilyn. Come kiss little Lucile, children."

"And you're Earnest carried out to a logical conclusion," Jubey said, clapping him on the back so Earnest couldn't get in a position to wring out a crushing handshake.

Minna dried her eyes and threw herself on Jubey's chest, quite a feat for a woman of her size.

"Oh, my own brother . . . to think you're here at last."

Everyone seemed delighted with Gay. "Why, she doesn't look one bit like a show girl, Jubey," Minna said in a rasping whisper. "I'm sure Mama would have approved of her *entirely*."

On the way from the station to the Schumacher's house, they passed the old monument. Earnest stopped the car and flung open the doors so everyone could get out and gaze up at it.

"Why, he's a darling," Gay said. "He looks like Teddy Roosevelt, only a little plumper."

In the interests of honesty Minna had to admit that Papa had been actually a little more plump than the sculptor had dared indicate. "He was always sensitive about being fat," Minna said. "Wasn't he, Jubey?"

But Jubey found he couldn't talk easily in the presence of this large likeness. The wonderful Sunday afternoon of the unveiling, when Mama had worn a pink and purple velvet wheelbarrow full of willow plumes, and Papa had had to wipe his eyes with his big handkerchief, had been blotted out by that dreadful day when the vandals had thrown red paint across the statue's head. He remembered how Papa had almost slumped to the ground in hurt surprise, how the crowd had stood around and gaped, and the crude blood-red letters across the pedestal had said, "Our disgrace." He felt actually sick at the memory, for he never had come to peace with it, and every detail was lying in wait to attack him.

"As long as we're this close, let's go up to the old house," he said rather thickly. "I'd like Gay and Lucile to see it."

"After dinner, darling," Minna said. "I've planned such a good dinner for us all. Everything you like, Jubey. I remember."

"It won't take long," Jubey begged. "Then we can just settle down for a nice long evening with you people." Suddenly he felt he must see the house, and get it all over with. He couldn't stand a stretched-out agony. He saw now that it would have been infinitely better if they had not come at all. Gay, not knowing the facts but realizing that he was painfully moved by all this, had come over to his side and had slipped her arm through his.

"Let's go now, Minna," she said. "Jubey's so anxious to see it."

"But I don't see why a few hours more or less would matter," Minna said ungraciously. "Well, all right, if you insist."

They drove up to within a few hundred feet of the old house. Then Jubey said, "Earnest, let me out here. I'd like to walk up to it, the way I used to when I was a youngster."

But it wasn't the youngster who walked up with him; it was the exile whom Rose Kramer had just given up, the strong-muscled boy who had wandered up and down the country a few days too long to see his mother alive for the last time.

Little Lucile had come leaping out of the car to walk with Daddy, and she was running along beside him, prattling in her high-pitched childish voice.

"Did Mummie live here, too, Daddy?"

"No, of course not," Jubey said impatiently. "You know where Mummie lived. You've been there dozens of times."

"She lived with Nanmother and Nanfather," the child said, being almost deliberately stupid, as if to distract her father from some old sorrow she couldn't possibly understand.

They were in front of the low redstone wall now, with the green iron lace fluted along its top. The big old mansion had a gaunt and cadaverous look, not exactly shabby but as if the spirit had gone out of it. There was a bald place in the center of the lawn, but the catalpa tree was the same, and the rhododendron bushes had grown so that they shrouded the out-lines of the massive stone porch. There were several lethargic-looking children running aimlessly about the grounds.

Lucile said, "Are those your little brothers, Daddy?"

"Of course not, Lucile."

"But I didn't know you had a niggra brother, Daddy."

"This is a home for children who haven't any place else to live. I told you on the train," Jubey explained wearily.

"Why haven't they any place else to live, Daddy? Do they like it here?"

"Of course."

"Well, I wouldn't like it. *I'd* run away. If you didn't live here, too, Daddy."

Gay came up then and hushed her offspring with one look which only a superior adult female could have given, and a knowing small female could have interpreted.

"I was only being nice, Mummie," Lucile said plaintively.

"Well, don't be," her mother said shortly. "Be quiet instead. At your age, that's even nicer."

"I was only talking."

"That will do, Lucile."

Gay stood there beside him and tried to see what he was seeing. She tried to think of a comforting question which might bring out some happy reminiscence, but none came to her.

"Places change, Jubey," she said at last. "It's only what we keep in our own mind that is safe."

"It looks about the same," he said stubbornly, unwilling to fall into any banality of discussion. "It looks about the way I remember it."

As a family vacation the trip wasn't really a success. Everything was too elaborate, and there were too many people who wanted to tell Jubal Our how much they liked his program, and why didn't he ever do that one about the baseball player and the schoolteacher again?

He sometimes said to Gay, "I suppose this isn't any fun for you. You had all you wanted of it. But to me . . . well, I get a kick out of it."

"Then have it, Jubey," she said. "Have it as long as it pays you back something valuable to you."

At the end of two weeks, they came back to New York and Jubey said he felt the whole thing had been most worthwhile for the Program. A man mustn't get too far away from his public. After all, how could you know what they wanted if you didn't live with them once in awhile?

The last few days of his vacation were agony to him. He wanted to get back to his work in the village. There was a baby being born, and the young mother needed someone to help her over the first days she had to face, coming back to her parents' house with no husband. There was an old man trying to die gallantly, who might be given a hand up the high step when the moment came. And most of all there was a plan in Jubey's mind for something the locked church might offer, locked though it was.

They got back to New York late Wednesday afternoon, and Jubey said, "Mind if I take a run down to the studio, dear?"

"I expected you to," Gay said.

"Well, you know."

"I ought to, Jubey."

Instead of going down to the studio, he telephoned from a cigar store on the way up to the bridge, telling Tumulty when to expect him.

"I'm back in town, Tumulty. But I've a couple of matters to take care of tomorrow. I'll be in Friday morning."

"Stuff has been happening around here," Tumulty said cryptically.

"So you wired me."

"I didn't put this in a wire. This is something I thought I'd just rather tell you about."

"Bad news?"

"Powerful good."

"Good news keeps," he said. "I'll hear it Friday, Sweetheart."

He drove across the bridge, singing. The car knew its own

way now, and he took the turns one after another, hardly noticing them. He reached Swiss Plains just after dark, and he
thought, "There are ten houses in this little town where they'd
be tickled to death to have me drop in for supper." It was a
thought permitted only to a man who was a millionaire in
brotherliness, he thought humbly.

He went first of all to the house of the dying man, and then
to the hospital where the baby had not yet arrived. One by
one he checked off his several compassionate errands. Then he
drove into the yard of the poorest family in the town, who had
the most children and the most love to share.

He went up to the door and listened a minute to the buzz
of life and familyhood within. Then he turned the knob and
called out, "Comp'ny! Comp'ny's here. And he's brought two
quarts of peach ice cream."

They came swarming around him, wanting to hear where he
had been the last two weeks, and why he hadn't come the last
two Thursdays, the way he always did.

"Gosh, we were afraid you were sick someplace, Mr. Our.
And we don't have any address for you."

"We just couldn't bear it if you got sick or something, and
we-all didn't know where you were," they said.

"I was doing a piece of work."

They sat around the kitchen table and talked awhile, and
then Jubey said it was time for him to run over to his place and
see how things were.

"And I wonder if I could borrow a piece of chalk from one of
you kids."

"Chalk? You mean school chalk, Mr. Our?"

"Sure. I got an idea that I'd like to write something on that
big blackboard in front of the church. Isn't any reason *that* has
to sit there blank. What'd you think?"

"You mean a Bible verse or something? The way churches
have that are getting along all right?"

"That's the idea."

"Go get Mr. Our the chalk, Howard," the mother said, brushing back a wisp of hair that always tormented her. "Get him a nice long piece now."

"Yes, ma'am. Would you like pink chalk, Mr. Our?"

"I think white would be better. If you've got any white."

"We got a whole flock of colors."

He drove down to his own place, and went through the tall gate, and stood on the quiet land, and it was almost as if he heard its heart beating.

I've got to tell Gay about this some day, he said to himself. But not until we're old people, I guess. A long time after everything is over and ended, I'll tell her.

He unlocked the door and went into the dark bare little room with its few comforts accumulated through the months, a second-hand chair, a plain table, the Franklin stove with its neat little pile of strong-muscled wood beside it. He knelt and built the fire, still in the dark for the sheer pleasure of having the room lighted by aliveness instead of electricity incarcerated in a bulb. The wood crackled and caught, and in a few moments there were huge shadows on the wall and ceiling, flickering excitedly. He sat in the chair a few moments, utterly happy and at home. Winter would come soon and he would know a new meaning in his place. Winter was the time for sitting before your own fire, and reading long good books. He would come down here just the same. The work in the village would go on, and the work in himself would go on.

He went out after a while and stood under his willow tree a long time, talking within himself in that way that had come upon him in the last few months. Was this praying? He supposed it was. But it hadn't anything sanctimonious or formal about it. It was just a kind of talking and listening, as if to a great wise friend. There was a Bible verse that expressed it . . . "face to face, as a man talketh to his friend."

At last he locked the door of his little house and went down the path and through the gate. He would walk to the church under the maple trees whose leaves, yellow and scarlet, had formed a rustling carpet on the ground. He kicked the leaves as he walked, just as he used to when he was a boy. The wonderful once-a-year sound of the rustling leaves! The best pleasures were such as this, the ones so simple you couldn't really mention them to anyone but yourself.

The church, white and forthright, stood in its neat lawn. It looked like a going concern. It looked as if people loved it and depended upon it. He went up to the big black bulletin board which stood on the lawn under its little peaked roof. He had noticed it the first day he came here, but not as he saw it now. It had not changed, of course; but he had changed, and that made it appear quite different.

Ever since he had first got the idea of writing something on the board, he had been trying to decide which verse to select. There were several he loved. The best one seemed to be the great commandment that Jesus had given:

"Beloved, love one another as I have loved you."

He took the chalk in his hand and scanned the words across the blank space, with his eye before he began lettering. But suddenly he realized he was not writing the words he had intended to write. Another verse was forming beneath the white chalk, a verse from Isaiah.

"Come let us reason together." (Isaiah 1:18)

Then he found that he was writing "5 P.M. Thursday. You are invited."

Yes, that was it! A great singing delight went through him. Why, certainly that was what it was all about!

There's nothing says the services have to be held inside the building, he cried to himself. We could get up a kind of informal get-together on the steps. Not real services. Just neighbors, after the day's work is through.

8

TUMULTY'S NEWS wiped out everything else. She had kept it out of the telegraphed report she sent him every day during his absence, because she knew it would have brought him bounding back to the city. Two important men from Hollywood wanted to talk to Jubey. They held the contract of a pale-faced little actor who had once been tops and now had slipped rather dangerously. They wanted to talk to Jubey about taking over his story and gags and making something new of the comedian's personality.

Tumulty had made the appointment for luncheon the first day Jubey was back at his job. During the first ten minutes they talked, one of the men said, "You're working too hard, son. Radio's for unskilled labor. You've got the kind of talent that Hollywood knows how to pay for."

"This starts out good," Jubey said with a grin. "Let's hear some more."

He knew the comedian, a sorry-looking mongrel named Sam Stem, whose clothes were always six sizes too big and whose lines usually bordered on the imbecilically obscene, as if he had no idea what he was saying.

"We're dissatisfied with what's been done with Sam," one of the backers said frankly. "The guy's got talent. He could act. He could be more than funny."

"Funny's quite a plenty," Jubey said defensively. "If it really comes off."

"But Stem might be funny plus."

"That's what I've always thought about him," Jubey said. "He could be the little timid guy that lives inside each of us. The little fumbler that tries too hard, and falls on his face."

"That's it. That's what I've been trying to say," the backer beamed. So Jubey knew from that moment he was "in" because of his old ability to phrase other men's words for them.

"I'd like to see him in skimpy pants, and a big coat with sleeves that drop down over his hands. I'd like him to have a shorter haircut, and he shouldn't talk much. He should look worried and panting to please. Maybe he could have one line that we could make a kind of trade mark, something that would catch on. He's got to look inefficient and useless, while every line of his skinny little body is crying out for somebody to find him big and important."

As he talked, Jubey's own huge body seemed to become emaciated, and his jovial face looked haunted yet hopeful. The two men sat back and gazed at him.

"Say, Our, you look more the way Sam Stem ought to look than he *ever* does!"

"He's always trying to help people, and all he does is snarl 'em up in messes. But he's so dripping with good will that he never realizes he's in a mess, so somehow he blunders out of it. He's got to win, usually. Because that little guy inside each of us needs to win so terribly. And he so seldom does come out on top."

During the next days the more he talked about Sam Stem, the more he loved him, as if he himself had been his creator. The studio had a story for him, a zany tale of mischances and trick shots, but so far, nobody had worked out a really good character for the melancholy little comedian. Jubey could have screen credit, they told him. "Extra dialogue by Jubal Our."

The little guy could sing, also, a faint plaintive kind of singing that wasn't like anyone else's. But nobody had ever found a way of using his voice. Did Jubey think he could write some songs for him?

"Could I write songs?" he said. "They're as good as written right now."

Now that he had been swept into the excitement of a new challenge to his talent, he was tingling with ambition again. The old thirst was in him.

The thought of his place, and the little white church and the humble gathering of neighbors on the steps that night two weeks ago, had become dim and distant to him now. Whenever he remembered, it seemed like a fever-dream in an illness from which he had now fully recovered.

I was living in a folk story, he said to himself sheepishly. I wouldn't want anyone to know about all that. I guess maybe I was tireder than I knew. I was exhausted. But I'm full of my-self again now. I'm as well as I ever was.

He pushed the memory of the town out of his mind every time it came, like a middle-aged love affair of which he was ashamed.

It's certainly time I had a new interest, he said to himself. If you believed there was such a thing as destiny taking care of you, you could say this chance was handed to me in the nick of time.

With all the new flattery and admiration from the motion picture men he felt young and handsome and sure of himself; he flexed his personality and his masculine charm as another man might have flexed his muscles.

The boy is back, he said to himself, and saluted himself in the mirror. But you had a close call, my brawny lad.

They began drawing up a fabulous contract. Jubey would need an agent. Carmichael and Swain, the two producers, assured him that they would insist upon an agent for him so Jubey would know he was getting a good deal. They themselves telephoned the sharp, white-haired boy that was now at the top of the heap of Hollywood agents, and he came straight out to New York, in order to fix everything and proper.

At the beginning of the negotiations Jubey had said, "I'll

have to talk it over with George Irving Compton. We'll have to work out a leave of absence, or something."

"He'll let you come. He'll see that it will be good experience for you," Carmichael and Swain assured him. The conferences went on throughout the next days, and it seemed that everyone, even George Irving Compton, was in agreement that Hollywood and Jubey would be of reciprocal benefit to each other.

Jubey walked through his life in a delighted daze.

"Of course I'm going on one condition, Tumulty," he said. "You know what that is."

"How'd I know?"

"If you think it will be all right for you to move Steve out to California."

It was the only time in all their experience that he had seen Tumulty undone. She put her big freckled paws up over her face and wept. Not like a woman but like a little girl, angry because she couldn't help crying.

"You're the only person on earth who would say something like that," she said. "My family and all my friends are always hinting that I ought to give Steve up as a bad job."

"You're married to him, aren't you?" Jubey said simply. "So what about moving him to California?"

"I asked the doctor yesterday," Tumulty mumbled.

"And?"

"He said it might do him good."

"Well, what're we waiting for?" Jubey cried, clapping her vehemently on her bony shoulder.

THEN AT BREAKFAST one morning, he suddenly realized something was wrong with Gay.

"Carmichael and Swain are going to have a subleased house all ready for us by the time we get there," he said, taking one of the digestive pills which seemed part of the successful creative man's occupational equipment.

"Oh? You're going to need a house?"

"Why, naturally, Gay. You wouldn't want to live in a hotel, would you?"

"I?" she said. "This is the first time anyone's asked me if I wanted to go to California."

He sat back in annoyance and stared at her, then he laughed and reached over and patted her hand. "Sorry, darling. I guess you're right about that."

She went on eating her cereal and saying nothing. So he realized the moves were for him to make.

"Very well, Mrs. Our, dear.' *Will* you please accompany your husband and child to California? They would both be very much pleased to have you."

She looked at him very seriously, and for the first time through all the years, she allowed the pity she felt for him to show in her eyes.

"No, Jubey. I'm afraid I can't come," she said.

"What are you talking about? *Can't?*"

She shook her head, and then put her elbows on the table and supported her clasped hands. "Jubey, I'm not going."

"Oh Gay, you wouldn't be difficult at a time like this!"

"It's always a time like this, in one form or other. And I've come to the end of it."

"The end of what? For heaven's sake," he said in annoyance.

"Of trying to be married to you."

"You mean . . . you mean you don't love me any more?" He felt himself blushing like a boy as he said the inadequate words.

"I think it's immoral for me to go on living with a man I'm *not* married to. The man I married has disappeared completely. There's a stranger here. And he's a man I have very little in common with."

He looked at her and weighed whether or not this was a place where anger would be effective. Once or twice through his spurting career, he had found that anger was an inspired strategy. He decided against it quickly, for this situation. Instead he let his face drop into weariness.

"I know we don't have much time together, darling."

"We have more time together than I really enjoy," she said softly.

Then he did get angry, strategy or no strategy. He felt his scalp prickling with rage, and he thought, This is one of those scenes they tell you about. I suppose I hurt her ego. Then something lost and almost forgotten wailed in him, Jubey . . . poor Jubey . . . this is your love you're talking about. This is Gay. Remember her?

He started to say something, and changed it and started again, and then stopped. Gay herself went on speaking, in a soft even voice, as if she had thought the words for years.

"You try to understand. Because it's not a clever kind of thought. It hasn't got any twist to it, or any switch, or any of the ingredients you're always watching for, Jubey. It's just a simple little fact. You've shut off the part of you that I loved. And the rest of you . . . the big famous part that everybody else is tickled to death about . . . just happens to be a man I'm not interested in."

The room whirled around him in a vertigo of rage and hurt

pride. His brain smarted as if a wasp had stung it. He remembered that first afternoon, when he had come home from his
interview with George Irving Compton. . . .

"You're jealous," he said in a whisper. "I've often wondered
why you weren't. I thought it was just that you were too dog-
goned sweet and big to be envious of my career. And all the
time . . . underneath . . . you've been boiling with it."

The room was very quiet now, and the maid, who should
have brought in fresh coffee at this moment, stayed behind the
serving pantry door with her eyes tight shut, praying on her
fingers and crossing herself.

"All right, Gay. I don't actually blame you. If you want me
to, I'll help you get back. You're still young enough, and you'll
always be beautiful. We'll make you a comeback. We'll go out
to Hollywood, and we won't say a word to anyone. But I'll
build you."

"And that would fix everything?" she asked sadly, and shook
her head. "There would be two of us then . . . just twice as
much of everything that fills this house with nonsense . . . and
that would be fine?"

"Well, what else do you want?"

She waited a moment, then she said it. "I want my husband
back."

He thought, Now we'll have to go round and round on this.
Nothing will satisfy her except more of my time, because that's
the only thing I haven't enough of.

Aloud he said patiently, "All right, dear. We'll take more
time together. I'll have Tumulty be more strict about appoint-
ments . . . or I'll give up looking at the mail . . . anyway we'll
work it out."

"I'm not coming with you, Jubey. Tumulty won't have to
work anything out, because I just won't be there. I told you
when I married you that I wanted nothing better than to help
you. . . ."

"You mean you'd like to help with the Program some way?

But Gay . . . you see, you were a dancer. I do talk about things with you . . . or at least I used to. But now, well, I get so fed up with it that when I'm home. . . . "

She watched him floundering along and she let him go to the very end of it. Then she said quietly, "I said I wanted to help *you*, Jubey. You act as if 'Program' and 'you' were synonyms. I'm not interested in the program. Or what you're going to think up for Sam Stem to say."

"You ought to be," he said, hating his own crudeness. "It's certainly bought you everything you could possibly want."

"Has it? I'm afraid not. It was you I married, Jubey. And the work we both believed in."

She could not let herself mention God in this conversation; she could not trust herself to say his name for fear Jubey would become angry and would split the earth between them in such a way that neither of them ever could bridge it again.

So instead she said, "You made me believe in things I'd never paid any attention to. All *that* in you was what I wanted to live with. But then you locked a door on it all and blithely lived outside. Well, that just isn't good enough for me, Jubey."

"But you agreed," he said. "There was nothing else to do at the time. This big opportunity came, and you agreed. . . . "

"We agreed we'd try it for a year."

"Most women would be grateful," he said reproachfully.

"I'm not most women. And you're not most men."

Unconsciously, out of tyrannical habit, he looked at his watch. Gay smiled and got up from the table, and then came over and touched his shoulder in a swift, dismissing pat.

"You'd better run along, dear," she said. "I know you've got all sorts of important things to talk about downtown."

"We'll finish this another time."

"It's finished already, Jubey."

He left for the studio, dutifully intending to think over what she had said, and get up the right answers. He must have

Tumulty order some flowers. A tight little round bouquet of rosebuds like the one she had carried at their wedding. She was a sweet thing, coming down to that ghastly little Pennsylvania town unexpectedly so they could be married in his church. His church! He veered away quickly from the humiliating words. His skin prickled with shame at the very sound of them.

You could say . . . or rather you might appropriately say it at the *end* of his life, "The only thing the man ever failed at was making sense out of a bickering, narrow-minded little church."

But the astonishing and wonderful part of it was that if he had not failed at that, he never would have been forced into this! This? What was this, anyway?

Then, quite without warning, another epitaph rushed across his mind: "He succeeded all his life in order to achieve a failure."

He laughed out loud in surprise at the neat balance of that, and he said to himself, Where in the dickens did that come from? And of course it doesn't mean anything.

Doesn't it?

Certainly not.

It means what Gay was trying to say. Only Gay never has that kind of words. Gay doesn't think with her brain. She thinks with her heart, which is smarter than brain-thinking.

The dialogue whipping back and forth in his mind infuriated him, as soon as he was able to stop it long enough to get self-respectingly angry at it.

The things you think of! he said disgustedly to himself. No wonder you're a swell script writer. Everything comes to you in the form of dialogue. But he knew he was cannily saying that to himself so there would be no foolish temptation to think there were two of them talking in his mind, himself and that Other.

In the elevator he thought, I'll phone Gay the moment I get

upstairs. She's a dear little woman. I've got to give her more of my time. Besides I'll need the woman's viewpoint when I get to working on the Sam Stem movie. And Gay's all woman, God bless her.

PART V

He comes to himself

1

As soon as he came into the office, Tumulty handed him the unopened telegram. "It says personal," she said with a shrug.

"Personal means you and me, Sweetheart," he said absent-mindedly. "But speaking of personal, I want you to order Gay the best little old bunch of roses to be had in the city. This is the way I want 'em done. . . . " He was opening the yellow envelope as he talked and then he stopped talking, taking in the words one by one.

ROBERTA ROSE KRAMER CRITICALLY ILL IN MASSACHUSETTS GENERAL HOSPITAL SHE INSISTS ON MY SENDING THIS TELEGRAM CAN YOU SPARE TIME TO COME IMMEDIATELY SIGNED DOCTOR RALPH PARTEN

Tumulty said, "What's the matter, Our? Bad news?"

"I'll have to go," Jubey said. "My oldest friend, Tumulty."

"I'll handle things," Tumulty said. "Don't worry about a thing."

"Carmichael was coming in this morning."

"I'll handle Carmichael," Tumulty said. "You want me to phone Gay?"

He stopped and thought a moment, then he said, "No. I'd better call her later myself."

"Maybe you'll want to take her with you."

"No. I don't believe so."

She got him a seat on the Boston plane, sent off the wire to Dr. Parten, and brought out the overnight bag he kept in the office for emergencies.

"You phone Gay later in the day, just to check," he said as he was leaving. "In case I don't get her. Don't try to tell her much about where I'm going."

"How could I?" Tumulty asked reasonably. "You haven't told me much."

He kept putting off telephoning Gay, because he couldn't seem to make up his mind just how much to tell her. He wondered why he had never before told her about Rose. There was no reason she couldn't have known. Except that it might be difficult for a girl like Gay to understand a woman like Rose. What nobody ever could have understood, of course, was her goodness. That was why he hadn't told about her. All the time he had known her, he remembered, that had troubled him. Nobody ever would have been able to see how *good* she was. They would have thought he was just an inexperienced boy who couldn't judge.

When he reached the Newark airport, he telephoned his apartment. The English housekeeper answered pleasantly.

"Oh, Mr. Our . . . Mrs. Our isn't here," she said. "She went out shortly after you left, sir."

"Did she say when she was coming back?"

"No. She said she was going to pick up Miss Lucile from school, and for us not to bother."

"Well, you tell her I've been called out of town. I'll phone her tonight from Boston, Mrs. Beale."

He felt relieved that it had fallen out this way; just showed you how unnecessary most worrying was. Gay had probably regretted her attitude this morning. All the time he had been thinking about sending the flowers, she had probably been thinking of some little present she would buy for him. Could he use that situation in a script? No, that was O. Henry's "Gift of the Magi" theme. Old and tired as the mischief. Funny how the brain of an experienced creator always tries on for size any item it encounters.

He got into the plane, looked over the other seven passengers, and then slumped down in a seat, pulling his privacy around him like a heavy curtain. This would give him some time to think about Rose, to remember her, to imagine what she would be like after all these years. It had been a long time. There must have been many persons close to her through this long interval. But somehow it didn't surprise him that she wanted him now. For one thing, the distance would have made their strange companionship more beautiful and more perfect than it actually was. When he remembered it, he always tried to allow for the poetic transformation time works.

But even so, it had been an unaccountably beautiful episode. Beautiful because of the very fact that from all outward appearances it would have seemed sordid and shabby. A thousand things had happened to him throughout his life, a thousand charming events in the last few years when everyone admired him and praised him. Yet none of them stood out with the same touching vividness as did those weeks with Rosie. Yes, one other theme stood out in the same way. *His place.* And that, too, was something faintly shameful and odd, which couldn't be told to anyone. Could it be possible that was one of the requirements for inner beauty . . . this protectiveness one felt about it, this quality of innocent secrecy?

He thought of Rose and *the place* together now, a counterpoint of revery. Rose would have understood *the place.* She would have loved it; she would have worked with him tidying up the weeds and bushes around the derelict, neglected old church. She would have felt that the old Franklin stove with its protruding belly was a kind of household pet; she would have loved a rainy day snug in the garage with a fire and a pot of boiled coffee, and homemade pie sent over by Mrs. Simpson. She was a runaway, like himself; that was why.

And what would she have thought of that five o'clock meeting on the steps of the church? Well, she would have thought

that was just crazy. Since that Thursday he had had no time
to digest that meeting, for Carmichael and Swain had happened
to him immediately after it.

He had come so far from the mood of that meeting that it
had receded into the past as if it had occurred years ago. It had
a faraway unreality about it, as if it had happened to a self
which never again could be located. And, to be sure, that was
exactly the situation, for with Hollywood looming up ahead of
him, the chances were he might never see *the place* again. And
if he did see *the place* . . . if he went down just for the purpose
of getting his telescope and a few books, he probably wouldn't
see the church, for he wouldn't have time to go over to it. And
why should he go over anyway?

Against his will, he found himself remembering the gathering on the church steps. Quite early the cars had begun coming
slowly down the street. Some of them had driven by, wanting
to make sure before they committed themselves that other people were accepting the invitation which he had written on the
hooded blackboard. Some people came on foot, and stood a
moment looking at the bulletin board, and asking each other
what did they think.

Jubey himself sat on the top step of the church, with his big
Bible beside him. He had no idea how he was going to pro-
ceed with this impulsive notion; he had kept himself from planning. Usually, everything he did was skilfully planned out be-
forehand, to get the maximum effectiveness out of whatever he
said or did. But somehow he felt an instinctive demand that
this should be different. Less Jubey in this; more of something
else.

There were too many of them to find seats on the steps, so
they began sitting on the grass. Children came, and sat down
quietly on the edges of the crowd, and three little trampish
dogs, wagging with inquisitive delight, ran around happily, and
then they sat down too.

Unexpectedly at five minutes before five, great rich bell tones began falling from the little steeple, and the group looked around and a few neighbors wiped their eyes, for they had missed the calling of the church bells. The peals stopped exactly at five o'clock, and Simpson, the real estate man, awkward and pink came around from the rear of the church, so that Jubey knew he had been the bell ringer.

All the faces then turned up expectantly to the top of the steps. Suddenly Jubey said a prayer in himself, an unexpected prayer. God, keep this man from being clever. You just do the talking, please.

He didn't even rise from where he was sitting; he had a feeling he had no business to be standing up in any posture of even momentary authority.

He said, "As long as we haven't any minister, and as long as what we all want is just some kind of worship, how would it be if we passed the Bible around, and all of us who want to could read it to the rest of us?"

There was a long silent moment, then someone called out earnestly, "You start, Mr. Our."

"All right. I'll start," Jubey said. He picked up the book and its weight in his hands was good.

"I'll read from the book of Psalms," he said.

The words flowed out like music. But not the music of a man's voice; rather it was a melody of meaning, a stirring of minds, intimately private. Jubey was scarcely aware of when he gave up the reading and passed the Book along to a stretched-out hand. No one thought about what others might be hearing, not Jubey nor the neighbors. Each was alone with the Book. There hardly seemed to be a break in the reading; it was as if one voice with many intonations was speaking.

He felt almost as if the same voice were speaking to him now in the plane, a voice made up of all the voices in the world ... the still, small voice that is louder than hurricane or thunder . . . which speaks within a man and waits forever until it is heeded. The voice of peace unspeakable which the world cannot give.

Then he realized he had fallen into a quiet sleep. The stewardess, a scrubbed-looking youngster, was leaning over and touching him because it was time to fasten his seat belt.

"We're coming in, Mr. Our," she said, beaming at him. "It's been quite an honor to have you with us. I listen to you every Saturday night. My family think you're just a scream."

Jubey came back from the vast distance, "Thank you, my dear," he said. "I guess that's what I am, all right."

2

AT THE HOSPITAL the girls at the receiving desk in the main entrance hall were watching for him. Surrounded by catastrophe as they were, they lived a dull existence, and the prospect of having Jubal Our come in, gave them quite a flutter of excitement.

Dr. Parten, young and athletic and carefree looking, hoped Jubey would have something to say that would throw a bit of light on how it happened that the drab little woman in Ward 913 could demand that a telegram be sent which would immediately bring the famous man to her side.

"I suppose Mrs. Kramer is a distant relative?" he suggested. But Jubey just let the supposition fall on the rubber-tiled floor. So the doctor hastily sketched in the history of the case.

"There's no use pretending that she's going to recover," he said at the end. "The mystery to us all is how she's kept alive so long."

Jubey allowed himself to say, "She has a great deal of life in her. I guess that's why, Doctor."

The doctor refrained from commenting that this was an unprofessional explanation straight out of folklore. Life as he saw it every day was a matter of tissues and blood, and had little to do with how much "life" people "had" in them.

"She's conscious most of the time," he said instead. "But it may happen that she will be in coma. In that case . . ."

"In that case, I'll wait," Jubey said. "I've nothing more important to do, Doctor Parten."

"Good," the doctor said, and they left his office and walked down a long hall teeming with nurses and orderlies and silently wheeled hand trucks to an elevator.

"The busiest places on earth these days, hospitals," the doctor said.

"When you're sick in bed, nobody can possibly expect anything of you. Or blame anything on you," Jubey remarked. Then, in case that sounded cynical he added, "Poor devils. All of us, I mean."

"Oh, I don't know," Dr. Parten said. "You're doing all right, Mr. Our. Nobody's blaming you . . . or expecting anything from you that you can't deliver pretty magnificently."

They were silent going up in the elevator, a small brilliant room crowded with a heterogeneous collection of hospital workers, technicians and visitors, nervously fingering their clothes.

Rose's ward was on a floor as noisy and as crowded as a railway station. Every possible kind of life seemed to be going on simultaneously. People in wheel chairs were plying their way cumbersomely about the shiny floors; mopping was being done; nurse's aides were carrying on enamored conversations with young internes; a little Negro child was sitting on the floor counting out pennies into small piles; and a visitor on a bench was solemnly eating lunch from a paper bag.

They went through the wide swinging doors of the ward, a long vista of illness and despair stretching before them on the right and the left. A few beds were partitioned off by white-sheeted screens. Behind one of these was Rose. Dr. Parten put his head around the screen.

"Mrs. Kramer, I've brought you a visitor."

She said nothing at all, and the doctor motioned to Jubey to step within the screened enclosure. She turned her head then and looked a long time at Jubey, while big slow tears gathered in her eyes.

"Now, if we're going to have anything like that, Mrs. Kramer," the doctor said threateningly.

"Like what?" she said fiercely, and Jubey knew it was the old Rosie.

He said, "I'm not complaining."

At that, her old gamin grin came back. So the doctor muttered some appropriate sound and withdrew. Jubey sat down on a chair which had been pulled up in readiness.

"I'd know you anyplace," he said.

"You're a liar, Jubey. And I wouldn't know you either. Not until you spoke, anyway."

"I've gotten prettier," he said. "I got my growth, Rose."

"I got mine, too. You helped me get mine, Jubey."

He saw she was finding it difficult to breathe, so he talked awhile to give her a rest. But she interrupted him, because she had to say something.

"I bragged about you, Jubey. People didn't always believe I really knew you. But I bragged about you everywhere I went. Was that all right?"

"That was swell."

"Sometimes I even told people you were my son. But I didn't want anybody to think you weren't doing right by your mother, so usually I said you were my adopted son."

"Maybe that's what I was, Rosie."

"No. That was never it," she said after a few minutes. "But now I don't care. Now it's all right that way."

He reached over to the thin mound of her, and took her hot dry hand and held it close.

"I haven't got my rings on, Jubey," she said apologetically.

"That's all right. You look fine any way."

"Maybe you don't think I've got any rings. It hurts me to look down and see my hand lying there without any rings."

"I'll run out and get you a ring for every finger you've got."

She squeezed his hand and said with some spirit, "That isn't at all necessary. I *have* rings. I tell the nurses and I can see they don't believe me."

"I believe you."

"It's only that I just had to borrow a little money on them. I thought surely I'd have them back before this. And I would have, too, except . . ."

Then her face convulsed as if in fright, and she said in a quick smother, "Jubey, I always promised myself I'd die with rings on my fingers. But now it don't look like I'll make it . . ."

"Let's don't worry about the rings," he said huskily. "The matter's all settled. Soon as I can tear myself away from your fascinating company, I'll go out and get them back for you."

She looked as if she would collapse in tears at that. "You can't, Jubey."

"What's to stop me?"

"They're in Memphis, Tennessee."

"So what's wrong with Memphis?" he said valiantly. "They run airplanes down there, don't they?"

She tried to sit up in bed at that, because a gale of laughter was shaking her, and she wasn't supposed to laugh.

"Oh, Jubey . . . now I *know* it's you," she said between wheezes.

"Don't laugh, Rose . . . suppose you ripped out the hemstitching, or something!" he said in consternation.

"Let it rip," she said. "You're *here*. So I'm not complaining."

"But about the rings. If you think I'd be gone too long, trying to redeem them . . . what'd you say if I just run out here in Boston and bring in a couple just like them? That could be done, couldn't it?"

"It could be done by you," she said. "Anything could be done by you, Jubey."

"So what kind of rings were they?"

She looked afraid to tell him, and then blushing, she blurted
it out. "One was a wedding ring."

"So you married somebody."

"No. But it was a wedding ring anyway."

"And the other one?"

"The other one was a diamond. A cock-eyed diamond . . .
but if you kept your hand moving a little bit, nobody ever
noticed that about it. It glittered swell."

"Do I have to find a cock-eyed one? If I can't locate anything
except a nice pure stone, will that do?"

She patted his hand, and he could see she wanted him to be
doing both things at once, sitting here beside her and at the
same time scampering out of the hospital, grabbing a cab, rushing up to Boylston Street, and then flying back with two little
boxes in his pocket.

"While they feed you your lunch I'll go," he said.

"Yes. They give me an i.v. feeding. It's revolting."

She snuggled down more securely in her pillows, and Jubey
realized now that despite the limp streaked hair and the tired
huge eyes in the creased old wrapping-paper skin, she had begun looking like herself to him.

"Tell me about what you've done," she said. "Not the stuff
I read in the newspapers. Tell me what you did when I left
you, Jubey."

"All right. I'll talk and you see if maybe you can fall asleep
a little while."

She gave him one of her old reproachful looks, and slapped
his hand weakly. He talked along, telling about Papa . . . even
telling that thing about Papa which he had never been able to
discuss with anyone. He told her about Papa's last letter, the
shameful, defeated letter. He found he knew the letter by
heart. " . . . I tried to be a good man, but only out of the good
in myself. That is not enough. . . . "

He wasn't sure some of the time whether she was asleep or awake. But whenever he let his voice trail off into silence, she opened her eyes indignantly.

"Jubey?" she said at last.

"Yes."

"You know I told you I brag about you to people I know. I told you that, didn't I?"

"Yes, you did."

"But there's something else."

"What, dear?"

"Inside of me . . . I've been disappointed in you."

"You have?"

"Don't get mad at me. I wouldn't tell you except that I'm dying. And when you're dying, things just kind of line up in a different way. What's really important comes to the top. Like cream does. And the other stuff kind of sinks out of sight." The long sentences nearly exhausted her.

"Yes, I suppose that's right," he said. "So you tell me, Rose."

"Inside, I've been ashamed of you. Because . . . well, you didn't do the good big thing. . . . "

"What good big thing?"

"Maybe you've even forgotten. That night when you talked to the . . . "

"I haven't forgotten, Rosie."

"You said things. There was something wonderful in you, Jubey."

"Maybe I was just a kid showing off. Maybe I was just a comedian cracking out of my eggshell. A famous comedian getting himself born."

"Hush." She raised her hand and tried to stop his mouth, but the hand hadn't the strength, and fell back. In a moment she went on with firmer breath. "You talked about God," she said.

"I didn't mention his name, Rose."

"You didn't have to. He was speaking in your voice. I heard

him myself. And there never was a day of my life after that, that I didn't look for him. And find him, too."

He got up from the chair, for he was trembling dangerously, and this was a very sick woman whom he must not upset if he could help it.

"Tubey?"

He turned his back so she couldn't see his face. That mimic's face of his which he could mold and remold into any shape he desired, couldn't be controlled now, and he dared not let her see what was happening to it.

"Rose, I tried," he said in a muffled voice. "You know what I did? I tried to be a preacher."

She waited a minute for him to explain, then she said harshly, "Then why didn't you *be* a preacher? Wasn't there enough money in it for that girl you married?"

"No. That wasn't it," he said. "I did all the hard parts. I did the studying and the practicing. I put in the manual labor . . . the janitor's work, you might say. But when I came right up to the head office . . . and asked for the job . . . "

"Yes?"

"Why, God just wouldn't hire me."

The moment the words were out in the air, he realized how monumentally true they were. In one swift summary he saw the whole history, split wide open to the core of the fact. He had been able to fool everybody but God about his fitness for that job. Himself, and Gay, the Seminary, old Hoppart, the majority group of the congregation . . . everybody but God! It came to him with a stunning impact, so that for a moment he forgot the dying woman in the bed.

All he knew was that God had shown incredible wisdom and integrity. He was the biggest thing in the world, and no mistake about it! He didn't argue with you. He held you off at arm's length if you wanted to argue and quibble and think yourself clever. But you couldn't fool him. If you weren't good enough for the job, he just didn't hire you. He put you where you belonged. If you were a clown with a defeated angel under your foot, he threw you into comedy. He gave you everything you thought you wanted . . . a beautiful wife, a bushel of fan mail every day, more rooms than you could possibly live in, so much admiration and praise that it turned your stomach, so much money that you had to hire people to spend it for you. He gave you everything, so that you wanted none of it. And that was hell enough for anybody.

"Jubey?"

"Yes, Rose."

"When are you going to ask him again if maybe he'll hire you?"

"I've already asked him," he said.

"And what'd he say?"

"I don't know. He hasn't told me his decision yet."

"He'll tell you, Jubey. You listen to him this time. You pay attention now."

He came back to the chair and sat down and they had no more to say for awhile. When he spoke her name he saw that she was deeply asleep. He sat there until he was sure she wouldn't want him for a while, then he went out and called the nurse.

"I have to do an errand."

"Yes, Mr. Our. I'll tell her you were sorry you couldn't stay."

"But I am staying. I'm staying just as long as she wants me to. I'll be back. You tell her I'll be back. She'll know where I've gone."

He got the cab easily. As soon as he was in it, he realized he should have phoned down to New York and tried again to reach Gay. The driver took him to a jewelry shop of his own selection on Tremont Street. Jubey looked out the window of the taxi and decided it wasn't good enough. Although if it were a cock-eyed diamond you wanted, you could surely find it here.

"I've got to have the best shop in Boston, Buddy," he said. "This is something awfully special."

"Whyn't you say so? I thought maybe you wanted a crucifix or something."

He picked out a wedding ring, and then a respectable diamond, rather ornately set as he imagined Rose would admire its being. He slipped them in his pocket without a box, then came back and got a box because he remembered she would be proud of the *Shreve, Crump and Low* name inscribed in gold across the top. The whole transaction had taken only a little more than an hour. Not until he was back in the ward did he remember again that he wanted to telephone Gay.

But she'll understand when I tell her, he said comfortingly to himself. He had forgotten the Gay of this morning, and had returned in his mind to the soft-eyed eager young wife who understood everything even before he spoke of it.

He slipped within the small improvised privacy behind the screens. Rose was still sleeping, a warm sleep with scarcely a breath lifting and lowering her narrow chest. She seemed infinitely tragic and childlike, like a little girl who has grown old trying to find something which she never could touch with the fingers she had. He took the rings out of his pocket and slipped them on her hot inert hand, first the wedding ring and then the diamond.

He said to her in his mind, Now, darling, you won't have to die without rings on.

Her hand gave a slight flutter in his, as if it were speaking its own language to him, as if it knew what he had done.

But the hand was all that knew, for Rose herself never woke from the coma.

3

It took Jubey nearly a week to get back from Boston. There was nothing very much to take care of, a simple little service which nobody attended except himself and three or four stray women sitting in the funeral parlor with the satin casket nearly concealed by a coverlet of pink roses.

Afterwards one of the women came and spoke to him, and said she was Roberta's roommate, and what did he want done with her "things."

"She didn't have anyone at all, Mr. Our," the woman said.

"She had you. So you keep the things. If they are anything you could use."

"There's a lovely coat. Cloth, of course. But it has a lovely collar. Whatever Roberta did have was always nice."

"I think she'd want you to have the coat," Jubey said patiently. Then he took some bills out of his wallet, and keeping them covered by his hand, out of deference to the place they were in, he gave them to her. "In case there are any unpaid items, or anything like that."

"I'm sure there isn't any. Roberta was awful strict about keeping things paid up."

"She always was. Good and strict," he said, and that served as her epitaph.

After the funeral he went to a movie, sitting in the dark and seeing nothing but his own thoughts. Then he walked around the streets, and finally wandered down to find Pier 7 in Charlestown where he had first made the acquaintance of the *Susquehanna*. Every few hours he telephoned his home, and the line rang and rang in a lonesome eerie way, but no one ever answered.

The morning after the funeral he telephoned George Irving Compton to tell him he couldn't make the next Saturday's program.

"Something's hit me rather hard, George," he said.

"I know, Jubey. Gay came in to see me yesterday to tell me she has left you."

So that was how he found out that Gay had really meant what she said. But the news didn't seem real to him, because he couldn't seem to locate the man whom Gay had left. The man who was with him now was someone Gay had scarcely known. . . .

He moved from the expensive hotel where he had first registered to a clean, plain little room down on the waterfront. Hours at a time he sat in a rocking chair by the narrow window, looking out across the harbor. Then he walked along the streets, thinking that surely by night he would be ready to go home. But as each night came he thought, Night's the time for getting things straightened out. I'll stay here until morning."

From within himself he saw the whole panorama, so that it fitted together into a coherent structure of meaning. It was the ancient pattern from Revelation, which Lucile had explained to him when he was too young to understand . . . the great red dragon waiting to destroy the good intention as soon as it was born. As Lucile had told the boy long ago, "Evil hates good . . . sometimes the murderous plot is within the very man who really wants to give the world a good gift." His life had been a series of such episodes. The most recent had been his curious, wonderful life in Swiss Plains, gradually growing to a climax in the meeting on the church steps. But even that the avalanche of worldly allurement had carried completely from his mind.

Just when he saw a spiritual fact, his own obsession came over his eyes like a mist and obscured it. The motif had happened over and over, in small ways and in great ones. He had been given a dozen chances; God had spoken to him over and over, through Geitzen, through that night in Union Square, in Papa's letter, through Gay, the lovely steadfastness of Gay, through the gauche sincerity of Hoppart, and Mike Pliven, and finally back to Rosie . . . over and over. Sometimes through others, and sometimes directly into his own mind as God was speaking to him these last few days . . . the divine dialogue had gone on patiently. And now, he was ready to listen.

Now he knew that never again would he starve himself on the husks. No wonder this lively peace was called the bread of life. . . . He went into a bookstore and bought a Bible. But he didn't read it. There was too much being said to him directly. The Bible would come later.

Suddenly, then, he was ready to go home, and he knew exactly what he had to do, step by step. It would require more moral courage than he had ever known in his whole life. But he had that now at last, layers and layers of it, beginning at the surface and going down to the very core of his being. Or perhaps it was the other way around. The inner court of his being was defined now and well built, and lighted so that nothing was hiding or calling itself by an assumed name. The streets of his thinking all led into that lighted area now, and he knew where he was doing his real living.

Going back in the plane he looked at a newspaper, the first one he had seen for days. The front page was full of Germany re-arming, of Hitler and aggression. He read the columns carefully, and they made him all the more certain of what he had decided to do. The world was starting on the long night. Nobody could know how long that night would last, before the morning came.

The world would have to reach its maturity, just as he had finally reached his own. The world had gone through the nonsense of childhood, centuries and centuries of it; then into a demented, delightful, tragic adolescence while more unheeded centuries flew past. But finally a gleam of wisdom would begin dawning. Just as it was dawning for him now. For the history of each man is but an atom-sized replica of the history of the race.

Laughter would not be good enough now; there must be joy itself. Jokes would not suffice, for the drunkenness of contrived mirth would pall upon the race just as it had palled upon him. There would have to be Light now, and nothing less would satisfy. Men like him who knew from crucifying experience where such Light could be found must stand up humbly and represent it. They must cast their votes, wherever they stood, the low and the high together.

From the Newark airport he went to Swiss Plains by bus and trolley and bus again, for from this day on, his life was going to be thrifty and simple. Part-way there, bouncing along in the bus, he began laughing to himself, for he recognized that this was the old Jubey dramatizing himself traveling by bus instead of taxi. There would be such histrionics to contend with, all right, for the clown would put on new make-up and try to pass himself off as a sanctimonious guy with a message! But he wouldn't fool the whole man; not any more, for the man had come to himself at last.

It had been more than half a year since that first spring morning when he had blundered into this little town, thinking he was having only a single day of truancy. He understood now that it had not been blundering at all; it had been answering the deep call of his own submerged destiny, stirring in its sleep and crying out imperative commands.

That had been a spring morning; this was a wintry twilight. The last of the leaves were gone from the trees, and there was a still, waiting look on them as if they yearned to be covered by snow. He expected to walk down to the end of the street and unlock his odd little house, build up a fire and get some life into the deserted place. Then later he would go about the town visiting his friends, catching up on the news. He wasn't planning how he would speak to them about the church. He knew that the words would come, and they would be the right words, for he would ask God to give them to him.

But he never reached his own land, for when he came within sight of the church, he saw there were lights in it, and through the dusk he could make out figures going up the path, and other figures coming down the shadowy street.

Someone was hurrying along behind him, and in a few seconds he was overtaken by Simpson.

"Oh, Mr. Our . . . I thought that was you."

"I'm just getting back," Jubey said. "I've been away."

"I know." Simpson looked at him almost in fear and then seeing Jubey's face was friendly, he said, "I guess you know a lot has happened, Mr. Our."

"Oh?"

"I hope I didn't do something that's caused you trouble," he said in a frantic voice.

"How's that?"

"Well, we all got to worrying about you. We had kind of got the idea that you'd be here the next Thursday after we had that first meetin' of ours. We thought you'd surely come for the next one. But that was more'n a month ago."

"You mean you people had another meeting the next Thursday?"

"Why, sure," Simpson said. "We've had one every Thursday. And we expected every week you'd come. But when you didn't, some of the neighbors got to worrying about you, thinking maybe you were sick or something."

"In a way I was sick," Jubey said. "I found that out."

"But then . . . you know there's always been a certain amount of talk about who you *was*, Mr. Our . . . "

"Who I was?"

"Well, you know. People are pretty familiar with your voice. And some of the neighbors insisted, and the rest of us said it just wasn't possible. So anyway, when you didn't come back,

they got me to telephone the studio. I hope you're not mad at
me...."

"I'm not mad," Jubey said. "They'd have to know sometime,
wouldn't they?"

"I was only planning to ask to speak to Jubal Our, and ask
him if he had a relative answering your description, and if he
knew where we could reach you. That was all I intended
doing." Simpson was perspiring with what he thought was the
enormity of his blunder.

"So you spoke to Mrs. Tumulty, my secretary."

"Yes. And she's the kind of woman that gets things out of
you."

"Yes. That's Tumulty," Jubey grinned now to reassure him.
"So she got it out of you, Simpson."

"I'm afraid I told her all about it. Just about everything, I
guess."

"What'd she say?"

"She said one of us was crazy, her or me."

They were standing on the pavement now, a few feet away
from the turn-in to the church. Jubey looked up at the lighted
church, its spire both modest and noble against the sky . . . the
way people who walk along with God are both modest and
noble.

"You got the church open, I see," he said.

"*We* got it open! *You* got it open, Mr. Our. We was going
to ask you would you come and be our preacher. But of course
we see now that you probably wouldn't think that was very
appropriate."

"What kind of meetings are you holding?"

"The same kind. We read the Bible, and if anybody has anything to say, why he says it. But what we want is a good preacher
now. What we all wish is . . . " He gulped on the words and
couldn't get them out.

They went up the path and mounted the steps. It was a

pleasant little church inside, white with touches of gold here
and there. A self-respecting dignity was built into it, and there
were organ pipes on each side of the pulpit. A handful of
neighbors were sitting quietly along the benches. Jubey's eye
embraced them quickly, and he thought, I know . . . actually
know . . . more people in this little church than anywhere else
in the world. They're my own people.

Then his eye stumbled and stopped. For on the very last
bench two women were sitting. One was a tall angular woman
with a freckled face and a hat that *Vogue* said was just fine for a
career woman. And the other was the most beautiful woman
on earth, as far as Jubey was concerned. She was wearing a
luxurious fur coat with a tight cluster of rosebuds pinned to it.
She turned her head when she felt his eyes, and her face flooded
with color and joy.

Simpson, goggling in astonishment, just stood and stared.
Then Jubey slid into the last row of benches beside Gay, and
took her warm hand in his and put both hands in his pocket.

"How did you know I'd come back?" he whispered to her.

"I didn't know you'd come here, Jubey," she said. "But I
knew you'd come to yourself."

"How did you know?"

"I know the story of the prodigal son."

The little church was nearly filled now, and Mrs. Orcutt who
taught music in the town got up and played the organ. She
went from very simple Handel into "Oh come all ye faithful,"
and the congregation stood up and sang.

Then there was a pause, and at last Simpson said, "I guess
there's no reason why we shouldn't have the same kind of meeting we have been having every Thursday."

The neighbors were shyly looking around at the last bench,
having heard one by one that Mr. Our had come back. Simpson,
fiercely ignoring all this said, "We might as well read the Bible,

the way we usually do. If someone would like to start off, I've brought the Bible."

"You start, Mr. Our," someone said. "As long as you've come back."

"All right. I'll start," Jubey said. He walked up the aisle to where Simpson was, and took the outstretched book. It opened of itself. He put his hands along the gilded top of the pages to turn them to the book of Psalms.

But someone in the crowd said, "Mr. Our, sometimes it's a wonderful thing to read just what the book opens to."

So Jubey let his eye go down the page. "This is the book of Isaiah, Chapter Twenty-nine," he said. Then he began to read:

"*It shall even be as when an hungry man dreameth, and behold he eateth; but he awaketh and his soul is empty.*"

He stopped reading then, and lifted his face.

"If nobody minds, I'd like to preach a sermon about that," he said. "I happen to know about that. You could say it's the story of my own life, that verse. I waked and found my soul empty. The thing is I know now how I can be filled. . . ."

THE END